Lucy King spent ~~~~ Mills & Boon w ~~~~ attention to her te ~~~~ dreamworld forev ~~~~ ~~~~ in languages and an eclectic collection of jobs. After a decade in Spain, Lucy now lives in Wiltshire with her young family where, when not writing, she spends time reading, failing to finish cryptic crosswords and missing the beaches of Andalucia.

With a background of working in medical laboratories and a love of the romance genre, it's no surprise that **Sue Mackay** writes medical romance stories. She wrote her first story at age eight and hasn't stopped since. She lives in New Zealand's Marlborough Sounds where she indulges her passions for cycling, walking and kayaking. When she isn't writing she also loves cooking and entertaining guests with sumptuous meals that include locally caught fish.

Kate Hardy has been a bookworm since she was a toddler. When she isn't writing Kate enjoys reading, theatre, live music, ballet and the gym. She lives with her husband, student children and their spaniel in Norwich, England. You can contact her via her website: katehardy.com

Foreign Affairs

Foreign Affairs: London Calling

LUCY KING

SUE MacKAY

KATE HARDY

MILLS & BOON

First Published in Great Britain 2023
By Mills & Boon, an imprint of HarperCollins*Publishers*
1 London Bridge Street, London, SE1 9GF

www.harpercollins.co.uk

HarperCollins*Publishers*
Macken House, 39/40 Mayor Street Upper,
Dublin 1, D01 C9W8, Ireland

FOREIGN AFFAIRS: LONDON CALLING © 2023 Harlequin Enterprises ULC.

A Scandal Made in London © 2020 Lucy King
A Fling to Steal Her Heart © 2020 Sue MacKay
Billionaire, Boss...Bridegroom? © 2016 Pamela Brooks

ISBN: 978-0-263-31879-1

Printed and Bound in Spain using 100% Renewable electricity at
CPI Black Print, Barcelona

A SCANDAL MADE IN LONDON

LUCY KING

For Flo, for all the support and encouragement.

CHAPTER ONE

WHAT ON *EARTH*...?

From behind his desk, situated on the top floor of the forty-four-storey building that housed the Knox Group, Theo Knox stared at the web page that filled the screen of the iPad that his head of security had just brought in and placed in front of him.

It appeared to be a table of information.

Harmony was the heading; below that came the details.

Geographical location: London
Age: 26
Height: 6' 1"
Vital statistics: 38-28-38
Hair: blonde
Eyes: blue
Tattoos: one
Interests: travel, books, music
Sexual experience: none

And the website? Belle's Angels, according to the elaborate logo involving entwined vines that shimmered in the top right corner. *'Matches made in heaven'*, apparently.

Which was all well and good, but of what use was any of this to him? And why did Antonio Scarlatto, a valued employee he'd previously considered competent and level-headed, think it would be?

Theo had absolutely no interest in dating sites, or in any kind of dating at all, since the occasional one-night stand when the need arose suited him fine. And even if he did, he had no time for it. As owner and CEO of a company that spanned the globe, employed thousands and was worth billions, he had a multitude of issues clamouring for his attention, the principle one of which currently was figuring out how he was going to persuade the ridiculously sentimental owner of the business he badly wanted to sell it to him.

'Why are you wasting my time by showing me this?' Theo demanded, lifting his gaze from the screen and levelling it at the man standing on the other side of the desk, who was way out of line if he thought Theo needed Harmony in his life.

'It relates to a current member of your staff,' said Antonio, not batting an eyelid in response to the dark look and arctic tone that usually had people quaking in their boots. 'She's registered on the site and this is her page. She tried to log in from her work computer twenty minutes ago. Our firewall flagged it up. As it's against company policy to access sites like this, I need to know what action to take.'

'It's a dating site,' Theo said flatly.

'It's not just a dating site,' Antonio countered. 'I wouldn't have disturbed you if it was. Scroll down.'

Mentally having to concede that point, Theo shoved a lid on his exasperation and switched his attention back to the tablet. He briefly ran his gaze over the table again, automatically registering and dismissing the information, then swiped up.

And froze.

Because to accompany Harmony's description were half a dozen photos. Of the woman in question in various outfits in various eye-popping poses. In the first four pictures, she was at least wearing clothes—short and tight and pretty revealing, but clothes nevertheless. In the last two, however, she wasn't wearing very much at all. Technically she had on a negligee, he saw, but she might as well not have bothered. It was so diaphanous it hid nothing that wasn't concealed under a few scraps of strategically placed lace beneath. Not her curves. Not the length of her limbs. Nothing.

And her face…

He knew that face.

It was Kate Cassidy.

Harmony, with her luscious body and dazzlingly striking looks, was Kate Cassidy.

The realisation hit Theo like a blow to the gut and he reeled.

What the hell was she up to?

Steeling himself, he scrolled down and read the text that accompanied the photos, and his blood turned to ice. Antonio had been right. Belle's Angels wasn't just any dating site and Kate wasn't after any kind of normal date *at all*.

As the implications of what he'd read and seen sank in, questions ricocheted around his head. What on earth was she thinking? Did she have *any* idea of the danger she could be putting herself in? More importantly, now he knew what she had planned, what was he going to do about it?

Because he'd definitely be doing *something*, he thought grimly as he clicked around the site, his horror growing with every passing second. Kate clearly needed looking out for. In fact, he should have been keeping an eye on her and her younger sister ever since their older brother Mike's death nine months ago. Discreetly. From afar. But nonetheless making sure they were as okay as they could be, because the debt he owed him was huge, because Mike had died because of something *he* could have prevented, and finally because they had no one else.

So why *hadn't* he done anything? Why hadn't he even been aware Kate was working for him? Guilt? Denial? The fact that these days he only seemed to function through sheer force of will?

Well, whatever it was, it stopped now because she, at least, was not okay. She'd evidently lost her tiny little mind.

Furthermore, by signing herself up to this particular website she'd put herself at considerable risk, and that was unacceptable. The potential consequences didn't bear thinking about, and a person hurt—or worse—because he hadn't done enough to stop it simply could not happen again. Twice in one lifetime was more than enough.

'What action do you want me to take?' asked Antonio, cutting off Theo's thoughts before they could scythe through the fog of Mike's death and hurtle down memory lane to his own turbulent teenage years.

'Shut the site down,' Theo said as he pushed the tablet in Antonio's direction and slammed a mental door on Harmony's bio and the photos. 'Whatever it takes, however much it costs, shut it down.'

The head of security acknowledged the order with a brief nod of his head. 'And with regards to the employee in question?'

'I'll deal with her.'

Not once in the five and a half months she'd been working at the Knox Group had Kate been summoned to the hallowed top floor of the central London building that housed it, and that was fine with her. Her position as a middle-ranking accountant didn't merit the dubious honour, and, quite frankly, the less she had to do with the horrible Theo Knox, the better.

Not that they knew each other well, thank God. He might have been supposed 'friends' with her brother—although she struggled with the concept that her uptight, aloof *über* boss could ever do anything as human as *friends*—but she'd only met him once. At Mike's funeral nine months ago, in fact. And since that had hardly been a cordial encounter, she hadn't expected him to be in touch.

He was the man, after all, who'd coldly told her he wasn't interested and then turned his back on her when she'd made the monumental mistake of asking him for his support. All she'd wanted was a quick drink after the wake. To talk. Nothing more. Everyone else had left and she'd been distraught, feeling so horribly alone she'd simply wanted to prolong the afternoon by talking about her brother with someone who presumably had known him well. High and mighty Theo Knox, however, had evidently interpreted her suggestion as an invitation, and had treated it with the disdain and contempt he obviously felt it deserved before spinning on his heel and stalking off.

Kate had stood there staring at his retreating figure, open-mouthed and dumbstruck, unsure whether to laugh or cry because had he *really* thought she was coming on to him? At her brother's *funeral*? How inappropriate, how downright absurd, *was* that? His arrogance had been breathtaking. She'd never encountered self-absorption like it. Even worse was the lousy way his unwarranted rejection had made her feel. She shouldn't have cared what he thought of her since he meant absolutely nothing to her, yet his response had pulverised what little self-esteem she had, and for one blazing moment she'd never hated anyone more.

So if she'd been in any position to turn down the offer of a job at his company that had come her way shortly after, she'd have done so. However, she had bills to pay and the salary she'd been offered had been too generous to refuse. Not generous enough, of course, to cover the stratospheric sums of money her sister's residential care facility required, nor the repayment of the ever-increasing debt her brother had accrued to cover it, but definitely generous enough to make her want to pass her probationary period. And that was why, when she'd received the call from Theo's assistant requesting her presence on the top floor at precisely six p.m., the time she should have been leaving for home, she'd obeyed instead of telling him where to stick his imperious demand.

The lift she was travelling in slowed until it came to a smooth stop, and the doors opened with a soft swoosh. Automatically reminding herself not to slouch, Kate lifted her chin and crossed the plush white carpet that covered the floor with a long-legged stride.

When she arrived at the reception desk, she was waved in the direction of a pair of vast wooden doors, and headed towards them. Taking a deep breath, she knocked, and didn't have to wait long before a deep masculine voice barked, 'Come in.'

Kate braced herself and did as he'd commanded. The minute she walked through the door her attention instantly zoomed in on the man sitting behind the oak monolith of a desk, the man who was looking at her with a dark intensity and a stillness that radiated powerful authority and suggested complete and utter control.

Of her surroundings—the sleek white office so vast her entire flat would fit in it, the crystal-clear wall-to-wall windows that allowed the early evening late spring sunshine to flood in, the luxurious furnishings and the colourful pops of modern art on the walls—she was only dimly aware. All she was conscious of was her boss, the rude, condescending, hurtful jerk, and the memory of the intense loathing he'd once aroused in her.

'Shut the door.'

She did so, then walked towards him, the office becoming increasingly hot and claustrophobic with every step she took. Which, given the state-of-the-art temperature control the building had, was odd, and not a little disturbing.

As was the automatic way in which she seemed to be taking a mental inventory of his looks. At Mike's funeral she'd been in too great a state to register much about any of the guests, least of all him. Now, though, she had to grudgingly admit that the gossip columns, which lauded his appearance as much as they lamented his enigmatic elusiveness, were right. With his short dark hair, obsidian eyes and chiselled features he was easily the best-looking man she'd ever seen. The shoulders beneath the suit were impressively broad and they were matched by an equally impressive height, which she knew to be true because even though he was now sitting down, she'd just had a brief flash of memory of how she'd been in the unusual position of having to look up at him when she'd suggested a drink that afternoon.

He was also immaculate, she thought resentfully, taking in the perfection of his appearance as she advanced. Did he *ever* shove his hands through his hair in frustration? Ever permit even the *hint* of a five o'clock shadow? She doubted it. And had he ever been paralysed by self-doubt or plagued by rock-bottom self-esteem as she continually was? Even more unlikely. The man was a machine. A high-performing, single-minded, ruthlessly brilliant one, if the business press was to be believed, but a machine nevertheless.

Well.

Whatever.

What he was and how he looked were immaterial. So he was staggeringly handsome, in enviable control of himself and a good three or four inches taller than her. He was still a deeply unpleasant human being.

Coming to a halt a foot from the desk, Kate pulled herself together and reminded herself to stay calm, since it wouldn't do to reveal either how little she thought of him or how vulnerable she could be if she kept remembering how wretched he'd once made her feel. 'Mr Knox,' she said coolly. 'You wanted to see me?'

Something flickered in the depths of his dark eyes, something that flashed and burned and swiftly disappeared but nevertheless made her pulse skip a beat and her blood heat. 'I did,' he said with a brief nod in the direction of the two modern armchairs on her side of the desk. 'Theo will do. Sit down.'

'Thank you.'

Deliberately taking her time, Kate folded her six-foot-one frame into a chair and then spent a couple of vital seconds tugging her jacket down and smoothing her skirt. She needed to settle herself. This pulse-skipping, blood-heating business was ridiculous, as was the strange restlessness that churned around inside her. Nerves, most probably, because she had no idea why she'd been summoned and despite what she thought of him he *was* a bit intimidating. Or dread perhaps, the kind that came from knowing that one false move and the many plates she had spinning would crash to the ground. But still, either way, it was absurd.

'How are you?'

She stilled for a second and fought back a frown. What? *Now* he wanted pleasantries? Well, okay, she could do that. She could forget how they'd met for now. She couldn't imagine *he* remembered in any case. He certainly didn't appear to recognise her. 'Fine,' she said brightly, as if she weren't wrung out with stress and exhaustion. 'You?'

'Fine. Coffee?'

She gave her head a quick shake. 'No, thank you.'

'Tea?'

'No.'

'Anything?'

'I'm fine.'

'How's the job going?'

Hah. Which one? As well as being an accountant, she now worked in a bar five nights a week and dog-walked at the weekend. What little time she had left when she wasn't visiting her sister, she dedicated to the freelance bookkeeping work she'd also started to take on. 'Extremely well,' she said with a beaming smile, determined not to think about how close she was to the edge or how terrifying that was. 'I'm enjoying it very much.'

'Good,' he said, leaning forwards in a way that for some bizarre reason made her breath catch and her pulse skip a beat all over again. 'So. Kate. Tell me about Belle's Angels.'

And just like that—*bang!*—there went her composure. Talk about being lulled into a false sense of security, she thought, her smile fading as the churning started up again in her stomach. What did Theo Knox know about Belle's Angels? And how? Surely he couldn't be a member. He'd have no trouble getting a date. But had he visited the site? Had he seen her page? She had no idea why when her pro-file had racked up over a thousand views since she'd rashly stuck it up last night but the thought of *him* looking at her photos made her feel quite weak.

'What about it?' she said carefully, since his expression was giving absolutely nothing away.

'You're on it.'

Ah. Right. Busted.

Since Mr Knox—*Theo*—was allegedly insanely sharp, Kate didn't see the point in trying to come up with an ex-cuse. 'I am,' she said, reminding herself that she had noth-ing to apologise for and nothing to be embarrassed about. What did it matter if he *had* seen her page? The photos were good. Empowering. Or something like that. At least she'd come up with a solution to the traumatic situation that had been robbing her of what little sleep she did get, even if it *had* had unexpected and rather unsettling consequences.

'You tried to access it while at work.'

Indeed she had. Earlier this afternoon. Her profile had attracted a great deal of interest, her alluded-to virginity in particular, and she'd been inundated with emails, some merely curious, some a bit odd, some downright creepy. Not having a clue what to do about any of it and wanting the deluge to stop, she'd decided to alter her account settings while she figured it out. 'I did.'

'Which is an infringement of company policy.'

At that Kate went very still, her heart giving a great lurch.

Oh.

Oh, dear.

That hadn't occurred to her. But it should have done because of *course* it would be. Belle's Angels, registered in Germany and possibly skirting the boundaries of legality in the UK, was just the sort of website that would be blocked by a firewall. Which was undoubtedly why it hadn't opened. She hadn't thought to reflect upon that. She'd just wanted to switch off the interminable stream of responses. But clearly she'd been an idiot. More than an idiot, actually. She could very well have put herself out of a job.

'That was a mistake,' she said as the potential ramifications raced through her head and a sweat broke out all over her skin. 'A one-off. It won't happen again.'

'You're right,' he said flatly, his eyes dark and inscrutable. 'It won't.'

A ball lodged in her throat and she swallowed it down with difficulty. 'Are you firing me?' she asked, the rising panic making her voice tight.

She needed this job, she needed *all* her jobs, but if she lost *this* one, she'd be in even more serious trouble than she already was. Fired accountants weren't exactly desirable potential employees and who knew how long it would be before she got another job? The bills were mounting up daily and the correspondence from the debt agency was growing increasingly threatening, not that her salary was anywhere *near* enough to cover the repayments or the cost of her sister's care, but Milly depended on her and *only* her since there was no one else now Mike had died, and if she had to leave Fairview she'd be devastated, and, oh, she *really* should have thought this whole crazy plan through.

'I'm not firing you.'

Phew.

'Then what do you mean?' she said as her racing heart slowed and the jumble of panicky thoughts faded.

'I had the site shut down.'

What? The tension that had ebbed a moment ago shot straight back.

No.

No.

This was *not* good.

'You can't do that,' she breathed, appalled, as it dawned on her that if what Theo was saying was true then he'd scuppered what, as far as she could see, was her only chance of making some serious, much-needed money fast.

'I can,' he said grimly. 'And I have.'

'How?'

'It wasn't hard.'

No, it wouldn't be to a man of his considerable influence and power, but— 'You had no right.'

'Probably not.'

'So why?'

His eyebrows shot up, the only sign of expression she'd seen in him since she'd walked in. *'Why?'*

'Yes, why?' What was it to him? Even if he *did* know who she was, which was doubtful, why would he care all of a sudden?

'You signed up to an escort agency, Kate.'

His tone was brutal and icily condemning but she refused to be intimidated. It was all very well for him and his billions in the bank. Lesser mortals had to think more creatively if they didn't want to firstly destroy the happiness and security of their vulnerable younger sister, secondly lose the home they'd once shared with their adored, much-missed brother and lastly be declared bankrupt and never work in the field they loved again.

'And so what?' she said, resisting the urge to lift her chin since a punchy show of defiance could well make him re-assess his decision not to fire her.

'How could you be so reckless?'

Reckless? She wasn't reckless. Desperate and exhausted and all out of options, yes, but reckless, no. 'I'm not. I did my research.'

'So did I,' he said ominously.

'Well, then.'

'Belle's Angels is basically an online brothel.'

'Possibly,' she had to admit, since there *was* that aspect to it, 'but it's a very high-class one.'

A tiny muscle began to tic in his jaw. 'That is utterly irrelevant.'

'No,' she said. 'It isn't. Because *this* one has different levels of service agreement, and I only signed up to level one.'

He looked at her as if she'd grown two heads. 'Did you honestly think someone was going to pay you a thousand pounds an hour for *conversation*?'

'Why not?' she said. 'My conversational skills are first class.'

'I have no doubt they are. However, believe me, your… *clients*…would have been expecting far more.'

'Yes, well, you obviously have more experience of such sites than I do.'

In response to her demure yet pointed little dig Theo's face darkened and the look he gave her was hard and for-bidding. 'I've heard stories,' he said flatly. 'None of them good. Do you have *any* idea of how dangerous it could have been?'

Kate opened her mouth to reply and then closed it be-cause he might have a point there. Truth be told, she hadn't exactly been thinking entirely rationally when she'd signed up to the site late last night. Another exorbitant bill had just come through from Fairview on top of a none-too-friendly email from the loan company Mike had used *and* a letter from her mortgage company informing her that she'd missed a payment, as if she needed reminding.

She'd had a couple of glasses of wine to dull the resulting anxiety, but they hadn't worked; they'd just made her feel even sicker. A documentary about webcamming had been on TV in the background, and in the midst of her despair it had suddenly struck her that sex sold. Extremely well, apparently. And while she wasn't desperate enough— yet—to perform for the camera, she'd figured there had to be other less extreme options.

It had been remarkably easy to find an appropriate site and register. When she remembered the stash of normal-sized clothes she'd bought over the years because it made her feel dainty and feminine just to know she owned them even though none of them actually fitted, it had seemed as though the stars had aligned. In fact, the most challenging aspect of the whole exercise had been mastering the self-timer on her phone.

Of course she'd considered the possible consequences of her plan—she wasn't a *complete* fool—but she'd been at her wits' end and as a result her assessment had been brief. Conveniently, the pros had vastly outweighed the cons. What cons there were—mainly concerning the sort of people who might use such a site—she'd presumed would be neutralised by the application of filters and a robust screening process.

Clearly, however, there'd been little of that because some of the creepier emails she'd received had been downright disturbing. The staggering sums of money she'd been offered for her virginity, not to mention the many ways it could apparently be relieved, had been even more alarming. And, actually, even the more moderate correspondence had hinted at something other than conversation, so maybe Theo also had a point about her would-be clients' expectations.

Perhaps, then, in hindsight, she'd had a lucky escape, even if it did mean that her only hope had vanished and she was now back at a terrifying square one. Because if she was being brutally honest, the reality of what the site offered was far seedier than in her naivety she'd imagined, and, regardless of the amount of money on offer, the thought of actually having to go through with some of the more lurid scenarios described made her want to throw up.

'It is absolutely *none* of your business,' she said, not inclined to admit that Theo could be right and give him the upper hand.

'That's not strictly true.'

No. Well. There was the small issue of pesky company policy, but still. He had no right to meddle in her affairs in this way. In *any* way. 'I don't need rescuing, Theo,' she said steadily. 'I'm twenty-six. I'm eminently sensible and perfectly capable of making my own choices.' Not that she had many at this precise moment.

'It doesn't look like it from where I'm sitting.'

Ooh, he was insufferable. 'Why do you even *care*?'

He stared at her silently for a moment, as if he couldn't work it out either, and the hard intensity of his gaze coupled with the way he seemed to be trying to see into her soul was sending a strange sluggish heat oozing through her blood, detonating tiny sparks along her veins and electrifying her nerves.

To her consternation she found she couldn't look away. She could hardly breathe. All of a sudden she wanted to get up, clamber over his desk and plaster herself against him. And then she wanted to—well, she wasn't quite sure what she wanted to do next since she had little experience of such things, but she wanted to find out. So badly she was ablaze with it.

Appalled at and bewildered by her reaction, she shifted in an attempt to alleviate the fizzing of her stomach and the prickling of her heated skin, but all that did was inch her skirt up her thighs, at which point Theo's darkening gaze dropped to her legs and lingered there a while, which sent the heat buzzing through her shooting straight down to the spot where she suddenly, *alarmingly*, burned.

Maybe she moved again, maybe she let out an audibly breathy gasp. She didn't know. But Theo jerked his gaze back up, his expression once again cold and inscrutable, and the tension snapped.

'I take it you need the money,' he said bluntly, and all she could think was money? What money?

Ah.

Well, of course she needed the money, she thought, tugging her skirt back down with annoyingly shaky fingers as the reminder of her precarious financial state obliterated the bizarre heat and dizziness and refocused her attention. Why else would she do it? She wasn't *that* desperate for a date. 'I do.'

'How much?'

'A lump sum of a hundred thousand, plus around five thousand a month on an on-going basis for the next sixty, possibly seventy, years.'

Up shot his eyebrows. 'That's a lot of money.'

Really?

'I am aware of that,' she said coolly. And now, thanks to him and his high-handed ways, it was a lot of money she still had to somehow find because, quite apart from the distressing threat of homelessness, she was *not* having Milly moved when she was so happy and secure where she was.

'It's a concern,' he said.

'You're telling me.'

'It's *my* concern.'

'How?'

'You're an accountant,' he said. 'You're about to finish your probation, at which point you will have access to certain aspects of the company's bank accounts. Fraud is a risk.'

What the—?

Kate blinked at him, for a moment completely lost for words. Was he being serious? 'Are you suggesting I might indulge in a little light embezzlement in order to pay my bills?'

'It's a possibility.'

'It is *not* a possibility because I am *not* a criminal,' she said heatedly.

'What do you need it for?'

Kate took a deep breath to soothe the outrage surging through her. 'I have a younger sister,' she said. 'Milly. She was in the car accident that killed our parents ten years ago.' She swallowed hard but made herself continue. 'She survived but she suffered catastrophic brain injuries. She can't live on her own. She needs twenty-four-hour care. The insurance pay-out only covers the most basic of facilities, which just aren't good enough.'

For a few long moments, Theo said nothing, just frowned. And then he nodded, as if something in his head had slotted into place. 'Your brother used to fund the rest.'

Ah. So he *did* know who she was.

Well.

'He did,' she said, steeling herself against the surge of grief that still sometimes shot out of nowhere and walloped her in the chest. 'And there was some money from his estate, but it's run out.'

'His flat?'

'Rented. A few months before his death he gave it up and moved in with me.'

'Life insurance?'

'He didn't have any.' If only. 'Believe me, if there was any money anywhere I'd have found it. After he died I discovered that he'd been taking out high-interest loans. They need repaying, like, yesterday.'

'I see.'

Did he? she wondered, swallowing down the tight ball of emotion that had lodged in her throat. She doubted it. The gut-wrenching combination of despair, guilt, anger, grief and dread she'd felt when she'd found out what Mike had done had to be unique. Besides, had Theo ever needed money so badly he'd do anything to get it? Unlikely. He'd made his first million by the age of seventeen and his fortune had rocketed year on year since.

'You'll have it.'

She stared at him in bewilderment. What was he talking about? Have it? Have what? 'I'm sorry?'

'Give me the details and I'll pay off the debt and set up a trust fund to pay for whatever your sister needs for however long she needs it.'

What?

Oh.

Right.

Wow.

'Are you serious?' she asked in stunned disbelief.

'Yes.'

'Why would you do that?'

His eyes clouded and she caught a glimpse of what bizarrely looked like…what? Guilt? Anguish? Regret? As if. By all accounts he didn't do emotion any more than he did friends, so who knew? It was most likely irritation that he'd had to interrupt his no doubt busy schedule to deal with what he perceived to be a problem. 'Because I can,' he said eventually.

That was undeniably true. He was one of the ten richest

men in the world according to one newspaper article she'd read. What she needed might amount to millions but to him it was a rounding error. Nevertheless, what ultra-successful reportedly ruthless businessman did something like that?

'Do you really expect me to believe you're that altruistic?' she asked, unable to keep the scepticism from her tone.

'I don't particularly care what you believe.'

Nice. 'Well, thank you,' she said primly. 'But I can't accept it.'

'Why not?'

Hmm. Where to start? Because she didn't like him and the thought of being indebted to a man she loathed was abhorrent? Because any man who could single-handedly close down a large, foreign website was to be treated with caution and she didn't trust him an inch? She could hardly tell him any of that. He was still her boss.

'It's too much,' she said instead.

'Not from my perspective.'

'Still no.'

'Where else are you going to get the money?'

'I'll think of something.' Hadn't her brief foray into the shady world of online escorts proved that? Surely she'd be able to come up with a workable solution, one that didn't involve seedy sex or overbearing men.

'It sounds like you'd better think of it quickly.'

Well, yes, there was that. She was running out of time. Fast. How much longer did she have? How much more could she take? She was *so* tired of worrying about the money. About the debt and the reduced quality of life her sister might have if she had to move because she—Kate—had failed. About losing her home and the precious memories she had of her brother. The responsibilities she now had, which landed entirely on her shoulders, were crushing, bewildering, overwhelming. Sometimes she wished she could just go to bed for a month and cry.

'Just out of interest, what would you want in return?' she asked, because even if she had been considering it, which she wasn't, surely that amount of money would come with strings.

'Nothing.'

She stared at him. 'Nothing?'

He gave a brief nod. 'That's right.'

'Why not?'

'Do I need a reason?'

'*I* would. You're in the business of deal-making. No one ever gets something for nothing. Even I know that.'

'You have my word.'

'I don't know what your word is worth.' What if hypothetically she agreed and he suddenly decided that his money gave him the right to influence Milly's future? What if at some point he decided to stop?

'I'll have a contract drawn up,' he said, clearly able to read the scepticism that must have been written all over her face. 'You can state the terms. I won't challenge them.'

'Things that sound too good to be true generally are.'

His jaw tightened. 'Just accept my offer, Kate. It's the only one on the table.'

True. But— 'I'd never be able to repay you.'

'There'd be no need.'

'I'd feel a need.'

'Then I suggest you get over it,' he said tersely, 'because you should know that I will be doing this, with or without your consent. Your agreement will merely speed things up.'

And quite suddenly, in the face of such intransigence, what remained of Kate's resistance suddenly crumbled. Why was she still fighting this? She was running on fumes and at her wits' end. What Theo was proposing would obliterate all her worries and stresses overnight. So if he could afford it and wanted to help, why shouldn't she let him? Maybe he *did* feel something after all. Maybe he and Mike *had* been good friends. Ultimately, did it even matter? She didn't need to like him, and his motivations were none of her concern. He was offering her a 'no strings attached' deal, which would get the debt collectors off her back and, more importantly, ensure Milly's comfort for the rest of her life as well as the best treatments available. So despite feeling as though she might be making a deal with the devil, she couldn't *not* accept his help. She just couldn't.

'Okay, fine,' she said with a brief nod. 'You win.'

CHAPTER TWO

HE'D WON, HAD HE?

Hmm...

Theo wasn't so sure. He might have achieved the outcome he'd been intent on getting, but in reality, given the massive debt he owed Mike, the provision of financial support for Kate and her sister was long overdue and it certainly didn't lessen the crushing omnipresent guilt he felt over the part he'd played in their brother's death. If anything, it made it worse because he hadn't known about the loans and he should have.

And then there was the battle for his self-control, which he'd started waging the moment Kate had walked into his office and detonated a savagely fierce and wholly unexpected reaction inside him. Was he winning that? By the skin of his teeth, and only then because he had years of practice.

He had not been prepared for her effect on him. The first and last time they'd met—at her brother's funeral, an insanely tough and gruelling experience for a number of reasons—had certainly given no indication. This evening, however, she'd come through that door and for some unfathomable reason every sense he possessed had instantly sprung to high alert. The way she'd moved—languidly and sinuously graceful—had mesmerised him, and as she'd approached his desk, that web page she'd set up had slammed back into his head. So much for thinking he'd successfully excised it from his memory. Clearly he'd merely drawn a veil across it, a veil that her appearance in his space had instantly swept back.

With every step she took towards him, his blood had

begun to heat and questions had started ricocheting around his head. Forget her vital statistics and her hobbies, he'd thought, his pulse thudding heavily and his body hardening. What he'd like to know more about was the tattoo. Where was it, and what was it of?

Then there was the tiny yet somehow momentous detail regarding her sexual experience. The 'none' of it implied that she was still a virgin, but regardless of its meaning, it shouldn't have been of the slightest interest. However, infuriatingly, he seemed to find it fascinating because all he could think was, why? She was twenty-six and it couldn't be from lack of opportunity. She looked like a goddess. Not, perhaps, conventionally beautiful, but certainly breathtakingly striking with her long blonde hair and big blue eyes and above average height.

And last, but by no means least, there were the photos, the last two in particular, which once seen could not unfortunately be unseen and were now indelibly etched into his memory. Those had had him instinctively thinking about the suite adjoining his office, the oversized bed he had in there, and her sprawled across it wearing nothing but that negligee.

Such a savage and unexpected assault on his senses had decimated his self-control and his body had responded— and was still responding—in the inevitable way, hence the subsequent battle.

However, he was concealing the attraction scorching through his blood effectively enough and he was well used to conducting a conversation that bore no reality to what was going on inside him. He might have been momentarily distracted when she'd shifted and the movement had exposed even more lovely long leg that he'd suddenly, *appallingly*, wanted to touch, but their discussion had remained—and would continue to remain—firmly on track. Kate would never have any idea of the fierce need pounding away inside him. It was purely physical and of zero importance anyway, and nothing she could do or say would ever entice him to yield to it. Not the blush on her cheeks, not the darkening of her irises, not the soft breathy gasp.

'Is there anything else you need?' he said coolly, his voice bearing not even a hint of the inner turmoil he was experiencing.

'No. Thank you. I have everything else under control.'

Lucky her. 'Let me know if that changes.'

'Of course,' she said, about to move again before clearly thinking the better of it, thank *God*, and adding, 'And, actually, thank you for your offer of help. That "you win" of mine was churlish.'

'It was.'

'Although, to be fair, you *had* just ridden roughshod over my plans without any consideration for my feelings.'

She had a point, just not one he could bring himself to apologise for. 'Perhaps.'

'Nevertheless, that's no excuse,' she continued. 'I apologise. My parents were particularly hot on manners. They'd be spinning in their graves at my lack of them...' She tailed off for a moment, a flash of sorrow flitting across her expression, but then gave herself a quick shake. 'Anyway,' she said briskly, 'I really am grateful for your offer. And since this seems to be the moment for it, I suppose I also ought to thank you for closing down that website.'

Sitting back and ignoring the desire to respond to that moment of grief because he didn't do emotion and it was no business of his anyway, Theo rested his elbows on the arms of his chair. 'Oh?' he said, arching an eyebrow since only five minutes ago she'd been outraged by what he'd done. 'Why?'

'There were emails,' she said with a shudder. 'Disturbing ones. There are some very sick people out there.'

'What did you expect?' he said, not even wanting to *think* about the offers she might have received.

'I'm not entirely sure,' she said with a naivety he envied because he'd give everything he had not to know the depths people could sink to. 'A few emails perhaps, maybe resulting in one or two regular clients with more money than sense. Certainly not *that* kind of a response. To be honest, it never occurred to me that my virginity would cause such a furore.'

He'd never have imagined taking such an interest in it either. He still couldn't work out why he did. 'You are pretty unique.'

Her eyebrows lifted and another blush tinged her cheeks. 'Am I?'

'In this day and age a twenty-six-year-old virgin is unusual.'

She appeared to deflate for a moment, but then rallied. 'I suppose so,' she said with a shrug.

'What's the issue?'

'It's none of your business.'

'True.'

She tilted her head. 'Why would you want to know anyway?'

Good question. He barely knew her. He didn't do personal and didn't need to know. He certainly had no intention of helping her out with it, and where the hell had that idea even *come* from? Nonetheless, he could tell himself all he liked that it was important to be in full possession of all the facts so he could stop her embarking on any further acts of recklessness, but the plain truth was that for some reason he just wanted to know. 'I'm curious.'

'It's hardly an appropriate topic for a boss/employee conversation,' she countered. 'And besides, I'm still on probation.'

No problem there. He'd spoken to her line manager in

the accounts department earlier just in case she did need firing. Fortunately, she didn't. Her work was superb and she was a reliable, valued member of the team.

'You're excellent at your job,' he said. 'You'll pass it. And we crossed the boss/employee line the minute you tried to access the Belle's Angels site from a computer I own.'

'Nevertheless, no.'

'Okay, fine,' he said, annoyed with himself for pushing it. He wasn't *that* curious, dammit. If she didn't want to tell him, so what? In fact, it was a good thing, because she ought to go. The battle he was having to keep his eyes off her legs and his mind off the rest of her was taking more effort than he'd anticipated. Their business was concluded and, frankly, the sooner he could get back to work, back to *normal*, the better. 'You can see yourself out.'

Kate watched Theo nod in the direction of the door and then turn his attention to whatever was on his computer screen, and thought that if that wasn't a cue to leave, she didn't know what was. As dismissals went it was unambiguous. She'd refused to play ball and he'd lost interest. Which was fine. There was no way she was going to share the issues surrounding her non-existent sex-life with her boss, of all people. Imagine the humiliation. It didn't bear thinking about.

Therefore his cue was one she was going to take. Right now. She was going to get up, waltz out and go home, where she could ponder at length this evening's whole surreal conversation and, when it came to her money troubles, pinch herself hard.

So why wasn't she moving? Why did her bottom appear to be glued to the chair? Why was her heart hammering at such a rate it might crack a rib and why was a cold sweat breaking out all over her skin? She couldn't actually be thinking of telling him what he wanted to know, could she?

No. It was out of the question. Theo Knox was the very *last* man she ought to want to confide in, although her brother had obviously had time for the guy and he *was* prepared to come through for Milly so maybe he wasn't all bad. But that was irrelevant. Spilling her innermost thoughts and fears to him would be insane. Complete and utter professional suicide. Not to mention epically mortifying. Besides, why would she even *want* to? She shouldn't. She *didn't*.

And yet, to her horror, it was growing increasingly tempting to think to hell with it and throw caution to the wind. She could feel the pressure to do exactly that building unbearably inside her, and the words were on the tip of her tongue, piling up one on top of the other, clamouring for release.

What was going on? she wondered in mounting panic, clamping her lips together as horror thundered through her. Had the stress of everything that had happened lately finally broken her down? Had Theo cunningly deployed some sort of reverse psychology that suddenly had her desperate to share every tiny detail? Or was it simply that now she'd experienced a smidgeon of his interest she wanted more?

Impossible, she told herself as she took a deep breath through her nose and willed the dizziness to subside. That would be utterly ridiculous. She wasn't that pathetic. She certainly wasn't so starved of attention that she'd forfeit her dignity and fall on any crumb dropped at her feet.

But when *was* the last time a man had expressed any interest in her? Ever? Okay, so Theo had made it perfectly clear at Mike's funeral he wasn't interested in her like *that*, and that was fine because it wasn't as if she wanted him to do anything about her little problem, was it? Heaven forbid. When she did finally get around to losing her virginity she didn't want him anywhere near her. He was rude, high-handed and unpleasant and made her bristle with loathing, although, come to think of it, it wasn't loathing she'd been bristling with for the last quarter of an hour. She wasn't entirely sure what it was, any more than she understood what that charged moment when he'd looked at her legs had been about. The blessed relief that her money worries were over, most probably.

It couldn't be anything else. It certainly couldn't be attraction. What a waste of time and energy *that* would be. Even if she *had* liked him, Theo Knox was so far out of her league he was on another planet. He was a staggeringly handsome, enormously successful billionaire. She was an inexperienced ordinary woman of significantly above average height, who managed to look passable on a good day in the right clothes, of which, truth be told, she had few since it was expensive to clothe well a body like hers. She was moderately good at her job and reasonably intelligent, but she wasn't beautiful. She wasn't special. In fact, she was the very opposite of special.

But regardless of her non-specialness, *something* about what she'd done had caught his attention enough to summon her up here and grill her when he could have just had her fired. And that was more appealing than it ought to be.

And so it seemed that—oh, dear—she *was* that pitiful and she *was* that starved of attention, because whatever the cost to her pride she wanted Theo's interest back. She wanted to matter to someone. It was undoubtedly stupid and she definitely didn't want to think about what it said about her, but the longer she sat there, the more inevitable it became, the more powerful was the urge to share, and she suddenly didn't have the strength to resist.

'Well, if you *really* want to know,' she said, vaguely wondering if she hadn't completely lost the plot, 'mainly it's my height.'

'What?' Theo snapped as he whipped his head round,

his deep scowl clearly indicating his displeasure at her continued presence.

'It's my height.'

'What the hell does that have to do with anything?'

'Everything.'

'Why? Lying down—or in most other positions, for that matter—height makes absolutely no difference.'

What?

Okay...

'Well, naturally I don't know much about that,' she said, hoping she wasn't blushing quite as madly as she suspected and wishing she had stronger willpower. 'But I hit six foot some time around my fifteenth birthday. I was lanky and clumsy and towered over the boys in my class at school. When it came to adolescent hook-ups they gave me a wide berth. There were plenty of other more normal girls to choose from.'

'There is nothing abnormal about you,' he said darkly, his gaze roaming all over her and setting her skin on fire.

'Others might beg to differ,' she said, determinedly ignoring it. 'It was a difficult time anyway. My parents had just died and my twelve-year-old sister was in hospital, fighting for survival. Life as I knew it had shattered. Most people were kind and full of sympathy. Others, not so much. Some didn't know how to handle it, well, me, really, and teenagers can be cruel, can't they?'

His eyes narrowed. 'What did they do?'

'It was more a case of what they *said*,' she said, her throat tightening as she recalled the grief, pain and confusion that had dominated her emotions during that time. 'There were a lot of stupid, nasty rumours going round. A few bitchy comments. On one particularly memorable occasion a boy came up to me and said that my parents must have deliberately crashed because death was preferable to the embarrassment of having such a freak for a daughter.'

There was a pause, during which Theo's jaw clenched imperceptibly and his entire body seemed to tense. 'I literally have no words,' he said eventually.

'No, well, that wasn't pleasant. It took me a while to get over it all, the loss of my parents, the new reality my sister faced, the bullying and then the guilt that my brother had been forced to leave university to come and look after me. And then when I did—which was no mean feat, I can tell you, not least because part of me was convinced that it wasn't fair of me to live my life when Milly's had been so devastatingly curtailed—it was to discover that even grown men are put off by my height. Apparently it's emasculating. Not to mention intimidating.'

A tiny muscle began to hammer in Theo's cheek. 'That's pathetic,' he said grimly.

'I know,' she said with a casual 'what can you do?' kind of shrug, as if the years of bullying and rejection that had crippled her self-esteem and destroyed her sense of self-worth meant nothing. 'But, well, it was what it was and on the upside, all that time my classmates and fellow uni students were dating I spent studying. I got a first-class degree and now have a career I love.'

'I find your height neither emasculating nor intimidating,' said Theo, his eyes not leaving hers for a second.

'Why would you?' she said as a tiny shiver raced down her spine. 'You're a hugely successful businessman with the world at his fingertips. I doubt you're intimidated by anything.' Or emasculated. He oozed such virile masculinity it simply wasn't possible.

'You'd be surprised.'

As his mouth curved into a faint smile, Kate thought that this was another of those occasions she wanted to look away. More than she wanted to know what intimidated him, which was saying something. The intensity of his gaze was making her skin feel all hot and prickly and yet again she was finding it oddly hard to breathe. She felt trapped. On fire. And suddenly, quite out of the blue, acutely aware of him.

Inexplicably, the tiniest of details began to register. The minute scar that bisected his right eyebrow. The slight bump on the bridge of his nose. And was that a silvery grey hair she could see at his left temple in amongst all the ebony? She rather thought it was.

And it wasn't only the physical details that she now noticed. She could sense the tension radiating off him and the power he was keeping tightly leashed. The non-verbal signals he was emanating gave her the impression he was furious. On her behalf. And although she had no idea why that would be the case it made her go all warm and fuzzy.

What would it have been like to have had someone like him on her side when she'd been at school? she couldn't help wondering as the silence stretching between them thickened. What would it feel like now?

Come to think of it, what would *he* feel like? He'd be hard and muscled, she was sure. All over. He wasn't the type to tolerate softness. Except maybe where his lips were concerned. Those looked nice and velvety. And what about the sprinkling of dark hair she could see on the backs of his hands? Would it be rough to the touch or silky? And where else might he have it? She had no way of knowing, and now, bizarrely, that, as well as the realisation she'd never find out how soft his lips actually were, seemed a shame.

'Anyway,' she said, baffled by the unexpectedly carnal turn of her thoughts and suddenly really rather keen to lighten the weirdly tense atmosphere, 'your experience of height has probably been far different from mine.'

Theo started, as if she'd jerked him out of deep thought, and his brows snapped together. 'Has it?'

'Has anyone asked you what the weather's like up there?'

'No.'

'Suggested a career in basketball?'

'No.'

'I bet you haven't ever had to put up with tiny little aeroplane seats and bashed knees.'

'I have a private jet.'

Of course he did. 'I always wanted a little zippy convertible,' she said with a whimsical sigh. He nodded and she thought for a nanosecond that maybe he did understand after all. 'Being hugged is a problem.'

'Is it?'

'Yes,' she said with a nod, although it wouldn't be a problem if it was Theo doing the hugging, would it? Her head would tuck into his neck perfectly. Her body would fit against his beautifully. And then she'd know exactly how hard and muscled he was…

'Doorways.'

What? Oh. 'Pendant lights.'

'Hotel showers.'

Not helping. But what was going on? Why was she so flustered by the thought of Theo in the shower? Why was she even *thinking* about Theo in the shower? And why did she get the impression he was thinking about her in the shower? Unanswerable questions all of them, so she put them out of her mind and focused. 'Much of the world is structurally tallist, don't you think?' she said, thankfully sounding more in control than she felt.

'It is,' he said with the glimmer of a smile so fleeting the minute it was gone she thought she must have imagined it.

'Sleeves?'

'My clothes are tailor-made.' Naturally. 'Shoes?'

'Nightmare,' she said. 'I'm a size nine. And I never wear heels. You?'

'Heels have never been my thing,' he said, that faint smile back again.

Kate nearly fell off her chair because, good heavens, was that a *joke*? Crikey.

'It's hard to be inconspicuous.'

He arched an eyebrow. 'Is that a negative?'

It was for her. She'd been taller than her contemporaries since the moment she'd learned to walk. Throughout her childhood barely a week had passed without someone commenting on it. She couldn't remember a time she hadn't felt different, and not in a good way. No amount of positive parental input had helped. She'd just wanted to be the same as everyone else. To fit in. Subsequently she'd spent so much of her childhood and teenage years hunching her shoulders and trying to appear shorter than she was her posture was abysmal. 'I imagine that depends who you are.'

'You command attention.'

Obviously he was using the 'you' in the general sense, not referring to her in particular, but nevertheless she weirdly found herself sitting up a bit straighter. 'Possibly,' she hedged.

'And statistically, taller people tend to earn a higher salary.'

Her eyebrows lifted. 'Really?' That *was* interesting.

'So I once read.'

'I must remember that at my next performance review.'

'I would.' He paused, then said, 'Light bulbs.'

'Maxi-dresses,' she batted back.

'You never have a problem reaching for something from a high shelf.'

'And you can always spot friends in a crowd.'

'Quite,' he said. 'Definite pluses.'

His words were spoken evenly enough, but something flickered across his expression and the smile faded, and it suddenly occurred to her that while she'd assumed he was too uptight and aloof to do friends, maybe it wasn't just that. Maybe it was more that it was lonely at the top. And so maybe he was as lonely as she was…

Or not.

The strangely electric heat surging through her dissipated and she went cold, because what planet was she *on*? A man like Theo would never be lonely. He certainly wouldn't lack for female companionship. Just because nothing appeared about him in the gossip columns didn't mean he was a monk. And a moment or two of banter did not make him a kindred spirit. She must have been mad to imagine he ever could be. And to think she'd even harboured the vague hope that he might have some advice for her about how to deal with an excess of centimetres. Of course he wouldn't. He clearly had no hang-ups about anything at all, and why would he? He was a god and she was about as far from goddess-ness as it was possible to get. She and Theo were poles apart in virtually every way. She had to be even more starved of attention than she realised if she was deluding herself with the idea that they somehow shared something unique. And as for the inappropriate little fantasies about hugging and showers, what had she been *thinking*?

The setting sun was casting an oddly seductive golden glow across his office and the sense of intimacy it created was messing with her head. That was the trouble. It spun a sort of web that rendered reality all blurry. That was why she found it so easy to talk to him. Why she'd been all of a flutter when he'd so casually mentioned the many sexual positions he'd obviously experienced.

The sooner she could get out of here, the better. If she stayed, who knew what else she might reveal? She'd already humiliated herself quite enough. Once she'd started talking she hadn't shut up. Besides, what with the rolling of her stomach and the bizarre way she kept going hot and cold at the same time, she was beginning to feel very peculiar indeed.

'So, anyway,' she said with a feebly bright smile. 'There you are. The reasons why I'm still a virgin. Basically no one wants me. And on that pretty mortifying note I should definitely go. I'm sure you have plenty to be getting on with and I've taken up more than enough of your time. So, sorry for the firewall breach thing and, uh, thanks for everything… I'd best be off. Unless, of course, there's anything else?'

CHAPTER THREE

ANYTHING ELSE?

Anything else?

God.

There was so much going on in Theo's head he didn't know how to even *begin* to unravel it. How he was managing to keep a grip on things he had no idea. If he'd known what chaos Kate was going to unleash by not leaving when he'd told her to, he'd have picked her up and carried her out instead of ignoring his better judgement and like an idiot encouraging her to continue.

When she'd been talking about everything she'd been through his entire body had started to churn. When she'd mentioned the short-sighted fools who'd rejected her over the years he'd had an irrational urge to demand a list of names. When she'd revealed that she'd been bullied and how, his hands had curled into fists and he'd wanted to hit something for the first time in fourteen years, six months and ten days. As they'd batted back and forth the pros and cons of being tall, for the briefest of moments he'd forgotten where and who he was and had found himself actually enjoying the conversation, until she'd mentioned friends and he'd crashed back down to earth with a bump.

And then there was the want, the searing, clawing, deeply inappropriate need to show her what the soft gasps and blushes meant and what her body was capable of. Of what they'd be capable of together, because when she'd looked him as if she was somehow imagining him naked he'd nearly combusted.

The strength of his reaction to this woman didn't make any sense. She was by no means the most beautiful woman he'd ever met and he'd always preferred sophisticated experience over naivety. He had absolutely no reason to behave and feel the way he did around her. It was too visceral, too dramatic, and wholly unacceptable.

Why did he even care about her issues anyway? And why had he taken such umbrage to her registration to that site in the first place? As she'd repeatedly told him, none of it was any of his business. She was obviously perfectly capable of taking care of herself. He wasn't responsible for her in any way. Yet hammering away inside him was the conviction that for some unfathomable reason it *was* his business and she *did* need his protection.

He'd never felt anything like it before, he thought grimly as she uncrossed her impossibly long bare legs and put her hands on the arms of the chair. He certainly didn't *want* to feel anything like it. In fact, he'd spent the majority of his adult life avoiding precisely this kind of thing. He'd experienced enough horror, confusion and unpredictability growing up to like his life now controlled, ordered and sterile.

The way he responded to Kate threatened that. It screwed with his head and made a mockery of everything he considered vital. So he ought to just let her go. She wasn't even making it difficult. By getting to her feet, smoothing her clothes and turning to head for the door, clearly taking his silence for acquiescence, she was actually facilitating the best outcome he could have hoped for this evening.

And yet, it wasn't the outcome he wanted. Not by a long shot. He wanted her horizontal and beneath him. He wanted to spend the evening running his hands over every glorious inch of her to see if she felt as silky smooth as she looked. He wanted to find out what sounds she made when she came, and with a primal instinct he'd never have dreamt he possessed, he wanted to be the first man to make her make those sounds.

The battle for control was one he was losing with increasing momentum. The desire thundering through him had grown too powerful to ignore. With every step she took away from him his self-restraint slipped that bit more and he found himself caring that bit less. By the time she reached the door, a hair's breadth from walking out of his life for ever, which should have been perfectly fine but wasn't, all reason had fled. His blood pounded in his ears and his body ached unbearably, and all he could think was, so what if he did respond to her with an unfathomable intensity? Was he really going to let her walk out of here with her self-esteem needlessly non-existent, thinking no one wanted her when someone very definitely did?

Was he hell.

'Stop,' he said roughly, pushing back from his desk and standing up barely before he knew what he was doing.

At the door, her hand on the handle, Kate froze, then turned, and he saw a combination of wariness and surprise filling her expression as she watched him stride across the carpet towards her. 'What is it?'

He came to an abrupt halt a foot in front of her, close enough to see the rapid rise and fall of her chest and hear the breath hitch in her throat. Close enough to reach for her.

'There is one more thing,' he said, jamming his hands into his pockets before he could act on the instinct hammering away inside him.

'Oh?'

'You're wrong.'

She stared at him, bewilderment flickering in the shimmering cobalt depths of her eyes. 'You *don't* have a lot to be getting on with?'

'About your desirability.'

The pulse at the base of her neck began to flutter wildly. 'What?'

'Those boys were fools.'

'In what way?'

'You are very, *very* desirable.'

Her eyes widened for a moment and then she frowned. 'And you are very, *very* funny,' she said. 'Or not at all funny, actually.'

'You think I'm joking?' said Theo darkly, gripped once again by an irrational desire to locate everyone who'd ever decimated her self-esteem and string them up. 'I am *not* joking.'

'Nevertheless,' she said dryly, 'experience would suggest otherwise.'

'You have no experience.'

'Which kind of proves my point.'

'And I can prove *my* point.'

'Oh, yes?' she asked, lifting her chin an inch and arching an eyebrow. 'How?'

Now was the time to retreat, yelled the little voice of reason banging away in his head, demanding to be heard. *Now.* He'd achieved what he'd set out to do when he'd told her to stop. He'd corrected her misconceptions. His work was done. He should take a step back and reinstate some desperately needed distance.

Yet he couldn't move. Her wide-eyed innocence and intoxicating scent were drowning out that voice in his head. The tilt of her face and the challenge in her voice were tugging at a viscerally primitive part of him deep inside. And then he noticed that her breathing was rapid, shallow, that she was staring at his mouth, and now, heaven help him, she was actually leaning towards him, and as a strange feeling of fate enveloped him what little remained of his control simply evaporated.

'Like this,' he muttered, and with one quick step forwards, he took her face in his hands and slammed his mouth down on hers.

* * *

Theo moved so fast, so unexpectedly, that for a nanosecond Kate had no idea what was going on. She was too busy trying to process the seismic shift she'd experienced when he'd demanded she wait and she'd turned to see him striding towards her with the intensity and focus of a heat-seeking missile. The set of his jaw, the hot look in his eye and the gruffness of his voice had made her shiver from head to toe. When he'd stopped just in front of her, the tension emanating from him palpable, something deep inside her had flared to life and rushed through her blood, making her head spin. And then his words. Her? Desirable? Yeah, right.

She didn't know what had made her demand proof of it and she had no idea what she'd expected, but now he was touching her, holding her, *kissing* her, seemingly as if his life depended on it, and she reeled first with the shock of it and then with the electrifying notion that maybe she'd been a bit too quick to dismiss his claims about her appeal. There certainly didn't seem anything half-hearted about the searing pressure of his lips on hers and he really didn't seem the sort of man who would do anything he didn't want to do.

Maybe though, just to check that he hadn't been lying when he said he wasn't joking, she ought to stop just standing there like a flake and start kissing him back. Then she'd know.

Before her courage could fail her or her hang-ups get the better of her, Kate closed her eyes and leaned into him. She put her hands on his waist and took advantage of his sharp intake of breath to part her lips and then crush them back to his. And in that instant the chemistry that she'd been too ignorant to identify before ignited. The second their tongues touched, Theo groaned and immediately deepened the kiss, pulling her closer, sliding his tongue into her mouth and blowing her mind with his breathtaking skill.

As she kissed him back with equal intensity but significantly less skill, she was sure, liquid heat rocketed through her veins and pooled between her legs. Instinctively, she moved her hands further round his back and he tilted his hips, and when she felt the huge rock-hard length of his erection pressing into her abdomen, she suddenly wanted it inside her with a clenching, gnawing, relentless ache that obliterated what remained of her wits.

All rational thought evaporated, and as her head emptied her senses took over with stunning ferocity. She was aware of nothing but Theo, the solidity of his broad chest hard up against the softness of hers, his heady masculine scent and the intoxicating taste of his mouth. The heat emanating from his body fired the flames in hers, turning her insides to molten lava and setting off so many tiny fireworks that her knees went weak.

It was as if some sort of devastatingly powerful tropical weather system had taken up residence inside her, she thought dizzily. And incredibly, it seemed as if Theo were caught up in it too because, in response to the sensory onslaught and the increasingly incendiary kiss, Kate gave a helpless little moan and suddenly he was pushing her back against the door and trapping her there with his big hard body.

And she wasn't complaining. Why would she when she felt so alive, so on fire? When, for the first time ever, it seemed that someone desired her? She was not going to look this gift horse in the mouth, so when Theo removed his hands from her face and clamped them to her waist she granted him better access by arching her back slightly and winding her arms around his neck.

In response, with one hand he shoved her skirt up just enough to jam one hard muscled thigh between hers and with the other he undid the button of her jacket and then tugged her shirt from the waistband of her skirt. And all the while he continued with the drugging, soul-shattering kisses.

As white-hot desire pounded through her, Kate instinctively shifted her hips to grind herself against his thigh and alleviate the burning ache, and then he was sliding his hand beneath her top and up, singeing her sensitised skin, then cupping her breast and rubbing a thumb over her agonisingly tight nipple. The lace of her bra might as well not have been there because she felt the heat of his hand like a brand. The friction was unbearable yet she wanted more. So she pressed herself closer, ground her hips that little bit harder and the hot sparks of electric pleasure jolting through her were so thrilling, so exquisitely powerful that she instinctively tensed and gasped—

And the spell that wild, desperate need had been weaving around them shattered.

As if doused with a bucket of iced water, Theo instantly froze. His hands sprang off her, and with a rough curse he jerked back. He looked stunned. His eyes were black and his breathing was laboured. And as he raked his hands through the hair that only moments ago she'd been threading her fingers through, somewhere in the midst of the hazy desire and intense disappointment that he'd stopped, it occurred to Kate that, yes, he *could* look dishevelled, he *could* be thrown off balance, and oddly enough it was something of a relief.

'That was not meant to happen,' he said roughly, clearly as poleaxed by the strength of the chemistry that flared between them as she was.

No, well, obviously not, she thought, righting her clothes with shaking hands, hugely glad that the door was behind her for support since she wasn't sure her legs were up to the job. 'I'm sorry.'

His gaze shot to hers and his brows snapped together. 'What?' he growled, rubbing his hands over his face and shaking his head. 'No. You have nothing to be sorry about. I do. I overstepped the line. I apologise.'

Oh. Right. 'I thought there was no line.'

'There's a line.' His dark eyes glittered and she shivered. 'And you should go.'

'Or what?' she challenged rashly, responding to the warning she could hear in his tone before she could reflect on the wisdom of her question.

He let out a quick, humourless laugh. 'You do not want to know.'

Oh, but she *did*. 'I do.'

'No.'

'Yes.'

'Fine,' he bit out. 'If you don't go, we cross that line together and your virginity becomes history.'

For a moment his words hovered in the space between them, charging the air with electricity and tension, and then Kate swallowed hard, her heart thundering and the blood drumming her ears. Dear God. What was he saying? Did he want her that much? Or was he merely teasing?

'Are you serious?' she said hoarsely.

'Deadly.'

'You want to have sex with me?'

His eyes drilled into hers as he thrust his hands in his pockets. 'Yes.'

'Why?'

'Why?'

'Well, is this a pity thing?' she asked, accepting the mortification that surged through her because she had to make sure. 'You know, help the poor orphan virgin with her pathetic self-esteem issues? Are you still trying to prove a point?'

His jaw clenched and he looked as if he wanted to hit something. 'No,' he grated, evidently hanging onto his control by a thread. 'You were right. I am not that altruistic. And believe me, pity is the last thing I am feeling at this precise moment.'

'I see,' she said, although really she was too bewildered, too stunned, to see anything.

'Good,' he snapped, taking a step back. 'So, for your own sake, Kate, I suggest you leave. Now.'

It was excellent advice. There was no doubt about that. The evening had taken an unexpectedly dramatic turn. Kate was so out of her depth she was in danger of drowning. With the way her head was spinning and her body was ablaze she ought to be feeling for the handle, yanking open the door and legging it to the lift, to *safety*, as fast as her trembling legs could carry her.

But she didn't want to leave. She didn't want safety. She wanted more of those wild kisses, more of the magnetic darkness and thrilling passion she could sense in him, and she wanted it all with an urgency that was breathtaking.

The strength of her feelings ought to have made her wary. Instead they were electrifying. She'd been hoping to offload her virginity for years. As unbelievable as it was, Theo appeared to be a hair's breadth from taking it, and she desperately wanted him to have it, because that attraction she'd so blithely dismissed as impossible earlier? Blazing.

So to hell with the consequences. So what if he was who he was and she was significantly less? It wasn't as if she were going to bump into him again. They quite literally operated on entirely different levels. Besides, recent events had taught her that life was short, and in all honesty she'd rather regret something she *had* done than something she hadn't.

She took a deep breath, licked her suddenly dry lips and opened her mouth to speak.

'Kate,' Theo cut in tersely, as if he was able to read her mind and found her thoughts deeply ill-advised.

'Yes?' she replied, knowing it was far too late for warnings when the decision was already made.

'Think very carefully.'

'I have.'

'Don't be a fool.'

'I know what I want.'

'I make no promises.'

'I don't want any.' Reality had no place here. 'Once is enough.'

He took a step towards her, his gaze cleaved to hers, and her entire body began to tremble with desire, excitement and anticipation.

'Last chance, Kate,' he said, his voice so low and gravelly it scraped along her nerve-endings.

'I'm going nowhere.'

And it was at that precise moment that Theo's patience, already stretched paper thin, snapped. He'd tried to warn Kate off—repeatedly—and he'd given her every opportunity to leave. If she chose to defy him then she was just going to have to face the consequences. She was an adult. As she'd told him earlier, she was perfectly capable of making her own decisions. He was only human, as much at the mercy of scorching desire as the next man, and so, really, there was nothing else to be done.

'Yes, you are,' he muttered, grabbing her hand and peeling her off the door as he inexorably caved in to the raging need he'd been holding at bay for the last five minutes.

'Not here?' she said with a little gasp of surprise.

Up against a door? Her first time? Not a chance. 'Not here.'

'Then where? The sofa? Your desk?'

'My bed,' he said, leading her straight past all the furniture and towards the door cleverly built into the wall and disguised as a bookcase.

'What—?' she started, pulling back a little, instinctively resisting the idea of walking into a wall, until he pushed the section he'd had constructed, the door opened and he led her through.

'Oh, wow,' she breathed, looking around the white minimalist room that was bathed in the soft light of the setting sun. 'You have a suite.'

He kicked the door shut, let go of her hand and strode past her towards the bed. 'I do.'

'It's incredible.'

'It's convenient,' he said, loosening the knot of his tie and pulling the whole thing off.

'For seducing the odd virgin who comes along?'

He looked at her. 'You're the first and you're not odd.'

'You're funny.'

'You're still talking.'

'I may be a bit nervous,' she said. 'Your bed is huge.'

Theo tossed his tie onto the armchair that sat in the corner of the room and undid the top two buttons of his shirt. 'If you change your mind—at *any* point—we'll stop.' It might well kill him, but he would.

Kate gave her head a quick shake and the relief that flooded through him was so fierce he didn't want to analyse it ever. 'I won't want to stop,' she said, staring at the wedge of his chest that was now exposed with a hunger he doubted she was even aware of. 'Especially not if you make it good.'

Good? *Good?* 'With chemistry like ours,' he said tautly, 'I won't even need to *try.*'

'Nonetheless, I'm expecting great things.'

'You don't know what to expect.'

Her lips quirked into a quick smile that for some reason stabbed him right in the chest. 'Ah, but that's where you're wrong, Theo. I've had orgasms. Good ones. However, I want more. I want fireworks.'

'Demanding,' he muttered, his pulse racing as his head

filled with images of how she might have gone about achieving all those good orgasms.

'Long-suffering and impatient and *extremely* ready to get on with it.'

'Then stop talking.'

'Tell me what to do.'

'Come here.'

She walked—no, *sashayed* towards him, pulling the band out of her hair so that it flowed around her shoulders like liquid gold, and it was all he could do not to stalk over to her, pick her up and tumble her straight down onto the bed before whipping the desire into a frenzy and then sinking into her. Instead, he drummed up a modicum of control to merely pull her into his arms and capture her mouth with another kiss that blew his mind.

There was nothing mere about her response, though. It was as fierce as it had been when he'd first taken her in his arms and they'd shared the kiss that had been utterly unplanned, deeply unwise and yet stunningly hot.

Now as they devoured each other, she wound her arms around his neck and pressed herself against him, every inch of her seeming to fit to him perfectly, and the desire beating through his blood erupted.

Somewhere deep in the recesses of his mind he was aware he shouldn't be doing this, that if he knew what was good for him he would stop and put as much distance between himself and Kate as was humanly possible. He was no Prince Charming and it wasn't his job to help with her issues. God knew he had plenty of his own to fix. Besides, one touch of her and he turned into a man he didn't recognise and liked even less, a man driven by the basest of instincts, a man without control.

Yet he couldn't have stopped now even if someone had been holding a gun to his head. He wanted her with a hunger it was impossible to ignore, a hunger that had had him pinning her up against a door and forgetting his name.

He could tell himself all he liked that if it wasn't him relieving her of her virginity it would be someone else—a notion that was so distasteful it made him want to retch—or that it was just because it had been a while since he'd taken a woman to bed, but in truth…well, in truth there was no reason beyond clawing need and a desire that demanded to be assuaged.

And it would be fine, he assured himself, his muscles tightening as she slid her hands beneath the lapels of his jacket and pushed up. Kate might be innocent when it came to sex but she wasn't stupid. She knew the score. His conscience was clear on that front at least. Once it was over that would be that. He'd put her in a cab and out of his mind, and the entire evening would be consigned to history. He'd lock up the memories and throw away the key. He'd have no need for them. In the meantime, however, he was going to focus on her, on *them*, and on getting naked as soon as was humanly possible.

Breaking off the kiss, he shrugged his jacket off and it fell to the floor. 'Anyone would think you'd done this before,' he muttered thickly as she moved her hands to his shirt and started tackling the buttons while he set to work on getting her out of her skirt.

'I did once get to second base,' she murmured, her breathing all ragged and shallow. 'But that was only because of a bet.'

What? A *bet*? Somewhere in the recesses of his mind Theo was aware that little bombshell needed processing, but there was no way it was happening now. Not when all his blood was rushing from his brain to a different part of his anatomy entirely.

'Doesn't matter.' Kate frowned and bit her lower lip. 'This isn't working,' she said with a little growl of frustration that had him leaning away to tug on the back of his shirt and pull it over his head and off.

He let it drop on top of his jacket and a moment later her clothes and his trousers had joined the growing heap on the floor. He ran his gaze over her, taking in every incredible inch of her, her skin golden and glowing in the setting sun and, aha, there it was. The tattoo. What looked like an upside-down bird the size of a two-pound coin at her hipbone. He'd wondered. Now he knew. He did not need to know what it represented. That was not what this was about. Instead he focused on the expensive cream lace of her bra and knickers and the intriguing contrast it made with the shapeless navy suit she'd been wearing.

'This is sexy,' he said gruffly, touching her hip and tracing the lace there with his fingertips.

He heard and saw her breath hitch in her throat and the knowledge that she was turned on so easily had the blood thundering in his ears.

'Underwear is about the only thing that fits me properly,' she said raggedly. 'I like to buy the good stuff.'

She had excellent taste, but— 'Lose it.'

'Help me,' she breathed. 'I'm all fingers and thumbs.'

Gritting his teeth against the pounding desire, Theo put his hands on her shoulders and turned her around. He unclipped her bra and he slid it off her, then swept her hair to one side and pressed his mouth to the spot where her neck met her shoulder. She shivered. Dropped her head against his shoulder and leaned back, and the sigh she let out hit him right in the chest.

He closed his eyes, the scent of her filling his head, and almost of their own accord his hands moved slowly down her back and then round, beneath her arms, to cup her breasts. As he took the heavy weight in his palms, she gasped softly and arched her back, which pushed her breasts further into his hands and her bottom into the hard, aching length of his erection, and it took everything he had to stay where he was instead of where he wanted to be.

He swore, low and guttural, the word smothered by her skin, as desire surged to an almost agonising level. While he continued to tease her breast and nipple with one hand, he stroked the other down the smooth silky planes of her torso, her abdomen, until he slipped it beneath the lace of her knickers and reached the soft curls at the juncture of her thighs. At the intimacy of his touch she tensed for a second, and he stilled.

'Want me to stop?' he murmured, hoping to God she didn't.

'Don't you dare,' she breathed, backing up her words by opening her legs and gripping his forearm.

He parted her with his fingers and stroked, and she was so wet, so hot, it nearly unravelled him. But she hadn't done this before, at least not with anyone else. He had to go slowly, be gentle and give her time to adjust, however much it killed him. He would not be that man who lost control and shoved her up against a door.

Abandoning her breast, he took her chin and turned her head slightly and kissed her, while lower he slipped first one finger into her slippery heat and then another. Slowly he rubbed and stroked, feeling her tremble, hearing her sigh and gasp, and automatically registered her responses. When she moaned into his mouth, then whimpered, however, the sound of it blitzed his brain and he couldn't help moving his fingers that little bit faster, that little bit harder.

One of her hands shot up to the back of his head and her kisses grew frantic. Her other hand covered his, urging him on, moving him exactly where she wanted him. Her hips twisted, minutely at first, then more frenziedly and suddenly she was wrenching her mouth from his, crying out and clenching around his fingers and it was so sexy, so intense, that Theo nearly came right along with her.

CHAPTER FOUR

KATE WAS STILL tumbling down from her first orgasm given to her by someone else when her legs were whipped from beneath her and she was picked up as if she weighed nothing. Her head was still spinning. Her entire body was still quivering, and little darts of ebbing pleasure kept shooting through her, and they hadn't even got round to the actual virginity-taking part of the evening yet.

But as Theo deposited her on the bed and then turned his attention to the drawer of the bedside table, the heat dissipated and the fireworks faded. With every second that ticked by she became aware that she was lying there naked and exposed and vulnerable, and the insecurities that had been nowhere to be seen moments ago kicked in.

It wasn't that she was ashamed of the wild, desperate abandon with which she'd responded to him. She wasn't. At least, not much. It was more that she'd been so caught up in the way he'd made her feel she hadn't given her body a moment's thought beyond the pleasure it was experiencing. And then there was the fact that from the moment she'd started shedding her clothing at no point had Theo been able to look at her properly. To judge.

But with her sprawled across his bed like this, he could now, and she couldn't help wonder what he would think. There was just so much of her. She might have the height of a supermodel but she did not have the frame. She had padding. What if there was too much? Best not to let him see, she decided, scooting beneath the sheets and clutching them to her chest, then watching him take a foil packet out of the drawer and rip it open.

Of course, in terms of surface area there was way more

of Theo, but in his case that wasn't a negative because he was quite the sight for sore eyes. She'd been right in her assessment of how hard he'd be. He had muscles everywhere. They rippled across the breadth of his shoulders and flexed in his strong powerful thighs. And she didn't have to wonder about where else he might have a smattering of hair any longer. She could see it sprinkled across the lean planes of his chest, then narrowing down to the erection onto which he was now rolling the condom with what looked like impressive efficiency although what did she know?

Moments ago, all that hardness and strength had been rubbing up against her back, the friction driving her wild. With any luck it would be soon rubbing up against her front, driving her even wilder. Assuming he didn't change his mind about the whole virginity-taking thing, of course. Which was a possibility because really he was out of her league in every single way. He might well take one proper look at her, wonder what on earth he was doing and leave her there feeling like a fool. And quite honestly, she wouldn't blame him.

'Stop it,' Theo muttered, his voice low and rough.

Jerked out of her madly oscillating thoughts, Kate lifted her gaze to his and saw that he was looking at her, his eyes dark and his face tense. 'Stop what?'

'Whatever it is you're thinking.'

Flushing, she bit her lip and glanced across at the curtainless windows. 'Is there some way of shutting out the light?'

'No.'

Right. 'Would you mind closing your eyes, then?'

'Yes. I would.'

'In that case, I'll just have to close mine.'

He stood there before her, enviably unselfconscious, and regarded her thoughtfully. 'You have no idea how much I want you, do you?'

'Well, I guess…that…is some sort of indication,' she said, waving a hand in the direction of his erection and vaguely wondering how on earth something of that length and girth was supposed to fit, 'but seeing as I have nothing to compare it with, no, not really.'

'You will.'

He leaned down, putting one knee on the mattress, and as he came down beside her he tugged the sheet down to her waist. When she tried to grab it back he took her wrists and held them to the bed. He ran his gaze over her for one long slow moment and a rush of heat surged through her. Her nipples tightened and a fresh ribbon of desire began to unfurl deep inside her.

'You are stunning,' he murmured and she wished she could believe it. At least he hadn't called her beautiful. If he'd done that she'd have known he was lying. 'And I am extraordinarily attracted to you,' he added gruffly, 'so stop worrying.'

Easier said than done. But the physical responses he aroused in her body did seem to obliterate her self-consciousness and whitewash her mind, so maybe she ought to trust it would work again. 'Make me,' she breathed, and he didn't need asking a second time.

Bending his head, Theo kissed her long and hard, and as she'd hoped, as before, her insecurities faded, and rational thought gave way to something primal, instinctive and way beyond her control.

As he continued his devastating assault on her mouth she softened inside with renewed need. He lowered himself, twisting slightly so he lay half on top of her, and the deliciously heavy weight of him pressed her down. So much strength and power, she thought giddily. So contained. And as for his scent, that was a dizzying combination of spice and wood and something she couldn't identify but tugged at a spot deep inside her.

Swept up in a maelstrom of desire and heat, and feeling slight and feminine for the first time in her life, Kate moaned as she kissed him back and writhed against him in a desperate, instinctive effort to get closer.

With a harsh groan, Theo tore his mouth from hers and moved it to her breast, and if she thought the sensations had been stunning when he'd touched her there earlier they were nothing compared to the electricity that zinged through her at the heat and feel of his mouth.

She clamped a hand to the back of his head and let out a strangled gasp as her stomach liquefied. He turned his attention to her other breast and as the desire rocketed through her with ever-increasing intensity, the need to touch him back became overwhelming.

She wanted to explore him. Everywhere and at length. With her hands and her mouth. She wanted to learn the texture of his skin and the strength of his muscles. She wanted to see if she could drive him as crazy as he was driving her. She'd read books. She'd seen films. She had a fairly good idea of what to do.

But what if she did it wrong? niggled the tiny voice in her head that managed to penetrate the chaos. He'd implied he wanted her a lot, and it certainly seemed that way, but what if her clumsy, naïve attempts put him off? What if he *laughed*? She couldn't risk it. And besides, she was getting impatient. Theo's kisses and caresses were divine but she wanted more. She *needed* more. Deep inside she actually ached.

The sheet that before had acted as a shield was now just in the way. It was stopping her from feeling the whole length of his body against hers, and she wanted it gone. She wanted nothing between them, not even air. So beneath him she wriggled and struggled, kicking at the fine white cotton, and Theo froze.

'What's wrong?' he said sharply, instantly lifting himself off her, and staring down at her, his eyes blazing. 'Do you want to stop?'

'Stop?' Kate muttered with a frown. 'Why would I want to stop?' Nothing short of Armageddon would make her want to stop now. Maybe not even that.

'Then what's the matter?'

'The sheet. I'm trying to get rid of it.'

'Are you sure?'

'Never been more so.'

'Thank God for that,' he breathed, yanking it off her and tossing it to one side.

Finally free, Kate bent her leg and, turning slightly, pressed her pelvis to his, her body clearly knowing how to ask for what it wanted. And Theo seemed to get it because he put a knee between her thighs and nudged her legs apart, and then he was between them, looming over her, his jaw clenched and his face dark and tight.

She could feel him at her entrance and she caught her breath, her pulse racing. It was about to happen, she thought, her entire body trembling and her heart swelling with a giant tangle of emotions she couldn't begin to unravel even if she wanted to. It was finally about to happen. After all these years. After everything...

She let her knees drop, parting her legs even wider, and then he was sliding into her, inch by incredible inch, giving her time to adjust to the strange feeling of being stretched and filled.

'Oh, my God,' she breathed, when he was embedded in her, deep and hard and strange.

'Are you all right?' he muttered harshly.

She took a moment to think about it. It might feel odd, but it hadn't hurt. She was getting used to it, and the promise of what he could do to her, how he could make her feel, bloomed inside her. 'Extremely all right,' she said, the desire and excitement building all over again at the thought of the pleasure to come. 'You?'

'Fine.'

Fine? Just *fine*? Oh, well. He had done this before. It was only momentous for her. Nevertheless, she sighed deeply and he grimaced.

'Don't move,' he said roughly.

'Why not?'

'Because if you do this will be over before it's begun.'

Oh. 'It was just a sigh.'

'That's all it'll take.'

He really wanted her that much? Perhaps he did. She could feel him pulsating deep within her. She could see the tension in his face and straining of his muscles. He looked as though it was taking every drop of his control to hold back, and it wasn't what she wanted. It wasn't what she needed.

'What if I can't help it?' she said, the ache spreading through her body demanding release with an insistence that was impossible to ignore.

'Try.'

'Impossible. Sorry.' It was too much. The need gnawing away inside her was too strong to control. Her hips shifted of their own accord, and Theo groaned.

'Heaven help me,' he said through gritted teeth before lowering his head and kissing her fiercely as he slowly withdrew, dragging along all her nerve endings, sending new thrills of desire coursing through her, and then plunged back into her.

The rhythmic pull and push of his movements stoked the flames inside her, melting her bones and boiling her blood. Her hands somehow found their way to his shoulders and she could feel his muscles shift beneath her palms with every strong powerful thrust of his body.

He was blowing her mind, and within minutes her breath

was coming in short sharp pants, her heart was thundering so hard it could well escape and all she could think about was racing towards a finishing line that was simultaneously rushing towards her.

Stifling a sob of desperation, Kate wrapped her arms round Theo's neck and her legs round his waist, and it must have been the right thing to do because suddenly he was moving faster and harder, pounding into her over and over again, pushing her higher and higher, until the unbearable tension within her snapped and, with a cry, she shattered.

White-hot pulses of pleasure, stronger and more powerful than anything she'd ever experienced, barrelled through her body. Stars exploded behind her eyelids and lit up her nerve-endings. She felt as if she were falling apart, and it was so intensely incredible that she barely registered Theo letting out a tortured groan, thrusting one last time and then burying himself deep and pumping into her over and over again.

As he collapsed on top of her and they lay there for a moment, all ragged breath, pounding hearts and long sweaty tangled limbs, Kate reeled with the intensity and magnificence of it all.

She'd done it, she thought, feeling weak, limp and completely wrung out. She'd actually done it. She wasn't frigid. She wasn't undesirable. All those years of disappointment and rejection, wiped right out. All those horrible mean comments, wrong.

The enormity of everything that had happened this evening suddenly struck and emotion welled up inside her, a swirling mix of relief and triumph, inexplicably tinged with guilt and sorrow, so massive, so overwhelming that she felt a tear escape and trickle down her temple.

But this really wasn't the time or the place to dissolve into a puddle, she told herself, choking off a sob and blinking frantically as Theo carefully levered himself off her and rolled onto his back. She'd save that for the privacy of home. Right now she needed to act as if everything was fine. Deep breaths and composure. That was what was called for here.

'So that exceeded my expectations,' she said huskily, with a nonchalance that sounded almost genuine.

'Good.'

'Thank you.'

'You're welcome.'

She thought she detected a note of aloofness in his voice that was at odds with the gruff impatience that had dominated his tone for the last half an hour, and glanced over. He was staring at the ceiling, and gone was the raw passion and the fevered tension, she saw. His expression didn't bear even the hint of a reaction to what had just happened. He certainly wasn't about to collapse into a quivering heap as she was. He was back in control, and this whole mad little interlude was over.

'So…ah… I should probably, really, go now,' she said, keen to leave before the situation could get any more awkward but unsure of the etiquette.

'You should,' he said, pushing himself up off the bed and, with barely a backwards glance, heading in the direction of what she presumed was the bathroom. 'Get dressed and I'll call you a cab.'

Kate spent much of the following forty-eight hours either breathlessly reliving the earth-shattering encounter with Theo in his office in gloriously vivid Technicolor or being battered by the emotions she'd managed to stave off when lying there in his bed.

At home, there was no one to witness the moments she drifted off into a sizzling daydream from which she generally emerged hot, flushed and trembling. Or the occasions when muscles she never knew she had twanged and she suddenly felt so vulnerable, so raw, it brought a lump to her throat and tears to her eyes. Alone, safely cocooned within her own four walls, she had no need for defences, which was just as well because any she might have mounted would have been crushed within seconds. The enormity of what had happened—not to mention the speed and unexpectedness of it—was simply too overwhelming.

She couldn't stop thinking about what it meant. She was no longer a virgin, was the bewildering, incredible realisation that kept ricocheting around her mind while she pottered about her flat achieving very little. She was no longer unusual. Well, not on *that* front, at least. She was still a great, unwieldy giant, and the boost that Theo's rampant need had given her would no doubt fade, but losing one's virginity was a rite of passage others took for granted and she'd finally made it.

And now she had, it was as if a light had suddenly switched on in her head, illuminating the shadows and making sense of things that deep down she'd always found baffling. Such as why she'd never found anyone willing to date her when out of a potential population of millions *surely* there would have been someone somewhere. It wasn't even as if she were particularly fussy, so how come she'd never met a single man who'd been up for it?

Maybe she just hadn't looked hard enough, she thought now. In fact, maybe she hadn't looked at all. Maybe it had been easier, safer, to resign herself to the status quo. Maybe she'd even become accepting of it. *Happy* with it.

And when she asked herself why that might be, it began to dawn on her that when she'd told Theo about the relationship between her height and her virginity she hadn't furnished him with the whole truth. What she hadn't revealed, what she hadn't even *known* at the time, was that for years she'd been scared. Of sex. Scared of doing it wrong and making even more of a fool of herself than she already felt.

It was so obvious now she could see it from the other

side. When she forced herself to look back to her troubled adolescence, to the time when her school friends had started losing their virginity and talked about it in great detail, she remembered she'd been fascinated and so excited about her turn, so desperate to be normal and fit in.

But when her turn never materialised, when it became apparent that she would always be on the outside, always rejected, she'd become quieter and had hidden her embarrassment and shame behind an air of mystery. Over the years that embarrassment and shame had escalated and had eventually turned into fear, which had put her off even more, creating a vicious circle that she hadn't even been aware of and which had possibly spread to other areas of her personal life, preventing her from trying new things in case they didn't work out and she made even more of an idiot of herself in the process.

But she'd had nothing to fear. Sex with Theo had been incredible. And momentous. And not only because she'd finally got rid of her virginity at the grand old age of twenty-six. Didn't it also prove that even though she would probably never be normal and would most likely never fit in, she might just *not* make a fool of herself? Theo certainly hadn't laughed at her, and he'd seen her stripped of not just her clothes but also of the protective shield she'd always kept wrapped round her.

So what was she going to do going forward? Was she really going to spend the rest of her life not trying things, just in case? Didn't that seem a bit of a waste? And hadn't there already been too much waste of life in the Cassidy family?

Surely she owed to it to herself, to her parents and her siblings, to make the most of what she had. To live life to the max. She'd allowed her virginity to hold her back by tethering her to a time of her life dominated by painful memories and teenage angst for too long.

Well, no more.

Now she'd recognised her fears she was going to confront them and let them go. So there'd be no more hiding. No more slouching. No more trepidation about the unknown. She was going to pull her shoulders back and hold her head up high as she sallied forth. She was going to be brave and bold and fabulous, and nothing was going to stop her.

CHAPTER FIVE

A MONTH LATER, Kate made herself a mint tea and took it into the sitting room to sit cross-legged on the sofa. It was one thing deciding to hold your head up and your shoulders back while you blazed a trail, she thought wretchedly, quite another to put it into practice. Because not only had it become apparent that decade-old deep-seated issues couldn't be wiped out quite as effortlessly as she'd assumed, but also life really did have the habit of suddenly walloping you about the head when you least expected it.

And to think that everything had been going so well. Theo, clearly a man of his word as well as action, had wasted no time in instructing his lawyers, and in the aftermath of a flurry of correspondence between her and his legal team, the monstrous debt her brother had accrued had been paid off and the fund Theo had promised for her sister had been set up.

As she'd hoped, the worries that had been hanging over her like the sword of Damocles disappeared in an instant and the relief was indescribable. Her home was safe and she'd been able to give up her extra jobs, and she had no regrets. Every time she visited her sister and saw how happy and settled she was, she knew she'd done the right thing, even if her visit the first Sunday after That Friday had momentarily shaken that conviction.

'Those are pretty,' she'd said to Milly, spying the huge bouquet of yellow roses sitting on the windowsill having dumped her bag on a chair and given her sister a hug.

'They're my favourite.'

'I know. But where did they come from?'

'Theo.'

At the mention of his name her pulse had leapt and questions had spun around her head but her smile hadn't faltered. 'That's nice.'

Milly had grinned. 'He's very good-looking, isn't he? He said he was a friend of Mike's. I liked him.'

And then her smile *had* faltered. 'He came here?'

'Yes.'

'When?'

'Yesterday.'

'What did he want?'

'To find out what my favourite flowers were.'

'Anything else?'

'I don't think so. I don't remember.'

The conversation had turned to the series Milly was watching on Netflix but Kate hadn't been able to focus. She'd been too concerned about why Theo had really shown up. When she'd questioned the staff, however, they'd reassured her that the only instruction Theo had issued was that Milly was to have whatever she needed. Kate had been sceptical, but gradually she'd come to accept it in much the same way she'd come to accept the flush of heat she experienced every time she looked at the fresh flowers that arrived weekly and reminded her of that Friday evening.

From the man himself she'd heard nothing, nor had she expected to. He'd been very clear about what he was offering and she had no reason to doubt that, which was fine because there was no future to be had with him. Apart from above average height and intense chemistry they had nothing remotely in common, and she'd neither seen nor heard any evidence to suggest he did relationships even if they had.

She hadn't bumped into him at work, thank God. As she'd suspected they trod completely different paths, so there'd been no awkward moments in a lift and no darting into nearby cupboards in an effort to avoid him. She kept her head down and worked hard, passing her probation and being given the pay rise she'd brazenly asked for after recalling what he'd said about tall people earning more.

So far, so fabulous.

But now…

Well…

Who knew what happened now?

Taking a sip of her tea to settle her churning stomach, Kate thought of the small pile of pink and white sticks on the vanity unit in the bathroom and felt her throat tighten and her head spin.

She was pregnant.

Not sick with a stomach bug as she'd assumed two days ago when she'd rung up and told her line manager she was too ill to come in.

Pregnant.

And there was no doubt about it. Because while one test might be faulty, all ten were unlikely to be, damn them and their over ninety-nine per cent accuracy.

But how could it have happened? she wondered for the billionth time since the breakfast she'd thrown up, when her brain had finally connected the random dots of early morning nausea, a missed period and recent sex. It didn't make any sense. She was no expert but she and Theo had only done it the once and he'd used protection. She'd even watched him rolling the condom on. They were supposed to be pretty infallible, weren't they, so how? Had he done it wrong? Had he ripped it? Had it somehow been *her*?

More importantly, more *relevantly*, since it was a little late to be worrying about the hows and the whys, what was she going to do? Because she couldn't have a baby. Still riddled with issues despite her best efforts to get over them, she was a mess. She was not equipped to bring up a child. She had no support network. None of her friends had children and her sister wasn't capable of understanding her situation. She had no mother to lean on and from whom to seek advice. She didn't even have grandmothers or aunts. And what about the baby's father? She couldn't imagine Theo wanting to be involved. She couldn't imagine *what* he'd think. She couldn't even *go* there right now.

And then there was the pregnancy itself. If she thought she was large and ungainly now, imagine how she'd look in nine months' time. Whales and ships in full sail sprang to mind, and, oh, the comments she'd get, the looks… How would she stand it all?

Yet the longing she felt… The *yearning* that filled every single inch of her to bursting… She'd only known about the baby for a handful of hours, but right down to her bones she wanted it. Desperately. Her heart and mind ached with it. She was so lonely and she had so much love to give. And an even greater capacity to receive it. A baby would never judge her and find her lacking. The love they'd share would be unconditional, and the mere thought of it was so intoxicating, so powerful that it shook her to the core.

There'd already been such loss in her life, she thought, her chest squeezing as she glanced at the photo on the bookshelf, the one taken of her, her parents and her siblings at the beach twelve years ago, all beaming carefree smiles and simple happiness. Such sorrow and grief. Such heartbreak. Here was her chance to rebuild the family she'd lost. To rediscover that happiness. To love and be loved. How could she not take it?

And so what if she did have issues? Who didn't? She could do it. Of course she could. Thousands of women had children in challenging circumstances and, really, how challenging were hers? Now she was debt-free and Milly was taken care of she could build her resources back up. And as for help and advice, there was always the Internet. It wouldn't be easy, but if she took things one step at a time and kept her head, surely she'd be able to muddle through.

And who knew? Maybe she wouldn't even have to do it on her own. There was only one way to find *that* out. Besides, Theo had the right to know about the baby, of that she was certain. And so while he'd had no reason whatsoever to contact her, she now had a very good one to contact him.

For the last four weeks Theo had found himself flat out, with a workload of Everest-like proportions.

The acquisition of the company he'd been pursuing for months was not going according to plan. Despite putting the best brains he had on it, including his own, he still hadn't come up with a way to clear the obstacles blocking the path.

Unlike every other deal he'd done, where the other side put up the semblance of a fight but inevitably collapsed during the negotiations, this one was proving trickier. Unusually, money wasn't the issue. The offer his corporate finance team had put together was the best on the table. The problem was that the current owner, a man with solidly traditional values and an extraordinary belief that ruthlessness wasn't a necessary ingredient for success, had more than enough money and was instead primarily concerned with the personality and integrity of the potential new owner. Incredibly, he appeared to have doubts about him, Theo, in this role.

Theo wanted to acquire Double X Enterprises with a hunger that gnawed away at him ceaselessly. It would be his biggest deal to date, the biggest the world had ever seen, and when he got it, it would be enough. He'd at last be satisfied. He'd have secured his place at the top, and the restlessness and the worthlessness that had dogged him for so long would be vanquished.

So he was *not* going to let it slip through his fingers simply because Daniel Bridgeman had an issue with him personally. He might be ruthless when the situation called for it but his integrity was without question. As for his personality, the aloofness and steel that the business press attributed to him suited him just fine. He was more than comfortable with being described as an ice-cool automaton. It was entirely accurate. Emotions were dangerous. They put a person at risk in so many ways just the thought of what could happen, what had *already* happened, made him break out into a cold sweat. He'd kept a lid on his for so long he doubted he had any of the damn things left anyway.

Regardless of the obstacles, though, he'd find a way to persuade Daniel Bridgeman to give him what he wanted. The man would fold eventually. Everyone did. He just had to identify his weak spot and drive a knife through it.

And in truth, the immense workload was welcome, especially today, the anniversary of his mother's death, which still hit him with the force of a sledgehammer no matter how major the distraction. He was no stranger to twenty-hour days. He'd been working all hours since he was fourteen, when he'd figured the only way he and his mother could escape his father's brutality was by being financially independent. He'd wheeled and dealed, buying low, creating value and selling high, grafting every spare minute he had with the sole aim of making enough to set them free, his relentless drive and grim determination to succeed surging with every muffled thud, every desperate cry, every sickening silence.

No one apart from himself had expected him to have such a knack for it. He'd shown little talent for anything at school apart from truancy and brawling. Yet he'd never forget the day he'd turned sixteen and told his mother that he'd amassed one hundred thousand pounds and that they should pack their bags.

He'd never forget her reaction either. The profound relief and gratitude and the maternal pride he'd been expecting were nowhere to be seen. Instead, once she'd recovered from her shock, she'd been appalled. To his bewilderment she'd refused to leave, and no amount of pleading on his part had moved her. Stunned, unable to comprehend it and devastated by her rejection and betrayal, Theo had left alone and had barely looked back.

It had been eight years since his mother died of a brain haemorrhage that he was convinced had been caused by his father although nothing could ever be proven, but the effects of how his sixteenth birthday had played out were deep-rooted and long-lasting. He'd never understand his mother's reasons for choosing to stay with a man who hit her instead of fleeing with a son who needed her, and he doubted he'd ever be free of the irrational guilt that he'd left instead of staying and trying harder to protect her despite her rejection.

And then there was the stomach-curdling knowledge that he bore his father's genes. As a kid he'd picked fights. As a sixteen-year-old he'd swung one proper punch that had had a devastating impact. Patterns by definition repeated themselves, and the risk that he might turn out like his father was sickeningly real.

But at least the cycle of abuse ended with him. He'd vowed never to marry, never to have children, and to never *ever* let anyone close enough to tempt him to break those vows. Even if there *was* no pattern, he couldn't be a part of anyone else's life. At least, not anyone he might be foolish enough to allow himself to care about. The consequences were too severe. He couldn't be relied upon. He let people down. And if he'd ever wished it could be any other way, well, he'd stamped out that kernel of hope and yearning many years ago before it had a chance to take root. Because in the long run everyone was better off if he remained alone.

But God, he didn't want to be alone right now, he thought, his jaw tight as he stared unseeingly at the city stretched out far below his penthouse, grey and wet beneath heavy clouds and relentless rain. Not with the darkness of his adolescence, the regrets and the guilt closing in on him on all sides. His entire body ached. His head throbbed. The emotions he preferred to deny he had were bubbling fiercely beneath an increasingly fragile surface, and the effort of suppressing them was pushing his formidable will to its limit.

Right now, he wanted to forget who he was and what he could never have. He wanted to forget everything. He wanted to lose himself in the oblivion of a warm body, long limbs and soft sighs. But not just anyone. He wanted Kate.

For weeks he'd buried the memories of the evening she'd spent in his bed. He'd put her in that taxi, set his lawyers to work, and that had been that: funding in place, desire assuaged, problem solved, the details shoved away in a corner of his brain and left to gather dust.

Today, however, with his iron-clad defences suffering a battering and the string of sleepless nights catching up with him, the memories were pushing through the cracks and invading his thoughts in scorching, vivid detail. He kept remembering the silk of her skin and the sounds she'd made. The taste of her mouth and the heat of her body. Her courage, her loyalty and her vulnerability and, most of all, the way that when they'd been talking she'd briefly made him forget who he was.

And he wanted it all again. He wanted *her* again. With a clawing ache that had his body as hard as stone and was becoming increasingly unbearable.

However, he was just going to *have* to bear it because while he could want all he liked, there was no way he was going to actually seek Kate out. He would not be that weak. One night was all he ever allowed himself. Two with the same woman represented the kind of risky behaviour he'd always spurned. He would not indulge it. Nor would he ever again put himself in a position that demolished his control, because without control, what was he? He didn't want to know.

The grim turmoil of today would pass. It always did. He just had to get through what was left of it. Tomorrow he'd be back on track and unassailable for another three hundred and sixty-four days. In the meantime, he'd find solace in work. While many who'd grown up in similar circumstances to his had found oblivion in drugs and alcohol, he'd always found it in the pursuit of success. It had worked for him for the past sixteen years. It would work for him now.

Setting his jaw, Theo swivelled his chair round. In the drawer of his desk he found a packet of painkillers, popped the two that were left and made a mental note to buy more. He turned to one of the three screens on his desk, and was in the process of opening his inbox when his mobile rang.

'Yes?' he muttered, forcing his attention to the latest email from the head of his corporate finance team, which came with a stark lack of suggestions for how he might push through the Bridgeman deal.

'I have a Miss Kate Cassidy in the lobby,' said Bob, the concierge who manned the desk twenty-three floors below. 'She wishes to see you.'

As the information hit his brain, Theo froze. His heart slammed against his ribs and his gut clenched. His concerns about the deal evaporated and his head emptied of everything but the knowledge that Kate was downstairs, bulldozing the boundaries he'd established and breaching his space, as if in his dangerously febrile need he'd somehow conjured her up.

But he could not see her. He was too on edge, his mood too dark. Her effect on him was too unpredictable, and the last thing he wanted was to be blindsided again. So he ought to instruct Bob to send her away and keep her away.

Yet what if she *was* in trouble? What if he had her thrown out and something happened? Could his conscience bear any more guilt? No. It couldn't. So he'd find out what she wanted, deal with it, and then get rid of her. And it would be fine. She was just one woman. He'd faced far worse. He might have once temporarily lost his mind with her, but he wouldn't lose it again. Weakness of will led to unpredictability, which led to damage and destruction, and that was unacceptable. So this time he would be prepared. This time he would be resolute and unflinching. This time would be different.

'Thank you,' he said curtly. 'Five minutes, then send her up.'

How much longer was she going to have to wait? Kate wondered as she perched on the edge of the sofa in the vast lobby of Theo's apartment building and rubbed her damp palms against her jean-clad thighs. It had already been four minutes and fifteen seconds since the concierge had told her to wait, and her nerves were shredded. Deciding to confront Theo and tell him about the pregnancy was all well in theory, but in practice it was lip-bitingly, heart-thumpingly terrifying.

How would he respond? What would he say? She'd had twenty-four hours to get used to the idea, but it was going to come as one massive shock to him. Would he be pleased? Would he be horrified? She didn't have a clue, and it was impossibly tempting to get up, spin on her heel, go home and leave it for another day.

But she wasn't going to do that, she told herself, sitting on her hands to save her nails. It went wholly against her recent resolution to be bold and brave. Besides, she had to tell him at some point, and the sooner she got it over and done with, the better. She might even be pleasantly surprised. And who knew when she'd get another chance? Just because she'd struck lucky with him being home today—a Saturday—didn't mean she would again, and it was hardly the sort of conversation she wanted to have with him at work.

So she'd wait for however long it took and try to refrain from chewing on her already raw lip. She'd admire her lavish surroundings instead. The giant dazzling chandelier that hung from the ceiling cast sparkling light across the polished marble floor and mirrored walls. The furnishings were tastefully leather and quite possibly cost more than her flat. The difference between the worlds that she and Theo inhabited could not be more marked.

What *was* he going to think?

'Miss Cassidy?' said the concierge a moment later, his voice bouncing off the walls and making her jump. 'Mr Knox will see you now.'

Finally.

'The lift on the right will take you directly to the penthouse.'

'Thank you,' she said, mustering up a quick smile as she got to her feet and headed for said lift on legs that felt like jelly.

The doors closed behind her and she used the smooth ten-second ascent to try and calm her fluttering stomach and slow her heart-rate. It would be fine. She and Theo were both civilised adults. They might be chalk and cheese, but they could handle this. What was the worst that could happen? It wasn't as if she was expecting anything from him. She just had a message to deliver. It would be fine.

But when the lift doors opened and she stepped out, all thoughts of civility and messages shot from her head because all she could focus on was Theo.

He was standing at the far end of the wide hall, with his back to a huge floor-to-ceiling window, feet apart, arms crossed over his chest. The interminable rain of the morning had stopped and sunshine had broken through the thick cloud. It flooded in through the window, making a silhou-

ette of him, emphasising his imposing height and the powerful breadth of the shoulders. Although clothed in jeans
and a white shirt, he looked like some sort of god, in total
control, master of all he surveyed, and she couldn't help
thinking that if he'd been going for maximum impact, maximum intimidation, he'd nailed it.

Swallowing down the nerves tangling in her throat, Kate
started walking towards him, her hand tightening on the
strap of her cross-body bag that she wore like a shield. His
gaze was on her as she approached, his expression unreadable. He didn't move a muscle. His jaw was set and he exuded chilly distance, which didn't bode well for what was
to come, but then nor did the heat suddenly shooting along
her veins and the desire surging through her body. That
kind of head-scrambling reaction she could do without. She
didn't need to remember how he'd made her feel when he'd
held her, kissed her, been inside her. She needed to focus.

'Hi,' she said as she drew closer, his irresistible mag-
netism tugging her forwards even as she wanted to flee.

'What are you doing here?'

The ice-cold tone of his voice stopped her in her tracks
a couple of feet away, obliterating the heat, and she inwardly flinched. So that was the way this was going to
go. No 'How are you? Let me take your jacket. Would
you like a drink?' He wasn't pleased to see her. He wasn't
pleased at all.

Okay.

'We need to talk,' she said, beginning to regret her decision to deliver this information in person. With hindsight,
maybe an email would have sufficed.

'There's nothing to talk about.'

'I'm afraid there is.'

His dark brows snapped together. 'Your sister?'

'She's fine,' she said. 'Thank you for what you did
for her.'

'You're welcome.'

'Did you get my note?' Shortly after he'd fixed her finances she'd sent him a letter of thanks. It had seemed the least she could do. She hadn't had a response.

He gave a brief nod. 'Yes.'

'She loves the flowers.'

'Good.'

'It was thoughtful.'

'It was nothing.'

Right. Beneath the force of his unwavering gaze and impenetrable demeanour Kate quailed for a moment and was summoning up the courage to continue when he spoke.

'Are you in trouble?' he asked sharply.

'That's one way of putting it.'

'What?'

'Sorry, bad joke,' she said with a weak laugh although there was nothing remotely funny about any of this.

'Get to the point, Kate,' he snapped. 'I'm busy.'

Right. Yes. Good plan. She pulled her shoulders back and lifted her chin. 'There's no easy way to say this, Theo,' she said, sounding far calmer than she felt, 'so here goes. There's been a…*consequence*…to our…evening together.'

A muscle ticced in his jaw. 'What kind of consequence?'

'The nine-month kind.'

There was a moment of thundering silence, during which Kate's heart hammered while Theo seemed to freeze and pale. 'What exactly are you saying?' he said, his voice tight and low and utterly devoid of expression.

'I'm pregnant.'

The words hung there, oddly loud and blatantly unequivocal, charging the space between them with electrifying tension, and Kate wished there'd been a less impactful way of saying it because something that looked a lot like terror flared briefly in the black depths of Theo's eyes, and it made her shiver from head to toe.

'Is it mine?'

'Yes.'

'Impossible.'

'Apparently not,' she said. 'Apparently it happens.'

'How?'

'I could ask you the same question.' He did, after all, have vastly more experience than she did.

'It makes no sense.'

'I know.'

His eyes narrowed. 'Are you *sure* it's mine?'

Ouch. 'Quite sure,' she said, choosing to forgive him for his scepticism since he was clearly in a state of shock. 'I saw a doctor this morning. I'm six weeks along and I haven't had sex with anyone other than you. I could arrange a paternity test if you need proof.'

He gave his head a quick shake, although whether it was to dismiss the need for proof or to clear his thoughts she had no idea. 'Are you going to keep it?'

'Yes,' she said with a firm nod, just in case he was thinking about persuading her otherwise. 'I am.'

'I see,' he said vaguely, and she got the impression that he'd gone to another place entirely.

'I don't expect anything from you, Theo,' she said. 'I thought you had a right to know, but that's it. It's entirely up to you how involved you would like to be. I can do this with or without you.' And it looked as if it was going to be without him because he was obviously *not* happy about it. Which was fine. 'Anyway, that's all I came to say,' she added. 'I get that it's a shock. So, take your time. Have a think about it and let me know.'

And with that, she turned on her heel and left the way she'd come.

CHAPTER SIX

Have a think?

Have a think?

How was that even possible when his safe, steady world had just been blown to smithereens? When his biggest nightmare, his greatest fear, the one he'd taken the utmost care to avoid for the whole of his adult life, had shockingly, horrifyingly materialised?

Only dimly aware of Kate's departure, Theo stood there, reeling. He couldn't move. He felt as if he were imploding. As if someone had punched in him the solar plexus and followed it up with a lead pipe to the backs of his knees. His chest was tight. His lungs ached. Dizziness descended and his vision blurred.

Breathe.

He had to breathe.

Before he passed out.

Pulling himself together, he dragged in a shaky breath and released it, and the minute the lift door closed behind Kate, he staggered back and sagged against the window.

How the hell could it have happened? he wondered numbly as he dragged shaking hands through his hair and swallowed down the nausea that surged up from his stomach. What warped twist of fate was this?

That Kate was telling the truth he didn't doubt. She'd been so calm. So matter of fact. He, on the other hand, felt as if he'd been swept up by a tornado, tossed about, and hurled back to the ground. He didn't need proof of what she claimed. He needed a drink. A damn time machine would be better. One that took him back to that evening so he could throw her out of his office instead of recklessly caving in to inexplicable desire and carting her off to his bed.

As for his involvement, well, that was a no-brainer. He wouldn't be involved at all. He couldn't. He was no good. It was highly probable he'd turn out to be worse than that. He could not be part of Kate's pregnancy or the raising of a child. Under any circumstances. He wouldn't even know how. To him the word 'father' didn't conjure up images of fishing trips and football games in the park. It represented fear and pain and desolation. He had no experience of anything different. None of the other kids he'd hung out with, kicking around the streets and causing trouble in order to avoid having to go home, had had positive father figures in their lives. He couldn't provide what a child needed. Hell, he didn't even know what that was.

All he did know was that he could not claim his child. The risks were too great. It would be in the child's best, *safest*, interests if he stayed far, far away. Emotionally. Physically. In every way that he could think of. He would not allow himself to give even a nanosecond's thought to what could be if he weren't so terrified of history repeating itself. He couldn't. The child deserved to live a life without fear.

So he would wipe Kate and the baby and the last fifteen minutes of his life from his head, and get back to the problems he *could* understand. If he focused on work and nothing else, the tightness in his chest would ease. The swirling blackness would clear. *Something* would come to him.

Although…

Hang on…

What if this latest development wasn't quite the horrendous disaster it appeared to be? What if it could, in fact, be the answer to the issue that had been plaguing him for months?

The questions slammed into his head, burying the chaos and turmoil with the cold clear logic that had rescued him from such situations many a time, and he instinctively clung onto them like a lifeline.

Were Kate and this pregnancy to become public knowledge, he thought, strength flooding back to his limbs as his brain started to teem with possibilities, it would definitely make him more palatable to Double X Enterprises' recalcitrant CEO. Especially if he stood by her. Daniel Bridgeman had been married to the same woman for fifty years. They'd had no children, but his wife was an integral part of his business. She was on the board of directors and appeared by his side at functions. He cited her as being behind every major decision he'd ever taken.

All of the above clearly indicated that the man valued such a partnership highly, so what if Theo presented one of his own? One he had ready-made. Surely that would allay any concerns the other man might have about his so-called ruthlessness and his less than acceptable personality? How much more touchy-feely could you get than a partner and an imminent baby?

So what if manipulating situations and faking a relationship *did* seem to smack of the ruthlessness and the lack of integrity he was aiming to disprove? The end more than justified the means. For the deal of a lifetime, a deal he'd *needed* to push through, he could—and would—do anything.

He foresaw no problem implementing this strategy. It wasn't as if any of it were for real. Once he'd achieved his goal he'd let Kate go and they'd be done. Should she put up any resistance, he had an arsenal of weapons with which to persuade her otherwise. And presenting to the world a facade he wanted it to see was second nature to him. He'd been doing it for years, ever since he'd learned at the tender age of seven to explain away the bruises and fractures and convince anyone who asked that everything at home was absolutely fine.

It was the best, the *only*, option on the table, so, ignoring the tiny voice in his head demanding to know what the hell he thought he was doing, Theo hauled his mobile out of his back pocket, hit the dial button and strode towards the lift.

'Kate Cassidy,' he said curtly when Bob answered. 'Stop her.'

Kate had got as far as the enormous slowly revolving glass door when the concierge caught up with her. Her thoughts on the scene that had just gone down up in the penthouse were mixed. On the one hand she was relieved that she'd accomplished her mission and had escaped unscathed, yet on the other she was gutted. She wasn't sure why. It wasn't as if she'd been expecting Theo to break open the champagne. She hadn't been expecting anything. So the disappointment didn't make any sense, which was yet another entry in the ever-growing canon of things about herself she didn't understand.

'Miss Cassidy,' called the man, puffing a little as he reached her.

'Yes?'

'Mr Knox requests that you wait.'

Kate stilled, her heart irrationally giving a little leap. He wanted her to wait? Why? What could that mean? Had he changed his mind? Did he want to be involved? *What?*

Well, she was about to find out, she thought, adrenaline surging and her pulse racing as her gaze shifted to the man striding across the lobby towards her. He seemed so energised, so full of purpose now that she found it hard to reconcile this version of him with the rigidly monosyllabic one she'd left up there in his penthouse. It had only been two minutes. What could possibly have happened in the interim?

'Thank you, Bob,' said Theo to the concierge before

switching his attention to her and virtually lasering her to the spot with the force of his gaze. 'Come with me.'

Before she could respond, he'd taken her elbow and was wheeling her in the direction of a room off the lobby. He led her into what was clearly a private meeting room, judging by the antique breakfast table and half a dozen dining chairs, and let her go.

'Are you all right?' she asked with a frown as she watched him close the door and then turn back to her.

'Couldn't be better.'

'I don't understand.'

'Marry me.'

Kate froze and stared at him, her jaw practically hitting the floor while her head spun. 'I—I'm sorry?' she stammered.

'You heard,' he said, something about the gleam in his eyes making shivers race up and down her spine. 'Marry me.'

'Don't be ridiculous.'

'I'm not being ridiculous.'

Her eyes widened. 'You're being *serious*?'

'Yes.'

Kate studied him closely for a moment and thought, no, well, he did look intense and steely and he wasn't the type to joke. But *marrying*? Her and *Theo*? What alternative universe was this? 'Why?'

'You're pregnant with my child.'

Okay, so there was that, but it didn't seem a likely motive in this day and age. There had to be something else behind it. But what? What could possibly have had Theo dramatically haring after her and issuing a proposal? He couldn't have suddenly realised he'd developed *feelings* for her, could he? No. That was impossible. He'd shown no sign of wanting her at any stage since he'd hustled her out of his office suite and bundled her into a taxi. Although presumably stranger things had happened. Somewhere and at some point…

Had her news jolted him into some kind of epiphany or something? He *had* been in a state of shock earlier. And he did have a reputation for knowing what he wanted, going for it and not giving up until he got it. So had she, however improbable it might seem, fallen into that category of being something he wanted?

Doubtful.

And yet…

What if this was her rock-bottom self-esteem making her assume the worst again? Just because no one had ever wanted to marry her before—or even date her, for that matter—didn't mean that no one ever would. So could Theo actually want her? For real? She had to allow that it was a possibility, for personal growth purposes, if nothing else. He *was* looking at her in a spine-tinglingly fierce kind of way. And he *had* just asked her to marry him, which he would not have done if he hadn't meant it.

So.

Maybe the circumstances were a bit of a surprise but people had married for less. Maybe she and Theo could work. Somehow. They already did on a carnal level, and imagine a lifetime of sex like that…

Hmm.

Perhaps it was best not to do that. Or get too carried away. Already excitement and a longing for what could be were drumming through her and scrambling her brain. She had to remain calm.

'Right,' she said, forcing herself to proceed with caution and fervently trying to keep the familiar fuzzy image of a cosy family unit at bay. 'I see. Well. This is rather unexpected.'

'Tell me about it,' he said, his eyes dark and his expression unreadable. 'I should clarify.'

Clarify? Yes. Good idea. 'Please do.'

'What I am about to tell you is highly confidential.'

A shiver ran down her spine as her heart thumped. Could this be because relationships between personnel at his company were discouraged? How thrilling. 'I understand.'

'I am pursuing the acquisition of Double X Enterprises.'

What? Oh. Right. Back to business. Odd. But never mind. His brain was famously nimble and at least it would give her fevered thoughts a respite. 'I'd heard.'

'It's not going as smoothly as I'd hoped,' he said, and she could hear a hint of frustration in his voice. 'To gain a competitive edge I need to acquire something I lack. To put it bluntly, a partner.'

Kate frowned. What on earth was he talking about? Why would he need a partner to seal the deal? From what she knew about him he was a lone wolf all the way. He didn't do partners. Besides, how could *she* help? She was way down the corporate food chain. And although she supposed it was flattering that he considered her a sounding board, what did any of this have to do with her and the pregnancy and his absurd yet intriguing offer of marriage?

'Would you like me to help you find one?' she asked, more than slightly bewildered.

'What? No. As I said, I want you to fill the role.'

She stared at him, still none the wiser. 'I'm afraid you've lost me.'

'I need a partner, preferably a fiancée,' he said flatly, his patience obviously stretched to the limit by her complete inability to grasp what he was getting at. 'Someone to accompany me to dinner from time to time. The odd gala or party. Lunch. Drinks.'

Huh?

'Daniel Bridgeman, the CEO of Double X Enterprises, values such a relationship so I need to provide him with one. For appearances' sake. Temporarily. Until he signs on the dotted line.'

Oh.

Oh.

As the true meaning of what he was after sank in Kate felt as if she'd been thumped in the gut. Her throat tightened and her ears began to buzz and a hot flush rocketed through her.

'Your company is all I require, Kate,' Theo continued, evidently unaware of the devastation he was beginning to wreak on her. 'Your time and your acting skills. Nothing more. Apart from complete discretion, naturally. I anticipate it'll take a fortnight. A month at the most. I'll supply you with the necessary wardrobe and a campaign plan. All you have to do is turn up when and where I tell you, pat your abdomen and smile.'

He stopped and looked at her, clearly waiting for a response, but Kate couldn't speak for the pounding of her head and the blurring of her vision. Oh, she was an idiot, she thought, swallowing hard to dislodge the knot that had formed there and turning away to blink back the sudden sting in her eyes. Why on earth would someone like Theo be interested in marrying someone like her for real? What had she been thinking? How deluded could she still *be*? They hardly knew each other. All they'd had was a one-time thing. He hadn't changed his mind about her. Why would he?

Of course, it would have saved her a whole lot of trouble if he'd started with the business angle to the marriage proposal in the first place, but obviously it hadn't occurred to him that he needed to. Why would it have when the notion was so laughably inconceivable?

That she'd got the wrong idea was entirely her fault, and it wasn't even the first time. There'd been the occasion that evening in his office when he'd told her she was unique.

For the briefest, headiest of moments she'd thought he'd been paying her a compliment, but all he'd meant was her situation—her virginity. Then, as now, she'd been stupidly filled with a hope that had been swiftly dashed, and she had nobody but herself to blame.

But while she might be naïve and hopeless, one thing was very clear. She was *not* going to be steamrollered into a fake engagement, marriage, whatever, just because it suited him. Self-esteem issues or no self-esteem issues, even she was not going to be used in that way, and there was no way she'd allow their unborn child to become a pawn in its unfortunate father's shady business deals. So she swallowed hard and stamped down on the emotions swirling around inside her.

'It's an interesting proposal,' she said, with a strength that interestingly she didn't even have to dig very deep for.

'A necessary one,' he countered.

'I see.'

'Excellent,' he said, with the flicker of a satisfied smile. 'I'll email you the details in the morning and—'

'No.'

The word was like the crack of a whip and for a moment it hovered in the silence between them.

Theo looked at her, his eyebrows lifting a fraction. 'What do you mean, no?' he said, sounding faintly taken aback, as if he was unused to hearing the word, which, she supposed, he was.

'I'm not going to do it.'

'Why not?'

She stared at him. *Why not?* She didn't know where to begin. 'Well, for one thing,' she said, opting for the least complicated reason, 'it wouldn't work. No one would ever believe it.'

'Of course they would,' he said, failure obviously a concept he was as familiar with as defiance. 'People do not tend to question me.'

Right. 'It's unethical.'

A flicker of irritation flitted across his face at that. 'It's business.'

'So find someone else.'

'I don't want someone else. I want you.'

'Because it's convenient.'

A muscle ticced in his jaw. 'Why else?'

At least he didn't bother denying it. 'Still no.'

His eyes narrowed minutely and the hairs at the back of her neck jumped up. 'Think very carefully, Kate.'

'I am,' she said, determined not to be put off by her body's infuriating response to him. 'Do you honestly believe you can basically say you want to use me and our baby for your own selfish ends, and I'd be all, sure, why not?'

'Yes.'

'Well, you're wrong.'

His jaw tightened. 'You will be handsomely compensated for your efforts.'

'I don't want your money.'

'You were happy enough to take it a month ago.'

At that, Kate went very still, her blood chilling and her heart thudding. Why would he mention that now? 'What are you suggesting?' she asked as a ribbon of trepidation wound through her.

'Nothing,' he said, not taking his eyes off her for a second. 'Merely stating a fact.'

'Then why bring it up?'

'Why not?'

'Because it sounds like a threat.'

'How you interpret it is up to you,' he said smoothly. 'However, there is also your career to consider.'

Her stomach clenched. What did that have to do with

anything? 'My career?' she echoed, the apprehension growing.

'The ICA may take a dim view of what you get up to online, don't you think?'

'But then again, they may not.'

'I imagine it would depend on who filed the complaint and how many favours they were owed.'

'There's no need for anyone else to know.'

'I couldn't agree more.'

And there it was.

The threat she'd heard earlier.

Now not even *thinly* veiled.

As the truth of what he was saying struck her like a blow to the head Kate went from icy cold to boiling hot, numb incredulity giving way to a burning deluge of emotion.

The *bastard*.

The complete and utter rat.

How could she ever have thought he wasn't all bad? He was just as cold and heartless as she'd originally believed. She'd heard he'd go to any lengths to get what he wanted, but there was clearly no line he wouldn't cross and no weapon he wouldn't use. He'd taken everything she'd told him that evening in his office, all those deeply personal issues of hers, her troubled adolescence and her worries about her sister, the money, and turned them against her.

How could he *do* that? she wondered, her entire body shaking as the silence thundered between them. How could he stoop so low? Oh, she was *such* a fool to have shared. She should have known she'd come to regret it. If only she hadn't taken his money. If only she'd been stronger. But how could he have insisted she'd owe him nothing and then demand repayment? Had he *no* integrity?

Something inside her withered and died, and she ruthlessly squashed down the surge of disappointment and hurt and who knew what else.

'You bastard,' she said, her voice hoarse with suppressed emotion.

His mouth twisted. 'If only.'

'What you're suggesting is blackmail.'

'That's an ugly word.'

'It's an ugly concept.'

'How this plays out is entirely up to you, Kate,' he said. 'The choice is yours.'

'It's no choice at all and you know it.'

'So we have a deal?'

He made it sound like a question, but it wasn't. He had her in the palm of his hand. She so badly wanted to tell him to go to hell but there was too much at stake. While she might be willing to forfeit her career and even her home to retain the moral high ground and never have anything to do with him ever again, she was *not* risking her sister's well-being. If she didn't comply with his wishes, Theo would withdraw his funding. She was sure of it. Because his word clearly meant nothing.

So fine. She'd accompany him to the odd social event if that was what he wanted. She could dangle off his arm and smile nicely for a month. Now she'd seen a glimpse of the man behind the mask she wouldn't be taken in again. Her guard would remain well and truly up and she would never forget what a low-life jerk he really was.

'We have a deal.'

CHAPTER SEVEN

THE FOLLOWING EVENING, Kate sat at her dressing table, peering into the tiny mirror while she fastened hoops to her earlobes and wishing she were somewhere else. Like Mars. Outwardly, dressed in a gown of green satin, all made up with her hair done, she looked a picture of sophisticated serenity. Inside, she seethed.

Theo had wasted no time in putting his diabolical plan into action. This morning she'd received a brief text informing her that tonight they would be going out to a black-tie function. Half an hour later she'd been summoned to an exclusive store in Knightsbridge that catered for the exceptionally tall, where a personal shopper had revamped her entire wardrobe. She'd then been whisked to a salon and had emerged three hours later with a sleek up-do and a face full of make-up that was way more than she usually wore but at least did a good job of disguising the effects of a sleepless night and continued morning sickness.

While she'd been sitting in the chair with people flitting around and dancing attendance on her it had occurred to her that what the makeover suggested was the height of insult but then she'd expect nothing less from a man who'd coldly and calculatingly used her honesty and her hang-ups to blackmail her.

Twenty-four hours after Theo had delivered his ultimatum she still reeled with the shoddiness of it. For some reason she'd thought he was somehow *more* than his reputation would have her believe. Foolishly, she'd allowed herself to change her mind about him. She didn't know why. The evidence had been flimsy at best, and, with the benefit of hindsight, granting him attributes he clearly didn't have had been a mistake of epic proportions. She couldn't have been more wrong about any of it, and the worst thing was it was her own fault because, while he might have manipulated her, he hadn't exactly tricked her. So not only was the disillusionment hitting her hard, she also felt stupid and naïve and unable to trust her own judgement. Again.

The buzzer sounded, shattering the quiet, and Kate jumped, the simmering anger and resentment she continued to feel towards Theo flaring up deep inside her. It was show-time—but, oh, how tempted she was to lift the window, lean out and tell him to get lost. But she didn't dare risk it. She didn't trust him one little bit. Not now.

There was no need to hurry, though, was there? Keeping him waiting another five minutes might be petty, but it would also be deeply, *deeply* satisfying. So Kate calmly redid her lipstick and gave her neck another squirt of scent. When the buzzer went again, she ignored it in favour of checking her phone for messages and emails before popping it in her bag.

It was only after the third, longer, more jabbing buzz that she figured if she didn't want him storming up here and dragging her out she'd better get going. So she slipped on her shoes, locked up and went downstairs. At the end of the hall, she took a deep breath and pulled her shoulders back, and opened the front door to see Theo leaning against a car, his hands thrust into the pockets of his trousers, looking decidedly unimpressed. Which was extremely pleasing and, frankly, only fair given his lousy treatment of her.

What *wasn't* fair, though, she thought, the sharp stab of triumph fading beneath an unwelcome surge of heat and an unforgivable thump of desire as she walked towards him, was how he could look so devastatingly handsome when he was so horribly, mercilessly *awful*. His tuxedo fitted him as if he'd been stitched into it. The snowy white of his shirt highlighted the strength of his jaw and the chiselled perfection of his features. Smouldering and dangerous were the adjectives that sprang to mind and, oh, great, now she was being bombarded with images of all the things he'd once done to her.

'You're late,' he said curtly, pushing himself off the car and turning to open the rear passenger door.

Kate snapped out of her trance and inwardly bristled at the icy annoyance in his tone. 'I nearly didn't come down at all.'

'We have a deal.'

'I know,' she said before adding pointedly, 'and I, for one, don't go back on my word.'

Wrenching her gaze from his, which was annoyingly harder than it ought to be, she slid into the car with as much elegance as she could manage and settled back against the soft leather seat. A minute later Theo joined her, closing the door behind him with a soft thud, and instantly it felt as if all the oxygen had been sucked out of the air. To her horror, her breath caught in her throat and her entire body hummed with a dizzying sort of awareness. Her dress, which had fitted perfectly a moment ago, suddenly seemed impossibly tight. As he shifted on the seat she realised he was too big, too near, and he smelled too good. She wanted to climb into his lap and get all up close and personal, and see if she couldn't do something about the tired lines that fanned out from his eyes and bracketed his mouth, which was simply insane when she loathed him with every ounce of her being.

Channelling the outrage that had dominated her emotions recently, Kate kept to her side and made herself look out of her window, but it didn't block the heat of his gaze on her or the corresponding flip of her stomach.

'You look stunning.'

'Thank you,' she said, refusing to acknowledge the brief stab of pleasure she felt at his compliment.

'How have you been?'

'Busy.'

'Shopping?'

'Among other things.'

'You maxed out my credit card.'

'This body costs a lot to clothe well,' she said, 'and all this,' she added, shooting him a quick glance and waving a hand around her face and hair, 'comes at a price.'

'It was worth every penny.'

She was *not* going to respond to that. 'Yes, well, you did say the budget was unlimited,' she said. 'And given how I ended up in this particular situation, it seemed the least you could do to make amends.'

'Did it work?'

'No.'

'Unusual.'

'In what way?'

'Money tends to fix most problems.'

'But not all?'

A pause. A flash of bleakness in his eyes. 'No,' he said with a faint frown. 'Not all.'

He was obviously thinking of the deal and the obstructive Mr Bridgeman, and Kate mentally high-fived the man she'd never met but who had to be the only person on the planet to defy him.

'So what's this evening about, then?' she asked, abandoning the view of the heavy traffic of central London through which they were inching, and shifting to bestow on him her iciest glare.

'It's a fundraiser.'

'What for?'

'A charity that helps young entrepreneurs who haven't had the easiest start in life.'

'Like you?'

'How would that be like me?'

The look that accompanied his response was dark and

forbidding, and she would have wondered what had caused the sudden tension radiating off him had she been remotely interested in digging deeper. 'Well, you started in business at a young age, didn't you? No handy trust fund or Oxbridge education.'

The tension eased. 'Yes.'

'A worthy cause.'

'Very.'

'Who's going to be there?'

'Business acquaintances mainly.'

But no friends. *How* unsurprising. 'The CEO you're trying to sweeten?'

'No. He's away.'

Oh. 'Doesn't that rather defeat the object of the exercise?'

'Not at all. Tonight is about building a narrative and spreading your news.'

Her news, she noted. Not *their* news. Right now she was useful to him, the means to an end, but once it was done she'd be on her own and she must never forget it. 'Why are you so keen to impress him?'

'I want his business.'

'I know, but why doesn't he want to sell it to you?'

'He has concerns.'

'About what?'

'My personality,' he said with a faint grimace that she found enormously satisfying. 'My integrity.'

Really? Hah. There were clearly no flies on this Mr Bridgeman. 'He knows you well.'

'We've never met.'

'Then he disapproves of your reputation.'

'Apparently so,' he said, as if he found it impossible to believe that anyone would dare.

'Astounding.'

'Quite.'

'Don't you think faking an engagement to facilitate a business deal falls somewhat short of the integrity you're keen on showing him you have?'

His jaw tightened and his expression hardened. 'Once the papers are signed it won't matter.'

Did he really mean that? He must. After all, she had direct experience how single-minded and immovable he could be when he wanted something, didn't she? 'How long do you think it's going to take?'

'As long as is necessary.'

'What if the deal never comes off?'

'That's not going to happen.'

Hmm. 'Yes, well, while your confidence is impressive,' she said, managing to inject a pleasing note of disdain into her voice, 'I'd be happier if we put a time limit on things.'

He arched one dark eyebrow. 'Conditions, Kate?'

'It's a fair one, you have to admit.'

'You're in no position to negotiate.'

Damn. He had her there. 'So that's a no?'

'That's very much a no.'

Then she'd better put her back into this ridiculous farce so that Daniel Bridgeman sold Theo his company asap and she could get on with her life. 'I have another one,' she said coolly. 'One that's not as easy to dismiss.'

'Oh?'

'I might have agreed to this little charade, fake engagement, whatever, but I do not consent to kissing or inappropriate touching or anything else like it.'

For a moment Theo didn't respond. Instead, his gaze dropped to her mouth and for some reason the temperature inside the car rocketed. Her head spun and her mouth went dry and an unforgivable punch of lust hit her in the gut.

'I wasn't aware I'd asked you to,' he said, sounding so in control, so uninterested, she envied him.

'Just making sure.'

'I'll keep it in mind.'

And she ought to keep in mind the reason she was here—the blackmail. 'So my job is to enhance your personality and show Mr Bridgeman your softer side?' she said, pulling herself together and focusing.

'Yes.'

'A Herculean task when you don't have one.'

'I have no doubt you are up to the challenge.'

'Aren't you concerned I might muck it up?'

'Why would you do that?'

'I've never had a boyfriend, let alone a fiancé.'

'You're a quick learner,' he said, something about his tone heating her blood and melting her stomach despite her resolve to remain cool and aloof. 'You'll soon pick it up.'

Kate thought of glaciers and straightened her spine. 'How do you know I'm not planning to sabotage things in revenge for the way you blackmailed me into this?'

'Are you?'

'I might be.'

'I wouldn't,' he said mildly, although she could hear his warning loud and clear.

'If only I still had my virginity to sell,' she said wistfully, half meaning it.

'Regrets?'

'Do you care either way?'

Something flitted across his expression, but it was gone before she could even try and identify it. 'No.'

'No, well, why would you?' she said, feeling the tiniest bit stung despite herself. 'When you own the world, I guess you don't need to worry so much about other people's feelings.'

'I guess not,' he agreed impassively.

'So brusque,' she said with a shake of her head. 'So serious. So *steely*.'

'Is that a problem?'

'Not particularly, although I guess it depends on your perspective. It seems to me, though, that a real girlfriend might expect the occasional smile. A fiancée definitely would, I should think.'

'How would you know?'

Ooh, that was harsh. But fair, she grudgingly had to admit. 'Well, what do *you* think?'

'Me? I have no idea.'

She stared at him, surprise momentarily nudging everything else out of the way. 'None?'

'None.'

'But you must have had a girlfriend.'

'Must I?'

'Haven't you? *Ever?*'

'I don't have the time.'

Oh, dear.

She'd assumed at least Theo would know what he was doing, but it now seemed as though it was a case of the blind leading the blind. How had he thought this approach would ever work? Was he nuts?

'Right,' she said, resenting him even more for putting her in this position. 'Well. Let's hope I'm not the only one who's a quick learner.'

Four hours later, having escaped to the bathroom after interminable drinks, a sumptuous six-course dinner and an auction of promises during which the extravagant luxury of the lots and preposterous figures whizzing around had blown her mind, Kate was exhausted. Keeping a smile fixed to her face and gazing at Theo in adoration when all she wanted was to stab him with a hairpin was draining.

He was not playing fair. Having no intention of giving him any reason to think she wasn't doing her best and therefore renege on his side of the bargain, she had thrown herself into her role. Theo, on the other hand, had not. He'd introduced her as his pregnant fiancée, and remained by her side, but that was pretty much it. He hadn't smiled at her. He'd barely even looked at her. She'd had to do all the work, and once tonight was over they were very definitely going to be having words.

Unexpectedly, however, there had been *some* positives to the evening. After the initial flurry of interest, Kate had become pretty much invisible, which was a novelty. Everyone was far more interested in the man at her side. His appearance in public was apparently something of a rarity, and, despite his giving off such chilly vibes he could cause frostbite, people couldn't get enough of him. The awe he was held in and the resultant fawning she witnessed made her stomach turn, but at least it meant she could observe instead of being observed for once.

And then there was the fact that he stood nearly a head above her. She had no need to slouch or try and make herself smaller. She could pull her shoulders back and hold herself straight and amazingly she still only just reached his chin. She might tower over everyone else but at Theo's side, for the first time ever, she felt normal. So normal, in fact, that next time they went out she might even wear a pair of the heels she hadn't been able to resist adding to the pile of new clothing she'd accumulated this morning.

Of course there'd also been some negatives, because unfortunately her body still hadn't got the memo about what a despicable human being Theo was. Her body kept wanting to take advantage of the fake engagement and, well, *snuggle*. So much so that she found herself actually regretting the no kissing and no contact condition of hers, which was wrong on practically every level there was.

At least the evening was coming to an end. She couldn't wait to get home and collapse into bed. She had the feeling that the continued attraction she felt, so obviously now one-sided, was going to become increasingly hard to handle, and she could only hope that Daniel Bridgeman got wind of the 'engagement', was fooled into thinking Theo's unfortunate personality had undergone a one-hundred-and-eighty-degree change, and announced his plan to go ahead with the deal just as soon as was humanly possible.

What she *couldn't* do was stay in here, much as she wouldn't mind taking a quick nap, because the door to the bathroom had just opened and people had come in, no doubt wishing to use the stall she was occupying.

Fighting a yawn and rolling her head to ease the kinks in her neck, Kate pulled herself together. She stood up and smoothed her dress, and was just about to slide the lock when something about the conversation on the other side of the door made her go very still.

'Yes, but who *is* she?' she heard one woman ask, the incredulity in her voice as clear as a bell.

'Apparently she works for him.'

'Theo Knox dipping his nib in the company ink? That doesn't sound like him.'

'I agree. But, well, it wouldn't be the first time a woman has trapped a man into marriage by getting pregnant, would it?'

'I guess not.'

'So, Miss Cassidy, what was it about gorgeous billionaire Theo Knox that first caught your eye?'

'Why, his sparkling personality, of course.'

Catty laughter.

A pause.

What sounded like a rummage in a handbag.

Then, 'No ring, I noticed.'

'I noticed that, too.'

'And he's not exactly *doting*, is he?'

'Well, would you be? Have you seen the size of her? She's huge.'

'I *know*.'

'Do you really think the baby's his?'

'No idea. Pass me a tissue, would you?'

The conversation stopped and then came the vague sounds of make-up being reapplied but Kate barely registered any of it. Her head was spinning, her heart was racing and she was trembling from head to toe. Every word had slammed into her, leaving her battered and bruised and sore. She didn't know why. Logically, they should not affect her. Her engagement to Theo was fake. She wasn't a gold-digger. She most certainly didn't want him to dote.

But they did. For some reason, they did. They sliced right through her and ripped her open, brutally exposing her innermost vulnerabilities and stabbing straight at them. When would she stop being a freak show? When would someone want her for real? What had she ever done to deserve any of this?

Her eyes stung and her throat tightened—blasted hormones—but she summoned up strength from somewhere deep inside and took a long, steadying breath, because *she* knew the truth. The gossip and these women meant nothing. And yes, she was abnormally tall, but there wasn't anything she could do about it, so she could either crumple in a heap of self-pity or let it go, and, frankly, this dress was too gorgeous to ruin.

Mind made up, she briefly looked up at the ceiling and blinked rapidly to dispel the threat of tears, then pulled her shoulders back and set her jaw. Clinging onto her courage as if her life depended on it, she opened the door, walked to a basin to wash her hands and, with a wide beam at the two bitchy women who stared at her in dawning shock and horror, sailed out.

CHAPTER EIGHT

BACK AT THE table that Kate had left fifteen minutes ago, Theo rolled a tumbler of thirty-year-old single malt between his fingers and tuned out of the conversation going on around him to run a quick assessment of the evening. Socialising was not his forte. He loathed small talk and sycophancy as much as he abhorred the idea of the press poking into his background and his personal life. However, things had gone well tonight, and he had no doubt that the news of his newly altered civil status would soon reach the right ears.

Despite her vague threat to sabotage his plans, Kate had embraced the role of fiancée admirably, although he could have done with fewer of her dazzling smiles and the occasional touches to his arm. Each of the former momentarily blinded him and each of the latter sent stabs of electricity shooting through him.

His irritatingly intense response to her was the only fly in tonight's ointment, and would have been a whole lot easier to ignore if he weren't so constantly aware of her. When she'd emerged from her building earlier, wrapped in green satin and looking so spectacularly sexy he'd gone as hard as granite, his gut instinct had been to grab her hand and take her back upstairs. In the car, which he'd always considered roomy, he'd had to fight for air. Her understandable spikiness, which ought to have doused the desire rocketing through him, had only intensified it.

But he'd held it together then and he was holding it together now. No one had any inkling of the battle that had been raging inside him all evening, and it would stay that way. Even if Kate hadn't imposed that no kissing, no inappropriate touching condition on their relationship, which now, perversely, was all he could think about, there was too much at stake to crack. He could not, and would not, concede even a millimetre of ground to anyone, let alone a woman who had once rendered him so unacceptably weak. Nevertheless, the tension gripping him was draining, and the minute Kate returned they'd leave. He'd drop her home and initiate the next step in the plan because, now, this evening, their work was done.

And here she was, he thought with a familiar bolt of heat, his gaze instinctively finding her as she wove sinuously between the tables towards him. Beneath the low, warm light of the chandeliers, she shimmered. Her hair gleamed and her skin glowed and the overall effect was irritatingly dazzling. But as she drew nearer, something struck him as wrong. The rest of her might be glowing but her face was pale. Her smile was too tight and no amount of smoky eye make-up could mask the fact that her eyes were overly bright.

Without even thinking to question why any of this was relevant, Theo abandoned his drink and got to his feet. He strode over to intercept her and took her elbow to draw her to one side, leading her through the French doors that opened onto the torch-lit terrace and into the warm jasmine-scented shadows. To his alarm, she didn't protest.

'What's the matter?' he said, noting the taut rigidity of her body and wondering whether it had anything to do with the pregnancy he was finding unexpectedly difficult to ignore.

She swallowed hard and stared at the ground an inch to his right. 'Are we done here?' she said, her voice strangely hoarse. 'Because I'd like to leave.'

Theo frowned and thrust his hands in the pockets of his trousers. 'Are you all right?'

'Of course.'

'Tired?'

'I'm always tired.'

'So what's different?'

'It's not important.'

Frustration speared through him. How could he help if he didn't know what was wrong? 'Anything that might affect what I'm trying to achieve here is important.'

'Ah, yes,' she said with a bitterness he found he didn't like. 'It wouldn't do to forget that.'

'What happened?'

'Nothing happened.'

'Tell me.'

'Okay, fine,' she said, sighing in exasperation as she *finally* looked at him. 'We're fooling no one with this whole fake engagement thing, Theo.'

'Oh?' he said, the hurt in her eyes that she was trying so hard to hide hitting him in the gut and for some reason knocking him for six.

'Apparently I'm a gold-digger who's played the oldest trick in the book and trapped you into marriage by deliberately getting pregnant.'

What the hell? 'According to who?'

'Some women I overheard in the bathroom.'

'I see.'

'There's no other possible explanation because someone like you would never see anything in someone like me.'

Wouldn't he?

'I did warn you,' she added. 'And they do have a point.'

No, they didn't. 'What are you talking about?'

'The glowering, Theo.'

He frowned. 'The what?'

'You've been glowering at me all evening. I've been working my socks off and you just, well, *haven't*. Aren't you supposed to at least be *pretending* you're interested in me?'

Pretending was the trouble, he thought grimly. He was

too interested. If he smiled at her, if he touched her any-where other than the elbow, he might not be able to stop and, quite apart from the unacceptable lack of control that would incur, he would *not* breach her no kissing, no con-tact rule.

'If you're not going to meet me at least halfway,' she continued, 'you could do the decent thing and release me from this deal. There has to be another way. You could just let me go.'

There wasn't another way. And let her go? For myriad reasons he didn't care to analyse, that was not an option. But neither was this state of affairs because, despite her attempts to brush off what she'd heard in the bathroom, it had clearly upset her and he wasn't having that.

'I have a better idea,' he muttered, taking her elbow again, wheeling her around and marching her back into the ballroom before she could protest. He came to a halt in the middle of the room, amidst the well-heeled, well-oiled guests milling about, and let her go. 'Where are they?'

'Where are who?'

'The women you overheard.'

'Oh.'

With a slight frown of concentration Kate scanned the room while Theo felt his displeasure rapidly morphing into anger.

'The woman in purple sitting over there,' she said after a moment, nodding in the direction of a table in the far cor-ner, 'and the woman in red next to her.'

He knew both and he'd have expected better. Too bad. He strode across the room and stopped at table twelve. 'Sa-mantha,' he said icily, looking down at the owner of the PR company he used.

'Theo,' Samantha simpered while batting her eyelashes up at him. 'So lovely to see you out. I was wondering if we might get together at some point to discuss—'

'The Knox Group no longer requires your services.'

In the moment of silence that followed, Samantha's eyes widened and her smile faltered. 'I'm sorry,' she said, giving her head a quick shake as if she'd misheard. 'What did you say?'

'Your contract expires at the end of the month,' he continued icily. 'It will not be renewed.'

'Oh, but—' she spluttered, turning pink. 'I mean… You can't do that.'

'I can.' He snapped his gaze to the brunette in the red dress who was sitting open-mouthed beside her. 'And you—Rebecca, isn't it? Stand down as chair or I'll find another charity to support.'

'Wh-what?' managed Rebecca, who, now he thought about it, was about as effective in her role as a wet dishcloth.

'You heard,' he said brutally. 'Do it. By nine a.m. tomorrow. And the next time either of you feels like gossiping about my fiancée, don't.'

If only Theo hadn't leapt to her defence like that, thought Kate, tossing and turning in bed that night as the memory of it circled around in her head and an unwelcome, unshakeable fuzzy warmth enveloped her.

She couldn't remember the last time someone had stood up for her, and the way he'd gone about it… The energy that had suddenly poured off him, the take-no-prisoners attitude of his and the sense of protectiveness… It was dangerously attractive and all too appealing to a certain someone who was starved of attention and achingly lonely. So appealing, in fact, that when they'd pulled up outside her building after a tautly silent journey, she'd inexplicably found herself wanting to ask him in for coffee, and maybe even more than that, which would have been unwise to say the least.

The trouble was, what he'd done made him so much harder to hate, and she needed to hate him because if she didn't, she could well end up liking him, and then where would she be? At the top of a very slippery slope that plummeted from the dizzying heights of excitement and hope to the miserable depths of disappointment and heartbreak, that was where.

But she had no intention of venturing anywhere near that slide so she could not allow his brief moment of chivalry detract from the rest of his lousy personality. She had to focus on the blackmail and the ruthlessness and not the feel of his hand on her elbow that burned her like a brand and the mesmerising eyes, dark with seething outrage and grim determination on her behalf.

She also had to accept that realistically there'd be many more naysayers like Samantha and Rebecca out there. Who knew what the press would make of the engagement? Of her? And then there were her colleagues. Her sister. How were they going to react?

She had no idea about any of it, but one thing was certain. If she had any hope at all of surviving the next few weeks, with whatever Theo or circumstances threw at her, ice-cool control and steely self-possession were the way to do it.

By lunchtime the following day, Theo had fielded more messages of congratulations than his limited patience could take, and the anger that had led to the instant dismissal of two significant business partners had swelled to fury.

How dared they? was the thought that kept ricocheting around his head during the three meetings he'd already held and wouldn't go away. How dared *anyone* attack what was his? Even temporarily his. So far the press had reported the facts without opinion, but if he ever heard *anything* in the way of sly accusation and measly insinuation again more heads would roll. Big heads. The biggest there were, in fact.

That he hadn't exactly behaved in an exemplary fashion himself was not on his conscience. Coercing Kate into a fake engagement by firing threats at her wasn't the most ruthless thing he'd done in pursuit of a goal, and what was at stake outweighed everything else.

What *did* trouble his conscience, however, was that she'd been right about his lack of input last night. He could have done better at playing the besotted lover despite having zero experience in the field, and if he hadn't been so wrapped up in frustration, he would have. It infuriated him now that he'd allowed himself to get so distracted, to lose sight of what was important.

However, it wasn't too late to rectify the situation. News of their engagement was out and in need of consolidation and that was precisely what he was going to do. In fact, he'd already taken steps, and by the time he was done no one would have any doubt whatsoever about its veracity.

Picking up the phone, Theo dialled the extension for the accounts department. 'Put me through to Kate Cassidy,' he snapped when his call was answered.

'I'm sorry, sir, she no longer works here.'

He scowled. What the hell? 'Why not?'

'She resigned this morning and was put on immediate gardening leave.'

'Where did she go?'

'Home, I believe, sir.'

'Thank you.'

Theo hung up, grabbed his keys, wallet, phone and the box he'd picked up this morning, and stalked out. As the lift whizzed him down to the garage he rang her mobile but the call went straight to voicemail. He left a curt message and got in his car, irritation pummelling through him as he negotiated his way through heavy London traffic. Without warning, Kate had gone off script and he didn't like it. Unpredictability led to confusion, which led to chaos, and he was not having his plans derailed by anyone or anything.

Half an hour later, he parked outside Kate's building, leapt up the five steps to her front door and pressed the buzzer for her flat.

'Hello?' came the tinny response an exasperating thirty seconds later.

'Kate, it's Theo. Let me in.'

There was a moment's silence and he thought grimly that she'd better not be deliberately keeping him waiting as she had done last night, because this afternoon he was in no mood for games.

'First floor on the right,' she said eventually and he let out the breath he hadn't even realised he'd been holding.

The door clicked and in he went. He took the stairs two at a time and swung to the right and there she was, standing in the doorway to her flat, still in her work clothes although barefoot. Was she pleased to see him? Surprised? Annoyed? He couldn't tell. Her expression was giving him nothing, which was fine because what she thought of him turning up like this was of zero importance. He just wanted her back in line.

'What are you doing here?' she asked coolly, as if totally unaware of the disruption she'd caused.

'What are *you* doing here?' he countered.

'I resigned.'

'I heard.'

She raised her eyebrows. 'So?'

'May I come in?'

She frowned for a second, as if debating whether to let him into her space, and then shrugged, as if it didn't matter either way. 'Sure,' she said, turning her back on him and padding into her flat.

Ignoring the inexplicable irritation he felt at her indifference, he followed, automatically assessing the space as he did so. Bathroom on the left. Two bedrooms on the right. Compact open-plan kitchen, dining, living room at the end, flooded with light that poured in through two huge sash windows.

'Nice place,' he muttered. But on the small side. How was that going to work when the baby came along? he wondered before reminding himself sharply that it was none of his business and he couldn't care less.

'Thanks.' She walked into the kitchen and shot him a glance over her shoulder. 'Tea?'

'No.'

'So what do you want, Theo?' she asked as she filled the kettle with water and switched it on.

'I want to know why you resigned.'

'My situation was…untenable.'

Damn, he knew it. He flexed his hands. 'What did they say?'

'What did who say?'

'Anyone. Give me names.'

'No one said anything. It just felt awkward what with you and me and—' she waved a hand in the direction of her abdomen '—this. You own the company. Beyond congratulations, my colleagues didn't know what to say. And in all honesty I couldn't see it getting easier. So I resigned.'

His jaw clenched. 'I see,' he said, dismissing the jab at his conscience when the sacrifices she was having to make because of him inconveniently struck. 'Do you want another job?'

'At some point.'

'I have contacts. If you want one, you'll have one.'

'Thank you,' she said with a chilly smile that didn't reach her eyes. 'But so do I.'

Of course she did, he thought as the kettle pinged and she poured the water into a mug and stirred it. She didn't need his help. But she'd have it anyway. 'Whatever decision you choose to make,' he said, 'I will ensure that you're financially secure. Both of you.' That much he could do. 'I'll set up a fund.'

'That won't be necessary.'

Too bad. 'Nevertheless, it'll be there.'

'But you won't.'

'No.'

'Just out of curiosity, why not?'

Well, *that* was a question he wasn't going to answer with the truth. 'There is no space in my life for a child,' he said, instantly crushing the brief, sudden surge of denial.

'You could make some.'

'No. I couldn't.'

'That's a shame.'

Not a shame. A necessity. 'That's reality.'

'Right,' she said, taking a sip of tea and setting the mug back down on the counter. 'So was there anything else?'

'There was one more thing.' He dug around in his pocket and pulled out the small blue velvet box he'd brought with him. 'This should help dispel any doubts people may have about us.'

For a moment she just looked at the box in silence. And then she stepped towards him and took it from him, her fingers brushing his and her proximity doing odd things to his equilibrium.

When she opened it, her eyes went wide and she let out a soft gasp that would have instantly transported him back to that evening in his office if he let it. 'Wow.'

'Do you like it?'

'Who wouldn't? Is it real?'

'Yes.'

She frowned. 'Borrowed?'

'No.'

'It's too much,' she said with a faint shake of her head as she closed the box and handed it back.

Theo felt the faint sting of something undefinable and

ignored it. 'Just wear it,' he said sharply. 'It's important. For the narrative.'

'Okay, fine,' she said with a careless shrug that somehow stung even more. 'But only when we're out together.'

'I don't mind what you do when you're on your own,' he said. 'As long as you remember your role when we're out in public.'

'I'm unlikely to forget with this on my finger.'

As was he. Which was, after all, the point. 'And speaking of which,' he said, dismissing as ridiculous the inexplicable urge to demand she put it on now, 'tomorrow night we're going to the opening of a new wing at the National Gallery that my company has funded. And this time, Kate, don't keep me waiting.'

A fortnight later, Kate eased off her shoes after yet another function, and with a grateful sigh flopped onto her bed.

To call the last two weeks a whirlwind of activity was an understatement. She'd attended eight events, one antenatal appointment and a hospital scan. She'd been to see her sister to explain the engagement and the pregnancy as best she could without going into detail, and had been relieved when Milly had accepted without question that she was going to be an aunt. In fact, her sister had been delighted, had immediately announced that she was going to take up knitting. Their WhatsApp chat channel was now filled with pictures of tiny bootees, hats and cardigans in various stages of progress and Kate's heart squeezed at every one.

She'd also been getting used to not going into work. Being at home on a weekday felt very odd; however, she hadn't really had any option. Once the news of her engagement had broken, her astonished colleagues had initially swooned but then backed off, as if any office gossip might reach Theo's ears at which point they could all well be fired.

She'd come to the swift conclusion that things would only get worse and had promptly handed in her notice, after which her entire floor had seemed to breathe a sigh of relief.

What she'd do about work in the future she had no idea. Discriminatory or not, she couldn't see a prospective employer jumping for joy about her condition. The hole in her bank account was still pretty big and any maternity benefit she might receive would hardly fill it. But she'd figure something out, maybe by reigniting the freelance bookkeeping she'd started, because she had no intention of ever touching Theo's money.

That he was going to set up a fund as he'd promised she had no doubt. Not so long ago he'd told her that there was barely a problem that couldn't be solved by throwing money at it and he clearly considered both her and their baby just such a problem.

As she sat up, it struck Kate once again that the way Theo had no interest in their child was strange. Weren't men, especially the alpha males among them, pre-programmed to instantly claim possession of their offspring, as a sign of their supremacy or virility or continuation of the bloodline or something? Wasn't it in some way evolutionary?

Well, Theo was as alpha and male as they came, yet he appeared to buck the trend. It was as if he was determined to distance himself from the very idea of it, and she couldn't help wondering why. Was it simply inconvenient? An obstacle en route to global domination? Was he really just too busy? Or did he genuinely not want a baby? She remembered thinking at one point, when she'd first delivered the news, that she'd caught a glimpse of pure terror in his eyes, but she must have been mistaken because she'd never met anyone less afraid of anything, so what was it?

However much it intrigued her, she could hardly ask. She'd already tried once, the afternoon he'd pitched up at her flat and filled her space with his dominating, disturbing presence, and had been firmly shut down. He didn't do personal and he didn't share anything other than the most superficial of information. The conversations they'd had over the last fortnight through necessity had been desultory at best, and, really, she didn't need to know.

To her surprise, though, he *had* taken on board her comments about his lack of participation when it came to faking their engagement. At the events they'd recently attended, he'd left no one in any doubt about his supposed intentions towards her. He no longer glowered in her direction. He even managed the occasional smile that flipped her stomach every time he bestowed it on her. He focused wholly on her, which was heady stuff, and ensured the ring he'd given her did not go unnoticed. And even though she knew it was all for show, that she shouldn't feel a million dollars when she was with him, her poor battered self-esteem lapped it up.

But she had to remember that this whole thing was nothing more than an elaborate charade, that the attention Theo paid her wasn't real, she told herself for the billionth time as she levered herself off the bed and unzipped her dress. He continued to show no remorse, no regret for the way he'd blackmailed her, and she couldn't fall again into the trap of crediting him with traits he didn't have. She had to stop drifting off into daydreams where every touch, every smile, was real. And she had to stop secretly putting the ring on at home, turning her hand this way and that so the beautiful stone caught the light and cast dancing sparkles on her walls, and pretending she had a man who loved her. The wave of longing she felt every time she succumbed to temptation did her no good at all.

Oh, how she wished she'd insisted on a time limit. There'd still been no word for Daniel Bridgeman and she didn't know how much longer she could keep it up. The pressure was immense. The battle between her head and her body was exhausting. And what was taking so long anyway? Their appearances in public had been noted, although thankfully with considerably less vitriol than experience had warned her to fear, and their performance had been entirely credible.

What if Mr Bridgeman had no intention of ever signing? Would she be locked into this absurd charade until Theo decided to release her? How would she bear it? She should never have agreed to it in the first place. She should have been tougher. She should have called his bluff and—

Her phone buzzed and she turned from the wardrobe where she was hanging the dress to reach down to fish it out of the evening bag that lay on the bed.

A message flashed up on the screen. From Theo.

Where was she to be paraded next? A charity ball? Business drinks?

No.

Italy, according to the text. On Friday. For the weekend. Because Daniel Bridgeman had finally, at long flipping last, been in touch.

CHAPTER NINE

'I CAN SEE why you like to travel by private jet,' said Kate, yanking Theo's attention from the document he'd been perusing for the past ten minutes with zero idea of its contents. 'I haven't bashed my knees once. It's heavenly.'

No, he thought grimly, watching her settle on the sofa as the plane climbed to thirty thousand feet and stretch her endless legs out. What was heavenly was the way she looked. And smelled. All the damn time.

Today she was wearing a pair of wide silky white trousers that clung to her legs whenever she moved and a blue top that matched her eyes. She looked fresh and lovely and she was immensely distracting. And even though he ought to be used to it after two weeks of outfit after incredible outfit and enforced proximity, he wasn't, because everything about her seemed to demand attention, whether she was with him or not, which was plain ridiculous.

His decision to give their fake engagement a hundred per cent had undoubtedly been the right one, but that didn't mean it had been easy. Keeping Kate's no kissing, no inappropriate contact condition at the forefront of his mind had required more strength than he could have possibly imagined. Every time he touched her elbow or her back, he wound up wanting to touch a whole lot more and wondering how far he could go before it became unacceptable. And then there was the ring, blinding him at every opportunity it got. With hindsight he should have gone for something smaller but at the time, for some unfathomable reason, he'd wanted there to be no doubt whatsoever that she was his.

All in all, the last fortnight had been a more gruelling experience than he'd expected, and Daniel Bridgeman's invitation could not have come at a better time. Because while he had no intention of ever giving up on his goal, he'd found himself seriously considering his options on more than one occasion, which was disturbing in itself because once he'd embarked on a course of action he never doubted it.

'I'm delighted you approve,' he said, deciding he might as well give up on work and park the perplexing nature of his response to Kate in order to sit back and admire the view.

'It's hard not to. It's very comfortable.'

'How do you usually travel?'

'I don't much.'

Oh? 'I thought it was one of your hobbies.'

Her eyebrows rose. 'Why would you think that?'

'It was on your profile. Along with music and books.'

'Oh. Right. Yes,' she said after a pause. 'I'm surprised you remember.'

'I remember it all,' he said. 'The pictures in particular.'

She flushed and looked away. 'Ah. Yes. Those.'

'They seemed out of character.'

'I was desperate and had had three glasses of wine.' She gave a slight shrug. 'Not a strategy I can currently deploy, unfortunately.'

'Do you need to?' he asked, wondering for a moment whether she was as unsettled by him as he was by her and finding it an oddly pleasing thought.

'No, of course not,' she said dryly. 'What could possibly be stressful about being blackmailed into a fake engagement?' Which, to his mild disappointment, firmly dispelled *that* idea. 'Anyway, my real hobby is numbers.'

'Numbers?'

She nodded. 'That's partly why I became an accountant. Outside work, I love puzzles and brainteasers and things, and don't get me started on calculus. But I couldn't exactly put that in my profile. Numbers are hardly sexy.'

They were when she was talking about them. Her whole

face lit up and her eyes sparkled. 'What do you like about numbers?' he asked with a baffling desire to expand the topic so he could see her light up some more.

'The reliability of them. They're black and white. They never let you down.' The look she shot him then was pointed. 'You know where you are with numbers.'

'Yet they're easy to manipulate.'

She arched an eyebrow. 'And you'd know all about manipulation, wouldn't you?'

He ruthlessly ignored the flaring of his conscience. 'I'm not going to apologise, Kate.'

'I'd be flabbergasted if you did,' she said. 'So what about you? How do you relax?'

'I don't.'

'Don't you have hobbies?'

'I don't have time.'

'All work and no play…'

'Are you suggesting I'm dull?'

She tilted her head and regarded him, her gaze leaving trails of fire in its wake as it ran over him. 'Dull is not the word I would use to describe you.'

'Then what is?'

'Single-minded. Devious. Merciless. Cold. Calculating. Completely lacking in empathy. Oh, and mercenary.'

The adjectives tripping off her tongue so easily were entirely accurate, yet, oddly, her opinion of him stung. 'Please, don't hold back.'

'You did ask.'

And he wouldn't be making that mistake again. He didn't know why he had. Her assessment of him didn't matter. Her attitude, however, well, that *did*. 'We're going to be under scrutiny this weekend, Kate,' he said deliberately flatly. 'It's in everyone's interest to wrap the deal up as soon as possible, so I suggest you lose the prickliness.'

She levelled him a look and let out a sigh. 'Okay, fine,'

she said with a shrug that made her silk shirt ripple entic-
ingly over her chest. 'I can do that. I can play nice. Anything to expedite the goal.'

'Good.'

'So what happens when we land?'

'We drive to the Villa San Michele.'

'And then?'

'Tonight we're having dinner with the Bridgemans. Tomorrow there are meetings, and in the evening is their anniversary party.' Which he could definitely do without.

'Ah, yes. Fifty years,' she said with a trace of wistful-
ness he'd never understand in a million years. 'Can you
imagine?'

No. He couldn't. He wouldn't. 'Unfortunately it can't
be avoided.'

'Did you get them a present?'

'No.' He saw little to celebrate about marriage however
long it lasted, quite frankly.

'Don't you think you should?'

'This whole weekend is purely about business. Gifts
are not required.'

She looked at him for a moment, as if debating whether
to push, but then, to his relief, said, 'It's your show,' and
she was right. It was. Not that he had any intention of explaining himself to her. 'And on Sunday?'

'Bridgeman doesn't believe in working on Sundays.'

'Extraordinary.'

'Isn't it?' he said, responding to her faint smile with one
of his own before he could prevent it. 'The final meetings
will take place on Monday.'

'After which you'll know.'

'Precisely.'

'What's so special about this particular company?'

'It's up for sale.'

'But there must be hundreds of companies up for sale.'

'Not of this size.'

'What are you going to do with it if you get it?'

'*When* I get it,' he corrected, 'the majority of it will be absorbed into the Knox Group and the rest will continue to operate independently.'

'Isn't your company big enough already?'

'No,' he said bluntly. 'Not nearly.'

'What can you possibly have left to prove?'

'Everything.'

She seemed to have nothing to say to that but her eyes didn't leave his. They merely narrowed slightly, as if she were pondering some enormous conundrum, which for some reason made him feel as if he were sitting on knives.

'What?' he asked, irritated by the way his body was instinctively reacting to her scrutiny.

'I was just wondering how on earth you and my brother were ever friends.'

He froze, her words cutting right through his discomfort, obliterating the heat and filling him with icy numbness. 'We weren't. We were acquaintances.'

'Oh? I got the impression you were friends. But I guess acquaintances makes more sense.'

'In what way?'

'Well, you're not at all alike. I mean, Mike was ambitious, sure, but you're on another level entirely. He lacked your killer instinct. He had lines. How on earth did you meet?'

'At the boxing club.'

She flashed him a sudden triumphant smile and for a moment he forgot how to breathe. 'Aha! So you *do* have a hobby.'

'I wouldn't call it a hobby,' he said, willing his thundering pulse to slow. 'More a means of keeping in shape.'

'Are you good at it?'

'Yes.' He'd had plenty of practice.

Her smile turned rueful. 'Mike wasn't.'

'No.'

'Did you box each other?'

'Only once.'

'Who won?'

'No one.'

'How come?'

'I collapsed.'

Her eyes widened. 'What happened?'

'I'd taken a blow to the ribs the week before. I hadn't given it any more thought but then when I was in the ring with Mike, my spleen ruptured. He got me to hospital. He saved my life.' Hence the debt that he should not have taken so long to pay back.

'I had no idea.'

'It wasn't something I wanted publicised.' The incident had rendered him weak, vulnerable, and had his competitors got wind of it they would have pounced within minutes.

'Are you all right now?'

'Yes.' Physically, at least.

'So what happened then?'

'Once I'd recovered we went for a drink. It became a regular thing.'

She nodded as if in understanding. 'An escape.'

'Yes. He was under a lot of stress.'

'I meant for you.'

'*I* have nothing to escape from,' he said, ruthlessly blotting out the great neon sign in his head that was flashing the word 'liar' at him.

Her eyebrows lifted. 'Not even work?'

'Not even that.'

'Hmm. So you knew what was going on with him?'

'Some of it.'

'Me, too.' Her cornflower-blue eyes filled with momentary sadness, and his chest tightened. 'I wish I'd known more, though. But he didn't once complain, not even when he had to leave university to come and look after me and Milly, *and* then find the money to move my sister when it became apparent she wasn't being looked after well.'

'What happened?'

'Nothing that awful. It was mainly little things. Cleanliness. The food. The size of the rooms. And then it became apparent that the staff—not exactly the warmest of people—were quick to medicate. Easier to manage the more unpredictable patients that way, I suppose. Fairview is about as different a place as it's possible to imagine. There's more space, outside as well as inside. The staff care. Milly moved just as soon as we could sort it. She's happy there, and well cared for.'

'She will have whatever she needs, Kate.'

'Thank you.' She paused. Then said with a sigh, 'I never appreciated the stress Mike must have been under. He worked day and night. We shared the day-to-day stuff, but financially he bore full responsibility. When he lost his job I wish he'd said something. He didn't have to carry the burden alone. I don't know how I didn't know, especially since he was living with me. I guess I didn't ask. He said he'd resigned to set up his own business and that he'd given up his flat to put the money into it and I just accepted it. But none of that was true.'

Theo frowned. 'No.'

'I feel so guilty.'

'If anyone is to feel guilty,' he said, unable to let her think she was in any way to blame and suddenly burning up with the need to confess and in some small way to atone for what he'd let happen, 'it's me.'

'Why?'

'His death was partly my fault.'

She stared at him in shock. 'What on earth are you talking about? He had an aneurysm. It was sitting there in his brain like a ticking time bomb. How could that possibly have been your fault?'

'I could have done more to help. To remove the stress. I should have insisted.'

'He had his pride. And he was stubborn.'

'That's no excuse.' And it wasn't because hadn't he already discovered what happened if he turned his back on someone who needed his help whether they wanted it or not? Hadn't his mother been enough? How many more people were to suffer before he learned? Whatever she chose to think he'd robbed Kate and her sister of their brother and he'd never forgive himself. 'I'm sorry.'

'There's really nothing to be sorry for,' she said. 'Truly. Did you know about the loans?'

'No.'

'Neither did I.'

'But I could have done,' he said bleakly. 'I should have done.'

'How?'

'A couple of weeks before he died, Mike mentioned he had something he wanted to discuss. I put him off.' He stopped and frowned, remembering how he'd instinctively kept the man at arm's length despite the huge debt he owed him. 'I regret that.'

'You came to the funeral.'

'It was the least I could do.'

She tilted her head, her gaze practically searing into his. 'Do you remember me suggesting a drink afterwards?'

He frowned. 'No.'

'You took it as a come-on.'

'Did I?'

'You did. And you said you weren't interested. But it wasn't an invitation at all. I just wanted to chat to you about my brother.'

'I apologise,' he muttered, now recalling how Kate's

grief had been too great for his guilt to handle and how in response he'd shut down, operating on automatic. 'It was a tough afternoon.'

'You're telling me.'

'How are you dealing with it?'

She bit her lip. 'I'm getting there. Most days I'm okay, but every now and then it hits me like a bolt from the blue. You'd think I'd be used to it by now. The grief, I mean. It's not as if I'm a stranger to it. I've lost more than most people do in a lifetime. Yet it still gets me right here.' She pressed her hand to her heart and rubbed. 'But there's nothing I can do about it. I can't change anything. So I have to just get on with it.' She tilted her head and regarded him thoughtfully. 'I do think, though, that if he'd lived, Mike would have been a good friend to you.'

The vice that had gripped Theo's chest in response to her suffering tightened. What could he say to that? He could hardly admit that he'd never have let things get that far. That the damage caused by his mother's rejection was irreversible and that the traces of it still affected the way he viewed every single person he met. 'Perhaps.'

'What are your other friends like?'

Non-existent. Which was fine with him. He didn't want or need friends. He was better off alone. Always. More importantly, other people were better off if things were that way. And this conversation was over.

'Quiet,' he said bluntly. 'Unobtrusive. They don't ask questions and they let me get on with my work.'

'Ah. Right,' she said with the flash of a grin that hit him square in the gut. 'Point taken. I'll leave you to it.'

They landed at Linate Airport mid-afternoon and the minute she stepped off the plane, Kate felt as if she could once again breathe, despite the thirty-degree heat.

How hard it had been to focus on her book when her

attention kept wandering, her gaze drifting over to where Theo was sitting, head down, his brow furrowed in concentration as he worked at his laptop. How hard it had been not to think about the suite at the back of the plane with its enormous bed just begging to be rumpled. And then there'd been the urge to strike up the conversation again, which had been so insistent that her jaw ached with the effort of keeping her mouth shut.

Truth be told, she found Theo increasingly intriguing. Now she'd had an unexpected taste of conversation that went beyond pleasantries, she wanted more because she had the feeling there was a lot going on behind that cold, steely facade. She saw it in the occasional flicker in his eyes and the way his jaw sometimes tightened.

Despite her best intentions to remain aloof and keep his ruthlessness at the forefront of her mind like some sort of shield, she could feel her opinion of him beginning to soften. She might have called him cold and merciless and lacking in empathy, but that wasn't all he was. His misplaced guilt over Mike's death and the apology for his behaviour at the funeral had been genuine. Then there was that hint of humour when he'd effectively told her to shut up, which was all the more attractive because of its rarity. And now there was the car that was waiting for them on the tarmac, a gorgeous bright red convertible, low, sleek and powerful. Was it at all possible that he'd remembered what she'd once said about always wanting a nippy little convertible? What would it mean if he had?

Nothing sensible, she thought, if the warm fuzzy feeling spreading through her at the mere possibility was anything to go by. And certainly nothing that merited further analysis. She could not afford to let herself get distracted. She must not seek rainbows where there were none. She had to keep control of her wayward imagination and her precarious emotions and focus on the reality of her situation.

'Nice wheels,' she said, watching in admiration as Theo hefted their luggage into the boot as if it weighed nothing.

'It was all that was left,' he said and slammed the boot shut before striding round to the passenger door and opening it.

Oh. Right. Well, that cleared that up. Good. And frankly what did it matter how this car had ended up here? She still got to ride in it. So that annoying stab of disappointment could get lost.

'Lucky me,' she said with a bright, slightly forced smile as she walked towards him. 'No chauffeur?'

'I like to drive,' he said, unhooking his sunglasses from the v of his shirt and putting them on. 'Get in.'

By the time Theo pulled off the road an hour and a half later and drove through a pair of giant iron gates, Kate had come to a number of conclusions.

Firstly, the northern Italian countryside in summer was stunning. It had taken a while to get out of Milan, but once they'd left the suburbs there'd been nothing but lush greenery and an abundance of beautiful wild flowers. Secondly, there was something impossibly sexy about a gorgeous man driving a fast car in the sunshine, with his shirt sleeves rolled up to his elbows and sunglasses on. And thirdly, it turned out she had a thing for competence.

The way Theo handled the powerful car was nothing short of masterful. Unlike many of the other road users, he didn't drive recklessly. In the city he kept his cool when everyone else seemed to be yelling and gesticulating wildly, and on the open road that had brought them to the edge of Lake Como, he stuck more or less to the speed limit and didn't overtake on blind bends.

Safe. That was how she felt with him. Everything he did was calculated. Measured. He liked to be in control and he was careful. Maybe that was why he refused to engage with the pregnancy. Maybe it represented a careless moment that he was in denial about. Or maybe he really just didn't care.

Whatever.

It didn't matter.

She was probably overthinking things anyway.

What *did* matter and what she *ought* to be thinking about was that they were here, and it was time to slip into the role of adoring, snark-free fiancée, which thankfully had become easier with practice.

The long wide gravelled drive was lined with soaring cypress trees and the warm late afternoon air was filled with the sweet scent of jasmine and honeysuckle. When the drive split, Theo took the left fork, and a minute later pulled up outside a surprisingly modest house that was ochre in colour, had petrol-blue shutters at the windows and elaborate iron balconies, and exuded old soft warmth.

While Kate smoothed her windswept hair, Theo climbed out of the car and strode to the boot. 'It should be open,' he said. 'Go on in.'

'Can we?' Kate asked in surprise. 'Oughtn't we wait for our hosts?'

'It's the guest house. It's all ours.'

Oh.

Oh, dear.

She hadn't anticipated she and Theo being on their own. In fact she hadn't given their accommodation any thought at all. But clearly she should have because this place didn't look big enough to have two bedrooms and what that might mean she didn't like to think.

In some trepidation, she pushed open the door and stepped inside, the sudden drop in temperature scattering goosebumps all over her skin. The flagstone floor was covered with a series of rugs in terracotta and white. The open-plan space was divided into cooking, dining and sitting zones. At the far end to her right was a huge fireplace. In front of it was a long, comfy-looking sofa and a table stacked with magazines. In the middle was a dining table that seated four, and on the left the kitchen. Off that was a utility room and a shower room, and then, up a wide flight of stone steps, the cool white en-suite bedroom.

Singular.

'Ah, Theo?' said Kate, heading back downstairs to where Theo was coming in with their bags and dumping them just inside the front door.

'What?'

'Bit of a problem…'

'What is it?'

'There's only one bedroom.'

His dark brows snapped together in a deep frown. 'Right.'

'I'm happy to take the sofa.'

'*I'll* take the sofa.'

'You're bigger than me.'

'You're pregnant.'

Ah, so he hadn't forgotten… 'Only just,' she said, not wanting to analyse the giddy pleasure and weird relief she felt at the knowledge.

'It's non-negotiable.'

It was ridiculous. 'We could share the bed.'

His jaw clenched. 'No.'

'We could put pillows down the middle or something.'

'No.'

'It *is* huge.'

'Kate,' said Theo tightly, fast running out of patience if his expression was anything to go by, 'the bed could be the size of Italy and it wouldn't be big enough if you were in it.'

Ooh, ouch.

His words landed on her with the sting of a thousand arrows and she had to fight hard to resist the temptation to curl in on herself. 'There's no need to be rude,' she said, feeling herself flush with mortification and searing disappointment that he thought of her like that.

'What?' he snapped, striding towards her and stopping a foot in front of her, his eyes suddenly blazing. 'No. I mean if we occupy the same bed, wherever you are in it, I will find you. And once I do, I can't guarantee there'll be no inappropriate touching.'

Oh.

Oh…

As his confession sank in Kate reeled, her breath catching in her throat and her head swimming. Was he really saying what she thought he was saying? Apparently he was. Which meant that, contrary to what she'd assumed, the attraction wasn't one-sided. He still wanted her. Intensely, judging by the hot, focused way he was looking at her.

Intriguing.

'I see,' she said huskily.

'Do you?' he said, his eyes dark and glinting. 'I'm not sure you do. But believe me, Kate, you do not want us sharing a bed.'

What if she did?

No. She didn't. She couldn't. Sex again with Theo, although no doubt explosive, would serve no purpose whatsoever. Besides, this whole situation was complicated enough and if she had any sense of self-preservation at all, she'd put it right out of her mind.

'Okay, fine,' she said, determined to stamp out the heat and desire pummelling through her and to regain control of her senses. 'Take the sofa.'

'Wise decision. Dinner's at eight.'

'And in the meantime?'

'You can do what you like,' he said, his expression now shuttered and inscrutable. 'I'm going for a swim.'

CHAPTER TEN

EARLIER, THEO HAD swum to the nearest promontory and
back. It had taken him two hours at full pace and it should
have exhausted him. It should have wiped out the ever-
present lust and the increasingly unbearable edginess. But
it hadn't. When Kate had emerged from the bedroom half
an hour ago in a simple black shift dress, her hair rippling
around her shoulders like a blonde wavy waterfall, all he
wanted to do was walk her back into the room, tumble her
onto the bed and to hell with dinner.

Of course there'd be only one bedroom in the house.
Everything about her, to do with her, was designed to torment him, so the less than ideal sleeping arrangements
were par for the course.

What *wasn't* par for the course, what had had him scything through the water as though a pair of great whites were
snapping at his feet, was Kate's response to his declaration
that he still wanted her. He'd had no intention of telling
her, hell, he barely admitted it to himself, but when she'd
jumped to the wrong conclusion about why they would not
be sharing a bed, she'd deflated right in front of him and
he hadn't liked it.

She'd certainly perked up when he'd recklessly corrected
her misconception. Her eyes had darkened to indigo and
her breath had caught, and he had no doubt if she knew
what she'd revealed she'd be appalled. He, on the other
hand, had experienced a jolt of surprise, inexplicable relief that he wasn't alone in this and, unbelievably, even
hotter, more desperate desire, which meant that this was
going to be one very long weekend because while the at-

traction might be mutual there was no way he was going to do anything about it.

'Drink?'

With Herculean effort, Theo switched his gaze from where Kate was chatting to Elaine Bridgeman over by the window of the elegant drawing room to his host, the man he was here to see and to convince. 'Whisky,' he said, ruthlessly blocking out the sound of Kate's laughter and the threat to his peace of mind she presented as he accepted the drink. 'Thank you. And thank you for the invitation this weekend.'

'It was time,' said Daniel gruffly. 'I've been following recent events with interest. Congratulations on your engagement.'

'Thank you.'

'Kate's very striking.'

'She is,' Theo agreed, resisting the monumental temptation to glance over at her.

'How long have you known her?'

'Not long. Seven weeks.'

'A whirlwind romance.'

Inwardly he recoiled, every cell of his body rejecting the idea, but outwardly he barely moved a muscle. 'Something like that,' he replied evenly.

'She used to work for you.'

'She did.'

'But she resigned recently.'

'Yes.'

'And you're okay with that?'

'Absolutely.'

'Has she got another position lined up?'

Theo felt a flicker of annoyance. He could hear the scepticism in Daniel's voice and he didn't like it one little bit. 'Not yet.'

'Pre-nup?'

'No.'

'Is that wise?'

It was irrelevant. Kate wasn't after his money. She wasn't after anything. Which was exactly how he wanted it. 'It's no one's business but mine.'

'Nevertheless—'

'Daniel.'

The older man looked at him shrewdly. 'Interesting. Well. Good. Glad to hear it. Very glad indeed,' he said, nodding and smiling as if he, Theo, had passed some sort of test. 'It may sound trite,' he added with a fond glance in the direction of his wife and sentimentality in his tone, 'but when you know, you know. I knew the second I laid eyes on Elaine that she was the one for me. We were married within eight weeks and I haven't regretted it for a second.'

It was a good thing Daniel didn't appear to expect a response to that because Theo didn't have one. What he did suddenly have was a churning gut, clammy skin and a thundering pulse, because whatever Daniel might be insinuating, Kate wasn't the one for him. She couldn't be. No one ever would be. She was a temporary fiancée, that was all. They barely knew each other. On Monday, with the deal in the bag, they'd go their separate ways. The all-consuming desire and the worrying sense of impending chaos would finally be gone and he couldn't be more looking forward to it.

'Have you set a date?' said Daniel, briefly yanking Theo out of the dark maelstrom of his thoughts.

'Not yet,' he said. Not ever.

'The pregnancy must be an added complication.'

The pregnancy wasn't anything except a means to an end. 'In some respects.'

'You're a lucky man.'

No, he wasn't. He wasn't lucky at all. Nor could he seem to get a grip. Because now not only did he feel as if he were about to pass out, but an image had slammed into his head, the image of a small child with his dark hair and Kate's blue eyes. No matter how hard he tried to wipe it out, the picture wouldn't budge, and suddenly his entire body prickled as if being stabbed with a hundred daggers.

Daniel continued to talk, but about what Theo had no idea. His host's words and his surroundings faded. His vision blurred. All he could see were the images that were whipping around his head, pushing aside everything else, making it pound and his heart race.

Why couldn't he block them out? he wondered, holding himself still through sheer force of will while inside he felt as if he were falling apart. He'd done so successfully so far. He'd hardly noticed the way Kate kept touching and stroking her abdomen. He'd got more than used to the ring blinking at him and tormenting him by making him wish for things he had no right to wish for and could never have. So what was different about tonight?

The pressure. That was what it had to be. Immense and crushing, it was bearing down on him like a thousand-ton weight and exposing hairline cracks in his armour. This weekend was the most important of his life. He couldn't afford any mistakes. Nor could he afford weakness. Ever. He had to plaster over those cracks and bury that weakness. Now. For good.

'Are you all right, Theo?' he heard Daniel ask as, with superhuman effort, he cleared his head of the images, the sense of suffocation and chaos, and refocused his attention.

'Couldn't be better,' he replied smoothly, savagely dismissing the fear that it was a lie.

'Then let's go through to dinner, shall we?'

To hell with playing nice, thought Kate grimly, passing by Theo as he held open the villa's front door after what had to be one of the most excruciating, most stressful evenings of her life.

What was wrong with him?

He'd been tense ever since he'd returned from his marathon swim, the progress of which she'd surreptitiously watched from the bedroom window while admiring the way he powered through the water, but tension was nothing new. It seemed to be embedded in his DNA.

However, the moment they'd gone through to supper, she'd noticed a dramatic change in his demeanour. He'd been even more on edge than usual, his mood black and rippling with swirling undercurrents that luckily it appeared only she had been able to detect. Outwardly he'd engaged, but inwardly he'd been somewhere else entirely and she'd lost count of the number of times she'd had to cover for him. He'd ruined for her a delicious dinner on a terrace that had the most incredible views with interesting and gracious hosts, and she badly wanted to know why.

'Okay,' she said, turning round to face him and crossing her arms over her chest as he closed the door and locked it. 'What's wrong?'

'Nothing's wrong,' he said flatly.

'Was it something I said? Something I did?'

'You were fine,' he muttered, moving round her and fixed himself a drink from the kitchenette. 'Want anything?'

'A glass of water, please.'

He filled a glass with some water and thrust it at her. As she took it from him, their fingers brushed and electricity arced through her, setting fire to her blood and charging the air surrounding them with a crackling sizzle.

'Thank you,' she said, firmly banking down the heat, ignoring the sizzle and getting a grip.

'You're welcome.'

'Well, *something* was up,' she continued, not planning to let it go any time soon despite his reluctance to share because she was done with guesswork and assumption and always getting it wrong. 'You were all right at drinks and then not all right at supper. What happened in between?'

'Nothing happened.'

Right. 'Is there anything you want to talk about?'

His mouth twisted and he took a slug of his drink. 'No.'

'Sure?'

His jaw tightened. 'Leave it, Kate.'

'Because if there's something I can do to help…?'

'Okay, fine,' he snapped, slamming his glass down and shoving his hands through his hair. 'Actually, you *are* what's wrong.'

Oh. That was a blow. 'But I thought you said I did all right,' she said, frowning.

'You did,' he said, stalking towards her with a look in his eye that had her instinctively wanting to retreat. 'Do you want to know what I was thinking at dinner when I should have been paying attention to the conversation?'

Did she? Suddenly she wasn't at all sure. Every drop of intelligence she possessed was telling her that if she had any sense of self-preservation at all she should get far, far away because she sensed he was on the brink of a confession from which there'd be no return. But she'd pushed for this and she wasn't going to back down now, so she ignored the warning voice in her head, and said, 'Of course.'

'I was thinking about you, Kate,' he said, his voice low and rough as he came to a stop just in front of her. 'In that bed upstairs. With me. And no pillows down the middle.'

His eyes blazed into hers with more heat than she could possibly have imagined and her body flamed in response. Her pulse galloped and desire pooled between her legs. 'Well, *that's* not going to happen,' she said a lot more breathlessly than she'd have liked. 'Let's not forget the only reason I'm here, Theo. Because you blackmailed me. I wouldn't sleep with you again if you were the last man on earth.'

'Wouldn't you?'

'No.'

His dark eyes glittered. 'Are you sure about that?'

'I've never been surer of anything.'

'I could prove you wrong.' His gaze dropped to her mouth and her breath caught in her throat. 'Easily.'

And now she did take a step back. 'I would advise against it,' she said with a tiny jut of her chin, even though every inch of her was demanding he get on with it. 'Anyway, I don't believe you.'

His gaze snapped back up, a deep scowl creasing his brow. 'What, exactly, don't you believe?'

'You wouldn't let a little thing like desire get in the way of this deal.'

'It's hardly little.'

'You know what I mean,' she said, refusing to get distracted by thoughts of what exactly he might be referring to. 'This is nothing more than a diversionary tactic. Something else was bothering you. I know it. I know you.'

As if she'd dumped a bucket of cold water over his head, the heat left his gaze and his expression turned stony and forbidding. A chill ran through her and she shivered.

'You know nothing, Kate,' he said icily, 'and you most certainly don't know me.'

'Then talk to me.'

'There's nothing to talk about.'

And quite suddenly Kate had had enough. If Theo couldn't see that this weekend would go a whole lot better if they worked as a team then that was his lookout. What did it matter if he didn't want to tell her what troubled him? They were nothing. She didn't need to know. In fact, it was probably better that she didn't know, because the last thing she wanted was to develop sympathy for him. Or *any* kind of feelings, for that matter.

'Okay, fine,' she said with a shrug as a wave of weariness washed over her. 'It's late. I'm tired. And I give up. Have it your own way. I don't care any more than you care about the fact that I've given up my weekend for this and for you and am therefore missing a visit to my sister for the first time in years. But you really ought to rethink your attitude, because I might have been able to cover for you tonight but I can't keep doing it, and Daniel Bridgeman is no fool.'

Annoyed by the inexplicable disappointment rushing through her and now just wanting to be anywhere he wasn't, Kate turned on her heel to head up the stairs. But as she did so the glass flew from her fingers and smashed into the wall, sending water flying before shattering into a thousand tiny pieces.

For a second she simply stood there staring at the broken glass lying on the floor, the echo of the crash bouncing off the walls, and then she snapped to. 'Terrific,' she muttered beneath her breath, stalking to the kitchen and yanking open cupboards in search of a dustpan and brush. Pregnancy induced clumsiness. Just what she needed.

But as she marched back and began to sweep up the glass, she caught a glimpse of Theo out of the corner of her eye, and something about what she saw made her stop. Straighten. And abandon the clearing up. Because he was utterly rigid. White. A bead of sweat was trickling down his temple and he didn't appear to even notice.

'Theo?' she asked in alarm, her frustration with him suddenly history. 'Are you all right?'

But he didn't answer. He didn't move a muscle. He seemed completely lost in his own world, and for some reason her heart squeezed. Before she could consider the wisdom of it and spurred on by an instinct she didn't understand, she walked over to him, avoiding the remains of the shattered glass, and lifted her hand to touch his face.

And then he reacted.

With lightning-like reflexes he grabbed her wrist and held it. Kate let out a startled gasp and for the briefest of moments they, time, everything, froze. She could hear nothing but the thundering of her heart, could see nothing but his eyes, which burned with myriad emotions she couldn't begin to identify.

And then a split second later the shutters slammed down and he let her go as if scalded and now it was her turn to remain rooted to the spot. She slowly lowered her arm and absently rubbed her wrist, but her entire body trembled and her mind reeled with the sickening suspicion that Theo's reaction had been the instinctive response of someone anticipating a blow. Expecting it. And the unexpected tumult of emotion that rushed through her at the thought stole her breath.

'So. Nothing to talk about, huh?' she said quietly when she could finally speak, her heart hammering and her entire body filling with a sudden and inexplicable burning rage towards whoever was responsible for it.

'Go to bed, Kate.'

As he watched Kate head slowly up the stairs and then disappear into the bedroom, the door closing behind her with a quiet click, Theo felt the icy numbness fade and into its place stormed such revulsion, horror and repugnance that his knees nearly gave way. The room spun around him and he couldn't breathe.

He'd grabbed her wrist, was the thought hammering around his head as his pulse pounded and his gut churned. Not tightly. But definitely firmly. He'd acted on instinct. He'd lost control. Not once in the years since he'd walked out of the squalid flat he'd grown up in had it happened. There'd been triggers, the occasional flash of memory, but he'd handled them. However, not so just now, and if he'd ever doubted the wisdom of his decision to stay away from Kate and the child that doubt was gone for ever. A better man would send her home.

What could she possibly think of what had happened? She had to be horrified. Maybe even terrified of what he might be capable of. At the very least she had to have questions. And since he wasn't a better man and he wasn't going to send her home, he had to give her the answers. He had no option. Despite every cell of his body rejecting the idea, he owed her an explanation. She had a right to know about the genes he carried and he couldn't have her looking at him with apprehension and uncertainty for the next forty-eight hours. He needed to clear the air. He needed to give her reassurance. Now.

Setting his jaw and galvanising into action while his brain shut down everything but the cold bare facts, Theo took the steps two at a time and banged on the door. 'Kate?'

'Come in.'

Bracing himself, although for what he had no idea, he opened the door and went in. Kate was sitting on the edge of the bed, her face pale and her eyes troubled.

'Are you all right?' he said grimly, scouring her expression for signs of pain and fear. He saw none, but he well knew that that didn't mean they weren't there.

'I'm fine.'

'Did I hurt you?'

'No.'

'Are you sure?'

'Yes.'

'Let me look.'

With a tiny sigh, Kate held out her arm and he stalked over to her, taking the wrist he'd grasped and examining it for marks, which thankfully didn't exist.

'You see,' she said softly. 'It's fine.'

He let her go and stepped back, shoving his hands through his hair. 'It's not fine.'

'Really.'

'I owe you an explanation.'

'No, you don't,' she said with a quick shake of her head. 'If anyone owes anyone anything, I owe you an apology.'

Theo frowned. 'What for?'

'Pushing. I had no right.'

'You had every right.' Because she'd been bang on when she'd confronted him on his attitude over dinner. Despite his conviction he'd dealt with it, he hadn't been able to shake the image of that child, and the realisation that his hold on his control wasn't as invincible as he'd assumed had been deeply disturbing and worryingly all-consuming.

'When you dropped the glass,' he said, addressing the part of the evening he understood marginally better and did need to explain, 'it triggered memories. Bad ones.'

She swallowed hard and lifted her shimmering gaze to his. 'Of abuse?'

He ruthlessly ignored those memories clamouring to be let out of the cupboard he kept them locked in and nodded once. 'Yes.'

Her eyes seemed to suddenly blaze. 'Who?'

'My father,' he said, totally in control, his voice utterly devoid of emotion as he relayed the facts. 'I grew up on the roughest estate in west London. We had virtually no money. Dad lost his job as a builder when he fell off a ladder on a construction site just after I was born. He never worked again. My mother was a cleaner. What little she brought in he drank, along with most of the benefits. When he'd had too much he threw things. Plates. Cups. Glasses. Anything he could lay his hands on. And when he'd run out of things to smash he took his frustrations out mainly on her, sometimes on me. Punches and kicks were his speciality.'

For a moment Kate didn't say anything, and Theo could understand her silence. What he'd just told her, the implications of it, was a lot to process. 'Did anyone know?' she asked eventually, her voice oddly gruff.

'No.'

'*Does* anyone know?'

'No.'

'What happened to him?'

'He died,' he said bluntly. 'Five years ago.' As the next of kin, he'd received the call. When he'd heard the news he'd felt nothing.

'And your mother?'

'She had a brain haemorrhage three years before that. Caused by him, I suspect, but the evidence was inconclusive.'

'She stayed with him?'

'Yes.'

'Why?'

His chest tightened for the briefest of moments and memory and emotion flared before he got a grip and shut both down. 'I don't know. Initially I assumed it was because she had no means of escape or subsequent support.' But it hadn't been because she'd refused every one of the many offers he'd made.

'Is your early business success any coincidence?'

'No.'

'You made a lot of money fast.'

'By the time I was sixteen I'd amassed enough to support us both. I had it all set up.'

'What happened?'

'She refused to come with me. She didn't want to leave him.'

She stared at him in growing disbelief. 'So you left on your own?'

'Yes,' he said bluntly, as a familiar dull stab of guilt hit him in the chest. 'I realise I should have stayed.'

'No. I don't mean that,' she said, suddenly so fierce that it sent a shaft of warmth burning through the ice inside him. 'I mean, how could she not have gone with you?'

'I don't know,' he said unflinchingly since he'd learned

to live with the fact that that was a question to which he would never know the answer a long time ago.

'I can't imagine what your childhood must have been like,' she said, her eyes filling with compassion that he neither wanted nor needed.

'I wouldn't ever want you to,' he said. 'I wouldn't want anyone to.'

She went very still. 'Is there any reason why they should?'

'Abuse engenders abuse.'

She stared at him, growing paler, other emotions that he couldn't begin to identify mingling with the compassion. 'Not necessarily.'

'The chances are high.'

'But not inevitable, surely.'

'It's a risk I will never be willing to take.'

'But—'

'No, Kate,' he interrupted, holding up a hand. 'Don't. I don't want to discuss it. I just wanted to explain what happened earlier. And to reassure you that you are in no danger from me. You have nothing to fear. I will make sure of that. There is no need to refer to the subject again. It needn't affect anything. It mustn't. I'll see you in the morning. Goodnight.'

Needn't affect anything? Kate thought, watching Theo walk out and close the door behind him while she tried to process everything he'd just revealed. How could he possibly think that? How could he think *any* of it? Most of all, how could he *ever* believe that she had something to fear from him? She'd experienced many, *many* emotions since she'd met him, but fear hadn't been one of them and never would be.

What he'd told her *did* affect things. Hugely. If he laboured under the heartbreaking impression that he might somehow be capable of harming her and the baby, it was no wonder he'd displayed such a lack of interest in and engagement with her pregnancy. And it certainly threw light on his fierce drive to succeed.

How had he ever got over his mother's rejection? she wondered, her throat tight and her eyes stinging as she struggled to process everything he'd said. Perhaps he hadn't. Did anyone? She'd learned to live without her mother, but her mother hadn't had a choice. His had, and she'd abandoned him. He'd had no siblings. He'd been all alone.

How tough and determined he had to have been in order to survive. How strong and resilient. It would hardly be surprising if that need for self-preservation was still deeply ingrained. She had first-hand experience of how old habits died hard. What had happened clearly continued to affect him. The way he'd presented her with the facts with such little emotion had spoken volumes, and it tugged on her heartstrings.

So where did she go from here? Should she try and make him see that history didn't have to repeat itself? That he posed no threat and that he could absolutely be a part of their child's life? Or should she leave well alone? On the one hand, she owed it to their child to at least try, but on the other, Theo had made it very clear that the subject was closed, and it was far too sensitive an issue for her to bulldoze her way through.

Whatever the options, now was not the time to subject him to her amateur psychology, she knew. This deal he was pursuing might well be wrapped up in his sense of self-worth and the need to prove something, and now she understood a bit more about why, there was nothing she would do to jeopardise it. So no matter how much she thought he needed to talk to someone about the trauma he'd suffered, no matter how much she wished she could help, all she could do was pretend that the last half an hour hadn't happened and carry on as if nothing had changed.

CHAPTER ELEVEN

THE TERRACE OF the Villa San Michele, the venue for the Bridgemans' golden wedding anniversary party, which was in full swing, had been spared no expense. Lights had been strung in and between the trees and around the railings. At one end, a buffet had been set up, the long wide trestle table laden with salads and cold meats and cheeses. A string quartet was playing something light and cheerful at the other, and in between a fountain tinkled with water that shimmered with gold dust. Earlier, boats sped across the lake that sparkled beneath the setting sun, delivering guests whose diamonds sparkled in the softening light and whose languages included English, Italian and who knew how many others. Now, champagne and conversation flowed and joy and sentimentality abounded.

It was absolutely the last place Theo wanted to be.

The noise was giving him a headache and the sense of suffocation that had dogged him all day was intensifying, tightening his collar and covering his skin in a cold sweat. He needed solitude. Time and space to deal with the fall-out from last night. Because while he'd had no option but to share with Kate the basic details of his upbringing, he had the stomach-curdling feeling that by giving her a piece of himself he'd put into play something that couldn't be stopped. Look at the plan he'd made for the free day they had tomorrow, which served no practical purpose and was in no way necessary other than to assuage the guilt he felt about the sacrifice she'd had to make this weekend because of him, which should not have bothered him but did.

He had the feeling impending doom was hurtling towards him, and for the first time in over a decade he was in the petrifying position of facing a situation for which he had no strategy.

If only he could block Kate out the way he blocked out anything that threatened his peace of mind. It wasn't as if he hadn't tried. And it wasn't as if he hadn't had enough to focus on today with the intense all-day meetings he'd had with Daniel.

But he couldn't. She invaded his thoughts without warning and he seemed to be constantly tuned to her frequency. Such as earlier this evening when he'd been standing on the terrace of the guest house, looking out over the lake as he waited for her to emerge. He'd left the house at daybreak after a sleepless night and hadn't seen her since, and he'd been brooding about how she would now respond to him. Would she believe that she had nothing to fear from him? Or would she view him with doubt and suspicion?

His entire body had started prickling with awareness, alerting him to her presence behind him, and he'd experienced a rare moment of hesitation before turning. But her gaze had been clear and she'd been wearing a smile that had hit him in the solar plexus, and the relief that she seemed to be all right had been indescribable.

That awareness had not faded. At every second of every minute of the last couple of hours he'd instinctively known where Kate was when she wasn't with him. The magnetic pull of her was irresistible and he was finding it increasingly hard to stop himself clamping her to his side and keeping there.

The way she'd called him darling and wrapped her arm around his waist when they'd been talking to the Bridgemans earlier hadn't helped. Why had she done that? She hadn't before. Didn't she know how close to the edge of losing it he was? How sick and tired he was of fighting the desire he felt for her? How much he wanted another night, two, with her before they went their separate ways?

If she'd had any inkling how close this evening he'd been to grabbing her hand and hauling her back to the guest villa she'd have been shocked. She wouldn't be sipping champagne and laughing as she chatted with an ease he could only envy. She'd be making arrangements to leave just as soon as was humanly possible. And he'd be cheering her on. Because he didn't like the way she made him feel. He didn't like the desire and the need slithering around inside him, rushing through his blood, making a mockery of his reason and battering his defences.

He particularly didn't like the way the guy she was talking to was leaning towards her. Or looking at her, for that matter. As if he was dazzled. Had the man no respect? What the hell was he thinking? Kate was *his* fiancée. His.

And yet Theo couldn't blame him for wanting to get close. She was blinding. The gold silk dress she had on was tight, which emphasised her phenomenal curves, and strapless, which revealed an expanse of sun-kissed skin that he ached to touch. It was knee-length and split to the thigh on one side, which left her lovely long legs exposed, and as for the stilettos she was wearing, well, those had him thinking of her naked beneath him with the spikes digging into his back.

The confidence she exuded tonight surrounded her like some kind of aura. She was enjoying herself, holding herself tall, as if she didn't care any more about her height or what anyone thought of her. She was no longer afraid, he realised with a start. No longer ashamed. Was she aware of the seismic transformation she'd undergone? Did she know how mind-blowingly attractive she was?

He did.

And as she laughed at something the man she was talking to said, everything in Theo's head disappeared beneath a wave of such intense desire it nearly took out his knees. The concern about what Kate might think of him… The terrifying notion that his grip on his control was weakening and that everything he'd spent so long building was about to implode… It all slipped away until all he was left with was a primitive need to claim and possess. And while on one level he realised he was allowing desire to surge and swell to such an extent it overwhelmed more complicated matters, on another he simply no longer cared.

Oh, dear Lord, Theo was coming over.

Up until this point Kate thought she'd been doing really rather well. Although she'd been aware of his gaze on her all evening, burning her up, making her unable to properly follow any of the conversations she'd been having, she'd just about managed to keep her cool.

How, though, she had no idea. She was by no means firing on all cylinders. She hadn't slept well. She'd ached too hard for the boy Theo had been and the man he'd become. When she thought about what he must have suffered… well, she didn't know and she wanted to, so after a few fitful hours she'd fired up her laptop and researched it, which had been a mistake because what she read tore at her heart.

She'd barely registered him leave the villa at dawn— she'd been in too much of a state—but she'd spent the rest of the morning in limbo, the hours dragging while her mind raced. She'd swum and sunbathed, caught up on the news and replied to a few emails, and then had lunch with Mrs Bridgeman, but she hadn't been able to concentrate through any of it, not even her hostess's cross-questioning about how she and Theo had met and her enthusiastic interest in their non-existent wedding plans, which somehow she'd managed to muddle her way through.

She hadn't seen Theo until she'd found him waiting for her on the terrace of their villa earlier this evening. She'd noted the tension in the rigidity of his shoulders and the lines of his tall, powerful frame, and at that moment all she'd wanted to do was hug him. Comfort him. Which was absurd since he didn't need her or anyone and she was supposed to be pretending last night hadn't happened, but there it was.

And when he'd turned round, looking so darkly, smoulderingly handsome in his black dinner jacket and white shirt it had stolen her breath, it hadn't been simple desire that thumped her in the gut. It had been something deeper and more intense. Something that grabbed hold of her heart and squeezed and made her think of that slippery slope she'd been so wary of. The lines that defined their relationship were blurring, and if she wasn't very careful indeed she'd be careering headlong down it.

Assuming she wasn't already, of course.

Worryingly, the fact that Theo had blackmailed her into this whole thing no longer seemed to matter quite as much as it once had. Those feelings she'd been so worried about had smashed through the flimsy dam of her resistance and were flowing through her, hot and fierce. And now he was striding towards her, his expression focused entirely on her, dark and forbidding, and her whole body was alive with anticipation. Shivers ran up and down her spine. Her pulse galloped. And she had the dizzying sinking feeling that she'd been waiting all evening for this moment, the moment he came to claim her.

With a murmured, 'Excuse me,' she moved away from the man she'd been talking to just as Theo came to a stop a foot in front of her. His eyes were dark and glittering with a hint of uncharacteristic wildness, and her mouth went dry.

'Dance with me,' he said, his voice so low and rough it was practically a growl.

Her pulse leapt, the tightly leashed hunger she could hear in his tone sending heat straight to her centre and detonating tiny explosions along her veins. 'I don't think that would be wise,' she murmured, swallowing hard and thinking that quite apart from anything else she never knew what to do with her arms and always worried she'd fall flat on her face.

His gaze darkened. 'I do.'

'Because it would look good?'

'No.'

'Then why?'

'Because I want to.'

Oh.

Well, so did she. Quite desperately. The sultry beat of the music that had replaced the string quartet was thudding through her body. The way he was looking at her was scrambling her senses. To hell with humiliating herself. She wanted to touch him in ways that were wholly inappropriate off the dance floor but entirely acceptable on it and the best thing was, he would never know. 'Then let's dance.'

Theo didn't need telling twice. He held out a hand and she took it and he led her onto the dance floor. And as he drew her into the circle of his arms, nothing at that moment seemed as important as his hands on her back, searing through the fabric of her dress and setting her on fire. Nor did anything seem as necessary as touching him. So she put her hands on his chest, the way his muscles tensed beneath her palms sending heat shooting through her, and slid them up and around his neck.

As they swayed in time to the music, she realised that the worst thing that could happen on a dance floor wasn't falling flat on her face. It was losing her mind. Because she couldn't help responding to the strength and hardness of his body and pressing closer. She couldn't help wishing they were alone so that she could get him naked and touch some more.

So what was to be done?

If the feral look in his eye and the thick, hard length pressing insistently against her were anything to go by he wanted her as much as she wanted him. But ever since that no kissing, no touching condition she'd hit him with he'd been careful about where and how he touched her, which meant that unfortunately it was unlikely he'd simply haul her off to have his wicked way with her.

Did she have the guts to suggest it herself? What would he think if she did? Yes, he obviously wanted her but she'd never met anyone with such control. What if she indicated she'd like a repeat of that evening in his office and he turned her down? Maybe she should steal a kiss, she thought dazedly, staring at his mouth and feeling her lips tingle. He wouldn't be able to reject that, not when they were in the possible presence of the person they were here to fool.

Fevered tension filled what little space there was between them, and the air sizzled and suddenly she couldn't bear it any longer. His mouth was mere centimetres from hers and all she could think about was how it would feel on hers and how desperate she was to find out.

Desire swept through her, drowning out reason and common sense until all that was left was instinct. Helpless to stop herself, she lifted her face and moved her head forward and touched her lips to his and it was dizzying until she realised he'd gone utterly rigid and was not responding and that headiness turned to excoriating mortification.

Flushing with a different kind of heat and feeling like an utter fool, Kate jerked away but she didn't get far because a split second later Theo had yanked her tight against him and crushed his mouth back to hers, kissing her with such heat and intensity that if he hadn't been holding her in his arms she'd have collapsed into a heap on the floor.

After what felt like hours, he broke the kiss, his breathing as ragged as hers, his eyes dark and his face tight with barely suppressed need. 'Enough,' he said roughly.

'Not nearly,' she breathed, staring at his mouth, longing to feel it back on hers.

'We're making a scene.'

'Isn't that the point?'

He tensed and when her gaze flew to his she thought she saw a rare flicker of uncertainty in his eyes. 'Is it?'

And she could lie and say yes, but she didn't want to and, besides, hadn't they gone beyond that? 'No.'

A muscle hammered in his jaw. 'Tell me what you want, Kate,' he said, and she instantly thought that the only answer to that was 'more' because she wanted another night. Possibly two. It wasn't as if she believed things would continue beyond that. She knew perfectly well that once this weekend was over, once the deal was signed, that would be that. But she didn't want to think about what lay ahead for her when she was home—unemployment, single parenthood, reality. She didn't want to think about what Theo had told her and how it made her feel about him. She wanted to lose herself in the heat and the passion that he unleashed in her and just for once live in the moment. 'I want us to go back to the villa,' she said, her heart thundering with anticipation and excitement. 'Together. Now.'

Flames leapt in his dark eyes and his hold on her tightened. 'You do know what will happen if we do, don't you?'

'Well, I know what I'm *hoping* will happen.'

'Then let's go.'

It took two minutes to say their thank-yous and goodbyes. Five to get to the guest villa. One to shove open the front door, hustle Kate in, close it and push her up against it.

For a moment Theo just stared at her, the moonlight flooding in through the window casting pale shadows across her face, losing himself in the depths of her eyes and not caring that she was able to see straight into his, into the empty black hole where his soul should be. With any luck she wouldn't see that. Instead she'd simply see the strength of his need for her and the relief that incredibly she was on the same page.

She was breathing hard. Her eyes were shining and she was shaking with what he hoped to God was excitement, and then she lifted her chin and arched an eyebrow as if asking what he was waiting for, and that was it.

As his control snapped he slammed his mouth down on hers and kissed her as if it had been months instead of minutes. Beneath the onslaught she moaned and opened her mouth and when his tongue met hers, desire instantly flared like a flame to touchpaper. She whipped her arms around his neck and tilted her pelvis to his and it was all the encouragement he needed.

He pulled her closer, devouring her mouth, her jaw, her neck. She pushed her hands beneath the lapels of his jacket, and, without breaking the kiss, he shrugged out of it. She clawed at his shirt, yanking it free while he found the zip of her dress and slid it down. He lifted the hem and she wiggled her hips, and a second later he'd peeled it up over her head and tossed it on the floor.

And then he put his hands to her waist and his mouth to her breast, and when she whimpered, he drew her hard pink nipple between his lips and she whimpered some more.

But it wasn't enough. It had been driving him mad not knowing what she tasted like, so he sank to his knees, and when she gasped and instinctively clamped her legs together, he slid a hand between her knees and eased it up. And when he reached the curls at the juncture of her thighs, he touched her there and stroked her lightly and she gave a soft sigh of surrender as her legs fell apart.

Unable to wait a moment longer, Theo tugged her knickers down and then off. He clamped his hands to her hips and put his mouth on her and then he knew exactly how she tasted. Sweet. Delicious. Irresistible. As he licked and sucked he felt her tremble and he held her more firmly, the desire rocketing through him almost unbearable.

Above him, there came a faint, 'Oh, God,' followed

by the gentle thud of her head against the door, and he increased the pressure, the tempo, while she sobbed and gasped, and then her hands were clutching at his head while she pushed against him and then, with a soft hoarse cry, she shattered.

Tight with the need for release, he kissed his way back up her trembling body until he was upright again. Her eyes were glazed. Her cheeks were pink and he didn't think he'd ever seen anything so beautiful, or anyone so desperate, and something shifted in his chest, something that might have concerned him if the way she was grappling with the button and zip of his trousers hadn't concerned him more.

'Stop,' he grated, summoning up every drop of his control to still her hand.

'Why?'

'I don't have a condom,' he said tautly, every muscle of his body screaming in denial.

Devastation flitted across her face. 'What?' she said dazedly. 'No.'

'Yes.'

'It doesn't matter. It's too late. You can't get me more pregnant. And I trust you, Theo. On this. On everything.'

His chest tightened. 'You shouldn't. Not on everything.'

'I know. But I do.'

Then she was a fool. But she had a point about it being too late. He was granite hard and the need to be inside her was burning through him like wildfire. There was no going back from this. Wild horses wouldn't drag him away from her now. So he crushed his mouth to hers, lifted her leg to open her up to him and thrust into her tight wet heat and it was heaven.

He gave her a moment to accommodate him but he couldn't hold still for long. Beneath his ravenous kisses she moaned and clung onto his shoulders. He began to move, knowing it wasn't going to take much when she matched his every thrust with hot, increasingly frantic demands of her own.

And it didn't. Within moments she was clenching around him again, gasping his name and sobbing and digging her fingers into his shoulders, and that was it. He felt his orgasm building in strength and momentum, and then it was barrelling through him as, with a roar, he thrust fast and hard, burying himself as deep as he could before fiercely and never-endingly spilling into her.

CHAPTER TWELVE

BY THE TIME Kate had recovered from the shuddering effects of two spectacular orgasms, she noticed that, encouragingly, Theo had got himself naked.

'Bedroom,' he muttered, grabbing her hand, his eyes so dark with the promise of more to come that incredibly she wanted him all over again. 'Now.'

But the only thing holding her up was the door, and she had the helpless feeling that if she moved, she might well crumple to the floor. 'I can't,' she said huskily, finally able to run her gaze over him, which only weakened her limbs further. 'Legs. Like noodles.'

So he scooped her up and carried her, all six foot one of her, as if she weighed nothing, and strode up the stairs and into the bedroom. And while he was doing so, it suddenly struck her that she didn't feel self-conscious at all. Moments ago, she'd been upright, bare, and totally exposed to him, and after her initial reservation, she'd loved it. Now her bits were jiggling and she was all squashed up against him, which wasn't exactly flattering, and she didn't even care. In fact, she felt incredible. As if she could do anything. Dance without falling over. Wear heels without towering above the man beside her. Take on the world.

And suddenly she wanted to find out not only how far she'd come but how far she could go. So when Theo took her into the softly lit bedroom and set her down beside the enormous bed, she planted one hand on his chest and pushed.

He landed in the middle of it, and stared at her first in shock and then with a slow smile that robbed her of breath. He lifted himself up onto his elbows and arched an eyebrow, as if daring her to go through with whatever she was planning, and while she didn't have a plan she was more than up for accepting the challenge.

'Where should I start?' she asked, uncertainty nevertheless making her hesitate.

'Wherever you want.'

'What if you don't like it?'

His eyes gleamed. 'I suspect there is nothing you can do that I won't like, Kate.'

Okay, then.

Gathering her courage, she joined him on the bed and let her gaze roam all over him. There was so much of him to explore, so she straddled him, the hard length of him pressing into her in the most delicious way, and ran her hands over his shoulders and then down his arms, feathering her fingertips over the dips and contours of his muscles and delighting in the way they tensed beneath her touch.

And now she wanted to taste him, so, remembering the pleasure she felt when he held her breast and teased her nipple, she bent down and touched her tongue to his and licked. He shuddered and hissed out a breath, so she did it again, the salty tang of his skin making her taste buds dance and sing, and suddenly she wanted to touch him and taste him everywhere. Thoroughly. The way she'd been too afraid to try all those weeks ago.

And though she'd never done anything remotely like it before, and though she was bound to be clumsy and inept, she'd never know if she didn't try. If he laughed she could always make him pay. Somehow.

Shifting herself lower, she ran a hand down his body, over the ridges of his muscled abdomen and the faint trace of a scar, and feeling him shudder. Tentatively she touched the head of his erection and then stroked her fingers along his rock-hard length. His skin there was surprisingly soft and velvety and she was gripped by the need to feel it properly, so she wrapped her hand round him and slid it gently up from base to tip and then down again.

Theo growled and thrust into her hand, which was intriguing. As was the bead of liquid gathered at the tip. She rubbed her thumb over it and his hips jerked. She bent her head and licked, and was about to do it again when he put a hand at the back of her head, his fingers tangling in her hair, and pulled her away.

'You need to stop,' he said, his breathing sketchy and harsh.

Her heart skipped a beat as her stomach plummeted. Oh. Had she been doing it wrong? 'Really?'

'If you don't, this will be over embarrassingly quickly.'

Phew. She hadn't been doing it wrong. And she didn't mind that he'd stopped her, because his rampant need for her and the tight desperation she could hear in his voice were sending shockwaves of desire pulsing through her and if she didn't get him inside her just as soon as she could she might well combust.

She kissed him because it had been too long since her lips had been on his, shifted again and pressed her pelvis into his. Acting on the need drumming away inside her she rubbed herself against him and it sent such sparks of pleasure through her that she did it again and again, until her head was spinning and she couldn't carry on kissing him because she couldn't breathe. She tore her mouth from his, her breath coming in short sharp pants, and all she could think about was racing towards a finishing line that was simultaneously rushing towards her.

'Kate,' he growled and she opened her eyes to see his brows drawn in concentration and his jaw clenched.

'Yes?'

'I know I said you could do what you want but there's a limit to how much of this I can take.'

That went for her as well. She was so close to the edge,

one more rub and she'd have been flying apart around him. But she wanted to come with him inside her again and she wanted it desperately, so she put her hands on his shoulders and pushed herself up. She lifted her hips, her pulse thundering, took him in her hand and angled him so that he was poised at her entrance. Then she lowered herself onto him, slowly, feeling every inch of him, hearing his low groan and shivering when he put his hands on her waist.

'I think I might start moving,' she said hoarsely.

'Don't let me stop you.'

Nothing could stop her. She was being driven by a force that she still didn't fully understand but was all up for going with. She rolled her hips experimentally and Theo moaned, so she did it again a bit harder and this time she moaned. He felt so good. He seemed to be touching her everywhere.

She leaned forwards to kiss him and gasped as the shift in angle meant he hit a spot deep within her and set off a whole new set of explosions. She felt his hands move to her hips, guiding her, moving her, while her breasts rubbed against his hair-roughened chest, the friction rocking her world.

As the delicious pressure inside her grew and everything began to tighten she found herself moving with increasing urgency and less coordination. Her control was history. The desire and need pounding through her was relentless. Unable to help herself, she whimpered against his mouth, she might even have begged. She didn't know. All she knew was that Theo suddenly tilted his hips up and buried himself deep as she ground down, and that was it. White-hot pleasure burst inside her like a firework and lights flashed behind her eyelids and her entire world turned upside down.

Explosive. That was what that had been, thought Theo with the one brain cell capable of functioning. He'd never experienced anything like it. He'd never ceded control in bed.

He'd never even considered it. But perhaps that had been a mistake because he'd just done exactly that and his mind had been blown.

The lack of self-consciousness with which Kate had explored him and the abandoned confidence with which she'd taken what she wanted was breathtaking. *She* was breathtaking. She was also lying naked beside him, uncovered and unashamed, stretching and practically purring with satisfaction, and incredibly he wanted her again.

But giving up control once was more than enough and her allure wasn't that irresistible. To prove it he would make himself wait. He would use conversation as a distraction. He might even try and get the answer to a question that had been bugging him for weeks.

Rolling onto his side, Theo propped himself up on one elbow. 'So what exactly is this?' he asked, trailing the fingers of his other hand over the tattoo at Kate's hip and feeling her shiver beneath his touch.

'It's an upside-down swallow,' she said with a breathlessness that made him briefly wonder why he'd thought it a good idea to wait.

'Why an upside-down swallow?'

'It represents me flipping the bird at the entire male sex. I was twenty and fed up with still not being able to get a date. I wanted to make a point.'

'It's pretty.'

'It's actually pretty pointless.'

'Why?'

'Because looking down on it from up here, it's the right way up, which does rather defeat the object of the exercise. I didn't think of that when I was all fired up and pissed off.'

Unexpectedly, Theo felt a faint smile curve his mouth. 'No, well, who would?'

'Ideally the tattoo artist would have had an inkling,' she said dryly. 'He supposedly had twenty years' experience.

But it's fine. I'm used to it. And now it seems rather irrelevant anyway.'

His smile faded and a ribbon of concern wound through him because he hoped she wasn't referring to them. They weren't dating and they never would. This was a one, maybe two, night thing at most. Which was all it ever could be. And that was fine. The thing stabbing away at him wasn't regret. It was guilt. Because now he came to think about it he'd been remiss earlier and it had been playing on his mind.

'You looked spectacular this evening,' he said, remembering how speechless he'd been when he'd turned and seen her standing there on the balcony.

'Did I?'

'Yes.'

'Thank you. I wasn't sure.'

'The mirror doesn't lie.'

'I wouldn't know.'

'Why not?'

'I don't much like looking at myself in a mirror,' she said, frowning and biting on her lower lip, which gave him all kinds of ideas he intended to put into action later. 'Not a full-length one anyway. There's just so much of me. I went to a hall of mirrors once at a funfair when I was six and was traumatised for weeks.'

'Yet you're now wearing heels.'

'I know,' she said, flashing him a quick grin that did something strange to his chest. 'For the first time in years. Isn't that great?'

Was it? He wasn't so sure. While he was gratified by the improvement in her self-esteem and confidence, he didn't like to think what she might see if she looked him straight in the eye. He liked even less the memory of how as they'd walked to the party, their strides in synch, it had briefly, unacceptably, occurred to him that they somehow matched.

'So come on,' she said, rolling onto her side so that she

faced him and fixing him with exactly the sort of disconcertingly probing look he feared. 'Your turn.'

'About what?'

'Tell me something about you that no one else knows.'

He tensed and frowned. 'I've already told you something no one else knows.' Many things, actually.

'Something else.'

'My childhood wasn't enough?'

'It doesn't have to be a big thing. It could be tiny. Humour me.' She shot him a wicked smile and for a second he marvelled at how quickly she'd gone from virgin to temptress. 'I'll make it worth your while.'

'All right,' he said, his body hardening all over again at the mere thought of just how she might go about doing that. 'I get headaches when I'm stressed. I didn't learn to read until I was sixteen. And I have a mild allergy to celery, which makes my tongue go numb.'

'There,' she said, her eyes shimmering with emotions he didn't want to even try and identify. 'You see? That wasn't so bad, was it?'

'Depends on what I want to do with my tongue.'

'And what *do* you want to do with your tongue?'

'Why don't you lie back and let me show you?'

Kate was in the kitchen making coffee on Sunday morning when there was a knock on the door of the villa.

How she'd made it downstairs in the first place she had no idea. Her entire body felt like jelly. Muscles she never knew she had ached. By rights, she ought to be exhausted. She'd only had a couple of hours' sleep. But instead she felt fabulous, on top of the world, exhilarated. Every sense was heightened. Colours were bright. Smells were intense.

Last night had been incredible. And not just from a physical point of view. When she and Theo had been able to take no more, they'd talked. Well, she had at least. His questions about her life—her upbringing, her job, that second-base bet—had been endless, his interest had been genuine, and she'd basked in the attention. She hadn't managed to get much out of him, apart from a few details about his journey to global domination, but that was okay. She had all day.

Because he was taking her to Florence. More specifically, to the Garden of Archimedes, which apparently was a museum of mathematics. He'd informed her of the plan an hour ago, when she'd suggested spending the entire day in bed, and when she'd heard it and realised that he'd remembered that numbers were her thing, her silly soft heart had melted. The plane was on standby, the finest restaurant in Florence was booked for a late leisurely lunch and she couldn't wait.

Whoever was outside knocked on the door again and Kate jumped. Abandoning the coffee pot and the lovely hot memories of last night, she walked to the door on legs that still felt a bit shaky and opened it.

On the doorstep, to her surprise, stood Daniel Bridgeman.

'Buongiorno,' she said, with the wide grin that she just couldn't seem to contain.

'Good morning,' he replied with an answering smile. 'May I come in?'

'Theo's in the shower.'

'No problem,' he said. 'It was you I wanted to speak to anyway.'

Oh? Why?

Kate felt her smile falter for a second and nerves fluttered in her stomach, but she held the door open for him and let him in because what else could she do?

'Would you like some coffee?' she asked, feeling a bit awkward about offering her host his own coffee as she watched him glance around the space as if for some reason checking it out.

Having apparently finished his perusal, he turned to her and shook his head. 'No, thank you.'

'The party last night was wonderful.'

'I'm delighted you enjoyed it.'

'We did.'

'I noticed. Watching you and Theo on the dance floor was revelatory.'

There was a twinkle in his eye and Kate found herself suddenly blushing. 'Yes, well, the music was good.'

'My wife has eclectic tastes.' He looked at her for a moment, his gaze suddenly shrewd, and Kate found that for some reason she was suddenly fighting the urge to squirm. 'Do you know why I invited you and Theo here this weekend, Kate?'

'To discuss the deal?'

'Partly,' he agreed with a nod. 'I wanted to meet you. And see the two of you together.'

'Oh?'

He shook his head and smiled. 'I may be old, but I am far from stupid.'

Her pulse skipped a beat in alarm. 'No, no,' she said, thinking that now would be a really good time for Theo to put in an appearance. 'Quite right.'

'How much do you know about the history of this deal?'

'Some,' she hedged cautiously.

'I had some doubts about Theo.'

'He said.'

Daniel's grey bushy eyebrows lifted. 'Did he?'

'Yes.' She smiled at the memory. 'He was very put out by it.'

'I've spent fifty years building up my business. I'm not going to sell it to just anyone.'

'No. Of course not.'

'One thing that did concern me was your engagement.'

Oh, dear. 'In what way?' she said lightly.

'A suspicious man might question the speed and timing of it.'

'And are you suspicious?'

'On occasion.'

Dammit, what was he trying to say? 'I can understand that.'

'It's a deal that's of huge benefit to both parties. There's a lot at stake. Theo isn't a man to give up easily.'

No, he wasn't. She had first-hand experience of that, although somehow it no longer seemed to bother her. 'He won't let you down.'

'So tell me why I should sell to him.'

What? 'Me?' Kate said, her eyebrows shooting up.

'You.'

'God, I don't know,' she said. 'I actually know very little about the ins and outs of it.'

'But you know him, I assume.'

Did she? She thought she did. A bit. Maybe more than a bit now. Enough to convince Daniel Bridgeman that he had no reason to doubt Theo's integrity, at any rate. 'You're right, I do,' she said, thankfully sounding more certain than she felt. 'And I can promise you won't regret it if you do decide to sell to him. Theo can come across as ruthless, I admit, but he is honourable. He's also incredibly loyal, protective and thoughtful.' Not to mention devastatingly handsome and unbelievable in bed, although she didn't think Mr Bridgeman would appreciate that level of detail. 'You have no idea how hard he's had to work to get where he is,' she said instead. 'He didn't have the advantage of a stellar education or buckets of money to support him. He's grafted his entire adult life and continues to do so.'

'I see,' said the older man, but she hadn't finished.

'And he's an excellent listener,' she said. 'When we met I had a few self-esteem issues but he's given me the confidence to get over them and believe in myself, and that is something I will always be grateful for.'

'Interesting.'

She blushed, suddenly aware that she might have gone a bit far in her defence of him, even if everything she'd said was true. 'Yes, well, he's a decent man.'

'You make a good team,' said Daniel.

'Er…right, yes, absolutely we do.'

'As I told him over drinks on Friday night, with a fiancée like you and a baby on the way, he's a lucky man.'

Oh, dear God. The suggestion must have conjured up his worst nightmare. No wonder he'd been so broodingly distracted at dinner. 'He certainly is,' she said.

Daniel headed towards the door. 'Thank you for sparing me some of your time, Kate, and I hope to see you again soon.'

And even though she and Theo didn't make a good team and she wouldn't be seeing Daniel Bridgeman again, Kate nevertheless fixed a bright smile to her face and said, 'I hope so, too.'

Upstairs in the bathroom, Theo gripped the edge of the basin, his head swimming and his heart thundering while a cold sweat broke out all over his skin despite the icy shower he'd forced himself to take.

He hadn't meant to eavesdrop. When he'd heard Daniel and Kate talking downstairs he'd fully intended to join them, especially when Daniel had revealed his suspicions about the engagement. But then Kate had begun extolling his non-existent virtues and he'd frozen, his body filling with dread and denial and who knew what else. The passion in her voice… The sincerity… It had made his stomach churn and bile rise up his throat, and he just couldn't swallow it down.

In no way did he and Kate make a good team. They

didn't make any kind of team. They would never match. And he'd been wrong when he'd told her there was nothing she could do he wouldn't like. He hadn't liked what she'd said. He didn't want anyone singing his praises. He didn't need anyone on his side. Ever.

One night of spectacular sex. That was all they'd had. He'd assumed she'd been on the same page, but it hadn't sounded as if she was. It had sounded as if she'd become... *involved.* And if he was being brutally honest she wasn't the only one.

When he thought of the uncharacteristic things he'd said and done since meeting her he realised that at some point he'd lost the sense of who he was. Despite blithely assuming he had everything under control, right from the beginning he'd allowed her to get under his skin and invade his thoughts.

Take the way he'd insisted on fixing her issues, issues that theoretically had nothing to do with him, out of some misguided non-existent sense of responsibility. Look at what he'd done with the thank-you note she'd sent him. He'd had no reason to keep it and he should have shredded it. Nevertheless he'd tucked it away in the top drawer of his desk in the office. Why? Who knew?

Then there was the red convertible parked up outside. It hadn't been the only car left. He'd had ample choice. But when he'd been presented with the options he'd recalled the wistful longing in her voice when she'd told him all those weeks ago that she'd always wanted one and he'd simply thought she'd like it. In much the same way he'd thought she might enjoy a visit to the maths museum in Florence.

And then there were the tiny snippets about himself that she'd asked for and he'd given her. She'd only wanted one. He'd given her three. Too many. Too much.

He should never have done any of it, he thought grimly as he pushed himself upright and rubbed his hands over his face. He most definitely shouldn't have slept with her again. However great the pressure of the weekend, however powerful his desire for her, he should have had better control. He'd been careless, weak and self-indulgent and that sense of imminent implosion was expanding with every second. If he didn't want everything he'd striven for to crash and burn, he had to put an end to whatever was or wasn't going on with Kate. Right now.

Shutting down and filling with steely resolve, Theo headed downstairs, and, on seeing that Daniel had gone, after muttering to Kate that he had something to take care of but wouldn't be long, left. And when he returned an hour later, the chaos churning around inside him had been dispelled. Cool, steady calm had returned and nothing, *nothing*, was going to threaten it again.

'Hi,' said Kate, greeting him with a brightness and enthusiasm that bounced straight off his armour and a kiss on the mouth that he didn't even feel. 'Are we off? Did you know that the museum has a section dedicated to Pythagoras? It focuses on puzzles inspired by his theorem and I can't *wait*.'

Too bad. 'Pack up your things.'

'Oh?' she said, staring at him in surprise. 'Why?'

'We're going home.'

Her grin faded and disappointment spread across her lovely face, and it bothered him not one jot. 'But the deal?'

'Signed.'

'So Florence?'

'Cancelled.'

'And…us?'

'Over.'

CHAPTER THIRTEEN

THROUGHOUT THE ENTIRE tautly silent journey back to a grey and wet London, Kate was accompanied by a level of disappointment that she didn't understand. The weekend might have ended abruptly and a day ahead of schedule, but she'd always known that once Theo's deal was signed that would be that. She'd always been more than all right with it, so what was this crushing sense of anticlimax all about? Why did she feel so stunned and so, well, *sad*?

None of it made any sense. Yes, she'd been excited about going to the Garden of Archimedes, but she could easily go on her own another time. She didn't need Theo to make her arrangements for her. And while another night of incredible sex would have been wonderful, it wasn't as if she wouldn't survive without it. In fact, she ought to be glad this ridiculous charade was over and she could get on with the rest of her life, starting with the visit to her sister that she had been prepared to miss.

Yet she wasn't.

Maybe it was the unexpectedness of it that was troubling her. Or the sudden inexplicable change in his mood this morning, which she still couldn't fathom. When she'd left him in the shower, he'd been thoroughly relaxed. She'd made sure of it. Yet, mere moments after the chat she and Daniel had had, he'd stormed off and returned in a very different frame of mind.

What could possibly have happened in the meantime? Had he heard what she'd had to say about him? Since she hadn't exactly been whispering he might well have done, but even if he had, why would that make him react so negatively? She'd only had positive things to say, and she was pretty sure that the false picture she'd painted of their relationship was what had got the deal signed. So really, he ought to be *thanking* her, not blanking her.

She didn't understand it, but when she asked what was wrong all she got in response were grunts and monosyllables, and that hurt because she deserved more. She *wanted* more. She wanted to know what he was thinking and what he was feeling. She wanted to burrow beneath his surface, find out what was going on and fix it. And not just because she found him insanely attractive. She also liked and admired him and cared about him. He was everything she'd told Daniel Bridgeman he was, and so much more. He was complicated and difficult and layered and fascinating. Challenging and annoying and brilliant.

And about to drop her home and drive off out of her life for good.

This really was it, Kate thought, her heart squeezing painfully at the realisation. The fake relationship that somehow no longer felt fake was actually over. Once she got out of the car she'd never see or hear from him again. Why did that hurt so much? Why did she feel as though she were being sliced in two? Was she actually going to be physically sick?

With fingers that were oddly trembling she lowered her window and turned her face towards it. The cool fresh breeze instantly calmed her churning stomach but it did nothing to alleviate the misery now scything through her body. Why had it had to end now? Why couldn't she have had one more day and one more night? Why couldn't she have had for ever?

At that, Kate instantly froze. Time seemed to skid to a halt. Her head emptied of everything but that last bewildering thought.

For ever?

What?

Why would she want that?

Why would she even *think* that?

Theo wasn't for ever.

But she was.

And, oh, dear Lord, she'd fallen in love with him.

As the truth of it landed like a blow to the chest, Kate reeled, her heart pounding, her skin tight and damp. She loved everything about him. He wasn't ruthless; he was dynamic. He wasn't lacking in empathy; he was understandably guarded. He was everything she'd ever dreamed of, plus he was sexy as hell and the father of her child and he'd been planning to take her to a maths museum.

All those feelings that she'd tried to prevent and then deny… The thrill whenever he called… The exhilaration when she was with him… The sympathy and the fury, and the leap of her heart whenever she looked at the ring… They all suddenly made sense. But how had it happened? And when? Only a week ago she'd hated him. What had changed that? Or had she never really hated him in the first place?

The questions spun around her head, tangling with the realisation that she was crazy about him, making her heart thump with hope and bewilderment.

And despair.

Because she couldn't possibly tell him. Love had never been part of the deal. She'd merely be setting herself up for brutal rejection and abject misery. He'd be appalled.

Or would he?

What if his feelings had changed, too? What if the chilly distance he'd put between them emanated from a similar epiphany? What if he too was battling feelings he wasn't sure would be reciprocated?

No. She would not think like that. She mustn't. When it came to speculation about what Theo might or might not be thinking she was always wrong. Besides, he didn't do uncertainty.

And, actually, with regards to one particular aspect of their relationship, neither did she. Because while she still needed time to process how she felt about him and figure out what she was going to do about it, if anything, suddenly she was damned if she was going to let him drop her off and drive away without at least having *tried* to persuade him to change his mind about his involvement with their child. She wasn't going to go back to the Kate of before, afraid and in hiding. She was going to fight.

'So, Theo?' she said, nerves nevertheless tangling in her stomach as he turned a corner and her building hove into view, an indication that time was running out.

His brows snapped together. 'Yes?'

'I was wondering… What are you going to do once the deal's gone through?'

'What do you mean?' he said, shooting her a stony glance that would have had her backing right off had she not strengthened her resolve.

'Well, once you've achieved global domination, what's left?'

'Nothing,' he said. 'I'll be done.'

'Will you?'

'Yes.'

'Are you sure about that?'

'Quite sure.'

She took a deep breath and mentally crossed her fingers. 'Because if you do need another project, there's one cooking away right here.' She indicated her abdomen and watched as his gaze flickered across and down, his jaw tightening in that familiar way.

'That won't be necessary.'

'Why not?'

'You know why not.'

'No. I don't. Not really.'

'Kate.'

'History doesn't have to repeat itself,' she persisted, ignoring the warning note she could hear in his voice because she was in love with him and she had to make him see she was right.

'As I told you before, it's a risk I'm not willing to take.'

'There is no risk.'

'However much I might wish otherwise, you are both better off—and safer—without me.'

At his choice of words, hope flared inside her, spreading through her like wildfire, dizzying her with its intensity. Could it be that he *did* want them but was simply so blinded by fear he believed he didn't deserve them? Could she convince him otherwise? 'You are not your father,' she said, her throat tight and her pulse racing.

'Leave it.'

'No. It's too important.'

'I don't want to talk about it.'

Too bad. He wasn't shutting her down again. Not now. And she'd chosen her battlefield wisely. There was no escape from a moving car. 'But you should,' she said heatedly. 'You need to. You need to see what I see: a man who would go to the ends of the earth to protect and defend those that matter to him. That man would never be a danger to anyone. That man would *never* hit anyone.'

He pulled over suddenly and parked, and then turned to her, his eyes bleak, his face rigid. 'But I did, Kate,' he said bluntly. 'I did.'

She blanched, the words hovering between them, the rain hammering down on the roof of the car. 'What do you mean?'

'Exactly that.'

No. He wouldn't. He couldn't. 'When? Who?'

'My mother. I was sixteen.'

She recoiled with shock, but right down to her marrow she knew that it couldn't be that simple. 'What happened?'

'Nothing happened.'

'I don't believe you. There has to be some explanation.'

'There isn't.'

'Circumstances, then?' she said, because she was not going to let this go and she refused to believe it of him. 'Tell me the circumstances.'

'The day I'd planned to leave,' he said, his voice flat and emotionless in a way that intensified the ache in her chest, 'I told her to grab what she needed. She said no. I begged. My father came home, off his head as usual. She told him what I'd asked her to do and he flew into a rage. He punched me in the stomach and I'd had enough. For the first time in my life I retaliated. My mother went to protect him and my fist caught her on the cheek. She told me to get out. So I did.'

He spoke matter-of-factly, but she could hear the trace of emotion behind what he said, the guilt, betrayal, the rejection, the abandonment. 'It was an accident,' she said, her words catching on the lump in her throat.

'Was it?'

'Yes.'

'That's who I really am, Kate.'

'It isn't. It really isn't.' She took a deep breath and stepped into the terrifying unknown. 'I've fallen in love with you, Theo. I don't know when or how, but I love you and trust you with every cell of my being.'

He barely moved a muscle in response. 'Then you've made a mistake,' he said flatly. 'I can never be the man you want me to be.'

For a moment her heart shattered, pain pummelling through her at the realisation he was adamant in his belief, but then, quite suddenly, anger flared deep inside her, rushing along her veins and setting fire to her nerve-endings. How dared he tell her she'd made a mistake?

How dared he dismiss her feelings? And how dared he continue to reject their child?

'You already are the man I want you to be,' she said fiercely. 'Everything I told Daniel was true. But you are also a coward.'

His eyebrows shot up at that, a chink in the icy facade at last. 'What?'

'You heard,' she said, burning up with frustration and hurt. 'You're a coward. History *doesn't* have to repeat itself. There are choices you can make. There are choices you've *already* made. You are not just your father's son. You're also your mother's. And when it comes to *our* child, you're only half the equation. I have never felt in danger with you, Theo, even when I pushed you and pushed you and you hated it. In fact, I've never felt safer or better protected.'

She stopped, breathing hard, but he didn't say anything. His fingers flexed on the steering wheel, his knuckles white and his face tight, but his simmering anger was nothing compared to hers.

'I think you're scared,' she said hotly. 'I think you're scared of rejection and abandonment and that's why you're not prepared to take a risk on us. And you know what? I get it. I'm scared, too. This pregnancy terrifies me. Everyone I love has a habit of leaving me one way or another. My brother, my father, even my sister. Right now, I miss my mother more than I ever thought possible and it hurts so very much. And then there's the guilt. My God, the guilt. Every time I see Milly, the fact that she will never get the chance to fall in love, have a family, crucifies me.' She shook her head. 'So I don't have a clue what I'm going to do and I'm petrified my anxieties will take over, but I no longer have the luxury of wallowing in my hang-ups. Of being selfish. I have a child to think about. You could, too. And you could have me. Because Daniel was right. We do make a good team. We could make a great one. We could be a family. The one that I want and the one that I know, deep down, you want. And don't you dare give me that "I'm better off alone" rubbish. No one is. Everyone needs someone.'

'I don't.'

'You *do*. Don't you *want* to be happy?' she asked, hearing the faint desperation in her voice but not caring. 'Don't you *want* to let go of the past and look to the future?'

Silence fell and stretched and for the briefest of moments she thought she'd got through to him and hope leapt, but when he spoke it was with an icy calm that splintered her heart and shattered her dreams. 'Why is it so hard to understand, Kate?' he said coldly. 'I don't need happiness and I don't want you.'

'But—'

'What I do want, however, is for you to get out of my car. Now.'

Shaking all over and in agony, Kate closed the door to her flat behind her and sank to the floor, her heart shattering as the sobs she'd held at bay while scrabbling to get out of Theo's car now racked her body.

His brutal rejection of everything she'd offered him was crucifying. Not only had she laid the possibility of a happy future, a happy life on a platter for him, she'd revealed her fears and handed him her heart. And he'd trampled all over it.

Tears streamed down her face and she curled up on the floor, exhaustion and despair descending like a heavy black cloud. She'd given it her best shot and she'd failed. If only she hadn't barged in there with her declaration of love. If only she'd stuck with the plan to keep it to herself for a while. If only she hadn't fallen in love with him in the first place.

She'd been such an idiot. She'd recognised the risk to

her heart he presented and she'd blithely assumed she'd be able to handle it. Why she'd ever thought that when she had zero experience in such matters and the physical and emotional attraction she felt for him was so strong she had no idea. But it was too late for regret because now here she was at the bottom of that slippery slope, and it was just as wretched and miserable as she'd imagined.

Why couldn't he have been willing to give them a chance? Why couldn't he have let her help him? Love him? She had so much to give. What if he just needed time? What if she gave him some space and then tried again?

But no, she told herself with a watery sniff as she angrily brushed away the tears that continued to leak out of the corners of her eyes. She'd be banging her head against a brick wall. She had to stop hoping and imagining and wishing. Theo wasn't going to suddenly and miraculously wake up one morning realising he was in love with her and deciding he *did* want them. He was too damaged. Too entrenched in his beliefs. He was determined to remain alone, an island barricaded from the soaring highs and wretched lows of life.

And however much that hurt, and, oh, how it did, she had to accept it, get up and move on.

CHAPTER FOURTEEN

IN THE DAYS that followed their return to London, Theo was convinced he'd done one hundred per cent the right thing by letting Kate go. He would not tarnish her with his darkness. His actions—and his inaction—brought about the destruction of other people and he would not destroy her, too. Or their child. He didn't deserve happiness and he had no right to take what she had offered. Despite what she believed, he wasn't, and could never be, the man she wanted him to be. And when he thought of the way she'd gone on the attack, which was all the damn time since he couldn't seem to get it out of his head, he was absolutely certain that there was nothing he would have done differently.

He knew he was no coward. She had no idea how much strength and courage it took to stand alone and apart and not seize what deep down he'd always tried to deny he craved. And he was not wallowing or selfish, despite what she might have implied. His concerns were current and real.

So as he'd watched her stumble up the steps to her building he'd told himself that she and her baby would be fine now. He'd driven home and poured himself one drink and then another and then another. The next day he'd gone into the office and thrown himself into work. The deal had been signed. The details were being hammered out. Everything was proceeding smoothly.

But now, two hellish weeks later, he found himself wondering, where was the peace? Where was the sense of achievement? Why was he still so frustratingly restless? And why couldn't he stop pacing?

The sense of impending doom he'd assumed would vanish once he'd dealt with Kate hadn't. Instead, it was larger and darker and more oppressive than ever. And as for order and control that he'd expected to return, he currently felt as if he were hanging on a cliff face by his fingertips. He was popping painkillers like candy and he was snapping at anyone who had the misfortune to cross his path.

What was the matter with him? Why couldn't he concentrate? Why couldn't he eat or sleep? And why hadn't he returned the ring to the jewellers? Kate had returned it to him by courier the day after they'd arrived back. The sight of it had cleaved him in two, but he'd kept it on his desk where it sparkled away at him all sodding day and he had no idea why.

Nor could he work out why he hadn't announced that he and Kate had decided to go their separate ways. The deal was sealed. The contract could not now be broken. A quick press release to announce that their engagement was off would be the easiest thing to do. So why did it feel like the hardest? Why was he still putting it off?

It was all as confusing as hell, but not nearly as confusing as the doubts that had started bothering him a couple of days ago and were now sprouting up all over the place. What if she was right and he was wrong? was the main one, the one that tortured his every waking moment. The minute he crushed it in one place, up it popped somewhere else, churning up his insides and driving him demented.

It couldn't go on.

He couldn't go on.

Not any more.

As the strength suddenly left his body, Theo sank into the sofa, his elbows on his knees, and buried his head in his hands.

He was so damn sick of it. Sick of the torment and the fighting and the bone-crushing loneliness. All his life he'd been alone. He had no siblings and he'd allowed no one to get close. Not even Kate, who'd made him doubt and fear and hope. Who'd pushed her way through his defences and stabbed at where he was weakest and who he might as well admit he adored.

He couldn't do denial any longer. His impenetrability was shot. As the walls around his heart crumbled, pain and regret sliced through him. She'd offered him everything he'd ever wanted and he'd thrown it back in her face. And why? Because she'd been right—he *had* been scared. He'd always been scared.

But, really, what was there to be afraid of? Hadn't he demonstrated time and time again that he had broken the mould? How many times had he been pushed yet stayed in control? He wasn't his father. He never had been. Never would be. Deep down he knew that. So what if that wasn't the real issue? What if he *did* fear rejection and abandonment?

He'd never forget the pain and the guilt, the distress and the trepidation that had gripped every inch of him when he'd shut the door on the flat he'd called home and what little family he'd had. He'd had money and a plan, but that first night he'd spent alone in a cheap nearby hotel had been so cold, so bleak, and the only way he'd been able to move forward was to accept the icy emptiness, adopt it and turn it into armour.

The actions of his mother had cut deep, but it had been fourteen years since she'd looked at him with accusation and disgust. There'd been nothing he could do to save her. He'd given her every opportunity to escape and she'd made her choice and it hadn't been him. There'd been nothing he could have done to save Mike either. Deep down he knew that because he'd done the research and asked the questions.

So he had to forgive himself and let it all go. Because how long was he going to deny himself the future he'd always dreamed of? How long was he going to be able to carry on knowing Kate was out there on her own because of his own blind stupidity?

God, he loved her. She was brave and forthright and confronted whatever life threw at her with her chin up and challenge in her eyes. He wanted her and he wanted their child. And he'd rejected them both.

When he thought of what he'd said to her, and the way he'd said it, he felt sick to his stomach. The ice, the disdain, the cruelty. He could recall every single word and they sliced at him like knives. What the hell had he done? he wondered, shame slamming into him as he broke into a cold sweat. And what the hell could he do to fix it?

The last fortnight for Kate had been something of a roller coaster. One minute she was doing fine, concentrating on putting one foot in front of the other as she got through the days, the next she was dissolving into tears, heartbroken and wishing for what could never be.

A week ago she'd gone to a doctor's appointment and when she'd heard the fluttering whoosh of her baby's heartbeat she'd completely lost it. When she'd visited Milly, who'd grilled her excitedly about the trip to Italy and bombarded her with questions about the non-existent wedding, she'd had to leave before she broke down. Swinging between intense despair and desperate hope that the fact that Theo hadn't issued an announcement about their separation might mean something, she was mostly a wreck and she'd lost count of how many tubs of ice cream she'd consumed.

But while acceptance that he wasn't going to change his mind still shredded her heart it *was* getting easier. Her appetite had returned and she'd stopped waking up in the middle of the night in tears. And look at the way she could now go without thinking about him for a whole five minutes. See how the urge to call him and beg him to give them a chance was gradually diminishing. That was huge progress.

And that wasn't the only area in which she was moving on. The day before yesterday, she'd grabbed a large plastic bag and filled it with the ill-fitting clothes she'd once bought because they made her feel dainty. Then she'd ordered a full-length mirror, which had arrived this morning. If she was going to carry on walking around in her underwear, which she'd taken to doing since everything else was getting tight, she figured she might as well see what she looked like doing it. So what if she was going to become the size of a whale and probably just as cumbersome? Her body was building a baby. It wasn't anything to be ashamed of. It was magnificent. And who cared if she didn't fit in? What was so great about being the same as everyone else anyway?

Besides, she wanted to be able to admire her fabulous new haircut properly. She'd wanted short hair for as long as she could remember but she'd always worried that it would make her look even bigger. And it probably did, but she didn't care, she loved it anyway. Statuesque was how she was going to think of herself from now on. Fearless. And strong.

Because she was all that and more. She'd been wrong about Theo being responsible for the changes she'd undergone. It had been her. All her. She didn't need him. She didn't need anyone. And when she was ready she'd find another man with whom she could wear heels and walk in synch. In Holland, perhaps. Dutch men were the tallest on the planet. They had an average height of one hundred and eighty-two point five centimetres. She knew. She'd looked it up.

In the meantime she had plenty to occupy herself. She had work to find. She had Milly and the baby to focus on. That was more than enough. She didn't need Theo. She didn't need anyone. She was more than capable of doing this on her own. She'd be fine. In fact, she *was* fine.

The buzzer sounded, making her jump and jolting her out of her thoughts. She put down the knife with which she was chopping onions for soup for supper and wiped her streaming eyes. Padding into the hall, she picked up the handset. 'Yes?' she said with a sniff.

'It's Theo.'

At the sound of his voice, the voice that had tormented her dreams and which she'd never ever forget, Kate nearly dropped the handset. Her heart skipped a beat and then began to thunder, the surge of love, need and hope colliding with doubt and wariness. Why was he here? What did he want? And what was she going to do?

The part of her that was still crushed by the way he'd rejected her was tempted to tell him to get lost. Yet him on her doorstep was precisely what she'd been dreaming of, and so even though she was so vulnerable where this man was concerned, even though he had the power to destroy her so completely she might never recover if she wasn't extremely careful, she knew she was no more going to hang up on him than she was going to be a petite size six.

'Come up.'

That was one hurdle cleared, thought Theo grimly, his gut churning with rare nerves as the door buzzed and he pushed his way in. Now for the rest.

As he took to the stairs, it occurred to him that for the first time in decades he had no plan. He had no idea what he was going to say. Once he'd realised how much of a fool he'd been, all he'd focused on was getting here. The only thing he *did* know was that he'd come to fight for the woman he loved and to get her back, whatever it took, whatever the cost, and he wasn't leaving until he'd achieved it.

His throat dry and his pulse racing, he banged on her door and a second later it swung open and there she was, standing there in a dressing gown, her eyes red and shimmering with unshed tears.

'Are you all right?' he asked gruffly, the idea that he could have done that to her, *had* done that to her stabbing him like a dagger in the chest.

'I'm fine,' she replied with a sniff.

Another thought entered his head then, a thought that chilled his blood and for a moment stopped his heart. 'The baby?'

'It's fine, too.'

'Then why are you crying?' he demanded, the indescribable relief flooding through him sharpening his tone.

She blew her nose and gave a shrug. 'Onions.'

He went still. 'What?'

'I've been chopping onions.'

Right. So. Her tears weren't because of him. They were because of onions. That was good. Wasn't it? 'In a dressing gown?'

She lifted her chin a fraction and arched an eyebrow, and he felt a great thud of lust and love slam through him. 'In my underwear, if you must know.'

He'd rather not. The images immediately flashing through his head were immensely distracting and did unsettling things to his equilibrium. Nevertheless, as much as he'd like to pull her into his arms, undo the belt and see exactly what she had on beneath, he kept his eyes up and his hands in his pockets. 'You've had your hair cut.'

'Yes.'

'It suits you.'

'I know,' she said. 'I've also bought a full-length mirror and am considering a move to Holland.'

The ground beneath his feet shifted. What the hell? 'Holland?'

She nodded briefly. 'Holland.'

'Why?'

'Why not?'

He knew of a dozen reasons why not. 'I thought you didn't travel much.'

She shrugged. 'Things change,' she said, and it hit him like a blow to the head that they had. She wasn't sitting at home pining for him. She was getting her hair cut and buying mirrors. She was moving on. Without him. And it was his own damn fault. He yanked his hands out of his pockets and shoved them through his hair, his heart pounding with the very real fear that he'd blown it for good. 'Don't go.'

'You don't get to tell me what to do any more, Theo.'

'I know I don't.'

'Then why are you here?'

'There are so many reasons, I barely know where to start.'

She frowned. 'Is there a problem with the deal?'

'No.'

'Then…?'

'May I come in?'

'No,' she said, folding her arms across her chest and straightening her spine magnificently. 'Whatever you have to say, you can say it out here.'

'All right,' he muttered, beginning to pace in an effort to untangle the jumbled thoughts in his head and calm the panic that he was too late, that he might have already lost her. 'First of all, I wanted to tell you that you were right.'

'About what?'

'Every single point you made in the car. Deep down, I *have* been afraid of rejection and abandonment and it's why I've always kept people at arm's length. But the truth is I ache with loneliness. I want to be happy, Kate, and I want what you offered. You. Our child. The chance to be a family.' He took a deep breath. 'Because I love you.'

She went very still and when she spoke it was almost a whisper. 'What did you say?'

'I love you,' he said, staring at her unwaveringly, unwilling to miss even a flicker of reaction. 'And I need you. You have no idea how much. You are incredible.'

She swallowed hard. 'But you threw me away.'

'Yes,' he said, the memory of his careless brutality skewering him.

'It hurt.'

At the pain in her eyes, his chest tightened as if caught in a vice. 'I know. And I'm sorry. For all of it. For the way I spoke to you in the car. For blackmailing you in the first place. For everything.' He cleared his throat. 'The thing is, Kate, for so long I've believed the world is a safer place if I'm alone and that detachment and distance was the only way to achieve that. It always has been.'

He paused and rubbed his hands over his face as he forced himself to continue. 'My earliest memory is of my father hitting my mother in the face. I can still see her on the floor, him looming over her, huge and angry while she curled up tight. We were terrified every time he came home. I used to wake up to the sounds of crying and shattering glass. I had nightmares. From the youngest age I wanted to protect her, but I couldn't and the sense of failure and hopelessness was all-consuming. I learned to shut down and switch off, and it became so natural I was barely aware I was doing it, or continued to do it. And, yes, I got out, but not before picking up a lot of other damaging belief, especially the "my way or the highway" approach to doing things, which could be attributed to my success or it could just as well be learned. And that's another thing. Success is an easy place to hide, and if no one ever challenges you it becomes even easier.'

He looked at her, willing her to understand and to forgive. 'But you did challenge me, Kate. You *do* challenge me. At first I tried to resist, tried to control it, but that was always going to be a battle I was going to lose. And

I have lost it. Which is fine, because I don't want to hide behind my hang-ups any more. I want to de-programme and learn to live my life with you and our child. You have no idea how badly I want to meet him or her. I can't stop thinking about who they'll look like. I want to be the kind of father I never had. But most of all I want you on my side. By my side. I want everything you have to give and to give you everything you want in return because you deserve to have it.'

He stopped and focused on her, but he couldn't tell what she was thinking and he went cold, his pulse thudding in his ears and dread whipping through him. 'But maybe I'm not what you want any more,' he said, his throat suddenly tight and his voice cracking. 'Maybe I'm too late. Am I?'

All Kate could do was shake her head. The lump the size of Ireland that was lodged in her throat was preventing her from speaking, and her heart was so full she could barely think. Theo loved her. He wanted her. He'd opened up to her, trusting her with his greatest fears and his deepest vulnerabilities and it was everything she'd dreamed of but thought she'd never have.

'You're not too late,' she said, her voice thick with emotion, the need to dispel the uncertainty in his expression and the tension gripping his large, powerful body all-consuming.

His breath caught. His gaze sharpened. A muscle hammered in his jaw. 'No?'

'No.'

'I am still what you want?'

'Yes,' she said with a nod. 'And more. I love you.'

'Thank God for that,' he muttered, striding forward, taking her in his arms and kissing her hard until her head spun and her stomach melted. 'I really thought I'd screwed up beyond salvation.'

'What took you so long?'

'As you may have noticed, I can, on occasion, be rather single-minded.'

She leaned back in his arms and arched an eyebrow. 'On occasion?' she asked with a giddy grin.

'All right. More than on occasion. Once I embark on a course of action I'm not easily derailed. I always know what I'm doing. I always think I'm right. There's safety and security in that. But then I met you and that was shot to hell. I found myself making reckless suggestions and behaving in ways I didn't recognise and it terrified me.' He looked deep into her eyes as if still unable to believe she was there. 'And then somehow you became the plan,' he said in wonder. 'I love you, Kate, and you should know I don't intend to let you go.'

'And you should know,' she said, pressing closer and winding her arms round his neck, 'that however tough things get, I will never walk away. I will always be on your side.'

'Will you marry me?' he asked, his eyes blazing with such love and tenderness that her own began to sting. 'For real?'

And as happiness burst through her like sunshine she tucked her head into his shoulder and sighed, 'I will.'

EPILOGUE

Two and a half years later

'SO APPARENTLY,' SAID KATE, sticking two candles into the dinosaur cake she'd spent most of the morning making, 'if you measure a child on its second birthday and double it, that's the height they're going to end up being.'

Theo glanced over from where their toddler son was ripping wrapping paper into shreds, his chest filling with emotion as it never failed to do. 'What's the verdict?'

'Five foot eight.'

His eyebrows shot up. 'Seriously?'

'No, only joking,' she said, with a blinding grin that still stole his breath. 'Six foot four, actually.'

'That's my boy.'

And in three months' time they'd have twin daughters.

Theo didn't like to think how close he'd come to throwing it all away. If Kate hadn't given him another chance… If she hadn't believed in him… But she had and she did. Every single day. The deal had taken a year to finalise, and once it was done, his company was indeed the biggest of its kind. But it wasn't that that had given him peace. It was his family. Daniel Bridgeman had once called him a lucky man. And he was. He was the luckiest man in the world.

* * * * *

A FLING TO STEAL
HER HEART

SUE MacKAY

CHAPTER ONE

'ARE YOU CERTAIN you aren't still in love with him?'

'Couldn't be more certain.'

Isabella Nicholson held back on saying more. Admitting the truth that she doubted she'd really loved her ex enough in the first place would be embarrassing, even if Raphael Dubois was her best friend.

Best as in she'd usually tell him everything, whenever the urge took her, even in the early hours of Sunday morning, which it was right now. Four a.m. here in Wellington, four p.m. Saturday in London, where Raphael worked at his dream job in obstetrics and gynaecology at the Queen Victoria Hospital.

Wait a minute. He'd texted to see if *she* was awake, and knowing she currently suffered insomnia it was a no-brainer.

'Hey, why did you call? Not to ask about Darren, surely?'

'Izzy, is that the absolute truth or are you afraid of the answer?'

Typical. The man never missed a beat when it came to asking the hard questions, whether of her or his patients. Yet he always ignored *her* questions whenever it suited him.

Two could play that game. Though she'd try once more to shut him down. 'Don't I always tell you the truth?' Minus some niggling details in this instance.

'You're good at leaving out the specifics when it suits,' he confirmed, chuckling so she knew he was letting go the subject of her failed marriage.

'So what brings you to call in the middle of Saturday afternoon? I'd have thought you'd be at a rugby game with the guys.' One of them had found the niche they were looking for—and it wasn't her. Two years ago she'd returned home to New Zealand with her new husband, full of hope and excitement based around Darren's promises for what lay ahead, and with the intention of finally stopping in one place and surrounding herself with family and friends. Instead, twelve months later, her marriage had crashed badly, leaving her dreams up in the air. The friends had been all his, and her parents were always busy with their own lives. Since then she'd gone back to what she was good at—moving around the world from job to country to anywhere enticing, only for a lot shorter periods than previously. A fortnight ago she'd finished a volunteers' job in Cambodia and returned to visit her parents while deciding where next. Only she couldn't bring herself to go just anywhere this time.

Find something more permanent kept popping into her head. *Go solo on that dream of settling down.*

'I've been delivering triplets,' Rafe replied. He'd settled in London, been there nearly three years, bought a house, was keeping some distance from his claustrophobic family at home in Avignon as he grappled with his own demons. He seemed content in a quiet way, which was not the Raphael she'd known most of her life.

Please be her turn next. Even if it meant remaining

single, which wasn't so bad. She was used to it. Nursing and midwifery jobs were fairly easy to come by, but after a childhood of moving around with her parents in the Foreign Service she'd hankered after settling back in New Zealand for ever when she'd married. Maybe that's where she'd gone wrong, put too much emphasis on where she lived and not who with. So here she was, minus the husband, ignoring the hole inside that needed filling with something unrecognisable, and which she suspected had to do with love. 'Triplets. Hard to imagine how parents cope with that many babies all at once.'

'This couple would've been grateful for quads if it meant becoming parents.' His voice fell into sentimental mode. 'You should see these little guys. So cute, looking tiny in their incubators hooked up to monitors, giving their parents heart failure already.'

'But they'll be fine, right?' He'd hate for anything to go wrong. When a baby in his care had difficulties that couldn't be fixed he'd get upset for days, distraught for the parents, blaming himself while knowing it wasn't his fault. She'd never been able to find out what was behind his extreme reaction that had only started over the last few years. Seemed they both kept secrets from each other.

'For triplets they're in good shape, though one of them is smaller than his brothers so I'll be keeping a closer eye on him. They made it to thirty-four weeks' gestation before the Caesarean, which means everything's on their side. The parents had fertility issues so we did artificial insemination and, *voilà*, the best of results.' Raphael's accent thickened when he became emotional.

'Great outcome for all of you.' Because he would've

been almost as invested as the expectant parents. 'You should go out and celebrate.'

'I'm meeting up with a couple of the guys and their better halves as soon as I've talked with you. What did you get up to last night?'

Huh? Her social life had never been of much interest to him before. There again, recently he had taken to expressing concern about how she was coping with getting over Darren. Worried she'd go back to the cheat?

'I went out for a meal and a couple of drinks at the local with a neighbour.' She hadn't stayed out late, preferring to head back to her parents' place rather than being eyed up by men obviously wanting one thing only.

Getting old, girl.

Or jaded.

'Beats staying inside the four walls feeling sorry for yourself.'

Again, huh? What was this all about? 'That's harsh, Rafe.' She preferred it when Raphael went all sentimental over the babies he delivered, not digging deeper into her messed-up life. 'I'll say it one more time. I do not love Darren. Any feelings I had for him died when I found Gaylene Abernethy's naked body wrapped around him in our bed.' If only it was that easy: blame Darren for everything and feel superior. But it wasn't. She'd taken his promises about their life together at face value, colouring in the gaps with what she wanted and not seeing that he'd never aspired to the same. Though the affairs were a different story. Her husband had gone too far there.

'That's positive. I had to ask.' That couldn't be relief in Raphael's voice. Then again, why not? The two men had never got on, were summer to winter.

'Sure you did.'

Naturally he hadn't finished. 'Love doesn't always stop the moment there's a reason to.' He spoke from first-hand experience. Was that what this was about? Would he finally tell her what had happened six years ago when his heart was torn out of his chest?

'I did love Darren, though not as much as I should've if I was committing to "until death us do part."'

'Does anyone say that any more? What if you both lived till you were ninety-five? That's a lot of marriage. At fifty who's the same person they were at thirty, let alone in their nineties?' asked the guy who'd signed up for ever with Cassie, only to get the boot within two years. Failed marriages were another thing they had in common.

'Typical of you to come up with that question.' If she fed him a little bit more about her relationship would he let it go? Not likely. This was Rafe. Neither did admitting how she'd failed come easily. She'd made a mistake marrying Darren. His promises of buying a house and having children didn't eventuate. Instead the parties, going to the rugby games with the mates and leaving her behind, the late nights at the office not working— found that out later—the weekends away with the boys… None of it ever stopped, actually became more intense, as though he was afraid to face what he'd agreed to do with her. She'd got more morose and by the time their first wedding anniversary came around she was blaming him for everything that went wrong in her life. Not accepting that she'd rushed in on those promises without asking herself if she really loved Darren as much as she'd believed. 'I'm fine. I made a mistake, and now I've put it behind me.'

'As long as you're sure,' Raphael muttered. 'I don't want you regretting leaving him further down the track.'

'Drop it, Rafe. We are not getting back together. It's over.' How many times did she have to say it?

'Right. Tell me about Phnom Penh, then. What made you stay on an extra month?'

She'd rather talk about her ex. 'A tragic case that I got too close to.'

'We're not meant to do that, Izzy.'

Tell her something she didn't know. 'It's different over there. When someone's sick or seriously injured the whole family's involved, from great-gran to baby brother, and I got swept up in it all.' To the point where she'd put the brakes on racing around chasing happiness while she thought about what she really wanted for the future. 'Can we change the subject?'

'Fine. So what's next? A summer at the Antarctic with the New Zealand science contingent? Or a month on one of the charity ships in Africa?'

There seemed to be another question behind Raphael's queries, but Isabella couldn't hear what it was. Strange, given how well they knew each other—apart from those secrets. 'Come on. I'm not that restless.' Though the past year said otherwise. Auckland, Melbourne, Cambodia. Maybe she was more like her parents than she cared to admit, and therefore she was never going to find that permanent happy place. Nothing wrong with Mum and Dad's thirty-two-year marriage despite rarely stopping in one place for more than three years at a time though. They just shouldn't have brought her into the mix. 'I spent six years in Wellington training and working as a nurse. Four more in London doing midwifery before—'

'*Oui*, I get it. But right now you'll be overthinking what you're going to do next. Stay in Wellington, move to Africa or America.' He paused. Then on a deep breath, he continued. 'With your attitude about failing, this breakup will still be winding you into a tight ball of conjecture. "Where shall I live? What's the next project to undertake? Am I more Kiwi or English?"' He sighed, then said, 'Tell me I'm wrong, Izzy.'

She couldn't. That was exactly who she was. Except that family in Cambodia had changed her in some indefinable way. But she wasn't ready to talk about it yet. Might never be. Isabella stretched the length of her bed, and tucked the thick woollen duvet around herself. 'You'll be pleased to know I can't imagine being stuck on an iceberg for months on end having to rely on in-depth conversations with penguins.' She pulled her pillow down around her neck. Autumn had thrown a curve ball today, sending a reminder of what winter would have in store in a few weeks.

'Penguins are probably more interesting than half the people you get to meet every day.' His laughter was usually infectious, but tonight it was sounding a little tired, fed up even.

'Something wrong at your end of the world?'

'No more than the usual. We're short-staffed and it seems every female in London over twenty is pregnant at the moment.'

'What about life outside the Queen Victoria? Love, life, laughter, those things?' Raphael was one of the most good-looking men she knew. Women fawned over him, fell in love with him without him having said *bonjour*. Yet, since Cassie, he'd not had one serious relationship, preferring the love 'em and leave 'em approach to relationships—when he found time for one. At least he didn't promise anything else and always warned the women he wasn't looking for a partner. In fact, he was so kind and careful about his approach they all still thought he was wonderful long after he'd said *au revoir*.

'Don't know what you're talking about.' At least his laughter was genuine now. 'Haven't got time for much than work and study.'

'That sounds as pathetic as my life right now.' What a scintillating pair they made.

'You think?' Raphael took a long, slow breath. 'Crunch time, huh, Midwife Nicholson? For you, not me,' he clarified.

'You sure about that?' she grumped, hating him for making her face up to what was bothering her.

'It's not me lying awake for hours every night trying to put the pieces of the puzzle back together.'

'You're right, and don't you dare gloat,' she added in a hurry. 'I do have some decisions to make.'

'Starting with?'

That was the problem. She didn't know where to start. 'Where to live?'

'What's wrong with where you are?' Straight to the point, as always.

'If I'm staying here I need to buy a property and get stuck in making it mine.' Isabella sighed. It was the truth, just not all of it. Try again. 'Funny how I always thought of Wellington as home and yet it doesn't feel like that.'

'You haven't exactly been happy there in the past. We all need some place to call home, but it doesn't mean we have to settle there if we're not getting what we require from it. Like me and Avignon.'

Yeah, where he got too much of what he wanted.

'Now there's an interesting city.' The ancient wall surrounding the city centre, the old fort on the other side
of the river, the famous Pont d'Avignon. The history
had drawn her, made her yearn to belong somewhere,
to feel a part of something—and so when Darren came
along she'd moved back to Wellington with him. Except now she'd probably leave again. Something was
missing. With the city? Or inside her? 'I think I want to
get back to friends who *know* me and where I've come
from.' Maybe even *where* she was headed.

Raphael should understand. They'd met on trips
with their respective schools to a ski field in the Swiss
Alps. Out of control on a snow board, she'd crashed into
him, and nursing bruises over hot chocolate in the café
they'd instantly bonded. His father worked in a bank in
Geneva while her dad was working at the New Zealand
consulate in the same city. She'd been used to making
friends quickly, aware how fast three years passed when
she'd have to move and start all over again. Raphael had
been homesick for his grandmother and cousins back in
Avignon, and resented his parents for taking him away
from them all. She'd wanted her parents to return home
and stop moving. Instead, when her mother obtained a
position in an international accounting company that
had her travelling a lot, Isabella had been sent to boarding school in England, leaving her feeling unconnected,
abandoned. Even when she returned to the family fold,
that disconnect remained. She'd done too much growing
up in the interim and had changed for ever.

Despite being two years older than her, Raphael had
gone out of his way to keep in touch, and they had remained close, despite living in different countries for
most of their friendship. She'd briefly worked with him

once in Tours, which had been great. Since then? Modern communications systems were the best thing to ever be invented.

Raphael asked, 'You're still coming over here for Carly's wedding, right?'

'Wouldn't miss it for anything. It was bad enough not making it to Esther and Harry's.' She'd been supposed to fly to London for that, but when the Medical Volunteers Charity asked her to stay on another month because the traumatised Khy family she'd been working closely with still needed her there as stability, she hadn't been able to say no. They'd needed her, and she'd wanted to be needed. Still did. 'Flights are booked.'

'Why not make it a one-way trip? Your girlfriends from midwifery training days are here and all working in the Queen Victoria, although for how long is anyone's guess with all these weddings going down. Then there's *moi*.'

Her laugh was brittle. 'You make it sound so easy.' It was. With an English mother getting a work visa for the UK was straightforward. But did she want to go there and be watched over like she was going to come out in a rash for being on her own again? Or questioned about every move she made? Every decision she arrived at? Because Raphael had changed. Since she'd left Darren, come to think of it. He was always questioning what she did, the jobs she chose, the countries they were in. No way did she want put up with any more of that, and living on his back doorstep wouldn't help. At least she wouldn't be *in* his house.

He continued in a coaxing voice. 'Okay, why I really rang. There is a nurse's position coming up on my ward if you're interested. With your midwifery qualifications as well as nursing you're ideal for the job. The girl who's leaving hasn't told anyone other than me yet, and she's agreed to keep quiet till I talk to you. What do you think?'

'How soon would I have to start?' She was stalling, not feeling the excitement that usually stirred when she had an offer on the table to do something new. Weighing up the pros and cons? Unlike her.

'Jasmine wants to be gone within three weeks. Something about a boyfriend in Canada and a road trip they've been planning to do over summer.'

Did she want to return to London? As in *really* want to? Or should she be staying put, making more of an effort to integrate into Wellington and stop blaming Darren for feeling confused? Making this the home base she'd always wanted?

'And…ta da, the best bit.' He paused for effect. Typical Raphael. 'Don't forget who's the charge obstetrician on the ward. Your call, but remember, we work well together.'

That they did. Working as a midwife for those few months in Tours just after she'd finished her midwifery training had been the best job she'd ever had; having her closest friend in the same hospital added to the pluses. He'd shown her the French lifestyle, taken her to Avignon to meet his maternal grandmother and his cousins, tripped all over the country on their days off to show her castles, cities, mountains. Then he'd taken up his current position in London, and she'd met Darren in France while watching a rugby game between the All Blacks and Les Bleus, and the rest was history. A rocky, sorry history, but what didn't kill her was going to make her stronger. Just not certain when. Not to mention how persuasive Raphael could be when he put his mind to it. 'You know what?'

'You're on your way.'

'I might be.'

'Hello? Where's strong, do-it-her-way-or-bust Isabella gone? You're coming or you're not. Which, Izzy?'

She had to make her mind up now? Why not? Raphael was right. She'd always approached life head-on, didn't usually waste time dithering over decisions, and accepted that when she'd got it wrong it was part of the gamble. Her marriage failure had set her off kilter, made her worry and fuss too much about getting things right or wrong, made her wary of trusting people. Then watching the closeness of the Khys as they struggled to keep their son alive and how they coped after it all went wrong had blitzed her completely.

'Izzy?'

If taking up a new position back in the city where her nursing friends and Raphael lived turned out to be a mistake, then she'd survive. If Rafe became too bossy she'd tell him what to do with that. But at least they were all there, the people who mattered the most to her. 'Got to go. Have to pack my bag.'

CHAPTER TWO

TWO WEEKS LATER, as Raphael paced the arrivals hall at Heathrow, Isabella's text pinged on his phone.

Landed.

About time. Something settled in his gut. Relief? No, this sensation felt stronger, not that he recognised it, but it did make him wary and happy all in one hit. He'd felt this way when Izzy said she was coming to London. His fingers flew over his phone.

I'm waiting in arrivals hall.

The flight was an hour late. Serve him right for getting here early, but he'd been ready to pick up Izzy since crawling out of bed first light that morning. Not even doing a round of his patients and checking on the triplets had quelled the need to get to Heathrow on time, which in his book meant early. Very early. He'd given his regular visit to the market a miss, cursed the traffic holdups all the way to the airport and ranted at the arrivals notice board every time it brought up a new flight arrival that wasn't Izzy's. Damn it, he even checked his phone app every time to make sure the board and the app were on the same page. *Oui*, of course they were. But this hanging around for Isabella was doing his head in.

He couldn't wait to see her. It seemed ages since she'd married Darren, who in his book was a complete idiot, and left London for what she euphemistically—in his mind, desperately—called home. It had been as though she'd been on a mission to prove something to herself, and she hadn't told him what it was, which worried him. Yet when Isabella suggested he pay them a visit in Wellington during his leave last year he'd pleaded prior commitments so as to avoid her husband. Unfair, but he and Darren had never seen eye to eye about anything, and especially about the woman they both cared about. Her husband could not get his head around the fact that Raphael and Isabella were close friends, not lovers and never had been, and he kept making digs about how she was *his*. Yeah, right. Look where that had got the guy. Single again, and still missing the whole point about commitment.

His phone pinged again.

Bring a trailer?

You've brought that much gear?

Yep.

Really? Isabella travelled light. Something she'd learned as a Foreign Service brat. While her parents had a container-load of gear follow them wherever they went, Izzy never packed much at all, said carrying only her regular gear around kept her grounded in reality.

Did this mean she'd come to London with the idea of staying long term?

Calmes-toi.

There was long term and then there was Izzy's ingrained version of staying put. They did not match. There'd been nothing to stop her settling in London permanently last time she lived here. But he wasn't being fair. She had decided to stay here and then along came the husband offering all sorts of carrots in Wellington. She'd always had a thing about returning to the city where she'd been born and partially brought up in, so Darren's promises raised her hopes of a life there. The failure of said marriage seemed to have screwed with that idea, and stalled her about making any serious decisions over what to do next. Odd, because Isabella was no stranger to being strong and getting what she wanted. But on the other side of that argument, she *didn't* always know exactly what she wanted. Hence fast-track midwifery training.

He texted back.

Great.

It was, actually. Could be she'd finally figured out what she was looking for. Given half a chance he'd go back to Avignon and the family tomorrow. But it wasn't happening any time soon. He'd return there only when he'd got over the guilt for the way Cassie had treated his nearest and dearest. And stopped feeling angry for the cruel blow she'd hit him with. His son, his parents' only grandson, dead at eight days from SIDS, and he hadn't even known he was a father. The pregnancy one more of Cassie's ways of paying him back for not falling into line with all her outrageous demands.

The doors from the other side swished open as a small group of people towing cases on wheels came through. Swallowing the familiar bitterness and hauling his concentration to what was important today, Raphael craned his neck trying to see around them. No sign of Isabella. Nothing on his phone. 'Come on. Where are you?' he ground out. No doubt dealing with the inevitable questions from immigration. He'd take another turn of the hall to fill in some minutes.

Except Raphael remained glued to the spot, his eyes never leaving the doors now that his phone had gone quiet. Hopefully that meant she'd soon burst through the doors like the hurricane she could be. Not that she sounded as revved up these days whenever he talked to her. Her ex had dealt some harsh blows to her confidence. Though there could be more to it than Izzy was telling him.

The doors opened again and more exhausted people spilled through, followed by a laden trolley being pushed by... 'Raphael.' The shout was accompanied by a small body hurtling through the crowd, aimed directly for him.

'Izzy.'

Oof. *Oui.* Definitely tornado.

His lungs huffed out every last molecule of oxygen they were holding as Isabella plastered herself against him. His arms wound around her like they never intended letting go. She smelt of travel and tiredness and excitement and—

Mais oui, Isabella. Soft, tough.

Careful. Friends, nothing else.

'Hello, Rafe. Good to see you.'

The relief expanded. Isabella *was* here. Izzy. He inhaled deeper, hugged harder and kissed her on both cheeks French style. Friendly style. Then, without letting go of her, he leaned back to gaze down at her fine features with dark shadows staining her upper cheeks. There was strain in her eyes, negating her usual go-get-'em attitude. Anger lodged behind his ribs. This was Darren's fault. The man had hurt her. But apparently it took two to tango, so had Isabella done something wrong too? He'd leave off the big questions until she'd got some sleep and was looking more like her normal self. Since the flat she'd arranged had fallen through she was staying with him for a little while—until they had their first row at least. Something not uncommon between them. 'Great to see you, *mon amie.*'

The familiar cheeky twinkle was back in her gaze, though the corners of her mouth were still drawn. 'You see me every other week.'

He relaxed enough to go with the change. 'Usually your chin is huge and your eyes somewhere above the screen. This way I get to see you properly. I can read your expressions,' he added to wind her up for the hell of it. Because that's how they'd always been with each other, and until now he hadn't realised how important it was. It kept him on track, especially at the times Cassie's betrayal got to him too much. He hadn't shared the details, but Izzy had always been at the end of a phone. They knew each other better than anyone, and had often relied on that to get through the upheavals life threw at them, yet there'd been apprehension in his veins since Isabella had agreed to come to London and take up the job he'd suggested. He didn't understand his apprehension, unless it was to do with the uncomfortable, almost painful, feeling that overcame him at her marriage ceremony where he'd stood beside her as she said her vows to Darren. A sense that he'd found out something important when it was too late.

'Next time I'll focus the camera on my slipper-covered feet.'

'Not the ones the neighbour's dog chewed.' Next time. Reality check. This wasn't a long-term move. Was that disappointment rapping his knuckles? And if so, why? He was used to her coming and going as it suited, or, when they were young, as her parents had decreed. Could be that his need to see her happy wasn't going to be satisfied. Could also be that his hope of spending more time with her wasn't going to be fulfilled. He looked around. 'We'd better rescue that trolley before someone crashes into it and the bags topple off.' This was going to be interesting. His car wasn't made for organising a complete house move. 'Did you leave anything behind?'

Her tight laugh had him wondering just what was going on. 'This is only the beginning. I'm shipping more belongings across. The container's due to arrive sometime in May.'

Raphael dived right in. 'So you're looking for somewhere to unpack properly? As in lock, stock and clothes?' This was nothing like her usual style of one backpack and the laptop.

Her laughter died. 'Don't be so shocked. Just because it didn't work in Wellington doesn't mean it won't here with all my friends around me.'

He reached for her, needing to hug a smile back onto her face. 'You're right, and I'm one of them.'

'I hope so,' she murmured against his chest before

pulling away, still without a smile. She'd never doubted him before. But before he could question her, she continued: 'There's a couple of pieces of furniture, some kitchenware and lots of books coming.'

He stared at her, a knot of unease tightening in his belly. She was serious about this move. He was thrilled for her, and him, and would help make it work, but... But he'd have to be careful about keeping his distance. Risking their friendship was not happening over some out of kilter emotions he'd felt on and off since her marriage. 'Truly?'

She nodded, her mouth twisted into a wry smile. 'Truly.' A sigh trickled over her lips. 'I'll add to them as soon as I find my own place.'

'Your own place?' The relief should be flooding in. It wasn't.

'A place to rent for a start.'

He sighed. *Stop being disgruntled.* His friend was back in town. Someone to talk the talk with, have a beer at the pub or take a ride out in the countryside. One day at a time and see how they went getting back to that easy relationship they'd always shared until she'd got married.

It goes back further than that, mon ami. *You've never shared much about your time with Cassie. Or the devastation she caused.*

'Thanks for putting a roof over my head until I find somewhere.'

'It'll be better than squatting under London Bridge.' Suddenly there was a bounce in his step. He'd been looking forward to this moment, and now Izzy was here. Right beside him. Recently his life had become all about work, and very little play. All too often he cancelled going to rugby with the guys, the only excuse being his patients needed him. But he needed to be more rounded, balance his lifestyle. Izzy was good at shaking him up, would take no nonsense about how he was a doctor before all else. Well, he was, but she always reckoned that didn't mean his work should fill twenty-four hours every day of the week. 'Let's get out of here.'

'Let's.' Isabella smothered a yawn with her hand. 'That was one hell of a trip. Crying babies, and an enormous man in the seat next to me who kept falling asleep and sprawling in every direction, mostly mine.'

'Sounds fairly normal.' Long-haul flights were hell on wings.

'One day I'm going to fly first class just to see what it's like. I did get some sleep though, which is a change. Probably because I had so little in the nights leading up to getting on the plane.'

'You done anything about that insomnia?'

Untidy auburn hair flicked across her shoulders as she shook her head. 'What's the point? I've tried everything except sleeping pills and I'm never resorting to them. Seen too many patients who've become addicted, and then any gains in the sleep department are lost. Besides, I'm used to getting by on a couple of hours at a time.'

This had gone on for almost as long as he'd known her, sometimes minor sleep deprivation, sometimes quite major, and in recent years it had cranked up a few more notches. Guess a person could get used to anything given enough time, though it wasn't good for her. 'Still, I think you should see one of my colleagues. He's good at helping people get to the bottom of what's causing the problem and might even be able to give you some practical advice.'

'Let me get unpacked before you start organising my

life.' Isabella gave him a lopsided smile, with a warning behind it. 'Okay, what've you got planned for tonight?'

Whatever she was trying to tell him, he'd leave it for now. 'Running three laps of the neighbourhood before digging up the back garden and putting in some plants.'

'Cool. Nothing for me to worry about. I can sit down and watch a movie on my phone, dial out for pizza.'

Raphael laughed, and it was like pushing Play on an old CD player, bringing back memories of fun times when his heart hadn't been ripped out of his chest. He halted the trolley to sling an arm over Isabella's shoulders and hug her against him again. 'You're on to it.' This was more like it. Cheeky Izzy not taking any of his nonsense seriously. It was one of the things he missed the most. Not even the overloaded, heavy trolley could put a dent in the sense of fun ahead now spreading through him. A familiar feeling he'd known the very first time they'd met, stronger than the pain in his thigh where her snowboard had struck hard. She'd been embarrassed at losing control, and tried blaming him for being in the way. They'd argued and laughed and shared hot chocolates and swapped phone numbers, and afterwards met up every weekend in Geneva when they could get away from school activities. 'I've missed you.' It hadn't been so easy to have two-hour conversations when there was a husband in the background, and he'd been very aware of how he might've felt if the situation had been reversed. He mightn't have liked Darren, but he understood the boundaries. And afterwards, Izzy had been a bit withdrawn with him.

'Same.'

'I would've headed down under for a week this past year to support you, cheer you up, get you back on track, but you were never there.' Her phone calls over the last twelve months had been quiet, and filled with sadness and, at times, something like despair that she'd never explained.

Again those auburn locks swished back and forth across her shoulders. 'You didn't have to do that. I'm a big girl. Anyway, I managed, and you were always at the other end of the phone when I needed to talk. You'd have been fed up with me by the end of the first day and champing to get away. I had to do it my way, and having you rant in my ear about my future when I couldn't hang up on you wouldn't have worked, for either of us.'

'You're probably right, but still…' He'd let her down. And himself. Again he wasn't sure why he thought that.

Raphael began pushing his friend's worldly goods towards the lift that'd take them to the car park. 'Bumped into Carly on Wednesday. She's pretty excited about you returning to the Queen Victoria.'

'She's more excited about her wedding. We've already got a night out planned with the other two from our training days' group. Funny how we're again all here at the same time. I wonder if that means everyone's settling down, becoming responsible adults, or is this just another stop along the way? Seems London's our place. My place?'

This sounded more like the Isabella he'd known for so long: always confident and putting it out there about how she wanted to live, and yet being gnawed at on the inside with her insecurities over people sticking by her, not breaking the bonds she desperately needed. Her parents had put her into boarding school when they felt she'd have better support and company than at home with them. They hadn't known a thing. He'd held her while she'd cried over being sent away. But after falling heavily for Cassie, and having her treat him so badly, he knew what a shattered heart felt like—and wasn't risking going there again. Nor hurting someone else similarly when he wasn't able to give enough of himself to her.

He said, 'Stop trying to second-guess everything, and enjoy being back amongst us all.' He would never desert her; he needed her friendship as much as she needed his. She understood him like no one else. If only he could stick with friendship, not let other emotions get in the way. 'You can do it. You have to believe in yourself.'

Then Isabella flicked him a look he couldn't interpret. 'Like you?' Her eyes were locked on his. 'I can follow your example? Work non-stop, get a home that I won't get to spend much time in?'

His happiness slipped. 'Is that what I've become? A workaholic?'

'It's what you told me only weeks ago.'

'I was probably trying to deflect you from your problems.' He'd been voicing his concerns about how everyone around him seemed to be finding love and making babies, while he was getting further tied up with work. What he hadn't said was how he wished he could find what it would take to try again, to finally put his past to rest. But he couldn't. Because of Cassie's selfishness, he'd lost a son and still wasn't able to make peace with himself about that.

'About those problems, will you always be here for me on the bad days?'

Where did that come from? '*Oui*, you can count on me.' She already knew it.

'Thanks. I can't tell you how good it is to spend time

with you. It's been a while since anyone told me what to do.'

'Most people are too scared to.' He laughed. 'Let's get this load home and go have a drink and a pub meal to celebrate your arrival in London.' Better out somewhere surrounded by people than stuck in his kitchen together. Only now was he beginning to understand the coming weeks sharing his house might not be as comfortable as he'd thought. Which was so far left field it was crazy. Izzy would get busy beginning her new life, and he'd be hanging on to the dull but predictable one he'd made for himself.

'Sounds good to me. I loved the pub food when I lived here last time.' Isabella's hand tapped her stomach, then a hip. 'Not that it ever did me a lot of good. But I'm in for tonight anyway.' She threaded her arm through his, ignoring how the trolley aimed sideways and caused him to put more pressure on to controlling it with the other arm. 'Honestly, Rafe, I keep wanting to pinch myself. It's been for ever since we last saw each other. Talking on the phone or through the internet doesn't quite cut it. I like to know you're within reaching distance.' She gulped, tripped, righted herself and stared straight ahead. 'Talking too much. Put it down to jet lag, if that happens so soon after a flight.'

This was different. He hauled the brakes on the hope beginning to unfold deep inside. In the long run he wouldn't be enough for Izzy. She needed someone to love her unconditionally. That wouldn't be him after the way Cassie had blown his trust out of the water because Izzy had her own issues about believing anyone would love her enough to stay around. Anyway, give her a few days to settle in at work and catch up with the girls and she'd be off doing all sorts of random things, and then he could relax around her. 'You don't suffer from jet lag.' He'd always been envious when he'd had to grapple with debilitating exhaustion for days after a long-haul flight, while this woman usually bounced off the plane ready to party.

'Always a first time.' Isabella remained quiet until they reached his car. More unusual behaviour.

Something was up, and finding out what was impera-tive if he was to be onside as she settled into London for good, but best left alone today. He tipped his head side-ways to stare at Isabella. Naturally he always wanted to help her when she was in difficulty, but normally he'd accept it if she refused to talk. But today he wanted to get behind the pain in the back of her eyes, see her achieve genuine happiness. Opening the car boot, he said, 'Let me do this. You get comfortable inside.'

'Like I'm your grandmother?' She smiled. 'How is Grand'mère, by the way? Fully recovered from her hip replacement?'

'Chasing the great grandkids with her crutch, ap-parently. Being her, she'll be back cycling around the city before she should,' he said with a smile. He adored Grand'mère. She was the only other person besides Izzy to support him in all his endeavours without criticism. His family loved him but always wanted to tell him what they believed he was doing wrong with his decisions. 'I was talking to her last night and she said whenever you need a change of scenery, pop over and spend time with her.' What she'd really said was, when Isabella was fed up with him, go pay her a visit and she'd sort her out. Grand'mère had a soft spot for the lost Kiwi girl who'd often hopped a train to go spend a day with her when she was working in Tours.

'Cool. I'll do that sooner than later. I love your grand-mother, and Avignon's one of my favourite cities.' She handed him one of the smaller cases.

He shook his head. 'That big sucker first.'

'She might be just what I need on the days when you're not available for chewing your ear off.' Fixing a smile on her face she made to shift the bags. 'The fam-ily still as smothering as ever?'

Typical Izzy. Here he was holding back on the big questions and she just leapt in. 'Out of the way. This is man's work.'

'Whatever.' Her eye roll made him laugh. At least she backed away from the stack of cases.

'What have you got in here?' he groaned. 'You must've paid a small fortune in excess baggage costs.'

'You avoiding my question?'

'You know I am. Now, get in the car before I put a bag on your seat and leave you to catch the train.'

Isabella snuggled into the soft leather seat and tugged her crumpled denim jacket across her chest to keep out the chill. From what she'd seen coming in to land, Lon-don had not turned on the sunshine in welcome, and the air out here was proving it. But Raphael had more than made up for the chilly welcome, hugging her tight as though he never wanted to let her go. There'd been re-lief in his gaze as she raced to him, as though he hadn't really believed she'd turn up.

Well, she was here, and right now she needed friends who didn't ask awkward questions. Count Raphael out, then. She sighed. He never let her get away with anything. There again, he knew how to help her without seeming too intense. Demanding an instant decision about the job in the Queen Victoria had been unusual for him but just what she needed to get out of the blues she'd dumped herself into. Since his phone call determination to get on with consolidating her life had started growing, begun to fill the empty place deep inside, even excited her. There was a long way to go, but a start was way better than nothing at all.

The car rocked as Raphael clambered in beside her. 'Ready?'

She nodded. Fingers crossed, for everything. 'I sure am. What's Richmond like?' It was the suburb where he'd bought his house. 'I hear it's very pretty.'

'It is. There're plenty of fabulous cafés, and I enjoy walking or cycling along the river when I've had a rubbish day and need to put things into perspective.'

'That would be often.' He gave his all to patients. Studying him as he drove out of the airport, shock hit her.

He's changed.

His face was drawn, his movements heavier, his words spoken more thoughtfully. Why? Another sigh. He wouldn't thank her for asking so she changed the subject. 'How's Pierre?' His cousin's son held a special place in Raphael's heart.

'In love with the girl next door. Apparently he's going to die if she doesn't kiss him soon.' Raphael chuckled. 'Everything's so intense at his age.'

'Too much so sometimes.'

Rafe had been seventeen when he'd helped Adele during the birth of her son. He'd been driving her through the country lanes headed for the birthing centre when her well-spaced labour pains went out of control. He'd told Isabella there'd been no time for embarrassment with Adele gripping his arm and screaming to do something about the baby. The first birth he'd seen and aided, and from that day on he'd known what he wanted to do with his future career in medicine. 'Pierre's now a robust fifteen-year-old, and also thinking of going into medicine. Though not obstetrics. He's keen on cardiology, though that might have something to do with his heart being in torment at the moment.'

'You think?' Shuffling down further in her seat, Isabella stared out the window as they followed the main road leading into the city. 'This is familiar. I like familiar. It makes me feel I might be doing the right thing coming back.' She did feel connected to London, something she didn't get often. Wellington had been the only other place, and Darren's infidelity had altered that. Sure, he hadn't been the only one to get things wrong with their marriage, but he had broken her heart by seeking solace in other women's arms, and wrecked her trust in people.

'Papa and Maman have returned to live in the family home in Avignon. Dad's left the bank. It was getting too stressful so now he's working part time with a importing company and aiming to enjoy time out with the family.'

'That's huge.' Monsieur Dubois had worked long and hard most of his life. 'It's great news, isn't it?' Then her heart stuttered. Would Raphael move home now? Just when she'd returned to London? When she wanted to spend time with him?

Rafe was leaning forward, his concentration fixed on the road and cars ahead. His tight grip on the steering wheel was another giveaway he was rattled. *'Oui.'*

'But?' she dared to ask.

His fingers loosened their grip, tightened again. 'I'm still not ready,' he said in a 'don't go there' voice she knew not to ignore.

She closed her eyes and tipped her head back, let the silence take over. Better than saying anything to upset her friend. Apart from his parents almost suffocating him in love she had no idea what was behind his refusal to return home. He seemed more content than in those dark days after he and Cassie broke up, but there were times Isabella wondered how happy he really was with his lot.

The silence became uncomfortable. 'We had such plans growing up, didn't we? Nothing turned out anything like them.' There'd never been any doubt Raphael was going into medicine. He had intended setting up a private practice in his home city, while she'd thought she'd go into marketing, then car sales so she could drive to-die-for vehicles. Running a bar came into the plans somewhere around that time. But nothing had felt right, like something was missing as it was in her family. Then hearing Raphael talking about working with patients and the pain and fear and love that surrounded people when they were sick, she understood she wanted to work with people too. Not by handing them a full glass over a counter, but soothing their fears when they were injured, caring that they got through whatever was frightening them. So she applied to start training as a nurse, and had been the most at ease in her life for the next four years. Until she was qualified, and once again restlessness overtook her so finally, in desperation, she came to London and signed up for the midwifery course. Being there for those babies, and sharing—albeit on the periphery—the love and excitement every baby brought its parents, had made her happier than she'd ever believed possible. Having two options to her career was a bonus, and she had no intention of doing anything else career-wise. It was the one thing she was absolutely certain about.

'I am so glad you're here, Izzy.' Rafe sank back against the seat, and flicked her a quick smile, his knuckles no longer white and tight. Then he stiffened again. 'Not that I'll have a lot of free time to spend with you.'

It sounded like a warning of some sort. He wasn't available for friend time? Again, her heart stuttered. Which frightened her. *Raphael was a friend.* Couldn't be anything else. Of course they were never going to be anything else. These oddball jitters just went to show how far out of sync she'd become with what she needed from life. 'I'll be busy too,' she told him with a dollop of self-preservation for her pride. 'Finding a flat to rent, catching up with the girls, starting my new job.' A yawn caught her. Bed would be good right now. Damn but she needed some sleep, although past experience told her she was best to stay up till a reasonable hour, and eat a decent meal. Even then, there'd only be intermittent hours of unconsciousness. Glancing over to Rafe, for the first time in ages, pure happiness surged through her. It was as though she had come home, not left it. And she suspected she wasn't only thinking about London and friends, but Raphael in particular. Whatever that meant, she was too tired to worry about it. She let the silence return. Until again she couldn't stand it. 'I can't wait to see your house.'

He sucked in a breath. 'You're going to be disappointed. I'd be lying if I said it's a work in progress. I haven't done anything about the paintwork or getting the kitchen altered and the bathrooms modernised. I never seem able to find the enthusiasm or time.'

'Maybe I can help.'

His eyebrows rose in shock. 'I'm not talking a small job here.'

'Have to start somewhere, and if I'm going to get my own place eventually I might as well practise on yours first.'

'You think?' He grinned. 'Afraid I'm going to have to turn your offer—' he flicked a finger in the air '—down.'

'Coward.'

'Pink walls and floral curtains are so not my thing.'

'Mine either.' Her tastes were more along the lines of pale colours—more white than anything, lots of natural light, big empty spaces. That came from the real estate programs she'd watched avidly back in Wellington when she'd begun collecting furniture for the future house she and Darren were going to buy. 'Dark blue walls and carpets, a dash of white in the curtains, lime green furniture should do it.'

'Excellent. We have a plan.'

Isabella smiled. It was great how he said 'we.' As if she had a place in his life. But then she always had. Did that mean she'd be looking for a home in his neighbourhood? Doubt she could afford a dog kennel in Richmond. The idea of moving too far from Raphael suddenly irked, when it shouldn't. Friends moved around, came back together, moved on. At the moment they were in the coming back together phase. Who knew for how long?

'Here we are.' Raphael parked outside a brick row house. 'Welcome home.'

It wasn't her home, only a stop gap while she found somewhere for herself, but she'd take the warmth that went with his words and enjoy. Shoving the door wide, she clambered out on tired legs and looked around. Trees lined the street, a dog barked from behind a house next door and puddles glistened in the sun that was making its way out from behind the clouds. Home. Yes, it felt exactly like what she'd dreamed of having in Wellington. A house in a quiet neighbourhood. Throw in friends nearby, and Rafe had got it right when he chose this place. It was perfect.

Nothing's perfect. There're always faults.

The warning didn't dampen the warmth pushing aside her exhaustion.

Following Raphael inside, she stopped and stared at the hallway walls. Eek. 'Magenta? This is so dark it feels like it's falling in on us.' Definitely a fault.

'Wait until you see the kitchen.'

That colour had to go. Sooner than later. It was hideous. She shivered and traipsed behind Raphael up the stairs with the smallest of her cases in hand. It soon became obvious nothing had been done to spruce up the house for a long time, probably well before he moved in. Every room she peered into was in need of a coat of paint, preferably a very pale, neutral shade to lighten them, and new curtains to match. At the top of the stairs on the third floor he dumped the heaviest of her cases. 'This is your room for as long as you want it. It's the best of the two spares, and anyway I use the smallest for an office,' he told her before heading back down to get the next bag.

Isabella looked around the neat but bland room, and shrugged. No magenta in here, thank goodness, but the pale mauve reminded her of an old lady's room. Still, it was somewhere to put her head down, and give her time to find somewhere to rent. So why the flicker of excitement? Sinking onto the edge of the bed she rubbed her arms through her jacket, and said aloud to prove she wasn't dreaming it, 'I'm back in London, in the other country I call home.' Her mother came from the Lake District and she'd only visited her relatives once last time she lived here. The welcome mat had been in storage that day, something to do with her mother marrying a New Zealander instead of the lord of whatever they'd planned on having as a son-in-law, and Isabella being the offspring of someone less desirable, despite her father's mega career in the Foreign Service, hadn't changed their attitude. They should've got over it by now, but it seemed some things weren't meant to be, and she'd quietly headed away, deflated but resolute she wasn't going to beg for recognition.

'I'm glad. For both of us.'

Hadn't heard Raphael returning with another case, had she? Blinking, she looked up into the steady but shocked gaze coming her way. Why shocked? He hadn't expected to feel glad she was staying with him? No. He wouldn't have offered if he didn't want her here. Or would he these days? 'I made the right call. Thanks for letting me know about the job.' She couldn't wait to start. It would be a bonus working alongside Raphael. Another was the girls were also all working at the same hospital.

'*Aucun problème.* Now, there's a bathroom on the floor below. It's all yours as I've got an en suite bathroom attached to my bedroom. Help yourself to anything you want. The kitchen pantry's full and the freezer's holding some of your favourite fish.'

'A shower's what I need. And some clean clothes.'

She sniffed her jacket and grimaced. 'Yuck. Long-haul travel has its own peculiar smell.'

He flinched, looked away. 'Take as long as you need. We're only going along the road for a drink and a bite to eat.'

Despite his reaction, that sounded so normal she laughed. This was what she'd come for. Normal. Whatever that was. At the moment everything felt right. Especially being with Raphael, knowing he'd never hurt her, no matter how far either of them pushed the boundaries of their friendship. Yes, packing up and coming here was a good move. Better than good; it was great, and filled with promise.

Believe it.

Yet she didn't feel quite normal with him. Yet. Still to come?

CHAPTER THREE

'HERE'S TO LONDON and your new job, and catching up with special friends.' Raphael held up his glass to tap Isabella's, just as loud laughter broke out further along the bar. 'Also to sorting out what's putting that sad look in your eyes whenever you think I'm not looking.'

Ignoring that last comment, Isabella tapped back. 'To spending time with you.' Except he'd already warned her he wouldn't be on tap all the time. They'd both opted to stick to soft drinks. She was wired. And exhausted. Even a little excited. Throw in worry about a whole heap of things she couldn't deal with right now, and she had the whole picture really. The trip in from the airport had touched her in an unexpected way. While it *had* felt like coming home, maybe being with Raphael was the reason. They understood each other so well, despite the awkward subjects they hadn't shared over the years. Cassie, the love of his life; and her truth about her marriage. She hadn't realised how much she'd missed his sharp remarks, though lately they seemed too sharp.

'Good luck with that. I struggle to find time to spend with myself.' His grin was lopsided and a little tight.

'Sounds like you need to find a life.' What was wrong? He wasn't known to forego having fun during his downtime, despite the serious side to the man who cared deeply for people worse off than himself.

'I bet you're about to sort me out,' he grumped. Then his grin became genuine. 'This could be a win-win for both of us. I could do with a kick up the backside.'

'Thanks for putting me up at short notice. I'll get on to other rental agencies ASAP.'

If I can't stay with you long term.

She choked. Stay with Raphael permanently? Where had that come from? So what was wrong with the idea? How about because they were friends? Sure, friends often shared accommodation, but she and Raphael had never lived in each other's pockets. Not even that time they'd worked together in Tours.

'No problem.' Raphael was suddenly intensely focused on the bar counter, his hands twirling his glass back and forth.

'I'll be out of your hair as soon as possible.'

I've only just got here, and I want to spend time with you. Need to, if I'm being honest, so that I can untangle the mess I've made of things by talking it out and then get on with living in London.

So she could get over this sensation of wanting more with him. Raphael usually kept her grounded. Today she was confused. Here was the reliable, helpful, caring Raphael she knew, and yet there was more. A deeper feeling that wanted to push hard at the walls, let him in in a new way. Into her heart. Her glass banged down on the counter. No. No way. She'd only let him down, and hurting him was not happening on her watch. Grabbing her glass again, she gulped down her drink.

Raphael had returned to watching her. 'Take your time. You've only just arrived.' His hand covered hers.

Whipping her hand away, she looked around the pub, frantically trying to still the wild thudding behind her ribs. 'Sure,' she muttered. This was not them. Glancing back at him, her heart did a funny little dance, while her eyes began tearing up. Rafe looked beyond stunning. He always had, yet she'd never really seen him as other women did. He was her friend. Nothing had changed. So why notice the stubble on his chin? Stubble was stubble, right? Or was it? Her palm itched. Reality check. Something had changed. Now she needed to focus on putting things back the way they used to be or move out of his house tomorrow. London Bridge was looking good.

'You cooked any French cuisine lately?' The question wasn't light-hearted. Was Rafe feeling her tension?

'Not really.' Darren had refused to eat anything he thought remotely French, all because of Raphael. So childish, but to keep the peace she'd thrown out the French recipe books and stuck with the boring basics: roasts, steak, sausages.

'We'll have to remedy that. Can't have you forgetting how to make a good béarnaise sauce.'

When she looked at Raphael she found a smile that held nothing back coming her way. Her stomach squeezed, while her heart filled with relief, returned to normal. See? Everything was fine. Time apart hadn't affected her perception of their friendship. It was the tiredness tripping her up, making her look at things differently. Today they were a little off centre, but that could be because she was now an ex-married woman he didn't know as well as he used to when she was single. 'Last time I saw you was in the bar further down this road. You'd put an offer in on a house and we were celebrating early because I wouldn't be around when the sale went through.' They'd also been toasting her moving back to New Zealand with her husband, though thinking back she remembered Raphael hadn't been too enthused about that. What she hadn't realised at the time: she was probably as much at fault as Darren. Which went to show she was utterly hopeless at relationships, not having had much experience other than snatching at friendships as and when they presented, because who knew how long she'd be staying around. Better keep that in mind if those odd feelings for Raphael returned.

'Oui.'

'You got drunk, and I had to get you home in a cab before you passed out.'

He winced. 'Sometimes your memory's too good.'

'What was that about anyway?' Rafe didn't do drunk, or drinking less than sensibly. Or very rarely and then only when something had gone horribly wrong for him.

'Can't remember.' He was looking everywhere but at her. 'Ah, here come the chips I ordered.'

Okay, the avoidance game. She should demand to know what he wasn't telling her, but she didn't want to spoil the rest of the evening. Past experience told her she'd eventually win, but she didn't have it in her tonight to do the hard grind to get there. Then she got a whiff of hot chips and relaxed. 'Yum. It's great to be catching up.'

That was the truth, no matter what else she might be feeling. Her legs were aching and her head filling with wool. But then she was starting over on the other side of the world to where she'd been two days ago, and for the first time ever, it was scary. Until now everything had been about making sure she had people with her, by her, there for her. After impulsively accepting the job at the Queen Victoria she'd then sat down and thought it through, and realised how tired of moving from one opportunity to the next she was. The Cambodian experience had shaken her, made her see how strong and enduring families could be for each other. It had made her understand she had to believe in herself before asking anyone else to. She couldn't keep winging it with any relationships. This move had to have a finality about it, *and* she'd go it alone so that eventually she might find herself equipped to give as much back as she needed for herself. More, in fact.

'Want another drink?' Rafe had the barman's attention. 'Izzy?'

Shaking away the questions filtering through the fog in her head, she pushed her drink aside. 'Can I have a water, please?' She studied Raphael for a moment. The gangly teen she'd first met had grown into a lean, muscular man with a face that said *Trust me*. A striking face that other women said made them think bed every time. Her stomach squeezed again, harder this time, showing how concerned she was becoming about him. Something wasn't adding up. Nothing to do with bed.

'You seeing anyone at the moment?' The question was out before she thought it through, but since when did she have to hesitate over asking him anything? He mightn't always be happy with her nosiness, or even give her an answer, but never had he made her uncomfortable over voicing what she wanted to find out. No idea why it felt so important to know where he was at with women, but it did, and she'd acted on those feelings. Being left in the dark was never an option. Knowing what was going on around her meant always being on top of problems before they erupted. Except when it came to her marriage.

Then she'd been scared to face the truth, to accept she'd made a monumental mistake.

'*Moi?*' He tapped his chest, mock shock on his face. 'This is Raphael Dubois you are asking.'

'Yes, you, Rafe.' Good-looking men didn't hang around being single for ever, especially doctors in a hospital filled with females of all ages. He'd had his share of women. She knew because he'd talked about them sometimes. Never a derogatory word, always admiration, along with the old wariness about relationships and not trusting they'd last for ever.

His shock was replaced with genuine resignation. 'No. Nobody serious and usually nobody at all.'

She sat up straighter and reached for her glass, took a mouthful. Definitely something out of whack. She'd give him a break from the quiz. 'Tell me about my new job. Anyone I might know on the ward?'

'Not that I'm aware of. Your girlfriends work in different areas, none on the maternity ward, but I guess you know that.'

'The emails have been flying back and forth. Carly's wedding is so close. Everyone's excited about that.' Now she had something genuine to grin about. 'Which reminds me. Do you want to come with me? The invitation is for Isabella and partner. You'll have to sit alone during the ceremony since I'm going to be a bridesmaid.' Once it was definite she'd be here for the wedding, Carly had insisted.

'No one else to invite?' He was smiling at her but there was a slight hitch in his voice.

'I want you to come. Otherwise I'll go on my own,' she added for good measure. Could be sounding pushy, because she didn't want to turn up at her friend's wedding without someone at her side. The other three girls were all loved up, and she'd only feel lonelier than ever. The odd one out. Unless Raphael was with her.

'Count me in, unless I'm on call that weekend. What's the date?' When she told him he scrolled through his diary. 'Free all weekend.'

'Great. You still happy with your position at the Queen Victoria?'

'Can't complain. It's turned out to be everything I wanted, and some.' He smiled. 'Perfect, really.'

What about Avignon? Returning there was always in the back of his mind. 'I'm glad. You deserve it.' Hopefully she'd be able to say the same about her new job. That would help steady her path to getting this move right.

'Same goes for you. You've just got to believe it.' His gaze was steady—and serious. He believed her, though maybe not fully *in* her. But then he did know her as well as she did herself.

'I will.'

'Say it again. This time with more determination.'

Heck, she'd missed that accent. Talking on the Net it didn't sound quite so deep and so French, more of a garbled mix. Oh, hell. This was weird. Rafe was a friend. 'I will,' she growled through her confusion.

'Isabella,' he growled back.

'So when I suddenly go into a tailspin and make a beeline for the airport with my passport, you'll stop me and tell me to think about what I'm going to do?'

'It won't come to that.' He smiled at her, deep and true.

Suddenly she wanted to cry, and laugh. Coming over

to join Raphael was *the* right thing to do. Which brought up more questions than answers. Thank goodness his phone rang then.

'Please be the ward,' Raphael muttered to himself as he tugged his phone out of his pocket. He needed to put space between Izzy's questions and himself. He'd gone from excited to see her to wary about spending too much time with her. Looking at the phone his heart sank. No reprieve coming.

'Hello, Cooper. How was the game?'

'Get your sorry butt up here now. Haley's in labour and you promised you'd be with us for the delivery.'

Okay, it was a reprieve. Haley was almost three weeks early, nothing to be concerned about. He stood and slipped his jacket on, the phone held between his ear and his shoulder. 'How far along is she?'

'The midwife said she's dilated four centimetres,' Cooper snapped. 'That was ten minutes ago.'

'Take it easy. There's a way to go yet,' Raphael told his friend. Fingers crossed the baby didn't suddenly decide to rush out. 'I'm on my way.'

Izzy stood up, drained her glass of water and slipped her bag over her shoulder.

Damn. Isabella.

'I'll come with you,' she said, solving his dilemma about taking her home and earning more wrath from his friend.

'Faster than fast,' Cooper growled, the stress growing every time he said anything. Fathers and their babies.

'See you shortly.' He nodded to the exit and followed Izzy outside. 'You could catch a taxi back to the house.'

Give him some time away from those sad eyes. 'You're exhausted.'

'True, but it's still early and I always try to stay up until my normal bedtime when I've come off a long flight.'

He didn't have time to argue, and a minute later he was driving down the street away from the pub and heading to the Queen Victoria faster than fast. 'I met Cooper and Haley at the hospital. He's a general surgeon and she's a radiologist. This is their first baby,' he explained.

'Exciting.'

That wasn't how Cooper had sounded on the phone. Raphael pressed the accelerator harder, and concentrated on getting to the hospital as quickly as possible.

'Which birthing suite is Haley in?' he asked Claudia as he charged on to the ward.

'Four,' the midwife replied. 'She's reached six centimetres and stopped. Baby seems in two minds about coming out.' Then she glanced past him to Izzy, charging along with them.

'Claudia, meet Isabella Nicholson. She's starting here next week.'

'Hi, Claudia.' Isabella smiled. 'Great to meet you.'

'And you.' Claudia laughed. 'We are having the night from hell, more babies than beds.'

Raphael slowed before he entered the suite, turned to Isabella. 'You want to sit in the office for a while?'

She pulled up short. 'Of course.'

A bell sounded throughout the ward. Claudia muttered, 'I've got to see to that. I'll be back as quickly as possible.'

'There you are.' Cooper stood in the doorway. 'The

contractions have slowed. Probably to give you time to get here.'

Raphael gripped his shoulder. 'There are a few speeding tickets coming my way you can pay for.'

'Who's this?'

'This is my friend I picked up from the airport this afternoon. Isabella, meet Cooper.'

As Cooper reached out to shake her hand, he asked, 'You're a nurse, aren't you?'

'Yes, and a midwife.' She never let that one go by.

'Come and meet Haley. She could do with a distraction.'

Isabella glanced at him. 'Okay?'

'Of course.' Raphael headed towards Haley, his teeth grinding. So much for putting distance between him and Isabella. 'Hi, Haley. I hear things have slowed down since Cooper phoned me.'

Haley grabbed his hand and burst into tears. 'I'm glad you're here. I thought I was going to have the baby without your help.'

'Not a lot I'll be doing other than monitoring the progress. You'll still be doing all the work.' He leaned down to kiss her cheeks just as a contraction tightened her body. His hand was in a vice. 'Breathe out slowly. That's it.'

'Easy for you to say,' Haley muttered as the tension let go. 'You're not the one going through hell here.'

'True. How far apart was that contraction from the previous one?'

'Five minutes,' Cooper answered for her.

'Five minutes, four, six. Who cares?' Haley began tensing again. 'Bet you haven't timed this one, huh? Standing around talking to your buddy like all is well in your world. Which it is. You're not the one going through this agony.'

Raphael struggled not to laugh. He'd heard it all before but to hear Haley talk so much was a surprise. 'And I thought you were shy.' She'd become a radiologist since they didn't have to talk to patients very often, mostly spent their days reading X-rays and MRIs.

'You can shut up too. Get on with making this baby come out.' Then she stared behind him. 'Who are you?'

Izzy stepped forward. 'Hello, Haley. I'm Isabella, Rafe's friend.'

'You made it, then. Raphael was unsure whether you'd turn up.'

I was? 'Hardly. When Isabella says she's going to do something, then there's no changing her mind.' She just didn't always last the distance.

Haley tilted her head at him. 'You've been on tenter-hooks ever since she accepted the job here.'

'Lie still. I'm going to listen to baby.'

And shut you down before Isabella starts getting the wrong idea.

'Ah!' Haley cried. 'Here we go again.'

Cooper took her hand, held tight.

Raphael moved to the end of the bed, and gently lifted the sheet covering Haley.

'Are you comfortable lying down through the contractions?' Isabella asked when the current one was over.

'I prefer standing, but when one starts I can't get off the bed quick enough to see it through. I know I should sit on the side, ready to be hauled to my feet by Cooper. It's just that every way I sit or lie it's uncomfortable.'

'Want to try standing next time? I'll help you.' Isabella began rubbing Haley's back, easing out the knots that were no doubt in her muscles, and she started relaxing.

'All right.' Haley was surprisingly acquiescing.

Raphael made the most of Izzy's distraction to examine Haley. 'Eight centimetres. You're back in business.'

'Knew the little blighter was waiting for you to get here. Now there'll be no stopping him.' Cooper's tension had backed off some since he and Izzy had arrived.

Isabella was still rubbing Haley's back. 'Walking around the room might help too, could ease the pain some and get the labour moving along faster. What do you think?'

'I'll try anything. I just want this over.' Haley sat up and slowly slid her legs over the side of the bed. Then another contraction gripped her and Raphael and Cooper took an arm each and hauled her to her feet.

Cooper held her against him, whispering sweet nothings in her ear and rubbing up and down her sides. 'You can do this, darling.'

'Not a lot of choice,' she groaned through clenched teeth. She'd barely got through the contraction and another came. As it finished, she growled, 'Don't think I'll be walking anywhere at this rate.'

'Let's give it a go,' Izzy encouraged. 'Anything's worth a try.'

Raphael watched her with Haley. She had a way about her that made Haley relax. She was going to be an asset on the ward. And when the next contraction came she was right there, encouraging her while Cooper held his wife and murmured in her ear.

'I'm feeling pressure, like I need to push. That's supposed to happen, isn't it?' Haley said some time later.

'Back on the bed,' Raphael told her. 'I'll take another look at what's going on.'

Izzy stood beside him. 'Looking good.'

'It sure is.' Raphael grinned. 'Baby's crowned. Let's get him out here so we can all met the little man.'

Cooper took Haley's hand. 'Come on, darling, give it everything you've got.'

'What do you think I've been doing?' This time there was no anger, only exhaustion, in her voice, and she gave her husband a smile before drawing in a breath and beginning to push.

Raphael glanced across to Izzy, who was back to rubbing Haley's tense back muscles. 'That's it. You're doing great.' She looked up at him and smiled as though to say, 'I love this job.'

He grinned. So did he. Bringing babies into the world had to be the best experience he could have. And when the baby was his friends' he couldn't be happier. 'And again,' he told Haley. 'The shoulders are out.' Then, 'One more push.' Moments later he held a tiny, new human being in his large hands, quickly checking him over before gently laying the baby on Haley's stomach. 'Haley, Cooper, meet your son.' Blink, blink. Damn it, he wasn't supposed to get emotional over this, but these two deserved this moment. 'Izzy, Cooper wants to cut the cord. Could you assist, please?'

'Sure.' She found gloves on the trolley to pull on and helped Cooper cut the cord when it had stopped pulsing.

Raphael watched as Izzy carefully wiped the baby with a towel. She looked so right doing that. What would she be like with her own baby? Besotted, no doubt. But like all midwives she'd probably be a nervous wreck over doing something wrong when she knew exactly how to look after a newborn. Now she carefully lifted the baby and wrapped him in a clean towel before handing him back to his mother, a look of awe on her tired face.

Raphael tapped her on the shoulder, nodded towards the door. 'We'll give you time to bond. Just holler if you want anything.'

For once Cooper was silent, and Haley seemed to have returned to her normal quiet self.

Outside the suite, Izzy leaned against the wall, and grinned. 'Wow. It never changes, does it? The thrill that comes with a baby arriving in our hands?'

'It certainly doesn't.' Not caring who saw him, he pulled her into a hug. 'Welcome home, Izzy.'

Her body tensed. Then relaxed. 'Yes, at last.'

Late the next morning Raphael nudged the shower off and reached for his towel. The tension in his legs put there by a harder than usual run had at last diminished under the onslaught of hot water. Outrunning the images of Izzy rushing at him in the arrival terminal, her wide-eyed gaze as she explored his house and yawning into her chips at the pub hadn't worked. Then there was the one after where they'd returned from the hospital and he'd helped her up the stairs to the third floor and the bedroom that was temporarily hers, her body struggling to put one foot in front of the other as exhaustion outdid everything else. He'd nearly swung her up into his arms to carry her up there, but common sense had stepped in just in the nick of time, forcing him to take her arm instead. Once he'd not have hesitated, but now the very thought of getting close to her and then letting her down was frightening.

After pulling on knee-length shorts and an open-necked shirt he tidied up his room, and made the bed. Earlier, when he'd popped into the kitchen to grab his keys on the way out for his run, he'd been saddened by the empty water bottles on the bench, evidence that Isabella had been downstairs during the night. The way she'd been all but comatose when they'd got home she should've slept right through the night without once opening her eyes. Something needed doing pronto about her insomnia. That sort of tiredness undermined everything a person did if left too long.

He hadn't reckoned on being quite so rattled on seeing her yesterday, and hearing her laugh and talk. Except it'd been Izzy with a difference. The laughter was strained, the conversations awkward. His heart had stirred at the sight of her, which once he'd have said was because of their friendship, yet now felt it might be about something more intense. They loved each other, platonically. But no denying that since the day he'd had to watch her marry Darren he'd felt he'd lost something, that he loved her in a way he shouldn't. Not that he trusted his feelings. Look where love had got him last time. He'd fallen fast and hard, and gave Cassie everything, only to have her continually complaining it wasn't enough. And that was before her final treachery.

When Isabella first told him she and Darren were splitting his heart had soared with selfish relief. Then, as the sordid details of their marriage registered, he'd been angry and distressed for her. Since then his emotions had run the gamut from hope to despair and everything in between for her. And for himself. Something he only admitted at four in the morning when sleep was elusive.

Now he had to cope with Izzy living in his own space, however temporarily. A space she'd slotted into last night as easily as he'd seen her shrug into a puffer jacket in midwinter on the Rhône years ago. Nothing unusual in that. Except he also had to ignore how his heart was involved. Cassie had finally taken a back seat. But not the loss of his child. He'd never forgive her for that, which meant his heart wasn't ready for anyone else.

Goosebumps lifted on his forearms. Rubbing hard did nothing to knock them down. Nor did the light woollen jersey he pulled over his head in the bedroom. His nose twitched. Coffee vapour was filtering up the stairs. Coffee. Had to be the answer. Obviously Izzy was in the kitchen. Damn, no dashing into the hospital for a bit of time out.

She was leaning one hip against the bench, a full mug wrapped in her hands, and a bewildered smile lifting her lips as she glanced down at the creature rubbing against her legs. 'You've got a cat.'

'I rescued her from the RSPCA.'

'Yeah, but you and a pet?'

'Since I was a little guy I've wanted a dog. Now that I'm settled it was time to do something about it.'

Isabella blinked, then laughed. 'Do I need to point out this is a cat?'

'Her name's Chienne.'

'Dog? You are so mean.' She put her mug aside and picked up the cat to snuggle against her breast. Ah, chest. Nope, definitely breasts, the rounded shape filling her T-shirt perfectly.

'That's me,' he muttered, and reached for a mug.

She rubbed her chin on Chienne's head. 'What was your real name before this mean guy got hold of you?'

'According to the RSPCA, Waster was on the tag around her collar. I was not going to keep calling her that.'

'So you came up with something even more original.' Izzy blinked and looked down at her furry bundle. 'I bet you're spoilt rotten. Raphael has never been mean.'

A band of warmth wrapped around him. It felt good to hear that, and while nothing was wrong in his life, who couldn't do with the odd compliment or two? 'Cover her ears while I say that I'd prefer a dog but they need so much attention and given my erratic and long hours it wouldn't have been fair to get one.'

Izzy began nibbling her bottom lip, which was new to him.

'What's up? You look like you're not sure where you are.'

She blinked and reached for her mug to sip the steaming liquid. 'I know exactly where I am, yet I feel kind of lost. Could be my brain hasn't kept up with the rest of me and will be arriving later.'

'Or it might be because this is the final move of your life.' That'd be confronting for her. If she meant it. Except she'd tried that once before and look where that got her. Back here. Though not alone. *I'm here.* 'I remember feeling a little bewildered the day I moved in here and dumped my few possessions on the table I'd ordered from the local furniture store, along with a lounge suite and a bed.' The second bed in the room Isabella was using had arrived on Friday after a frantic phone call to organise that and a chest of drawers for her. 'I struggled to believe this was *my* home.' He tapped his chest with his knuckles. 'And that I got to stay here until *I* decided otherwise.'

'It's real, isn't it?' Isabella seemed to be holding her breath.

Expecting the right answer from him?

Sorry, Izzy, but I only know what's right for me, and I'm not sure I've got that right yet.

'It's as real as you want it to be.'

Her mouth quirked. 'Back at me, huh?' Then she hit the serious button. 'No regrets?'

'Honestly? No. Sometimes I think about how my life might have turned out if I'd let Cassie talk me into moving to Paris, but…' He shrugged.

Izzy's eyes widened at the mention of his ex, but she just stroked the cat.

Raphael filled his mug with coffee before topping up hers. Time to get on to something normal and ordinary. 'I'm going in to see Haley and baby as soon as I've had this. Want to come?' Gulp. That was not what he planned on saying.

'Give me ten to take a shower, and fix up the face.'

It was going to take a fair amount of make-up to hide the shadows under her eyes, but he wasn't saying. 'There's no hurry.' Tell that to his taut body. He wanted to be doing something other than standing in his kitchen drinking coffee and smelling Izzy's perfume instead of the coffee. But he'd have to be patient.

Oui.

'I'll introduce you to whoever's about. You can also meet the three little guys I told you about a couple of weeks ago. They're something else. Their mum wants a quick word with me too.'

She paused on her way out of the kitchen. 'They've got to you, haven't they?'

'Just a little.' He'd love to have a family of his own. There'd be no replacing the son he lost but could it be time to think about moving on?

No. He wouldn't survive that sort of pain again.

CHAPTER FOUR

'HELLO, HALEY,' ISABELLA said to the happy woman cuddling her son in the single room where she'd been transferred after the birth. 'How're you feeling today?'

'Isn't Ryan the cutest baby ever?' Haley's eyes lit up. 'I can't believe I'm a mother.'

She'd soon get used to that with sleepless nights and nappies to deal with. 'Believe me, you are. I saw it happen.'

'So did I.' Raphael laughed from the other side of the bed. 'Can I have a hold?' He held out his arms.

Haley reluctantly handed him over. 'One minute.'

'Then it's my turn,' Isabella said. 'How are you doing with breastfeeding?'

'Eek. That's no fun. I can't quite manage it yet, but I've been told that's normal.'

'Certainly is. You'll soon get the hang of it. Don't stress though. That only makes matters worse.' She looked at Raphael. There was a look of relief in his expression. As though he didn't quite believe the outcome of Haley's labour would be so good. Which didn't add up considering there were no complications. Or was he thinking about children, as in his own? Why not? Could be his biological clock was ticking? That wouldn't be just a woman's prerogative. Deep in her tummy she felt a twinge, as though her clock had come to life. Her mouth dried. That was not part of the plan to settle here. Not yet, not until she'd got all the other factors right. In the meantime she'd get her fix holding other people's babies. 'Time's up.' She held out her arms for Ryan, and laughed at Rafe's reluctance to hand him over.

Haley was watching her son, hunger in her eyes, and Isabella couldn't not pass Ryan back to his mum. 'There you go. I'll have another turn before we leave.'

'Come and meet the triplets,' Rafe said as they left the room.

The moment they walked into the nursery Isabella felt the same awe she'd seen in Raphael's face when he talked about the three little boys. They lay in their cribs lined up side by side, blinking at any movement made by the two people leaning over them, smiling and chatting as though the boys understood. Raphael went straight across and gazed down at the babies too, warmth in his eyes. But also a shadow of something else. Anger? Pain?

'Hello, Raphael.' The mum turned to him. 'You didn't have to come in on your day off.' Her gaze shifted to Isabella. 'I know you don't get a lot of time to yourself as it is. Your partner must get fed up with you being called out all the time.'

He blinked and those emotions were gone. He was back to professional doctor mode. 'Melody, it's fine. I was coming to see another patient anyway. And this is Isabella Nicholson. She's a nurse and midwife, and will be starting on this ward later in the week.' Not his partner. Though he hadn't actually put it into words, it was there. Raphael nodded at the man gazing down at the boys with a besotted look. 'Isabella, this is Ollie, the doting dad.'

'Hello, Melody, Ollie. Your boys are gorgeous.' Isabella smiled. 'Look at them. They're so busy, moving their arms and kicking their little legs. You're going to have your hands full when you get them home.' Even the smallest boy, still attached to more monitors than his brothers, was staring up at everyone.

'Aren't we? And I can't wait.' Ollie grinned. 'Antony's taking a little longer to get up to speed, but really, we've been so lucky. These other two are already putting on weight. The sooner we're all at home, the better.'

'I don't want to rush things,' Melody said with a worried glance at Raphael. 'What if I can't cope?' She looked to Isabella. 'I've never had much to do with babies before. To have three at once is daunting. Not that I don't want them,' she added hastily. 'We've waited too long for this as it is.'

Ollie brushed a kiss across his wife's forehead. 'You'll be fine, sweetheart. With the folks dropping in to help and the daily visits from the district nurse, we'll manage.' He grinned. 'You'll soon be telling everyone to get out of the way and let you get on with looking after your boys.'

Raphael nodded. 'You'll be more tired than you've ever been, and there won't be enough hours in the day, but you'll manage. I promise. Even mothers with one baby for the first time go through the same concerns that you have. If you'd taken them home within a couple of days of them being born as usually happens when it's only one baby, you wouldn't have had time to think about all the things that need doing—you'd be doing them.'

'So everyone keeps telling me.' Melody sighed. 'But what if I'm useless as a mother?'

'Stop it,' Ollie growled softly. 'We're going to be the best parents ever. We're doing this together, remember?' He turned to Isabella. 'I've turned our back bedroom into an office so I can work from home for the foreseeable future. Whenever clients need to see me I can meet them there or at the company rooms in town.'

The worry in Melody's eyes only increased, as though nothing was registering except she had three babies to look after and all the things that could go wrong. Was she a candidate for postnatal depression? Isabella glanced at Raphael, and relaxed. He was on to it. Of course the same thought would've occurred to him.

He said, 'I'll arrange for you to talk to someone about how you're going to cope, Melody. Try not to get too wound up about everything. Make the most of this time in here where you can learn a lot about being a mum in preparation for going home. Enjoy your babies. They grow up so darned fast you'll soon be wondering where the time went.'

Ollie lifted one boy—Shaun, according to the card on his little cot—and held him out to his mother. 'Here you go, Mum.'

Melody immediately relaxed and placed her son against her breast, rubbing his back as though she'd always been doing that.

'See, just like a pro.' Isabella nodded. 'He's as happy as can be, snuggling against you.'

'He's hungry.' The father picked up Antony and held him in a similar position.

'Aren't they always?' she said, and leaned over the third crib. 'Hello, Morgan. Aren't you the cutest little guy?' He was blinking and moving one hand in the air. So innocent and trusting. What would his life be like? All their lives? Would the three of them watch out for each other? Or compete over everything? If she'd had a sibling she was certain her life of moving from country to country would've been different. There'd have been someone who was always there, a constant, someone of a similar age to understand what she'd longed for, to share the good and bad times, to love always. Not all siblings got along though. There was that. No point thinking about what couldn't be changed. She was grown up now, and making her own way without having to do as her parents demanded. Besides, she'd had Raphael in her life since she was a teen. Still did. As good as a brother. *Brother?* These feelings she was getting for him had nothing to do with a brother.

Behind her, he was talking to Melody. 'I hear you've got another infection in your Caesarean wound.'

'Yes, but why when I've been taking antibiotics? It's not fair.' Melody sounded close to tears.

'We'll try a different antibiotic. Mind if I have a look first?'

Melody shook her head.

'Isabella, do you want to get me some swabs?' Raphael asked when he saw Melody's inflamed wound. 'They're in the trolley outside the door.'

'Sure.' She pushed the trolley into the room and slipped gloves on before handing him the swabs. 'You want the antiseptic fluid?'

'Please.' He cleaned the area and dabbed the yellow liquid all over. 'There, that should help. I'll make sure someone does that regularly. And I'll sign a prescription for the nurses to collect. Any other worries?' When

Melody shook her head, Raphael said to Isabella, 'I'll go check on my other patients. You okay finding your way around?'

'You can introduce me to whoever's at the station and I'll go from there.' Though right now she'd be happy lying down for a nap. 'If you can't find me I'll be curled up somewhere out of the way.'

Raphael was quick to look at her, worry now in *his* eyes. 'Are you all right? This is so not like you.'

'The jet lag's new, I admit. But I haven't been sleeping well for so long I hardly notice.' Ever since she'd been forced to face up to the fact she hadn't married Darren purely for love but mostly for the security and one-stop life he'd promised. That had been as important to her as love. Maybe even more. It had taken her reaction to finding her husband in bed with another woman to bring her up sharp, and to start thinking about why she'd married in the first place. She hadn't liked the answers. They had her questioning her ability to have a loving, caring relationship. She'd been selfish in wanting the lifestyle Darren offered before anything else. Didn't mean he had to betray her though. How was she supposed to trust any man with her heart again?

'We'll talk some more about this when we're back home.'

'Ah, no, we won't.' She wasn't ready for that. It was history, and she was getting on with *now*. 'Come on, play nice and introduce me to whoever's here.'

Two nurses were sitting in front of computers in the work area, and looked up at the same time. 'We were wondering if you'd drop in, Raphael. Mrs Baxter has been seen by the duty specialist and has settled down again.'

'No one let me know that.' He didn't look happy. 'But since I'm here I'll talk to her.'

One of the nurses was on her feet instantly. 'I'll come with you.'

'First let me introduce Isabella Nicholson to you.'

The same nurse turned to her. 'You're starting here later this week, aren't you? I saw your name on the roster. Hi, I'm Annabel, and this is Mary. What are you doing in here today? Should be making the most of your days off.' Annabel's eyes flicked from her to Raphael, a question in her gaze.

'Hello. I came along for the ride.' Not going to explain why she was with the handsome doctor who obviously had one of the nurses in a bit of a lather. Which was odd, because she was usually quick to let women know she was his friend, not his lover.

'Can you show Izzy around, Mary?' Izzy, not Isabella. Rubbing it in how friendly he was with her?

'Sure.' The other nurse stood up. 'Anything would be better than doing the stock figures.' Then she grimaced. 'Sorry, Isabella. That sounded all wrong. Take no notice of me.'

Isabella laughed. 'Don't worry. I'll get over it.'

'Want a coffee first?'

It might help her stay awake. 'That'd be great.'

'Come through to the staff kitchen, then. The lockers are along here too, and uniforms are next door.'

'It's all coming back.' When Mary shot her a puzzled look she explained, 'I trained as a midwife in this hospital, and spent many nights on this ward.'

'In that case, shall we grab coffees and go back to the station so I can keep an eye on things while interrogating you?' It was said with a smile, and Isabella laughed.

'Not sure I've got anything interesting to say, but let's give it a go.' As long as she didn't want information on Rafe. That would not be happening. His details were not for her to share.

'Actually, I did hear you'd worked here before. It slipped my addled brain. Esther and I are friends.'

'How is she? I only got here yesterday so haven't had a chance to catch up with her or our other two friends. The four of us trained together, and now we're all back here again.'

'She's great. Totally in love with Harry with stars in her eyes all the time.'

'Isn't it awesome?'

Mary handed her a mug and pushed the coffee jar in her direction. 'Help yourself.' Leaning back against the bench she watched Isabella. 'You're close to Raphael? Since he brought you in I figured you must've been together when he got the call,' she added hurriedly when Isabella tightened her mouth.

'We're friends from way back.' That wasn't divulging anything that could be twisted into something more interesting. 'It's been a while since we had time together.'
And that's all I'm saying.

'Lots to catch up on, then.'

Time to change the subject. 'So do you do all shifts or weekends only?'

'I cover all the rosters just like you're going to do. Most of the staff do, apart from two nurses who work nights only, and one who only does weekends. Where were you last working?'

'Based in Wellington, New Zealand, but I volunteered in Cambodia recently.' When they were seated in the workstation sipping coffee, Isabella filled her in on her working background and avoided questions about her private life. She was here, that's all that mattered. In fact, that was a good line to follow herself. 'What's the social life like here? Does everyone get together for drinks at the end of the week?'

'Some of us do. You up for that?'

'Absolutely. It's the best way to get to know people.'

Her eyes were heavy, and her head thick with sleep. She shook herself and straightened up in the chair. Where was Raphael? He seemed to be taking a long time.

A phone rang and Mary reached for it, then brought up the computer screen. 'Here we go. Knew the quiet spell was too good to be true.'

Isabella looked around the work area, saw nothing unusual to ask about. All fairly standard. It wasn't going to be hard to slot in with everyone. A yawn slipped out and her eyes drooped.

'Wake up, sleepy head.' A firm hand shook her gently.

Isabella dragged her chin up off her sternum and blinked up at Raphael. 'Guess I didn't make the coffee strong enough.'

'Let's get out of here. You're giving everyone the wrong impression.' He winked.

All very well to make a joke of it, but she probably was. There seemed to be more people wandering around the area now. Saturday afternoon brought friends and family out in their droves. 'I'll be fine by the time I start work on Wednesday.'

Mary laughed. 'Seems I bored you to sleep talking about shifts and who's who on the roster.'

Didn't hear any of that. 'Sorry. I'll do better next time. I'm still getting over my flights.' She stood up slowly, picked up her bag from the floor where it had fallen. 'See you when we're on the same shift.'

Mary nodded. 'Or handing over.'

'Do people know I'm staying with you?' Isabella asked Raphael as they waited for the lift to take them down to the car park.

'I haven't mentioned it to anyone except Jacki, since she's the head nurse for the ward, and I figured she needed to know since I put such a good word in for you.' He grinned. 'It's none of anyone else's business though. Not that it's a secret, but I don't want someone saying I'm favouring you once you're working amongst us.' The lift rattled to a stop and the door cranked open. 'Come on, let's get out of here and go do something interesting.'

'Like what?'

'For you that means getting some sleep.'

'If I sleep during the day I won't get much during the night.'

'The problem with that theory is that you're already dropping off every opportunity you get. And you don't sleep at night anyway.'

Isabella grimaced. 'True. How about I have a snooze, then we go for a walk along the river?' The exercise would do her good.

They climbed into Raphael's car and started for home.

'Want to talk about why you're so tired?' he asked quietly as they waited at traffic lights.

'Not really.' It wouldn't change things. But this was the one person she used to tell everything.

'Don't blame the jet lag. This is worse than normal.'

'Didn't mention the jet lag.'

'It's to do with Darren, right?'

Just spill the beans, get it off your chest. What's

Raphael going to say that you haven't already said to yourself?

'I stuffed up big-time.' She paused, stared out the window at the tail lights on the car in front. 'I'm talking about my marriage. Our bust-up wasn't all Darren's fault.'

'There're usually two sides to these things.'

Yeah, but she was uncomfortable with her contribution, or lack of. 'I didn't love him as much as I should've.'

'Then why did you marry him?' There was genuine confusion radiating from Raphael. Maybe a hint of disappointment.

Shouldn't have told him. But she'd started, so might as well get it over. 'Because I thought I did. I *believed* I did. Right up until it all began disintegrating.'

No, earlier than that. I stayed in denial for as long as I could.

'The pain wasn't as deep as you'd expect?' Forget disappointment. Raphael was looking confused. Which made no sense at all. More to think about when she wasn't so tired.

'Yes, it was, but for the wrong reasons. That took a bit to figure out but when I did it hurt more than ever.' She drew a deep breath and rushed on. 'Darren promised a home and family, and to live in the same city for the rest of our lives. I so desperately wanted that I didn't look beyond to anything else. By marrying him I let him down. Hell, I let myself down. And you know what's the worst? I don't know with complete certainty that I've learnt my lesson. What if I make the same mistake again? I was so intent on living the life my parents had denied me I got it all wrong, and it worries me.' What if she fell in love again, only to find she'd made another mistake?

They'd stopped at another set of lights and Raphael's fingers were playing a silent tune on the steering wheel. 'We all make mistakes, Izzy.'

'I got wrong the one dream I've had most of my life.' She swallowed a bitter mouthful of pain. 'Which is why in the meantime I'm sticking to running solo and making a home of my own, by me for me. I don't want to hurt someone else. Better to play safe.' Get it, Rafe? Actually, it was her she needed to remind of that.

'I think you're being hard on yourself.'

'Yeah, right,' she growled. 'Easy for you to say. Darren did some bad things like those affairs and spending more time with his mates than me, but if I'd loved him as much as I'd professed, then he wouldn't have had to. He might've stayed home more often, might've been happy to go house hunting instead of skirt chasing.' She was grasping at straws. According to the partner of one of his mates, Darren had always had a roving eye. Not that it was his eye doing most of the work. But apparently she wasn't the only partner he'd cheated on, just the first wife.

'He could've talked to you about it, not buried his head in the sand.'

'Like Cassie did with you?' Isabella snapped, and instantly regretted her words. This was about her and her messed-up relationship, had nothing to do with Raphael's history. But he didn't seem to accept she was at least trying to take some of the blame in an attempt to soften the hurt Darren had created and that riled her. As he said, she was usually so honest it could be awkward. 'I shouldn't have said that.'

'*Non.* You shouldn't have.'

Silence took over in the car, tense and uncomfortable.

Isabella stared out at the passing buildings, not really noticing them, instead seeing Wellington on a bright summer's day with the harbour sparkling and the ferries passing further out. Her heart didn't flutter with longing, instead seemed to sigh with relief. Yes, she'd done the right thing in leaving there, as she had in walking away from her marriage. And from now on she was dropping the worry about that, looking forward, no more doubts. Hopefully then the trust issue would start to resolve itself, and she could consider a new relationship. She'd make herself get on with it. Now. Not tomorrow or next week. Now. 'So what did you have in mind for us to do this afternoon?'

Raphael drew in a lungful of air and sighed it back out. He could hear Izzy's distress, understand her fear of repeating her mistake—because he knew it all too well himself. Cassie had torn his heart to shreds, and he was reluctant to try again. Hell, in the beginning he'd given Cassie *everything*. His love, his life, his family, trust. He'd only put his foot down about living in Paris because he already had the job he needed to set up his career as he wanted. It had been the only thing he'd denied her, and it had backfired, brought out her fickleness. So no, he wasn't getting involved with anyone else. Certainly not the woman sitting beside him. Then he went and messed with that idea. 'Thought we'd get the bikes out and go for a spin alongside the river.'

'We what?' Shock filled her face. 'Me? On a bike? Think you've got the wrong person in mind for that.'

He'd made her forget what she'd been gnawing her lip over though, hadn't he? Her lip was swollen. A kiss might help ease the soreness. Swearing under his breath, he scrabbled around for something inane to say. 'One of the doctors was selling her bike last week so I bought it for you.'

'Hope you got crash pads and a helmet and padded clothing to go with it. And a pair of those thick fancy shorts that make butts look bigger.'

Butts. Bigger. Fitted shorts. He swallowed hard. Sure. 'You forgot the steel-capped boots.' Even to his ears, his laugh sounded strained. But he was glad to have made her smile, though he was still sour about her snide remark over Cassie, even if it was true. That was just Isabella putting up the wall to keep him away. Though she had gone for the jugular, not something she usually did.

He'd never told her the whole story. Certainly hadn't mentioned the baby he'd only learned about when he'd tracked Cassie down a couple of years later. Nearly as bad was coming to terms with the fact Cassie should've been more upset, but relieved their baby hadn't suffered. Her new career in acting had been taking off and a baby would've been a hindrance. Later he learned the bit parts hadn't flowed into roles of any significance, had instead ebbed away to the point she now worked in a sleazy bar on the outskirts of Los Angeles, struggling to make ends meet. It was the last time he'd seen her, and he'd woken up. They had nothing in common, and he'd wondered how he could've loved her so much. They said love was blind, and he'd found out the hard way how true that could be. He didn't want to lose his sight ever again.

'Honestly, Rafe, I haven't ridden a bike since I was a teenager.'

'Which means your backside and legs will ache afterwards.' The way Izzy's backside filled out her shorts and trousers set his body aflame. 'No, you're right. Better I go alone and get home earlier.'

'You're backing out now?' She turned to face him.

There was no winning with Izzy. 'Let's stop somewhere for a late lunch instead.'

'Your shout for winding me up.' Her mouth spread into a cheeky smile and they were back on track, tension about their pasts forgiven.

But not forgotten. One day he'd find the courage to tell her the rest of the Cassie story. But not today. He'd hate to see pity in her eyes. 'Wouldn't have it any other way, *mon amie.*' Except friends didn't make his gut tighten over a smile. This was getting out of hand. He needed breathing space, which would be hard to find while they shared his house and worked on the same ward.

'How about we have a French week?' She'd know exactly what he meant. It wasn't the first time, and probably wouldn't be the last. 'Everywhere we go except at the hospital.' Probably get locked up for speaking nothing but French there.

'Je ne veau pas faire de vélo.'

'Dure.'

Too late he realised how intimate spending time talking in his native language might be. He grimaced, then went with cheeky. 'I don't need to teach you to ride. Your body will remember how to push the pedals even if you cry foul, so toughen up.'

'Does this mean you're cooking dinner tonight? I'd like coq au vin.'

'Say that in French and I might oblige,' he replied in French. Actually, she wasn't too rusty, but he'd keep at her as it'd been a while since she'd been submerged in the language and he intended taking her back to Avignon to visit Grand'mère in the next few weeks.

And that idea had nothing to do with the feelings he wasn't admitting even to himself.

Or did it?

CHAPTER FIVE

RAPHAEL SLIPPED INTO the seat opposite Isabella in the hospital cafeteria with a mug of coffee in one hand and a large egg mayo sandwich in the other. 'What are you doing here?'

'Initiation course.' At eight that morning Isabella had received a call from the head nurse of the maternity ward to come in and do the drill all newly signed-on employees had to partake in.

'Damn, sorry, I was meant to tell you about that.'

'Apparently.' Forcing a laugh, she tried not to notice how Raphael's shoulders shaped his suit to perfection. That *perfect* word again. It popped up a lot around Rafe. But how his body filled his clothes? This was Raphael. Seems when she got jet lag she got it bad. 'No problem. It's the same old, same old. Work in one large hospital and you know the routine for any others you go to.' She'd spent the last few hours learning the ropes of where fire extinguishers and staircases were, as well as all the safety rules involving staff. 'Lunch is the best bit so far, even if beyond late.' It was nearly two and she was starving.

He blinked. 'Not same old food, then?'

'Nothing different about that, but it's far more interesting being in here.' Her hand swept the room. 'There are real people in here, not sheep following Miss This-Way-Folks all over the hospital.'

Raphael's laugh sent ripples of warmth through her. He was watching her closely. Looking for what? 'You seem a lot more awake than I've seen since you arrived. The jet lag must be wearing off,' he said.

'How was surgery?' He'd left home before six as his surgical list had four ops, one of which he thought might throw up some complications, and he'd wanted to be prepared. Nothing unusual there.

Now he nodded once, a grim expression on his face as he glanced around them. 'The woman I told you about? The cancer has gone through to the uterus, as I'd suspected. Then when we had that sorted she haemorrhaged from the large bowel and we found another growth. I had to call in David Stokes, one of the general surgeons, to take over when I'd done all I could.' He shook his head. 'Some people get a raw deal.'

It wasn't sounding good for the woman. 'Take it easy. You've done all you can.' Isabella reached for his hand, squeezed it before letting go in a hurry. That wasn't a normal gesture from her to Raphael. But he was so distressed she could almost see anguish oozing out of his pores. It was also there in the tightness of his shoulders and the white lines around his mouth.

'I know. It's up to the oncologists now. She's only forty-one.' His frustrated sigh cut through her, had her wanting to take his pain for him.

One reason for preferring midwifery to nursing patients that specialists like Raphael dealt with was not having to face some of these grim cases. 'If you're not too late finishing tonight do you want to go out for a

meal?' In her lap her fingers crossed of their own accord. Knowing doctors had little control over their private hours she didn't really expect an instant acceptance.

'Sounds like a plan.' Where was the enthusiasm?

'Look, we can give it a miss if you'd prefer.'

He looked straight at her. 'If I knock off about six will
you hang around in town? I'm thinking we can go along
the river to this bar everyone frequents. You'll like it.'

'That's a yes, then.' Raphael hadn't said no, or maybe;
he'd said he'd be there. Yippee. Suddenly the ho-hum
day had become bright and exciting.

*Careful. This is your friend. He won't see it as a hot
date.*

Nor should she. Yeah, but it was growing on her that
she'd come home, as in found her niche. Being with Raphael relaxed her in ways she hadn't known for a long
time—for two years, really. Was that what close friends
did? Or was there another reason for this deep sense
of belonging whenever she was with him? If only she
could sort out her mixed-up feelings for him. Slowing
her breathing, she went for calm. 'Great, I'll be around
here somewhere. Might see if Carly wants to go for a
coffee and catch up while I wait for you. She's on days
this week.'

'I need to tell you—you'll probably get a call asking
if you mind starting on the ward tomorrow instead of
Wednesday. We're three staff down and as busy as can
be,' Raphael told her. 'Don't feel pressured to say yes.
I know you're still tired and taking naps like a toddler.'
His smile sent ripples throughout her body, which was
frankly weird. He shouldn't make her feel like this. Except apparently he did.

'I'll be fine, might even be better for doing something.

If not, there's the weekend to catch up on sleep.' Now she was becoming boring. Though it wasn't boredom rippling through her body as the impact of that smile continued blasting her. Since when did Raphael's smiles disturb her in any way? Isabella had no answer so went with devouring her now cold pie. Their relationship was changing. Hopefully for the better.

'Have you made appointments to look at flats yet?' No grin now. More of an intense scrutiny of the bottom of his empty mug.

So he wanted her gone sooner than later. Her shoulders slumped. She hauled them tight. She would not be upset. 'I've hardly had time,' she snapped. 'I didn't think there was that much of a hurry.'

'There isn't.' Now he locked eyes with her. 'I just thought you were in a hurry to get started on settling down.'

'Should've known.' She'd reacted too quickly and come up with the wrong answer. 'I'll get on to it shortly. I need to decide where to live that's not too far from the hospital and yet in a bit of a community. If that's possible close to the city centre. I do like the area you're in but rentals there are probably exorbitant. You wouldn't want me too close keeping an eye on what you get up to either.'

He stood and gathered his plate and mug. 'Not true, Izzy. I'm thrilled you're staying in my house, and about to start working on my ward. It's been too long since we spent time together, and we mustn't let that happen again.'

Quite the speech. One that sounded false. She didn't fully understand, and suspected there was something more behind the words. But thrilled? Really? Good.

Great even. One thing she knew for certain. 'I agree. It's been for ever since we could sit and shoot the breeze.' For some reason the thought of not having Rafe nearby, if not right beside her, was beginning to feel wrong. As if they were meant to be together. The last crust of her pie fell to the plate. She and Raphael? Together? As in a couple? Come on. That's what she'd been avoiding admitting since arriving in London.

'I'll text you when I'm done tonight.' He was smiling, happiness shining out of his cerulean gaze. 'Want me to take your plate, or are you going to finish that pastry?'

Pushing the plate at him she shook her head, and tried to find something to say. But nothing sensible came up, so she remained quiet. She was off balance, and Raphael wasn't helping by looking at her like he wanted more from her. They knew each other inside out. Ah, not quite. See? She'd never have thought that before. Okay, but since when hadn't she been able to read whatever he wasn't saying? Usually she could do it with her eyes shut. Not today. 'I'll see you later,' she muttered. Yes, she still wanted to have dinner with him. More than before. Really? Yes, really. As in more than catching up. As in getting to know him when she already did. As in trying to understand why she was so off centre around him. Was she on the rebound from Darren? But if this was a rebound, why pick her friend?

Because he's safe and kind and I know where I stand with him.

Oh. That was a wet blanket smothering her. If she did fall in love again, it would be for the right reasons.

I never truly fell completely in love in the first place.

Anyway, no rebound in sight. She was totally over

the man. He wasn't as sexy as Raphael, nor as kind and selfless, or as gorgeous.

Shoving upright, Isabella headed for the exit. The cafeteria had become too small and airless. A few minutes alone outdoors might help unscramble her mind. Might not, either, but she had to try.

'Where are you headed now?' Raphael stood beside her as she peered left, then right.

'Thought I might go introduce myself to the rest of the gang on the ward.' So much for heading outside. She turned in the direction of the lift bank, walked away.

'Isabella.'

She stopped, turned back slowly. 'Yes?'

'This is going to work out for you.' His smile was fleeting, as if not quite believing what he'd said, or not accepting she'd meant it about stopping moving around.

'I hope so.'

Doubtful he heard her quiet reply as he strode away, hands at his sides, back ramrod straight, head up. In Raphael coping mode. What was he coping with? Her decision to live in London? Did he want her here? Or gone by sunrise? He'd suggested she move across the world. Had he changed his mind now it was real? Who knew? She certainly didn't. She needed to get over herself. His mind was more likely to be on his patients, particularly the woman with secondary cancers.

Yet there was a nagging sensation going on at the back of her head saying there was more to this. Isabella slumped against the wall, out of the way of people charging in both directions like they were on missions she was not party to. What was happening to her and Raphael? To their easy, accepting friendship? Never before had she felt awkward with him, yet right now she had no idea what he was thinking or wanting, and that'd happened a few times over the past couple of days.

Her phone rang as she reached the nurses' station on the maternity ward. 'Hello, this is Isabella Nicholson.'

'Jacki Jones, Isabella. I'm ringing to ask a favour.'

Isabella glanced around, saw a woman talking into a phone not more than two metres away. Holding the phone against her chest, she called, 'Jacki? I'm Isabella.'

The head nurse spun around on her chair. 'Oh, hi.' She shoved the phone on its stand and stood to meet her. 'Talk about timely.'

'I've finished the safety course and thought I'd drop by to introduce myself.'

'I was ringing to see if you'd mind starting earlier than first agreed. Tomorrow? We're down on staff and it's bedlam in here.' She had a strong Welsh accent, making Isabella smile. She also seemed to be holding her breath.

Glad of Raphael's warning, the answer came easily. 'Not a problem. Whichever shift you need me on.'

'Thank you.' Jacki's relief was loud and clear. 'Raphael said you probably wouldn't mind, but I still worried you'd say no. It's a bit desperate up here at the moment.'

'Do you want me to put in a few hours this afternoon? I'm signed off on the course and all set to go.'

'Thank you again, but we'll manage today. I know it's only been a couple of days since you arrived in town. Go home and make the most of your time off. You'll be busy enough tomorrow.'

Since her head was starting to pound, she agreed. 'You're probably right.'

A nurse stuck her head around a corner. 'Jacki, I need you in here with Rosalie.' She sounded desperate.

'Coming,' Jacki said calmly. 'A very prem birth, twelve weeks early,' she told Isabella before heading away. 'Raphael's on his way and everything's under control.'

And I'm in the way. Totally get it.

'I'll see you at seven tomorrow.'

'Thanks again, Isabella. I really appreciate it,' Jacki called over her shoulder.

Waiting for the lift again, Isabella texted Carly.

Want a coffee when you knock off?

Not expecting an immediate answer, since Carly was working, she headed for the main entrance and the fresh air. Talking with Carly and hearing more about the man she'd fallen in love with would put everything into perspective, and she'd be able to see Raphael as she'd always done. The best friend ever, who had her back, and had once told her they could rely on each other for anything any time.

Ping. A text landed in her phone.

Three-thirty at the café left of the hospital. Casper's.

Oh, yay. Awesome. Isabella's step picked up as she walked outside. Now what? Nearly an hour to fill in. She'd go for a walk along the Thames and soak up the atmosphere. Stop worrying about everything. Seemed lately she made problems out of anything. Especially her and Raphael. Like she was looking for trouble, when nothing had changed. But it had. She was different. She'd made a serious decision to move here.

You did it in a blink when Raphael made the suggestion.

Raphael. Everything came back to him. She needed to get to the bottom of these niggling concerns, and the sooner, the better. Needed to relax and be happy, more like.

The sun was weak but it didn't matter, the air so much better than the overheated hospital rooms and corridors. The sky was blue with a smattering of fluffy clouds, while boats of all shapes and sizes were making their way purposefully up and down the flowing waters of the Thames. Already there were lots of tourists on the pathways and bridges, cameras busy, selfies being snapped, excitement high, voices loud and excited. This was London. She recalled the first time she'd come here and feeling exactly the same. Hugging herself, she smiled widely at the scene before her and relaxed. The thumping in her head began quietening down.

Strolling along amongst the tourists, hearing a babble of languages and laughter, she let the city take over and push aside everything bothering her, and went with the flow of people all around her. For the first time since landing at Heathrow she didn't feel like falling asleep on her feet despite only a short time ago wanting to crawl into bed, and the tightness in her belly that had been plaguing her had taken a hike.

Isabella lost track of time and had to scramble to get back to the café before Carly gave up on her and headed away. If she hadn't already. Staring around the crowded café she couldn't see her friend.

'Isabella, Izzy, here.'

Relief and excitement had her charging through the spaces between the tables to where Carly stood waving from a table.

Laughing, she reached Carly and was instantly wrapped in a tight hug with a baby bump in the middle. 'It's been a long time.'

'Hello, you,' Carly murmured against her.

'Blimey, this is amazing. I've missed you guys so much.'

'Know what you mean.' Carly stepped back and sank onto a chair, her hand doing a loop of her belly. 'There's so much to talk about. First, go grab yourself a coffee. I had to get my mint tea when I got here so we could have this table.'

When Isabella returned, with an overfilled mug and a bottle of water, Carly was texting, but put her phone aside at once, her face all soft. 'Adem.'

'Look at you. All loved up. I'm so happy for you.' They should've been celebrating with wine, but with a baby in the mix this was the next best thing, as was the talk and laughter as they caught up on day-to-day news. Then Isabella said, 'Tell me all about Adem. When am I going to meet him?'

'Not telling all.' Carly chuckled. 'Izzy, he's everything I've ever wanted and more.'

'As is obvious from your face.' As her friend talked nonstop about her man and the baby they'd made, a mix of happiness for her and an unknown longing for herself rolled through her. 'I am so happy for you. Look at you. You're sparkling.'

'Isn't it great?' Then Carly's perpetual smile dipped. 'How are you now? Completely over that jerk?'

'Have been since the day I caught him out with one

of his floozies.' Again, there were things that this close friend didn't have to know. She'd told Raphael in the end, because he was too perceptive for his own good, and she hadn't wanted it hanging between them. Didn't mean Carly needed to learn how stupid she'd been.

'Honestly?'

'Yeah, honestly.'

'Great.' Carly eyeballed her. 'You up for finding another man to have in your life yet? A hot doc, maybe?'

'You're rushing me.' Raphael was as hot as they came. And a doc. Her cup hit the table hard. Can't be. Other women said that about him, not her. Even thinking it was beyond weird.

'I know. I haven't forgotten what it's like to have the man you think you love turn out to be different to your expectations. But I've moved on, and definitely for the better. I only want the same for you.'

'Thanks.' It was a kind thing for Carly to say and it had the longing expanding, had her being truthful. 'Yes, I do eventually want to try again at marriage.' Despite trying to convince herself otherwise. She wanted to fall head over heels in love and not come up for air for a long time. 'This time with someone who doesn't stray.' Raphael would never do that. Gasp. The cup shook when she picked it up again. What was going on? Her head was all over the place. Couldn't blame this on the long-haul flight. She was the problem. Or Raphael.

'How's Raphael? It's cool that you're staying with him.' Then Carly took on a surprised look. 'Raphael's single. You get on brilliantly with him. Now there's a thought. I can see that working.'

'Carly,' Isabella snapped. 'Stop right there. We are friends,' she ground out, not liking how Carly had come to a similar conclusion she was working her way towards. 'You know, as in talk, and laugh, and do things together, but not have sex or kiss. Or set up house and have babies.' Who was she trying to convince here?

Carly merely laughed. 'You think? He's hot, knows you inside out. Okay, not quite, but that can easily be fixed. Seriously, what's wrong with the idea?'

'Everything.' Nothing. Her fingers trembled, her head spun. No way. This conversation was not happening. 'You're doing what everyone who's just fallen in love does—trying to set up your single friends to have the same experience.'

'Too right. And Raphael's perfect for you. The whole situation's perfect. You're living in his house, spending lots of time with him. Make it happen, Izzy. Can you honestly say you haven't looked at him as other women do and gone, wow, he's gorgeous?'

That *perfect* word again. Better get on the phone to make appointments with the letting agents ASAP. Except when could she find time to go looking when she was starting a new job tomorrow, and needed to see the dressmaker for a fitting for her bridesmaid dress, and still got tired without trying? She refused to think about putting this other aberration to bed. Alone. 'I haven't,' she muttered. It used to be true. Not so long ago in the cafeteria she'd noted how well he filled out his suit. Friends didn't do that. Did they? She hadn't in the past. Damn, this was getting too complicated. So much for relaxing with Carly. Now she was wound up tighter than ever. 'Concentrate on Adem and leave my life to me.'

Carly's reply to that was to laugh.

'Thanks, friend.' After this conversation it was apparent she'd have to be wary about how often she mentioned

Raphael. Couldn't have Carly keeping an eye on her and Rafe to see if there was anything growing between them. Oh, damn, he was going to the wedding with her.

The moment Isabella sat down beside Raphael in the pub she'd agreed to meet him at after she'd said goodbye to Carly, any thought of moving vamoosed. Only to return when she realised he was hardly talking. But why rush into any old flat just to put space between them when they got along so well? Except they weren't so easy with each other at the moment. Okay, she'd make time to visit the rental agencies. In the meantime staying with him might fix this strange idea he meant something else to her now from expanding further. They'd inevitably quarrel over the dishes left in the sink or about one of them emptying the milk and not replacing it. That's what flatmates did. It was normal. It would ground her in reality. Or it could grow, expand, take over her common sense.

'Here, you look like you need this.'

She grabbed the wineglass Raphael was holding out to her, took a mouthful. 'Thanks.' The wine was cold, and calming. She took a breath, had another mouthful, felt the tension begin to ebb away. 'I see you're on the lemonade.'

'The joys of being on call.' He settled more comfortably on his stool. A good sign. 'I hear you've agreed to start tomorrow.'

'Jacki talked to me briefly this afternoon—when she wasn't running round like a headless chook. The ward was frantic.'

'Don't call her that to her face, or she'll put you on cleaning bedpans for a week.'

'Not the nurse I saw talking about a woman who'd

gone into labour twelve weeks early. She seemed so calm, while a few doors away the woman was crying loud enough to be heard all over the hospital.'

'The baby came in a hell of a hurry and is now in PICU, attached to every monitor ever invented. Joseph Raphael Gleeson. Fitted into my hand like a newborn puppy when I transferred him to the incubator.' Rafe held up his hand. 'Doesn't matter how often I deliver these prem babies, I never get used to that. If all goes well, one day he'll be an adult, working, playing, maybe having his own kids.'

'A puppy? You and your dogs. Better keep *that* to yourself or no one will want you near their babies.' Isabella laughed. Placing her hand on his, she squeezed gently, her eyes watering. 'They named him after you. That's cool. Bet it gave you hiccups when they told you.'

'It did. Apparently Joseph, his grandfather, is thrilled too.' Raphael turned his hand over and wound his fingers between hers.

Oops. Bad move. She carefully extracted her fingers. 'How many Raphaels are out there because of you?'

'Not too many, *merci*. Imagine if I'd been given a really horrible name. There'd be all these poor little blighters cowering at the school gates every day, waiting for the teasing to begin.'

She laughed again, and withdrew her hand. Reluctantly, she realised with a jolt. 'I can't think of any names that bad.' They'd briefly held hands. As in how friends didn't do. More laughter bubbled to the fore. She held it in, afraid Raphael would want to know what was funny. Happiness wasn't funny, and she'd swear she was very happy, happier than she'd been in ages. Did Carly have a point? More to think about. Later. When she was tucked up in bed—on her own. What? As if anyone would be with her. Her gaze flicked to the man sitting with her. This was becoming beyond bizarre. And yet the happiness still bubbled through her.

Raphael was doing that staring into the bottom of his drink trick again. It happened quite a lot. 'I'm attending a conference in Cardiff this weekend. Won't be around to take you shopping.'

'As if I need you for that. I do know my way around. I'm also hoping to look at a couple of flats on Saturday morning. The woman I dealt with from Wellington rang to say she had some places that might work for me.'

That could not be disappointment flickering across his face. 'That's quick.'

'Yes, well, don't want to hang around harassing you for too long. You might regret getting me the job and I need it.'

'Don't go making any decisions that you'll regret later.'

'I'll run everything by you if I find a place I like.'

'Do that.'

'I got a text from Jacki an hour ago, asking if I'd fill in on Saturday night. I said yes.'

'There's no holding you back, is there?' Raphael sipped his drink. 'Let's order. I've got some notes to go over when I get home.'

'For the conference?'

He nodded. 'On Sunday morning, along with the man who still mentors me, I'm speaking about two cases of early menopause we had this year.' A wry smile crossed his mouth. 'Not sure why he wanted me there, since most things that will come out of my mouth came from him in the first place.'

'Is that what you were doing in your office late last night? Working on your talk?' She'd gone downstairs for a glass of water and seen Raphael hunched over his computer, completely focused on the screen. 'You looked like nothing could interrupt you.'

'Obviously you didn't.' He grinned.

'You know me, quiet as a mouse.' Looking around, she noted the place was filling up. 'Want to share a pizza? I don't want to be out late either. Starting a new job in the morning, you know.'

Raphael couldn't forget that if he wanted to. He'd spent the night tossing and turning, thinking about Isabella and their relationship. So much for wishing for her to come to London, and to work with him. He'd got what he'd asked for all right, he groaned as he snapped off the vinyl gloves he wore and dropped them in the theatre's bin.

At 6:10 they'd caught the same train into the hospital, Izzy up early and ready to go long before he'd got his act together. She'd even looked more focused than he'd felt. But the usual evidence of her not getting through the night without going down to the kitchen had been there when he'd finally made it to the coffee machine—all primed and ready to share its life-saving liquid. Maybe she hadn't gone to bed at all.

His work phone buzzed. It was Jacki. Can you look in on Milly Frost sooner than later?

So he wasn't going to avoid seeing Izzy throughout the day. Not that he could avoid going on the ward for eight hours, but thankfully surgery had kept him busy until now. 'So much for lunch,' he muttered as he dried his hands and checked his tie in the mirror.

'Should've studied grass growing if you wanted meals at set hours,' one of the theatre nurses quipped.

'See you back here, hopefully on time,' he threw over his shoulder as he headed out of the theatre suite.

'Isabella noticed the foetal heart rate's stressed,' the head nurse explained when he strode into Milly's room. 'I've checked and agree.'

Jacki would've been keeping a close eye on everything Isabella did today. It was always a strain taking on new staff, no matter how highly recommended they came. Raphael nodded. 'I'll listen to the heartbeat as well.' Three heads were better than one. Finding a smile he turned to his patient. 'Hello, Milly. Aaron.' He nodded at the woman's husband. 'I understand your labour is going well, but baby might be distressed. I'm going to listen to the heart and watch the screen here to get a clear picture of what's happening.' If Isabella and Jacki were correct, he and Milly would be going to Theatre shortly, and as those two nurses were good at what they did, and wouldn't have made a mistake, he had an unexpected operation ahead of him. Nothing unusual in that, just meant he'd be later getting home. Again, nothing unusual, but for the first time in years, he regretted it.

Thought you were wanting time away from Izzy?

Face it. He didn't have a clue what he wanted.

'Is Evie going to be all right?' Fear darkened Milly's eyes as she scrabbled around for Aaron's hand.

Milly's question put him back on track. 'Let's see what's happening before I answer that.'

On the other side of the bed Isabella was lifting back the sheet in preparation to pull Milly's gown up and expose her baby tummy. Then, 'Another contraction, Milly?' As their patient rocked forward, pain marring her face and tightening her grip on her husband's hand, Isabella rubbed her back and waited for the spasm to pass.

Raphael also waited, watching the screen on the foetal heart rate monitor. Thankfully baby's heart rate did not slow any further during the contraction so no recovery afterwards, but it was already too slow and the contraction had done nothing to alter what was going on with baby. Next he listened through his stethoscope. 'Has baby been moving as much as usual?'

'Not for the last little while,' Milly cried. 'I didn't say anything. I thought he was resting. We've been going at this for a few hours now. It's all my fault.'

'It's nobody's fault.' Had there been any indicators he should've seen earlier? Before labour started? No. He knew there weren't, and playing the blame game did no one any favours. 'I see Isabella's noted he slowed down very recently.' He straightened up and delivered the news Milly and Aaron would not want to hear. Even though saving their daughter's life was the priority this wasn't how they'd planned on welcoming their baby into the world. 'I'm going to do a C-section. Baby's distressed and it isn't safe to leave her in there.'

'Is Evie going to be all right?' Milly repeated, this time with fear echoing around the room.

'Is our daughter in danger?' Aaron shouted.

This never got any easier. 'Surgery is the safest option. There's some risk of meconium being in the amniotic fluid. I don't want her breathing that in, so urgency is required. Isabella will prepare you to go down to Theatre, while I go organise the emergency team and scrub up, Milly.' He paused for a moment, fully expecting a load of questions, but the parents were both stunned—gripping their joined hands and staring at each other in raw silence. 'Isabella—' he nodded '—stay with Milly and Aaron until they go into Theatre.' Then he was striding away, talking on his phone to the head theatre nurse. 'My next procedure has changed. Urgent C-section to save full-term baby.'

'Do you want to cancel any surgery on this afternoon's list?' Kelly was very matter of fact. No wasting time on trivia.

'Not at this point. Let's see how we go.' Which meant he'd do all the listed procedures. Cancelling an operation was hard on patients when they were mentally prepared to go under the knife. He reached the scrub room and began preparing, his mind busy with every step of the procedure he'd done innumerable times. Milly and Aaron's daughter was going to get every chance on offer and more.

Evie Frost was delivered within minutes of Milly reaching Theatre. Raphael checked her breathing for abnormalities, and gave the mother a smile. 'All good. No meconium in her lungs.' Relief thumped behind his ribs. 'Evie's heart rate's normal for all she's been through.' He watched as a nurse handed Milly her daughter, and felt the familiar lump of awe build in his throat. New parenthood was wonderful, special. There weren't enough words to describe the amazement covering mums' and dads' faces when they met their child for the first time. Aaron was looking gobsmacked. Love spilled out of his gaze as he stared at his wife and daughter.

Raphael moved away. Despite how often he'd witnessed that scene it never grew stale. The awe he'd known the day Pierre slid into his shaking hands had never left him. That tiny boy had grown into a wonderful, strong lad with a great enthusiasm for life and an abundance of confidence. Raphael felt proud for being a part of his arrival, although he'd actually done little more than make his cousin comfortable and catch Pierre as he shot out into the world.

'Well done.' Kelly walked alongside him.

'Thanks. He's a little beauty.' He'd done a good job for baby and parents. Then the usual flip side of the euphoria hit. Anger filled him. What about *his* baby? What had he looked like? Who did he follow? Blond or dark? Short or tall? Cassie had refused to tell him anything, saying it was best he didn't know. Best for who? She'd never answered that question. He spun away, headed for the lift. He needed air and no friendly faces while he swallowed this particular pill yet again.

Then he'd return to Theatre and lose himself in work.

When Raphael called in on Milly after his last operation for the day Isabella was there. 'Evie's so cute. But then I say that about them all.' She'd been keeping a close eye on mum and baby all afternoon.

Now she and Raphael moved out of the little room to stand in the corridor. 'You ever think about having your own brood?' It was one thing Izzy had never talked about. Probably because it hadn't been an issue until she'd married Darren and then he hadn't wanted to hear her say yes. As for him, yes, he'd wanted children. Still did, but… Joshua, his little boy he'd never met… How did he cope with getting someone pregnant and waiting out the nine months until he got to hold his child? He was watching Izzy, wondering what she would say even as he dealt with his own pain.

She blinked, appeared to think about it. 'I've always presumed I would one day, and thought it would come about when I married. Now, I can't say I've been planning on it happening any time soon, if at all. It's filed with other things I hope to get to do some time, and when I do, be grateful if all goes according to plan.'

In this job they saw enough times when people's dreams of having a family went horribly wrong to know there were no guarantees. But was she referring to that, or her expectations for her future? Not asking. Not here anyway. 'What will be, will be,' he quoted.

Isabella nodded. 'Everyone thinks it's a given we'll get pregnant when we want to, but working in this job I've learnt how wrong that assumption can be.' Then she shrugged and perked up. 'We're being glum when there's a very lucky little girl in there with two of the happiest people in the world.'

'True. Weren't you meant to knock off an hour ago?' He still had patients to see, but surgery was finished, and suddenly he was exhausted. That often happened after a big day in Theatre and on the ward. Especially after a sleepless night. Add in the confusion Izzy was causing him and he was screwed. 'Feel like picking up some Italian on the way home? I'll be at least another hour.'

'I'll get the take-out and see you at home.'

At home. A soft sigh escaped.

If only you knew, Isabella Nicholson.

Putting his hand in his pocket for his wallet, he smiled when she shook her head.

'My shout.'

'Fair enough.' He knew better than to argue. He wouldn't win. 'See you later.' The sooner he checked on his patients, the sooner he could go home. Home. The connotations of that word had never been so huge. So frightening. Yet the need to settle grew the more time he spent with Isabella. She wasn't the only one wanting to find that special place in life. At least she'd made a start at getting on with it. Wouldn't it be great if he and Izzy could get what they wanted—together?

Stop right there. She's been hurt once. You can't risk putting her through that again.

No, he couldn't. It was his role as a friend to keep her safe, which meant putting some barriers up between them.

CHAPTER SIX

'THANK GOODNESS FOR FRIDAYS.' Isabella slammed the front door shut and stared along the hallway.

'You didn't even do a full week,' Raphael called from the kitchen at the far end. 'Come on. I've been waiting for you to get home so we can have a drink.'

'Good idea.' She was entitled to one after the hectic few days she'd spent on the ward.

'Dinner's not far off.' Raphael's glass of red wine with dinner was a nightly ritual. Another French habit he'd picked up from his family back in Avignon.

At the door into the kitchen she paused, gazed at Rafe as he stirred a sauce in a pot while at the same time squeezing garlic into it. She hadn't seen him so relaxed. It suited him. 'That smells divine.' Beat take-out any night of the week.

'Boeuf Bordelaise.'

'Yum.' So was the sight before her. 'What happened to heading to Cardiff today? Isn't that why you took the afternoon off?'

His shrug was a little stiff. Not so relaxed now she was here? 'No rush. The conference proper doesn't start till nine tomorrow. I'll head away first in the morning. Won't miss much if I'm a bit late.'

Warmth filled her. It wouldn't be a night alone after all. 'Cool. I'll get changed.' That wine was sounding better and better. She'd spent an hour with Carly, discussing the wedding, and love. She'd mostly listened, trying to ignore the flare of sadness that she wouldn't be walking down another aisle any time soon. There'd also been her selfish wish that Carly didn't have a man to rush home to, could go out on the town with her. But deep down, she was more than happy for her friend, and got over her funk quickly.

Up three stairs and she hesitated. Again it felt as though the ceiling was coming down on top of her and the walls crowding in. 'That colour has got to go.' Or she was more tired than she'd realised. She headed upward again, in a hurry to get away from the darkness.

'Izzy?' Raphael had come along the hall and was looking up at her. 'What are you on about?'

'That magenta is hideous. It's so dark and brooding, makes the hall seem smaller than it really is.' Not even the cream paint of the stair rails softened the atmosphere, instead accentuated all that was wrong with the paintwork.

He shrugged. 'Like I said the other day, changing it is on the list. I just don't happen to have forty-eight hours in every day.'

'When you've poured that wine can you get out the colour schemes you said came with the place?' Not waiting for an answer, she continued upstairs.

'Oui, madame.'

They'd never got around to the French week, but it didn't really matter since they flipped from English to French and back again all the time.

Pausing, she looked back down at Raphael. 'I have

more free time than you, and I like redecorating.' She could help until she moved. When she found some free time that was. 'I'll wow you with my skills.'

'Oh, no. You are not going to paint my hallway.'

'Why not? It's not like I haven't done this sort of thing before.' Being useful, instead of feeling a bit redundant, might help her sleep at night, too. 'Find those charts.'

His mouth twitched. 'You know how to make a man feel guilty.'

He had to be pulling her leg. He'd be more than happy to have the *problem* taken out of his hands, and having her do that shouldn't be getting him in a twist. 'You can't come up with a reason for me not to do it, can you?' Fist pumping the air, she grinned. 'Love it when I win.'

Raphael shook his head at her before heading back down the hall.

There was a small pile of charts on the table when she returned showered and in clean clothes. 'What are these?' she asked, tapping some pages of notes.

'The interior design suggestions that came with the house. Like I said, I'm not the only one who hasn't got around to doing up this place.'

'It's not everyone's idea of fun,' she conceded, flicking through the pages and pausing at a design for a new kitchen layout. 'Wow, I like this.' Glancing around the kitchen, she nodded. 'Lighter for one. Far more functional for another. And modern.'

'That's not hard to achieve when you think how old this must be.' Raphael was also staring around, looking as though he'd never really seen it before. 'I wonder if the design company's still got the in-depth plans?' Excitement was beginning to crowd his gaze. 'They're based on the other side of Richmond.'

'Only one way to find out,' she drawled.

He grinned and pushed her glass in front of her. 'Drink up and stop being annoying.'

'Why is wanting to help being annoying?' The wine was delicious, a perfect end to a busy day.

Ignoring her question, he went with some of his own. 'How do you feel after your first week on the maternity ward? Glad you joined us?' He gave the sauce a stir before leaning against the counter and stretching his legs before him. Legs that went on for ever.

Gulp. He'd always had those legs. Why were they any different tonight? Another gulp of wine. What was the question? Oh, right. 'I'm loving it. And yes, I believe it was the right move. Though only time will really be the judge of that.' Following his example, she perched on another chair and reached for the colour charts, noting the ones that had been circled with a marker pen.

'I'll add my bit to making it happen.'

'Tell me something I don't know. You'll be a dog with a bone.' Looking around she spied Chienne on her cushion. 'Sorry, not trying to insult you, Cat. You're too good for bones.' The cat was getting to her, making her feel more and more at ease. But then she did like to share the bed in the darkest hours of the night, or curl up on her lap when she came downstairs for a glass of water and some upright time in an attempt to get into a fall-asleep zone.

'Don't listen to her, Chienne. Izzy likes to con everyone round to her way of thinking.'

'Why not if it gets me what I want?' She grinned. Then focused on the colours that had been circled with a marker pen, rather than stare at those thighs filling his black jeans. 'Who suggested these colours?' They weren't bad. The colours? Or the thighs? She could live with them. Both of them. Gulp. Nice wine. Hope there was more in that bottle for after dinner.

'Believe it or not, in the first months when I was fired up to get on with fixing the place up I visited the paint shop and the woman I spoke to was very helpful with suggestions. Said these were the latest in colour schemes and if I want to sell the place would appeal to more buyers.'

'You're thinking of moving? Already?' First she'd heard of it. She didn't like it. She was getting used to Raphael being here and had hoped they'd live in the same vicinity long term. Was he really considering moving again? Of course she'd known he would eventually return to Avignon. That's why. He'd always felt a pull towards his family and hometown. As she had with Wellington. Look where that got her. It hadn't been Wellington at fault, more her and the man she'd returned there with. Whereas Avignon might very well be the best thing for Raphael. Her heart stuttered. Didn't she want him to be happy? Deep, deep breath. Yes, she did. More than anything. More than her own happiness. Truly? A sip of wine. Truly.

'Can't guarantee anything's for ever. But I'm here for the foreseeable future at least.' He spaced the words, loud and clear, as though it was important she believed him.

The relief was strong. 'Glad to hear it.'

'What are you looking for in a flat?' He sipped his drink as he waited for her reply.

'Two bedrooms, though I guess one would suffice. Located near a train station, of course, and close to shops and food outlets.'

'Sounds ordinary.'

'I guess it is, but ordinary's fine for now.'

'As long as it doesn't bore you, Izzy.'

'I'm not about to dash away again. This is a permanent move. I'm determined to keep it that way.'

Raphael went back to stirring his sauce. 'You ever feel it's not working out please tell me.'

'Why?' The word shot out of her mouth.

Tipping his head back, he stared up at the ceiling.

And she waited, sensing if she uttered one word he'd not answer her.

Finally his head dropped forward, and he took a small mouthful of his merlot. 'I like having you back in London.'

So? She liked being here. But was that what this was about? She waited, breath caught in her throat.

His words were measured as he continued. 'I've lived here for two years, and when I say lived I mean I've come and gone, and not really noticed the place. It is four walls and shelter, comfortable in a less than desirable way. It's a house, not a home.'

What did that have to do with her?

'Since you arrived, it already feels different, more like the home I intended making it. *My* home. I think about coming back at the end of the day now, not just going somewhere to eat, shower, study and sleep.' He stopped.

What to say to that? Her mouth had dried, and there didn't seem to be any answers forthcoming to what Raphael had just said. Inside, that feeling of finally getting her life right expanded a wee bit more. They did fit well together, but how well? Were they becoming more than friends? Was that even wise given there'd been no attraction in the past? Could people suddenly want someone physically after spending most of their lives not noticing each other that way? 'I'm glad you're finally enjoying your home.'

Crass, Izzy, crass.

Totally. But she couldn't tell him what she'd been thinking. For one, she hadn't been here very long, and secondly, she had to haul on the brakes. She wasn't reliable in relationships, and Raphael was vulnerable after how Cassie dumped him.

'I've surprised you.' Raphael was studying her.

What was that about? 'A little.' It would be a relief to tell him how she felt, but then there'd be a whole other can of worms to deal with. Best shut up. She began flicking through paint charts, the colours one big blur as thoughts of holding Raphael, of kissing him, being kissed back, rose and heated her before she could squash them back in place.

At five next morning, fifteen minutes before the alarm was due to go off, Raphael dragged himself out of bed and into the shower, then stared at his puffy face in the mirror as he shaved.

'Don't lose any sleep over where I'll find a place to live,' Izzy had said over their beef dinner. How prophetic.

She'd blighted his night with thoughts of what it might be like if she didn't find a flat, and instead stayed on with him, moved down to the second floor and his bedroom. Of course none of that had been suggested, but he hadn't been able to think of anything else as he'd watched her swing her small but shapely legs while she sat on the stool. The relief had been immense when he'd put dinner on the table and she'd had to shift. But then he'd been subjected to seeing her fork food through those full lips, and conjuring up thoughts of her mouth on his skin.

The razor slipped. He swore. Dabbed the blood away. 'Concentrate, man.' Hell, now she had him talking to himself like some brain-dead moron on P.

It was far easier to blame Isabella than take a long, serious look at himself. If he did that, he'd have to admit he was floundering here, and hell, he didn't usually get into a quagmire over his own emotions when it came to women. Only Cassie had done that to him. Until now. Now Izzy was having a damned good go at tipping him upside down. At least she was on the good side of the barometer, not like the hellhole Cassie had shoved him into. But then it was not as though he was falling hard for Izzy like he had for Cassie. If anything he was getting there slowly, carefully, and with a whole heap of concerns to deal with.

Focusing entirely on removing the last of the growth on his face, he managed to quieten his thumping chest for a few minutes. No more nicks on his skin. Yet the moment he rinsed the shaver the thumping started up again. This strange sensation Izzy brought on threw him whenever he wasn't totally engrossed in work or study or any other blasted thing that didn't start with *I*. He couldn't go on ignoring his feelings for her. Nor could he do a thing about it until he returned from Cardiff. Taking a mug of coffee up to her room and saying, 'Oh, by the way, I think I might want to spend the rest of my life with you. Can't talk now. Lots to sort out first. See you tomorrow night,' wouldn't win him any favours. Not that he had worked out how to approach this yet, only understood the time was coming when he'd not be able to stay uninvolved. All he knew was if Izzy laughed at him, he'd die inside.

Now his alarm woke him up. As in out of his stupor and into getting ready for the trip to Wales. Swiping the screen of his phone to shut the infernal noise off, he tossed it into his overnight bag along with his shaving gear, and got dressed in his latest swanky suit and tie. Bag zipped shut, he headed downstairs for a quick coffee and toast before hitting the road. He was early due to that lack of sleep, but hopefully that meant the roads would have less traffic to contend with.

'Hey, coffee's ready and waiting. I put it on when I heard you moving around up there.' Izzy sat at the round table at the edge of the kitchen, a mug in one hand, and Chienne on her lap schmoozing against her other hand.

'Morning.' He hadn't smelt a thing. Too distracted. Then, 'Cheeky.' He nodded at the cat. 'You'll do anything to get attention.' He wouldn't ogle Isabella in her sleeveless top with no bra underneath. Was that a pyjama top? Guess so, if the matching loose shorts Chienne was stretched across were an indicator. So she—Izzy, not Chienne—still wore shapeless PJs. Or had she reverted to them once Darren had left the scene? He'd seen enough on washing lines throughout their lives to know she'd never been one for matching bras and knickers, let alone fancy lingerie of any kind, but who knew what being in a relationship might've done for her? Turning away, his mind filled with an image of her in black sexy lingerie. And he swore.

'Pardon?'

Did he say that out loud? Sloshing coffee into the mug waiting by the coffee machine, he drew a slow breath and looked over his shoulder. 'Sorry. I spilled coffee, that's all.' Grabbing a cloth he made a show of wiping down the bench, which was coffee-free. If this was what not sleeping did to him, then how did Izzy manage day to day on the little she got?

'I take it you didn't sleep again? Perhaps you should stop drinking coffee.'

'One step ahead of you.' She waved her mug at him. 'This is tea. Not that I'm giving up entirely on my caffeine fix.'

Then he noticed the paint charts once again spread over the table. Showed how much attention he'd been paying to Izzy and her PJs if he hadn't seen those. 'You are serious about getting the decorating under way, aren't you?'

A rare worry flickered through her eyes. 'Does that bother you?'

He shook his head. 'Not at all. I should've known you'd get stuck into sorting my mess out.' It was what she'd always done. Only difference was this was a large, hands-on job, not like making sure the rowdy guys in the room next door at university stopped banging on his door in the middle of the night when he was trying to study.

Her shoulders softened, and Chienne got another stroke. Lucky cat. 'It's okay. You'll recognise the house when you return tomorrow night. I've got too much else on today.'

'Thank goodness for that,' he retorted. 'Can't have you taking over completely.' The coffee was blistering hot and he needed to be on the road. 'I'll put this in a travel mug. Got to go.'

'Fine.' Izzy sipped her tea. When her tongue did a lap of her lips the thumping started up in his chest again, only harder and faster.

Just as well he was going away.

* * *

Except as Raphael and his colleague, Jeremy, stood on-stage receiving a hearty round of applause at the end of their talk on Sunday, he knew he wasn't hanging around for the afternoon's workshops. 'I'm out of here,' he muttered in an aside.

'I'm not surprised. You've been miles away since you got here. Except during our talk,' Jeremy added hastily.

'It's a miracle I managed to get through that without making stuff up.' Though he had concentrated hard, determined Isabella wasn't going to wreck everything about this weekend. He missed her. Had done from the moment he'd backed out onto the road in Richmond yesterday morning. It had taken strength not to text to see what she was up to. He just wanted to be with her, even when that twisted his gut and tightened muscles best ignored. Sure, he wouldn't be able to do what he really wanted to—kiss those tantalising lips and hold that soft, curvy body against him—but he could give her cheek and laugh, and make her a mug of tea.

'What's playing on your mind?' Jeremy asked as they stepped offstage.

'Nothing to do with work,' Raphael was quick to re-assure his mentor.

'I didn't think so.'

Right. Now what? He hated lying to anyone, and par-ticularly to this man who'd been nothing but kind and helpful to him from the day they met in the gynaecol-ogy department when he'd come on board as the newest specialist. 'Just some personal stuff.' Hopefully Jeremy would get the hint and drop the subject. Not that he'd ever done that if he really felt it important to get to the bottom of something. The man could be a hound when he put his mind to it.

'Woman trouble?'

Got that right. Now what? He wasn't talking about Izzy to anyone. He tried to laugh it off. 'Isn't it always about women?'

'Not with you, my friend. You make sure of that; no repercussions when a fling is over. Everyone comes out smiling. Even you.'

Yes, and could be that was the problem. He had got not getting involved down to a fine art. *Magnifique*. He was getting nowhere fast. Try the truth line again, diluted, of course.

'My close friend Isabella is staying with me at the moment.'

'And you want to get home to spend time with her. Why didn't you say so?' Then Jeremy's eyes widened. 'Oh, oh. I sense trouble.' He tapped Raphael's chest. 'In there.'

'Stick with gynaecology, will you? You're better at it.'

Jeremy didn't laugh. Not even a glimmer of amusement showed in his face. 'This Isabella, I've met her on the ward. She's a very competent midwife. So she's special? You've known her a long time?'

'Since I was an incompetent teen.'

'And now you're not incompetent. Nor do you want to remain just friends.'

Mon amie. Izzy. Special. More than a friend.

Jeremy gripped his arm. 'What are you going to miss by not being here for the rest of the day? Nothing you don't already know. It's time you put your personal life before your career. You need a balanced life, Raphael, one where you have someone to go home with at the end of the day.'

'Don't I know it.' Yet it was a new idea, one that began filling him with hope from the day he'd picked Izzy up at the airport. No, not new, because two years ago he'd seen what he wanted and had had to bury the longing, to focus on the other thing necessary to him—work. Not Isabella. 'Thanks, Jeremy. I'm out of here.'

Not that he was heading home to spill his heart. No way. There was a lot to work through before he was even close to admitting his love. Time spent with Izzy, laughing and talking, or more likely arguing over next to nothing, was always time well spent. Hopefully he'd be relaxed and she wouldn't pick up on these new feelings because he had to get them under control and back in the box.

The house was locked up when he arrived home. Inside, as he walked along the hall, he called out, 'Izzy? You about?'

Silence greeted him.

The vacuum cleaner stood against the wall, still plugged in, as if Isabella had been interrupted, and fully expected to come back to the job she'd started.

There was no note on the table explaining where she was. Nor on his phone. Not that there should be. She wouldn't have been expecting him home this early, but still. The anticipation that had been growing as he'd negotiated highways and roads filled with weekenders with nothing better to do than get in the way evaporated, leaving him feeling like an idiot. Of course Izzy would be out doing her thing, hadn't been sitting here pining the hours away. Why would she?

He'd text and see where she was. Might go join her for

a drink or some shopping or whatever took her fancy. It was yesterday she'd gone to look at flats. Had she found one she liked and gone back for a second look? That could mean she'd be out of here soon and he could get back to his quiet life—which he didn't want any more. Truly? Yes. Didn't mean he knew what he was going to do about it though.

Raphael sighed, then reverted to normal and went in to the Queen Victoria to see how his patients were faring.

'I'll get you a new tumbler,' Isabella told Brooke. 'It's not a problem.' Her patient was stressing out over every little thing as the contractions got harder and closer together.

'You're so calm, it's annoying,' Brooke growled through gritted teeth.

Isabella chuckled. 'You're not the first to complain about that.'

'Wait until you have a baby and then see how composed you are.' The woman blinked. 'Or have you had children of your own?'

'Not yet.'

Not yet? Like there was a possibility in the near future? Raphael flashed across her mind. As he'd been doing all weekend. No wonder she'd agreed immediately when asked to come in and work the afternoon after one of the nurses had gone off with a stomach bug. But Raphael and babies and her? All in the one sentence? As if that was happening. Although they were getting on in a closer way than ever before, and she had no idea where that was leading, there was always an air of uncertainty between them. Besides, her dream of babies with Darren had been stolen from her. She wasn't ready to be that vulnerable again.

'Got to get a man first,' she told Brooke.

But not before I get that tumbler.

Heading for the water dispenser and the stack of plastic mugs, she glanced at her watch. Less than an hour to go. It had been a frantic few hours, babies arriving in all directions.

Raphael had been quiet. No texts asking what she was doing, or telling her how the conference was going. He'd have finished his talk hours ago, could possibly be on the road by now. Wonder what he'd like for dinner?

After giving Brooke her water and checking how baby was doing, Isabella went to see Caitlin Simons, who had delivered an hour ago. Since the door was open she popped her head around the corner of Caitlin's room to make sure she wasn't interrupting anything, and stopped, a gasp whispering across her lips.

Raphael was sitting awkwardly on a narrow chair. Baby Simons swathed in light blankets was cradled in his arms. The usual look of relief was in his gaze as he looked down at the boy, but there was something else too. Something like—pain? But it couldn't be. What was there to be sad about here?

A sharp pain stabbed her chest. A lump blocked her throat. Breathing became difficult. Rafe would make a wonderful father. Despite that intense look there was something so tender about him that blindsided her. Shook her to the core.

She could never imagine Darren like this.

She stared at the beautiful man holding the tiny baby, and the floor moved beneath her feet. The air thickened, breathing became impossible.

This was Rafe, the man she'd known for so long. This was Raphael, a man she'd begun falling in love with. She couldn't do a thing about that because she wasn't settled, could not risk hurting him. Raphael was polar opposite to her ex. How could she have thought she loved Darren? This feeling she'd been denying since arriving in London was so different to anything she'd felt for him. Strong and soft, caring and gentle, hungry and fulfilling.

Isabella closed her eyes, counted to ten, opened them. Her eyes filled with tears. She and Raphael made great friends. What would they be like as lovers? He deserved someone who would stick by him through thick and thin, and she couldn't guarantee that was her, no matter how hard she was trying to settle here. The picture before her would've been perfect if that was their child. As she swiped at her cheeks her heart crashed against her ribs. Now what? How could she return to his house tonight as if nothing had changed? She had to get away. Turning around she froze when Raphael called out.

'Hey, Izzy, come and meet Fleur.' Raphael's eyes locked with hers, nailing her to the spot.

She took an unsteady step, then another, and another, until at last she stood before him and looked down, down at the baby but mostly at Raphael. Saw him as the man she wanted to spend her life with.

'Want a hold?' He lifted the child towards her.

'I've already had a hold.' She took a step back, afraid she'd drop Fleur. Which was plain stupid, considering how many babies she'd held during her career.

'Have another.'

'Okay,' she whispered.

'Come on. She's so cute.' Raphael stood up, held out the precious bundle.

Taking the baby, she stared down at the wrinkly, pink face of the girl she'd help deliver earlier, and who now opened her eyes wide. 'Hello, Fleur.' Then she couldn't say another word, fear of telling Raphael about the mass of emotions tying her in knots.

'Izzy?'

'Isabella, Brooke's asking for you,' Claudia called across the room. 'I don't think we've long to go now.'

'On my way.' Gently placing Fleur back in her bed, she turned to Caitlin. 'She's gorgeous. Well done, you. Anything I can get you?'

'My mum. She's gone for a coffee, and I need her here.' Caitlin was a solo mum, the father having done a bunk when he learned about the pregnancy.

'Not a problem. I'll dash down to the cafeteria right now.' Phew. That'd give her some space from Raphael. 'Make that after I've checked on my other patient.'

'I'll go see Mrs Johnson, Izzy,' Raphael said.

So much for getting away from him while she cleared her head. But what could she say? She might be one of the midwives on the case, but doctors came first. Always. Glancing across at him, she saw he was looking more like his normal self, the longing and awe now under control. 'Fine.'

'How long have you been on shift?' he asked as he made for the door.

'Started around lunchtime, and should be finished shortly.' Not regular shift hours but who cared? If she was needed here, then that was fine by her. Ignoring any further questions Raphael might come up with, she said to Caitlin, 'Fleur's lovely. Thank you for letting me hold her.' Then she shot away to find Mrs Simons, who'd hopefully put a smile back on her daughter's face.

It was hard for the women who had to go through labour without their soul mate. A friend or family member was well and good, but not the same thing as a doting husband or partner.

'Isabella, wait.' Raphael was right behind her. 'Are you all right?'

'Yes,' she muttered. 'I got side tracked in there when I should've been with Brooke.' Not that she'd done anything wrong. Brooke had not been ready to give birth when she left the room.

'You find a flat?'

'Yes.' Her mouth was dry, her hands damp. Snatching a plastic cup at the water dispenser she filled it and turned to head for the lift only to come to an abrupt stop in front of Raphael. She couldn't read his expression at all. 'You came back early from Cardiff.'

'I'd had enough of being squashed into the hotel conference room.' His reply was terse.

'Thought you were meant to be getting a life outside these walls.' And who dropped the housework to come in here when Jacki called to say she was desperate for staff for the rest of the day shift? Who hadn't gone home when the next shift arrived?

'I won't hang around after I've seen Brooke. But first, are you sure you're okay? You looked a tad pale, and are as jumpy as a frog on steroids.' Nothing but concern radiated out of those blue eyes.

Damn it. Think of something to say that'll keep him happy. Think, girl. 'Just didn't expect to see you holding Fleur like you never wanted to let her go, that's all.' Wrong. All wrong, and she couldn't take back a single word.

'What?' Raphael glanced at her. 'Never.'

Shrugging aside her mood, she asked lightly, 'Never want your own family? Or never like that with anyone else's child?'

'You know the answer to both those questions. Or I thought you did.'

She nodded. 'I suppose I do. Lack of sleep catching up.'

'I saw the crossword on the kitchen bench when I got in. How many hours did you get last night?' The concern had returned, but this time annoyance was in the mix.

And she owed him an apology. 'Actually, I did sleep quite well for me, and the crossword was breakfast entertainment.' Not saying she'd started it at three in the morning. 'Now, I'd better get cracking. It's busy in here.' She nudged past him, striding down the hall to the room she was needed in.

'For the record, in case you've forgotten, I do want children of my own with a woman whom I love, and no, I don't get all possessive over someone else's baby.' Raphael was right beside her, his mouth grim. This conversation wasn't over. It was going to be a barrel of laughs at home tonight.

Maybe she'd go to visit Carly. Except she and Adem weren't going to be home tonight. Something about having a meal with family members. All part of the wedding build-up. Lucky girl. Isabella took a sideways look at the man who had her heart in a flutter. What was it like to be planning a wedding with the man of your dreams? Not once had the small celebration she and Darren had turned her heart into an out of control bongo drum. The planning had taken a few hours on the phone, and the dress had been in a sale in the local shop.

Damn it, Isabella, why did you not see how wrong that was at the time?

Because she'd been so desperate to have the life she'd been promised she hadn't seen past the hype. And if she had? Would she be feeling differently about Raphael now? No answer dropped into her head, nothing stopped the tailspin she was in.

Raphael tapped her on the shoulder. 'I'll wait and give you a lift when you're done.'

'That's not necessary.'

'Maybe, but I'll wait anyway.'

CHAPTER SEVEN

'RAPHAEL, CAN YOU take a look at Janice Crowe?' Jacki asked as he left his patient's room. 'Baby's breeched.'

There went any chance of snatching a coffee. 'Room?'

'Three. Janice is eighteen, hasn't been to antenatal classes or seen a doctor for three months.'

So she'd be terrified and blaming everyone else. Raphael sighed. Young women without family support always had a hard time of their pregnancies. 'Bloods?'

'Haemoglobin eighty-six, MCV and MCH indicate iron deficiency. Still waiting for the results on the blood group, iron and liver functions.'

He raised his eyebrow. 'Drugs?'

Jacki shook her head. 'There's a distinct yellow tinge to her skin and eyes.'

Inside room three Isabella was trying to calm the distraught girl. 'Janice, breathe deep. That's it. Keep at it, and you'll help baby.' She glanced up and relief flooded her face when she saw him. 'Here's Mr Dubois, the obstetrician. He's going to help you and baby.'

'Hello, Janice. Call me Raphael,' he said in an attempt to put her at ease. He had her notes in his hand but didn't look at them, instead kept eye contact with his patient. 'I hear your baby's turned the wrong way round.'

Janice nodded, her teeth biting deep into her bottom lip.

Izzy held her hand.

'I have to examine you. Is that all right?' It'd be a problem if she refused as there weren't any female doctors on duty today. 'Or would you prefer Isabella does it? Though I do like to see what's going on myself.'

Janice's mouth flattened, and she stared at him.

He held his breath as he waited for her approval. It went better when the patient was on the same page. This baby was going to be all right. It had to be.

'Okay.'

'Good.' Slipping gloves on, he watched as Izzy talked Janice into lying back and bending her legs, placing her feet apart.

'Now, I am going to lift the sheet up to your waist. At least the room is nice and warm.' She was good with the terrified girl. 'Hold on. That's another contraction, right?' Izzy immediately went to hold Janice's hands until it passed. 'Breathe. You're doing great. That's it.'

Tears spilled down Janice's face. 'It hurts so much.'

'Yes, but the painkiller should be working by now. You need to relax.' Izzy smiled. 'I know. Stupid thing to say, right? But believe me, if you can relax a bit the pain drug will work better. Now, lie back and let Raphael see what baby's up to.'

Raphael positioned himself for the examination. 'Do you know if you're having a boy or girl, Janice?' Chances were she hadn't had a scan, but keeping her talking would make what he was about to do go easier.

'No. When I had my scan it was too early to find out. I want a boy though.'

'Why a boy?' Isabella kept the conversation going, while ready to pass him anything he might require.

Janice shrugged. 'They seem easier.'

Raphael laughed. 'You think? My mother wouldn't agree with you.' His hand felt the baby. Definitely breech, and there was the umbilical cord below the presenting part of baby. His laugh snapped off. They had a problem. This had become urgent. Drawing a breath, he prepared to tell his patient what the next move was. 'Janice, baby is trying to come out feet first and that doesn't work. There's also a complication with the cord being flattened by baby so not enough blood is getting through. Do you understand?'

'I think so. Is my baby going to die?'

'No. I am going to do a C-section. Urgently.'

'You're going to cut it out?'

That was putting it bluntly. 'Yes, I am. It's best for baby, and for you. It doesn't take very long, and means no more contractions. You'll be sore for some days afterwards and need help with baby, but someone will talk to you about that later.'

Izzy pulled down the sheet to cover Janice. 'You're being very brave.'

'Can you stay with me when he takes the baby out?'

Izzy looked at Raphael, one perfectly shaped eyebrow lifted.

'As long as Jacki doesn't mind losing you for a while, it's fine with me.' He had to have a nurse there anyway, and why not Izzy? He liked working with her. 'Right, I'll get the ball rolling.'

'I'll get Janice ready.' Her smile warmed him right to his toes.

There were no hiccups with the C-section. The baby

girl was healthy and Janice seemed to have forgotten she wanted a boy as she gazed down at her precious bundle.

Raphael felt the tension between his shoulder blades back off as he accepted that another baby had made its way into the world and was going to be all right. There were a lot of hurdles ahead for Janice and her daughter, but he'd done his bit for them and got it right.

He and Izzy. He watched as she tended to Janice, getting her a drink of water, wiping her face, constantly keeping an eye on the baby, showing Janice how to hold her, to rub her. Oh, yes, Izzy was good at this.

His mouth dried and his heart thumped. What was he going to do?

Just after midnight on Wednesday Isabella lifted the ward phone and speed-dialled Raphael. 'You're needed. Tania Newman's showing signs of puerperal sepsis.'

'I'm putting you on speaker phone so you can fill me in on the details while I dress.'

That she did not need to think about. 'Heart and resp rates are high, BP's down, and she's running a temperature. White count an hour ago was slightly elevated but no indicators of infection.'

'Any abdo pain that's nothing to do with contractions?'

'Yes, and she's started vomiting.'

'I'm heading out the door now. Take another blood for CBC, mark it urgent,' Raphael told her. 'Always happens at night time, doesn't it?' Click. He was gone.

Had he really had time to haul on some pants and a shirt? Guess he was used to dressing in seconds. There was always a pile of clothes on his dresser, no doubt just for moments like this. Isabella rushed back to Tania's room with the phlebotomy kit in her hand. 'Mr Dubois's on his way. He wants another blood test done.'

Katie, the nurse on with her, nodded. 'You take the sample while I wipe Tania down again.'

Isabella set the kit on the bed beside the terrified woman. 'Tania, I know you don't like needles but this is really important.'

'Do whatever you have to,' the thirty-four-year-old woman grunted through her pain. 'Just save my baby.'

'We're doing everything we can, and like I said, Raphael is on his way. Pushing his speed to the limit, I bet.'

'Hope he's careful. We need him here,' Dominic Newman said as he held his wife's hand, looking lost and nothing like the notorious criminal lawyer he was. Babies were great levellers. 'What can I do? There's got to be something other than sitting here like a useless lump.'

'You're on keeping Tania calm duty.' It was a big ask. The woman was frantic with worry and fear.

'I read about puerperal sepsis on a website,' Tania cried. 'It's bad. Really bad. Baby might not make it.'

True, sepsis at this stage of pregnancy was not good. 'Sometimes I wish the internet had never been invented.' Isabella slid the tourniquet up Tania's arm. 'Tighten your hand into a fist. That's it. Now, a small prick.' She hit the vein immediately and released the tourniquet as the tube filled.

'Why do you always say that? It's not the first time I've had my blood taken,' Tania shouted.

'It's routine.' Isabella drew the blood, placed a cotton ball over the site and slid the needle out. 'There you go. All done.' She named the tube and filled out a form, marked it urgent. 'I'll get that up to the lab now. Hopefully we'll have the results by the time Mr Dubois gets here.' Hopefully the lab tech would make a film when he received the sample and not wait to find out what the white count was. The film would be required to do a white cell differential count to ascertain the number of neutrophil band forms which were indicative of infection. The more bands and even earlier forms of that particular white cell, the stronger the infection.

'Agh!' Tania cried, and straightened out on the bed, grabbing at Dominic and gripping his wrists like a vice.

His face paled, but he didn't budge, let his wife squeeze as though her life depended on it.

'Deep breaths,' Isabella said, and rubbed her shoulder constantly until the spasm passed. 'Well done.'

'Like I had any choice,' Tania snapped.

'Hey, steady, darling. Isabella and Katie are here to help us.'

'It's all right.' Katie grinned. 'We've heard worse.'

'I'm sorry.' Tania looked contrite. 'I really am. It's just so painful, and then this puerperal infection. I'm terrified.' She struggled upright and leaned her head in against Dominic, who took over the rubbing.

'Can I take a look at your cervix?' Isabella preferred asking rather than just saying that's what she had to do. A simple question gave her patient some sense of control over a situation where she had absolutely none. Especially in this case. As soon as Raphael got here there'd be a lot going on, and Tania wouldn't be given a chance to say anything. Urgency was now a major factor in this delivery. If this was PS, then the infection would run away on them if they weren't careful. Antibiotics had already been administered, but Rafe might up the dosage.

'Why have I got an infection down there?'

Katie answered, 'You said your breasts were sore when you first arrived, and I thought it looked as though you've got a small infection in your nipples.'

'The other doctor gave me antibiotics for it. She said it would be all right for baby to take them.'

'The infection could've already spread, and the symptoms have only just begun showing up in the last little while.'

Isabella waited until Tania gulped hard and nodded at her. 'Go for it. Hopefully baby's nearly here and we can get this nightmare over and done with. What if he gets the infection too?'

That was the problem. 'Mr Dubois will explain everything when he arrives.' Ducking for cover, but it wasn't her place to fill this couple in on what might happen. Times like this she was glad to be a nurse and midwife, and not a doctor. They could have handing out the grim news. She'd seen how much it upset Raphael. Tugging on gloves she positioned herself at the end of the bed and waited for Tania to lie back. 'Okay, try and relax.'

It didn't take long to get the measurement and Isabella felt relief. 'Nine centimetres. We're nearly there.'

'About time,' Tania grumped. 'I've had enough.'

There was still the pushing to undertake, but best keep that to herself for now. No point in upsetting her patient any more than she already was. Hopefully Raphael would be here before they started.

'Hello, Tania, Dominic.' The man himself strode into the room minutes later, looking beyond calm.

But Isabella knew better, saw the tell-tale sign where his mouth tightened in one corner. 'That was quick.'

'The roads were fairly quiet for a change. Right, let's

see what's happening, shall we? Tania, tell me about the pain in your belly.'

From then on everything happened fast. A phone call came from the lab alerting them to the CBC results and the raised white cell and band form counts. Raphael administered another antibiotic intravenously. Tania began pushing before she was told to, and reluctantly stopped, only to have baby make her own mind up that it was time to come, and soon it was over. Baby Sophie met her parents, had a brief, safe cuddle from each before being whisked into the specialised cot and wiped over extra carefully because of the infection mum had.

'I'm going to give Sophie antibiotics too,' Raphael told the worried parents. 'We don't know yet if she'd caught the infection, but I prefer to be on the safe side. You have to understand what this means.' He ran through what could go wrong, then reassured them it was unlikely, but they had to know. 'Then she'll go to PICU where they'll monitor her continuously.'

Tania was crying. 'I want to hold her. I want her here, not on a different floor.' She hiccupped. 'I know what you're doing is the right thing, but it's so unfair. We've waited years for her and now we can't keep her with us.'

Dominic wrapped his wife in his arms, tears streaming down his face to mingle with hers. 'Shh, darling. It's going to be all right.'

Raphael talked to the couple some more, working at pacifying them.

When he'd finished, Isabella looked at him and Katie, and they nodded agreement, then left the room quietly, pushing Sophie's cot ahead of them.

'Phew,' Isabella sighed. 'It never gets any easier with distraught parents.'

'The day it does is the time for you to walk out of here and go work as an interior decorator.' Raphael chuckled. 'Me, I'll learn to play the banjo and sit on my back step all day.'

Katie agreed. 'I'll find a rich man and retire for good. Right, come on, Sophie, let's get you settled in PICU.'

As Katie headed down the corridor at a fast clip with her special cargo, Isabella's heart went with the wee tot. 'She's so vulnerable.'

Raphael moved closer. '*Oui*, they all are. I wonder how something so fragile and tiny can be so strong. It scares me sometimes.'

'Would we be worse parents because we know all the things that can go wrong?'

'I'd say so. I've seen it often enough with colleagues who've had babies on my watch. Their pregnancies are hard work.' He didn't blink at her use of 'we'.

But then she hadn't meant it as in we, us, together. Had she? Oh, hell. Get busy, find someone who needed her attention. Raphael would go home soon. Fingers crossed.

But now he looked worried. 'Who can tell with these things? Right, I'd better go interrupt the couple and do some more checks on Tania before I head away.'

'Hopefully you'll get home before it's time to get up and come to work.' She still had five hours to get through before knocking off at seven. By the time she reached home Raphael would be back here. Ships in the night. It should be ideal. No talking about things that got her in a knot, or brought that faraway look to his eyes when he was watching her. No wishing she could sit down and tell him the truth. To say out loud that she wanted more from their relationship but was afraid to act on it for fear of hurting both of them, especially Rafe. To explain she could not give him what he deserved after how Cassie treated him, and still she wanted to try.

'I'll do my best.' He shrugged. 'You got anything planned for the day once you've had some sleep?'

'A second inspection of the apartment I'm renting.'

His face dropped. Had he not believed she'd move out? She'd thought he'd be only too happy when that day came. Seemed it wasn't only her who was all over the place in what they wanted.

Friday and the end of a particularly drama-filled week with patients. Raphael felt his body come alive at the thought of a free weekend ahead. What would he do with it? Spend time with Izzy when she wasn't working? Go and see where she was intending to move to. Visit the shops. There was quite a bit of shopping for kitchenware and furniture going on at the moment, and the landing on his second floor was filling up with packages and small cartons. Every time he walked past to his bedroom his heart slowed. She was definitely setting up her own home. Getting on with her life. He could learn from her. Find the courage to do the same.

Raphael let himself into the house and stopped. Paint fumes hit him. A foreign lightness in the hall made him gape. Wow. What a difference. Should've done it years ago. Except there'd been no motivation before. Izzy had changed everything.

She stood at the bottom of the stairs, dressed in over-large paint-spattered overalls with a roller in one hand and a wide grin on her face. A paint smear streaked across her cheek. Cute. Sexy. 'What do you think?'

I think I want to kiss that spot.

His stomach crunched, his blood hummed.

I think I want to kiss your soft lips and taste you.

Forget humming. There was a torrent in his veins. He was over waiting, being patient, giving her time. He had to do something about his feelings for her.

Dragging his eyes away from the sight that had him in meltdown, he looked around at the white with a hint of grey walls, woodwork, ceiling, and felt his mouth lifting into a smile that grew and grew. 'Amazing. Who'd have believed getting rid of that magenta could make such a difference. This hall is twice the size it was when I went to work this morning.'

'That's a relief.' She placed the roller in the clean tray.

'You were worried I wouldn't like it?' He stepped closer, put his keys and phone on the bottom stair and stood there watching the varying emotions flitting through her beautiful old-wood-coloured eyes.

'Not really.' Her teeth nibbling her lip told him otherwise.

He had to force himself not to reach over and place a finger on her lips to stop her action. 'Why wouldn't I? It was me who bought the paint two years ago.'

Izzy shifted her weight from one foot to the other, then lifted her head enough to lock those eyes on his. 'I worried I've overstepped the mark by doing this without telling you what I was up to.'

Izzy never worried about upsetting him. Carrying on with whatever *she* thought best was a trademark of their friendship, always had been, and was one of the reasons he adored her. Something was off centre here, and it frustrated him not knowing what that was. 'Relax. I'm more than happy with what you've done. In fact, I'm blown away.' He waved a hand at his new hall. 'This is amazing. It fires me up to get on with doing up the rest of the house.'

He hadn't noticed the tension in her shoulders until they softened, and a smile touched those lips. 'Thank you, Isabella.'

Her eyes widened and she glanced away, came back to lock eyes with him again. The tip of her tongue appeared at the corner of her mouth. 'Phew.'

Raphael could not stop himself. He reached out, placed his hands on her arms and drew her closer. 'Again, thanks. By doing this you've starting turning my house into a home and up until now I hadn't realised how important it is if I'm to continue living here and become ensconced in a London lifestyle, not just working at the hospital every available hour.'

She was shaking under his hands.

His thumbs smoothed circles on her arms. 'Izzy.'

Her breasts rose, stilled, dropped again. 'Rafe.'

Afterwards he didn't remember moving, couldn't recall anything but his mouth on hers at last. Soft. Sweet. Isabella. Strong, tough Izzy. Returning his kiss. Returning his kiss! She tasted of promise, of fun and love, of life. And then her tongue nudged past his into his mouth and the world stood still. While his body fizzed, the thudding behind his ribs frantic, his groin tightening, and tightening further. It felt like an out-of-body experience, yet his feet were firmly planted on the stair below her. His hands were holding Izzy's arms, now sliding around to bring her in close, closer, up against his body, chest to breast, her thighs against his groin, mouth to mouth. Kiss for kiss.

Yes. This was what he'd been waiting for. Izzy. She'd always been there, in his blood, his heart, but not like this. Until that day she married someone else and he woke up.

She moved, slid her mouth away, leaned back to stare up at him.

She'd better not have read his mind right then.

Her tongue was licking her bottom lip. Tasting him? Her throat bobbed. Her eyes were saucers, big, golden globes of heat and desire. 'Oh, Rafe,' she whispered through what sounded like need—for him.

His own need was pulsing throughout his body. 'Izzy? You all right? With this?' *Please, please, please say yes.*

A slow nod.

'I…' He hesitated. Talk too much and kill the moment. Don't explain where he was coming from and risk having her change her mind, and running for the hills. 'I want to be more than friends. Have for a long time now.'

Another nod. This time with a hint of concern darkening that golden gaze.

'You don't agree? I should stick to being friends?'

Raphael wants me.

Isabella wanted to let go her grip on his shoulders, to step back, take time to think this through. But if she removed her hands, couldn't feel him under her palms, she'd curl up and die. She wanted him. Yes, she was admitting it at last. She wanted Rafe. But that fear was still there, lurking at the edges of her mind. What if she failed him? What if it didn't work out? She'd lose the most important person in her life.

He was waiting. Patiently. Yet there was tension in his muscles. She felt it under her hands, saw it in his jaw, knew it in his eyes. Had he thought beyond this moment? Of course he would've. This was Raphael—

not Mr Spontaneity, not Mr Take-What-I-Can-Get-and-to-Hell-with-the-Consequences. Friends or lovers? She could not continue being neutral. Had to stop playing safe. Digging deep, she found it wasn't so hard to ask, 'Want to go upstairs?'

He lifted her off the stairs, held her against him. 'Thought you'd never ask.'

Slipping her arms around his neck she gazed at this man she'd always known and was now going to learn about in an entirely different way, and let go all the hang-ups, the questions, the need to be someone, and went with being who she was, who she had. Raphael. Nuzzling his neck, she smiled when his arms tightened around her as he carried her up to his bedroom.

He lay her on the bed.

Oh, no, you don't.

She leapt up, stood in front of him and reached for the first button on his shirt, slowly slid it through the buttonhole and leaned close to kiss the spot she'd revealed. Then the next button, and licked his skin, smiling when he groaned. The third button, and Rafe's hands skimmed down her back to clasp her butt.

The fourth button and her head was spinning with need.

Those strong hands were lifting her up against his erection. His manhood pressing into her belly. OMG.

The fifth and— She had to stop or this would be over before it got any further. She couldn't stop. Her whole body was crying out for release, yet she wanted so much more, wanted to touch all of him, every inch of skin. Forget the buttons. She jerked the shirt out of his waistband and pushed it up.

Rafe lifted his head enough for her to tug the annoying shirt off. Then she went back to kissing and licking that smooth skin, and absorbing the hits of sharp desire stabbing her belly, her breasts, her centre. Hands on her waist, then she was wobbling on her feet as the domes of the overalls were pulled open. The oversized boiler suit fell to her hips, then to the floor, unaided by Rafe's hands now intent on lifting her T-shirt and touching her—everywhere.

A groan slid across her swollen lips as his thumbs rubbed her nipples, arousing them further, tightening them into painful knobs of pulsing need. Her own hands were claws against Raphael, trying to caress while tightening further as the need in her deepened to the point she lost all comprehension of what was happening. 'Rafe. Please,' she begged. 'I can't take any more.'

Her bra hit the floor, her panties slid down to her ankles with the help of one of those hot hands. He quickly grabbed a small packet from the drawer beside the bed, tore the packet open and rolled the condom on. Then he was lifting her to his waist, turning around to lean her against the wall as she wound her legs around him. 'Izzy,' he growled.

His hot tip touched her centre.

She tried to reach for him, to hold him intimately.

Another throaty growl. 'Not yet. Won't last.' And he was filling her, giving to her.

Her head tipped back against the wall and she rocked with the need exploding throughout her body. 'Rafe,' she screamed.

Then with a guttural roar he took her, his body tense as he came.

They lay on his bed, legs and arms tangled, lungs working hard, eyes closed.

Wow. Isabella sighed. Never would've thought she could feel like this. As if she'd found something so special it might break if she wasn't careful.

'Don't go there, Isabella.'

See? He knew her too well. Rolling onto her tummy and sprawling half across him she eyeballed him. 'It's hard not to.'

He winced.

Immediately she lifted up to kiss him. 'I am not sorry.' Kiss. 'I'm mind-blown.' There was no comparison between her feelings for Raphael and those she'd believed she had for Darren.

A return kiss that lasted longer than hers to him, and started clouding the subject. 'That's two of us.'

There was so much she wanted to tell him. How she loved him, wanted to always be with him. But what if she did let him down? That was too awful to contemplate. She still didn't know if she'd got it right. Look what happened last time she told a man she loved him. Not that she was ready to utter the L word. Afraid to, more likely. Rolling onto her back as he got up to dispose of the condom in his bathroom, she stared up at the ceiling that was desperately in need of a coat of paint. 'Pinch me.'

He came back into the bedroom and lay back down next to her. 'Please don't say you're already regretting this.'

Reaching for his hand, she held on tight. 'Not at all. Why would I?' Hell, what if Rafe only wanted sex, and had no wish for a future with her? Hadn't thought of that, had she?

Raphael rose onto his elbow and gazed down at her. If she didn't know better she'd say that was love coming her way. But it couldn't be. Not the 'this is for ever, sexy, everything together' kind of love.

When he remained quiet, she had to ask, 'What?' Her heart smashed against her ribs as she waited for him to reply.

At last, 'Nothing.' That was it? Then he kissed her and her muscles loosened a little.

Wrapping her arms around his strong, muscular body, she pulled him into her. She'd hopped off the fence on the side of go for it, and was ready to give this everything she had. But not ready to talk about it. That might ruin everything.

Raphael gathered her into his arms and began making love to her like he had no intention of ever stopping. She could live with this for as long as it was on offer. Reality would step in some time, but for now she was safe from the demons that liked to wreak havoc with her dreams.

Raphael yawned. It was his turn not to sleep. How could he with Izzy wrapped around him like a limpet? A warm, soft one. Okay, not a limpet, but the best damned thing to have happened to him in a long time, if not in for ever.

Sensationnelle.

He'd poured years of emotions into his lovemaking during the night. Had he always loved her?

But if that were true, then he wouldn't have been so devastated by what Cassie had done to him.

He shivered. Slow down. Think it through. Last night had been amazing, but it didn't change anything. He and Izzy were still friends, and despite being intimate, that hadn't changed. Other than to put pressure on him to get it right. Big pressure. Izzy was vulnerable, still coming to terms with Darren's treachery. She didn't need him trying to get too close, too fast, and then finding he wasn't ready to commit to her either. Because he was still struggling to accept the loss of his child, and why. Especially the why. If he told Izzy about Joshua it might free some of the knots holding him back, but he didn't want her to see his vulnerability. That was saying he wasn't as tough as she believed him to be.

His body tightened, and not in the way it had often during the night as they made love. He had to tell her. It would be a lie not to. She was entitled to know everything, otherwise he would never be able ask her to become a part of his life when he was ready. If he was ever ready. *Thump, thump* went his heavy heart.

'Rafe?' Izzy muttered.

'Oui, mon amie?' Stick to friend, keep this real.

Her reply was a small snore.

So, not ready to talk. Thank goodness. He could continue the dream by lying here, holding her warm, sexy body against him, feeling her hot breaths on his skin, knowing she was relaxed with him as she hadn't been since she arrived. But this was Isabella. There'd be questions and concerns scooting round her mind about whether they were doing the right thing, how long this could last, was it for ever or a rerun of her marriage. Knowing her meant he was forewarned.

And this *was* Izzy. He couldn't hurt her in any way. He had to back off until he sorted out his mess. Had to. No other way to go forward. But how, now that he knew Izzy intimately?

How, when she was living in his house for another few weeks?

When he was going to the wedding with her?

Damn, he'd made the situation between them worse, not better.

CHAPTER EIGHT

OUT ON THE DECK, Isabella stretched onto her toes, leaned back to ease the rest of the kinks out of her muscles that a long soak under a hot shower hadn't fixed. What a night. What a lover Rafe had turned out to be. She'd never known sex to be so wonderful.

And then she'd slept like she hadn't in for ever. Right through to ten in the morning. Why? She'd have thought the excitement of making love with Raphael would've kept her awake all night, not knocked her out. Had she found her safe place with Rafe? No, couldn't have. Must've been because he'd exhausted her with his lovemaking. But she did feel different. Relaxed and happy.

Why wasn't he here? It had stung a little to wake up and find herself alone in his bed. He hadn't been downstairs when she made her way to the kitchen. There'd been a note saying he'd gone for a run and might go into work afterwards. As though putting distance between them. Was he regretting last night already?

Her heart sank. He wouldn't. He might.

Then what? She'd have to suck it up and get on with her plans of setting up the flat she was about to rent. She had to do that anyway. Just because they'd become lovers didn't mean she would change everything. She still had to make her own life work for her. Preferably including Raphael. But she was not going to follow him or anyone to do what they wanted without keeping herself true to herself. She'd messed up once. It wasn't happening again, if she could help it.

Her phone rang.

Rafe.

She snatched it up. 'Hey, good morning. Where are you? I didn't wake up for hours. I feel so good.' Shut up, let the man say why he rang.

'Could've set a bomb off and you wouldn't have woken. Guess I've got my uses, then.' He laughed.

'Seems like it.'

'Feel like going to the movies and dinner tonight?'

Pardon? 'As in a date?'

Silence. Then, 'Yes, a date.'

He could sound more enthusiastic. 'You sure that's what you want to do? I mean, if last night was a one-night stand say so.' Get the pain over with now.

'Yes, Isabella, I do want to take you out. And…'

She gritted her teeth. 'Go on.' He was about to break her heart.

'I don't want it to be a one-night stand.'

Phew.

Then, 'But I admit I'm uncertain where we're going with this.'

How about into a relationship that would blossom into love? 'We don't have to rush it, Rafe.' Her heart was squeezing painfully. 'I've got things to think about too.'

'I know. That's also what's holding me back. So, you still want to go out tonight?'

Did she? 'Yes, I do.' She could be setting herself up for a fall, but sometimes she had to take a chance.

'See you about six, then.' And he was gone.

She stared at her phone. Did that just happen? He hadn't said where he was. It was the weekend and he wasn't rostered on the ward but bet that's where he was. It was his bolt hole, she realised. Put a bed in a corner, and fill a cupboard with his clothes and he'd never come home. No wonder he hadn't got around to redecorating.

Chienne rubbed against her leg.

'Hey, you. At least I know where I'm at with you.' She lifted the cat onto her shoulder for a cuddle. 'I've got a date with your dad.'

A date meant dressing up in something decent. And if she wanted a repeat of last night whatever she chose to wear had better be more interesting than jeans and a shirt.

Raphael stared at the apparition in red standing in his lounge. *Sacré bleu.* This was Izzy? He could feel his heart exploding against his ribs, while his groin was tightening. 'I want to rush upstairs and tear that dress off you.' It had to be the sexiest dress he'd ever seen, and yet he wanted to remove it?

'That bad, huh?' She grinned.

'Oh, yes.' This had to stop or they'd never make it to the restaurant and as much as he wanted to make love with Izzy he was taking her on a proper date so they could calm down after last night. Put some perspective on things. Except she'd gone and raised the bar to impossible heights. Somehow he had to be strong, stop being diverted by a red ball of sex on amazing legs and ladder-high shoes. Reaching for her hand, he tugged her close and began walking to the front door, past the stairs that'd take them up to his bedroom. 'Let's get out of here while we're still capable.' Except her hand was soft, small in his, and adding to the need clawing through his body. So much for pulling back.

Hopefully the movie would be scintillating and he'd forget all about his companion. As if.

A couple of hours later Raphael had to admit it hadn't been too bad. He had forgotten Izzy enough for his body to quieten down. 'What did you think?'

'That I prefer romance movies to fantasy.'

'Got that wrong, didn't I?' He looked around. 'Let's give that bar a go. Or do you want to choose since I got the movie wrong?'

'There's good.' She wasn't sounding as excited as she had earlier.

Which might be good since he was trying to slow things down. 'Wine?'

'Please.' She found them a table in the back of the room and shuffled her cute butt onto a stool.

And his body went back to tightening and wanting. While his mind tried to deny everything.

In his pocket his personal phone vibrated. He ignored it. He shouldn't have brought it with him, but who knew when it might be needed in an emergency. For the first time in ages his hospital call phone was on the table at home since he wasn't on call. There were other specialists to cover his patients if the need arose. No one was interrupting them tonight.

'How is Grand'mère?' Izzy asked. 'Back on her bike yet?'

'Not quite. Or she's not admitting it if she is. I'd have to tell her off.'

'Yes, and she'd laugh at you, so no problem.'

'She rang today. She wants me to go home for a visit sometime soon.' He paused.

Izzy sipped her drink, her gaze fixed on him over the rim of the glass. 'To spend time with her? Or is there something else happening?'

Was this Izzy's way of asking did he still intend moving home one day? 'Only that she wants to catch up and it's easier for me to make the trip at the moment. She suggested you tag along too.'

'I'd love to.' Izzy was still watching him like she was looking for something more. Of course she was. She'd be thinking that if he was over Cassie enough to have a fling with her, then he could very well be ready enough to move back to France. She might be right, and how would she feel about that? Her growing excitement and determination to make London home would come down in a rush, sending her back to wondering if she could ever settle anywhere and be happy. She could relax on that score. He wasn't going to wreck her newfound happiness, even if that meant ruining his own before he got started.

Raphael gazed at Isabella, his mind stumped with the way he'd been blindsided with their lovemaking. He'd felt as though he'd found something he'd been looking for all his life. Yet it scared the pants off him. He wasn't ready. Might never be. But to walk away without trying might be beyond him. It might be too soon for Isabella as well. Not to mention the Joshua hurdle for him to get over. He'd never thought it would be so hard to tell Izzy. Sure, no one else knew either, but this was so much more important. It scared him to reveal the depth of his pain and anger. Holding on to those emotions was the one grip on keeping himself complete he had. Airing it might undo him so much that he'd never be the same again.

'Earth to Raphael.' Her warm hand covered his. 'Where have you gone?'

Quick, come up with something. 'Thinking about when we can manage to go over to Avignon together.' Together? He really wasn't keeping back from this, was he?

'We'll have to pick a weekend we're both off.'

'Of course.'

Their pizzas arrived, looking and smelling delicious. And tasting just as good.

Izzy asked, 'I know Grand'mère says she's getting out and about as though the hip operation never happened, but do you think she might've slowed down? Might be starting to think about the future in a different light?'

'I do. She says she's not ready to move out of the family home, and is thrilled Maman and Papa have moved in. As soon as she's getting around properly she'll take the downstairs rooms and save herself those horrendous stairs now that she's had a fall.'

'Bet she already thinks she's capable,' Izzy said, those golden eyes focused entirely on him. 'It's your family tradition for someone from each generation to live in the family house at some stage, isn't it?'

'*Oui.* Though my parents have taken a while to get there.'

'You haven't thought of skipping a generation and moving in yourself?'

Damn. Should've kept his mouth shut. 'Izzy.' He reached for her hand. 'I live here. I'm still not ready to return to Avignon.' *Please believe me.* Why should she when he didn't?

Tipping her head to one side, she studied him so intently she must've been able to see everything he was striving to keep to himself. As bumps lifted on his skin, she said, 'As long as you're sure. And happy.' Then she picked up a slab of pizza and ate so calmly that he struggled to believe she'd been any different moments ago.

If Isabella remained determined to make London home, then he might have to factor that into any decisions he made about his future. His heart slowed. He did want to return home one day. He also wanted to have Izzy in his future once he'd laid everything else to rest.

As soon as the pizza was finished, Izzy pushed her plate away and stood up. 'I'm ready to go home.' The gold returned to her brown eyes. 'I'm whacked.'

'You and me both.' Physically and mentally.

Isabella could feel her heart pounding on the quiet drive home. She couldn't make Rafe out. He was on edge, like he didn't want to be with her while at the same time he enjoyed her company.

What had changed since last night? Had he got cold feet? Raphael, Mr Confident, running scared? Couldn't be. Was he going to let her down too? Hardly. He hadn't made any promises about anything. Could be it had been a one-night fling. Except she couldn't accept that. They were too close for that. Or was that the problem? They were close and he was afraid they'd lose it all? *That* she could understand.

Pulling into the drive, he said, 'Thanks for the night. I enjoyed it.'

That was it?

'Me too.'

She shoved the door open and clambered out in an

ungainly fashion with her high heels. So not used to wearing anything so far off the ground. Making her way inside she waited by the front door until Raphael joined her.

'I might do some work on the computer,' he muttered, looking everywhere but at her.

Isabella placed her arms around his neck and leaned in against him, tipping back enough to look into his startled face. 'You really want to do that?'

'I think it's best.'

For who? She stretched up on her toes and placed her lips on his mouth.

His hands took her hips. To pull her forward? Or push her away?

She pressed her mouth over his, slid her tongue inside. Tasted him. Slipped out and back in.

'Izzy,' he groaned. 'Stop.' His hands tightened their hold of her, tugged gently so her stomach touched his need.

And he wanted her to stop? Try again, Rafe.

Now he was kissing her, possessing her, giving as much as she was offering him.

Pressing her peaked nipples against his chest sent ripples of desire racing through her, heating her body, fizzing her blood.

'Isabella.' Strong hands lifted her away, put space between them.

Isabella.

He was serious. 'Don't you dare say we can't do this. Not now,' she growled.

Not when I'm pulsing with need for you.

'You don't understand.'

'Damn right, I don't.'

'I can't promise you anything, Izzy.'

She relaxed at Izzy. 'I haven't asked you to.'

'I know.' He was still holding her. 'I might hurt you.'

True, and she might hurt him. 'I'm a big girl, Rafe. I'll take whatever happens on the chin.'

'Yes, but…'

She placed a finger over his mouth. 'But nothing, Raphael. Make love to me. Please.'

Those dark eyes locked on her, searching for what she had no idea. There was apprehension in his gaze, which was slowly replaced by excitement. 'If you're sure,' he said as he swung her up into his arms and carried her upstairs.

Very sure. If there were consequences, then she'd manage. It would hurt but she could not walk away from tonight.

Isabella looked through the window to the beautiful garden beyond where Carly and Adem's wedding ceremony would take place in a few minutes. She was so happy for her friend. She also couldn't help wondering if she and Raphael would ever get to this point. They'd had an amazing week, making love every night, but there was an obvious hesitation in his approach to her, as though he wasn't ready. Which he had kind of intimated on their date night. Well, she wasn't one hundred per cent ready either but she was up to giving it a chance by working hard to keep the doubt gremlins quiet, and believing in herself. The past was over, the doubts brought about by Darren finished with. But she wasn't here to think about that. This was Carly's day.

'Isn't this a gorgeous setting?' she said to Esther. The

gardens were colourful with roses and peonies and other flowers bright in the sunshine.

'Magic. And don't we all look swish in our silk dresses?'

'Not bad at all.' Raphael was standing with her friends' men, looking completely at ease. The moment Carly knew he was accompanying her to the wedding, he'd been told he'd be Isabella's escort when they stood with Carly and Adem as they exchanged their vows. What was he thinking? Would he ever want to get married again?

'Lily, no.' Esther grabbed Lily's hand before Carly's bouquet of blue flowers was destroyed. 'Come on. We'd better get this show happening before little miss here does something we'll all regret.'

'Group hug first,' Carly said as she approached them. She looked beautiful in her dress with her hair falling free over her shoulders, and a small baby bump beginning to show.

Tears threatened to spurt down Isabella's face. 'You look stunning. And so happy.'

The four women gathered close to hug, tears on everyone's faces. 'So much for the make-up,' Chloe laughed.

'Me.' Lily pulled at her mother's skirt. 'I want a hug.'

She got four, then Isabella, Chloe and Esther gathered around Carly to lead her out to the garden to get married.

The ceremony was short, spoke of love and commitment and had every female in the garden in tears. Glancing sideways at Raphael, panic struck. Here was a man she truly loved, with everything she had. Yet she couldn't celebrate. He wasn't showing signs of loving her back. What if she was doomed to another broken heart? This time would be far harder to get over than her previous mistake. Swallowing hard, she dragged in air to calm the banging in her chest. She could not get upset or worried today. Not when her girlfriend was celebrating finding the love of her life, and *she* was standing beside Raphael.

'Knew I'd need this.' Rafe handed her a handkerchief. 'Brand new, just for you.' His smile was soppy, like he too was feeling the love going on. And why wouldn't he be? There wasn't a soul in the garden who didn't look the same.

'Ta,' she sniffed, dabbing her nose and eyes, and doing her best not to mess up her make-up. Mascara under the eyes was such a great look. Except by the time Carly and Adem slid rings onto each other's fingers the make-up was long gone, and Raphael had passed her a second handkerchief, pocketing the first one, sodden and stained blue-black. When Adem leaned in to kiss Carly, Isabella clapped, hiding the sudden spike of jealousy.

'You're such a softie.' Rafe grinned, then blinked, looking away.

'And you're not?'

'Un peu.'

'Sure.'

A little? Underneath that serious specialist façade was an emotional man who was good at hiding his feelings when he felt they'd be used against him. She gave a little gasp. Was that the cause of his hesitation to talk about the future? He had something to hide?

Not now, Isabella.

True. She was wasting a wonderful occasion worrying about herself. Today wasn't about her. Or Raphael. 'Weddings do that some people.'

'Not me usually. But for some reason today feels extra

special.' He was looking into her eyes, right in, while smiling that sensitive, loving smile she adored.

What was he saying? 'It is.' She gave him back a smile. One that told him the words she hadn't managed to utter yet. *I love you.* 'There are weddings, and then there are other weddings. This is one of the best kind.'

Raphael's lips brushed her brow. 'You look beautiful, Izzy. Inside and out.'

'How many handkerchiefs did you bring?' she asked around a lump in her throat. Gone was her ability to fob off words she didn't know how to deal with by saying something witty or growly.

'It was a three-pack.' He stepped back and looked around the garden, suddenly very interested in the roses.

Great. She'd gone and lost him again. He was doing that more and more. She loved it when he kissed her. He made her feel cherished and at ease with her life. Yet all the time those doubts kept surfacing. How long was this going to last? Would they get more involved, or would he walk away? What did he want out of life?

An image of Raphael holding a baby in the maternity ward snapped into her head. Babies. He wanted a family. Still, there was a 'but' hanging around that he hadn't explained. And she still had to conquer her fear of letting him down. Drawing in a breath, she flipped from her worries to her friends. 'Right, I'm going to hug the bride.'

'I'm coming with you.'

Thought he might. 'Carly, I am so happy for you.' Isabella wound her arms around her friend.'

'You're next,' Carly whispered against her.

Her happiness plummeted. Don't say that. Might be

tempting fate. 'Oh, that's a long way away off. I'm just enjoying the sex,' she whispered back.

Carly pulled back, stared at her in astonishment. 'You're not certain this will come to anything?'

'Just being cautious, that's all. Now I need to give Adem a hug.' And shut Carly down. She moved sideways to the bridegroom. 'Adem, congratulations. You look beyond happy.'

'I am, Isabella. Way beyond.' He wrapped her up in a hug, then turned to shake Raphael's hand. 'Right, can we get a drink now? Or do I have to abstain all afternoon?'

'Let's go inside. There's cocktails for everyone, and the dinner will also be in there.' Carly was waving to someone else, and when Isabella turned she saw Chloe and Esther coming their way.

'We're heading inside,' she told them.

'Good idea,' Esther said, nodding at the greying sky. 'It's chilled down a little out here, and doesn't look like improving. These dresses are amazing but they're not made for warmth.'

'Off the shoulder leaves a lot of bare skin,' Isabella agreed. Checking that Raphael was still talking to Adem, she saw that Xander and Harry had joined them, and more handshakes and stiff male hugs were going on. The four men got on very well, which made it easier for her and the other women. Nothing worse than a partner who didn't fit in with your circle of friends. Isabella spied Lily about to step into the garden and went to take her hand and head inside. 'Do you want something yummy to eat?'

'Chocolate?'

'Maybe later. How about some little cheese bickies first?'

'Will I like them?'

'We'll get some and find out.' All the other guests were now inside the understated room that spoke of class, and accepting the glasses of champagne being handed around. Izzy grinned. 'Just like old times.'

'What? Us together?' Chloe nodded. 'It is, isn't it?'

'I'm hungry,' Carly said. 'I was too nervous before the wedding, and the baby needs food.'

Isabella agreed. 'I'll bring one of those of hors-d'oeuvre plates over from the table.'

The day disappeared into evening while they ate dinner and drank toasts, and people made speeches, and had a wonderful time. Then Adem stood up and placed his hand on his wife's elbow to bring her up beside him. 'Thank you for sharing our special day, everyone. But now, we're going to leave you and head to our hotel.'

Everything wrapped quickly after the newlyweds left.

'Ready to hit the road?' Raphael asked.

'I guess. We're all done here.' Suddenly she didn't want to go back to the house and find out if Rafe was going to make love to her or if tonight was one he said he had work to do. Like he had twice last week. 'Or we could go clubbing.'

He shook his head. 'Not me. I'm more than ready to hit the sack.'

With or without me?

'Fine. Let's go.'

'Isabella, I'm sorry if I've let you down.'

She sighed. 'It's all right. Really. I'm feeling a little deflated after such a wonderful wedding, that's all.'

The ride was so slow and yet sped by. Isabella couldn't wait to get out of the car yet didn't want to stop. She couldn't face being turned down by Raphael heading to his office to work. As if he really had any that needed dealing with tonight. Was this when she stepped up? Put her feelings out there? Let him know she wanted more, not less? Her chest ached with the pounding going on behind her ribs. *Be strong, be brave.*

The moment Raphael shut them in the house she turned to him, reaching her arms up and around his neck.

He tensed. 'Isabella.' Never a good sign when he used her full name.

'You're not working tonight.' Then she stretched up to kiss him, long and hard, and he kissed her back, demanding, giving, sensual.

Yes. She smiled under his mouth, and ran her hands down his back and under his jacket. Tugged his shirt free, touched his skin with her fingertips, absorbed his groans through their kiss. Yes.

Raphael pulled away, stared down at her. 'Izzy.' Better than Isabella.

She put her finger on his mouth. 'Don't say a word.' Then she pushed his jacket down his arms and let it drop to the floor. The shirt was next, and then his belt and fly and his trousers landed around his feet.

Raphael stepped out of them, and waited, his reaction to her obvious and large in his boxers.

Afraid he might still change his mind, she kissed him, slowly, while she touched him, rubbed the head of his erection. Arousing him further. And then she was lifting her leg around his waist, trying to wrap herself around him. She wanted him. Now. Hard. Fast. Satisfying.

Raphael moved, took her around the waist, lifted her into his arms and charged upstairs to his bedroom, his manhood knocking against her butt.

What was wrong with where they were? She didn't ask. With her finger she teased his nipple, made it peak and him cry out. Then they were on the bed and she was tugging her panties off and tossing them aside. Raphael pulled her dress up to her waist and bent down to lick her.

'No. Now. You, me, together.'

He quickly sheathed himself, then rose above her and thrust into her. Hard and fast. She cried out and pushed up towards him to take him again.

It was over almost before they started. She'd been desperate to make love to him. To show him how she felt.

Isabella fell back against the pillow, her breast rising and falling rapidly.

Raphael sprawled out beside her, and draped an arm over her waist.

'Rafe.'

'Shh...don't say anything.'

She stared up at the ceiling, seeing nothing in the dark. He didn't want to talk. *She* wanted to tell him she loved him, but the words kept getting stuck in her throat. She still didn't quite trust herself to be one hundred per cent certain she loved him, and at the same time she did. That was the trouble. She knew, bone deep, he was the only man for her. But she still needed to know that these feelings weren't about settling down and making the life she'd craved since she was a kid. She'd done it once, had truly believed it was right, that her love had been for Darren and not just that picture, and she couldn't have been more wrong.

Raphael listened to Izzy's breathing as she slowly got her breath back. Did that really just happen? She'd been like a wildcat, taking him without preamble, turning him on so fast he'd hardly kept up. He'd tried to slow down, but she wasn't having it.

Hell, he'd tried to avoid going to bed with her altogether. After seeing the sadness lurking in her eyes as she witnessed her friend's betrothal he'd known he had to stop leading her on. Not that he was deliberately playing with her, but he didn't think he could promise her what she so desperately wanted—a for ever love, marriage and children. Yes, he had been moving on from Cassie a lot faster now, and believed she was history. She'd left him, and that was that.

As for Joshua, he had a way to go on that, and probably would never completely get over the pain. But before he could move forward he had to tell Isabella, and then his family. And he just wasn't sure how to do it. It meant exposing his heart, his vulnerabilities. Izzy knew him well, but still. It wasn't easy. He'd never talked much about the things that mattered, had kept them in wrappers so no one could use them against him.

Tell her now.

She wasn't sleeping. Her breathing had returned to normal, wide awake normal. He opened his mouth. Closed it. No. Not yet. He rolled away, stretched the length of the bed and prepared to wait the night out.

At last Raphael's breathing deepened.

Isabella carefully slid out of bed and crept out of the room. In the bathroom she took a short shower, then dressed in track pants and a sweatshirt before heading downstairs where the crossword book lay on the bench. She was done with trying to sleep, and with thinking about her and Raphael. There were no answers at the moment.

The sky was beginning to lighten and the birds were waking up, chirping happily, lucky things. Her body ached. Her heart was heavy. Her head pounded. Despite the number of times she'd not known what to do with her life, she'd never felt quite this bad.

A phone began ringing. Raphael's tune. Looking around, she couldn't see it. Listening harder, she followed the sound out to the hallway and his jacket. As she removed it from the pocket the ringing stopped.

At least it won't be work, she thought.

It rang again.

Raphael's mother's name showed on the screen.

'*Bonjour*, this is Isabella.'

'Is Raphael there?' Celeste sounded stressed.

'He's up in his bedroom. Hold on, and I'll run up there.'

'Izzy? Who is it?' Raphael appeared at the top of the stairs.

'Your mother.'

He jogged down and took the phone. 'Maman, what's happened?'

Izzy held her breath as she blatantly listened to Rafe's side of the conversation.

'When did that happen? During the night?' Rafe looked to her and held the phone away from his ear. 'Grand'mère's in hospital. Fell down the stairs. Again.' He put the phone back to his ear. 'Maman, what are her injuries? Are they serious?'

Izzy reached for his free hand and gripped it. 'Is she going to be all right?' Grateful she understood French,

Izzy stayed still, and waited. Fingers crossed nothing too serious had happened.

'She broke her other hip? And her femur?' Raphael looked shocked. 'And she's unconscious?'

This did not sound good. Raphael had to go home and see his grandmother, as soon as possible. Isabella headed for the kitchen and her phone, tugging Raphael along with her. Typing in London to Avignon on her airline app, she waited for the flights to come up.

'Being in a coma is worse than broken bones.' Raphael shoved a hand through his thick hair, his gaze clouded with worry. '*Oui*. I'll come as soon as I can. Yes, today if possible.'

Isabella tapped his shoulder, said, 'There's a flight at 5:45 out of Heathrow.'

He raised his thumb. 'Maman, Izzy's on to it already. I'll send the details as soon as I have them.' His phone clattered onto the bench. He did the fingers through his hair thing again, while reaching out to her with his other hand. 'You heard? She's in a coma after falling down the stairs going down to her room, which she's not meant to be using yet. Stubborn old lady.'

'I know those steps. None too forgiving for old bones. Or her head.' Grand'mère was strong but still. Who knew what the outcome would be?

'I need to see for myself, find out all the details from the doctors. Let me look at that flight.' Moments later, 'Yes, I'll take it. But I'd better talk to someone on the ward first, make sure they can cover for me for a couple of days at least. Not that I'm not going to Avignon.'

'You do that while I fill in your details here.' She paused, drew a breath. Now was not the time to be sulking over their relationship. 'Would you like me to come with you?'

He hesitated, locking his eyes with hers, then nodded. 'Yes. I would, very much. *Merci beaucoup*, Izzy.'

Raphael stood staring out the window, his shoulders tight, his back straight, as he talked to two different specialists about his patients. 'Thanks, Jerome. I'll call as soon as I know what's what over there. Won't be until tomorrow though, as I don't touch down until somewhere around ten tonight.'

'You wouldn't have your passport number on your phone by any chance?' Isabella asked as soon as he'd finished his calls.

Tap, tap. 'Here. And here's my bank card. Thanks, Izzy. You're a champ.' He was rubbing her neck as he watched over her shoulder as she finalised their bookings for one-way flights. 'Sorry about this.'

'Hey.' She twisted around on the stool. 'Don't apologise.' This could be good for them. Time together dealing with Grand'mère's accident and learning what the consequences would be. Serious compared to fun. Real life. And she'd be able to see for herself how determined he was to return to Avignon in the future, because not even Raphael would be able to hide the longing if it was what he wanted.

Leaning over, he brushed his lips across her brow. 'You're sure you don't mind coming?'

'Absolutely. That's what friends are for.'

He stared at her. 'Of course.' Then he turned away. 'I'll go and pack.'

CHAPTER NINE

'OH, GRAND'MÈRE, LOOK at you,' Rafe croaked around a throat full of tears the next day. 'Is she going to be all right?' he asked the hovering consultant.

Isabella reached for his hand, and held tight. She might be a nurse, but the sight of his grandmother's colourless face and her long, dark grey hair a knotted mess on the white pillow had shocked her.

'What to say? She's in a coma. Sadly.' The older man lifted a shoulder. 'There've been no signs of her coming out of it yet.'

'What about the fractures?' Raphael and the consultant got into a discussion about injuries and treatment.

Izzy extracted her hand and leaned over the rail that had been put up around the bed in case Grand'mère managed to move and fall off the bed. She reached for one of the cold, thin and wrinkled hands on top of the sheet. 'Hello, Grand'mère. It's Isabella.' Her heart sank. This accident could change Grand'mère's life for ever. But that was getting ahead of things. 'I haven't seen you for years. Raphael and I were talking about coming to see you as soon as we both had the same days off from the ward, but seems you beat us to it, got us hurrying across.'

Not a blink. No movement. The hand lay limp in hers.

She rubbed her thumb back and forth over the cold skin on the back of Grand'mère's hand.

Rafe's hand gripped her shoulder. 'I'm staying here for a while. I don't want to leave her on her own. Silly, I know, but I can't help it.'

'Rafe, it's okay. You're only feeling what most people do in these situations. Useless, and worried. Your doctor hat is no help to you in this case. In fact, it's worse because you know all the things that can go wrong.' He'd have a mental list scrolling through his mind non-stop.

'Don't pull any punches, will you?' he grunted. 'But you're right. I'm a doctor with no role to play here.'

'Yes, you do. Grand'mère will want you giving her cheek and telling her to hurry and wake up. That's your job here. We can go back to the house for some sleep later.' They'd got very little last night by the time they'd landed in Avignon and then sat up talking with his parents. Nor had they the previous night, trying out that bed in various ways. At least when she went to bed to sleep she did actually sleep now. Had been since the first night with Rafe. It gave her a sense of knowing she was doing the right thing by staying with him, and believing they could make a go of this.

'Couldn't get two more different nights if I tried.' Seemed he could still read her mind even when distressed. Better remember that.

She glanced up at him. 'Know which one I'd prefer.'

Some of the gloom had lifted and he sounded a little more relaxed. 'Me too. Thanks for being here. It means everything. I don't feel so alone.'

Raphael wasn't alone. There was a large family in the city and surrounds. 'Don't get all sentimental on me, Rafe, or I'll have to paint your bedroom orange when I get back to London.' His least favourite colour by a long shot.

'Ha. When you've finished there you could come over here and do up the family house. Despite everything going on, I couldn't help but notice how tired and dated it is, and instantly I was thinking you would turn this into something special.'

Except I live in London. Not Avignon.

'What? Because I painted one hall, I'm a decorator extraordinaire now?' Was this where his thoughts were heading? Was he already considering moving back now that his grandmother might need him? Where would that leave her? Back in London where she had stated categorically her intention of living permanently, or moving to France on yet another attempt to stop and settle down? *Whoa. Slow down.* Just like the long-term future plans, she hadn't started on settling into her flat yet.

And don't forget you wanted to know what his thoughts were on moving.

'I've never seen her looking so frail and old, Izzy. It's a reality check. She's getting older by the week.'

Nothing to say to that, so Isabella reached for his hand again and held him.

'Even once she's out of the coma, it's going to take time and patience for her to get back on her feet. I'm not sure how well she'll cope either. Her bones are fragile, and healing takes so much longer at eighty-five.'

He wasn't even considering she might not regain consciousness. Isabella liked his determined positivity. 'Nor is she known for her patience.'

'True. But what worries me most is that her confidence will have been knocked badly. I've seen it happen often enough in the elderly to expect it, but this is Grand'mère. You know what I mean?'

'Yes, Rafe, I do. She's special to you, and this is the last thing you want for her.' He'd have pictured her always being there in his life, even when that wasn't possible. '*I'm* struggling with the idea of her not getting around, bossing everyone she meets, while listening to people when they needed an ear to bend.'

'It'll be a role reversal. Strange, but only a few weeks ago she was telling me that if anything happened to her she did not want to go into a rest home. Apparently those are for old people.'

'I'm surprised she was even thinking about it. Like she'd had a premonition.' Grand'mère was a person who knew exactly what she wanted and did everything to make it happen. 'Did she say where she'd like to go?'

'She'll stay downstairs as previous generations have, and if necessary we can employ full-time care, though that won't be fun for the nurses.'

'I see.'

They pulled up chairs and sat with his grandmother for another hour when Raphael suddenly stood up and stretched. 'Let's go for a walk through the city.'

'Some fresh air would be good.' She tapped the back of his grandmother's hand. 'We'll come back soon.'

Inside the wall the city was busy with locals and tourists crowding the streets and cafés. Isabella wandered beside Raphael, taking in the sights and scents, looking at the ancient stone walls. 'It's wonderful.'

'Coffee?' Raphael indicated a vacant table on the side of the street.

'Please. Then can we stroll through the market? I want to smell the spices.'

'I remember how you spent hours in there, buying spices that I bet you never used.' Rafe smiled and pulled out a chair for her before heading over to place their order. Then he took his phone out of his pocket and punched some numbers before wandering to the side of the café. Who was he talking to?

Isabella tried not to watch him, instead looking around at the people taking their time to walk the street, laughing, talking, pointing at buildings. Yes, she remembered that feeling of wonder the first time she visited Avignon. It was still there, making her happy when she should be worrying about Grand'mère, but there was nothing she could do for her, so might as well make the most of time spent in the city.

When Raphael finally returned he held two cups of coffee in one hand. 'I need to stay here for a few days at least, maybe more than this week.' He cleared his throat. 'I've just talked to my colleagues and they're more than happy to cover for me for as long as I need.'

Talked to them before her? She supposed it made sense to get his priorities right. But still. 'You have to do what you feel is right for Grand'mère. After all, she's always been there for you.'

'I'm glad you understand.'

That stung. 'Why wouldn't I?' Her voice was sharper than she intended.

'Izzy. Sorry. I don't want to upset you. I know you have to go back tomorrow, and I'll miss you. You're a great support.'

'You say the nicest things when you're trying to dig yourself out of a hole, Raphael Dubois.'

'Did it work?'

As quickly as that they were back on even ground.

The tension that had begun tightening her belly backed off. 'You know it did.' Being here, seeing Grand'mère, had created a new depth of understanding, sharing, helping one another. Rafe needed her to be strong and there for him. Not crashing at the first hurdle. If she got too lonely she'd get over herself, or come back here on her days off.

'Adele wants to discuss things with me tonight.'

'Things? Like what?'

'Family stuff.'

That was putting her in her place. Seemed she wasn't getting as close to him as she'd hoped. He was gazing round the area, smiling in a way she wasn't familiar with, almost as though he was at home. Guess he was. He knew these streets like the back of his hand, having spent most of his early childhood here before his family moved to Geneva.

That was what she wanted, only in London. With Raphael. Was she expecting too much? Draining her coffee, she stood up. 'I'm going to the market. I'm going to get some pastries and cheeses. Coming?'

'Yes.' He looked baffled. 'Why wouldn't I?'

She didn't have an answer. 'Tell me what I can get for your mother for tonight's dinner.' Adele wasn't the only one coming. All the Dubois family would be there.

'Maman will have everything sorted, believe me.'

'Then I'll buy flowers,' she said as they entered the Halles d'Avignon and breathed in spices and coffee and freshly baked bread.

'Leave those until we've finished wandering around or they'll be bruised from bumping into people by the time we're done in here.' There was a deep happiness in Raphael's voice that had been missing for a long time.

Isabella felt her heart drop. Not even their hot nights had brought that on so strongly. He really belonged here, and now he was starting to look around and see what he'd been missing out on all because he'd been so stubborn.

The buzz around the family dinner table later that night only increased Isabella's unease. Despite the reason for Raphael coming home everyone was laughing and talking non-stop and Rafe was right in the thick of it.

'Izzy, have some more beef. I know it's your favourite.' He didn't wait for her reply, just spooned more of the delicious stew onto her plate.

'Give her a break,' Adele laughed. 'You'll be frightening her away if you keep doing that.'

She wasn't staying long anyway. Swallowing hard, Isabella smiled and tried to relax. It wasn't easy when Raphael was enjoying himself so much. Of course she was happy for him, but with each passing hour she had to wonder if he'd ever get around to going back to London. He would. He had a job that he relished there, a home and a cat. But he belonged here too.

Raphael wound his arms around Izzy and cuddled her against his naked length as they lay in bed in his old bedroom from when he was a teen and where he stayed whenever in Avignon. It had been a bit awkward last night when they headed to bed. Maman had prepared another room for Izzy. He hadn't wanted that. He needed her with him at the moment. Selfish, maybe, but she'd come to support him, and he was grateful.

The sun was up, and he was ready to get out. 'Want to walk into the city and have breakfast by the bridge?'

She tossed the sheet aside and sat up, letting his arms slip away. 'Let's go.'

'Mind if we visit Grand'mère on the way?'

'Of course not. She's why we're here.'

Something wasn't right with Isabella, hadn't been since they arrived in Avignon on Sunday night. 'Talk to me.'

She sank her naked derriere onto the side of the bed and faced him. There was a sadness in her eyes he didn't like. 'Your family ties were strong, and couldn't be more different to mine. You are so lucky.'

Rafe nodded. 'I'm starting to think that.' Then he looked closer and felt like he'd been punched in the gut. 'You can be a part of it too, Izzy. They adore you.' Everyone had jostled for her attention last night at dinner. They'd never been like that with Cassie.

'I was made to feel special,' she admitted, still looking directly at him.

'Then what's the problem?'

'I don't know where we're going with our relationship.' She seemed to let go of some knot inside her as those words slid out of her mouth. 'Do you?'

Crunch time. He sat up fast. This wasn't how he wanted to tell her, nor where. But maybe he should just get it out of the way. Reaching for the water bottle by the bed, he tried to drink down some fluid and moisten his suddenly dry mouth, but his throat wasn't playing the game. His gut was churning. His head was banging. His heart had a whole new rhythm going on.

Izzy was watching him closely, concern filling her eyes. 'Rafe? You're frightening me.' Then she leapt up, strode across to stare out the window. 'Talk to me.'

If there was anyone he'd tell it would be Isabella. He

had to tell her. She knew so much about him, what was one more thing? Except this was huge. But if he wanted to banish that despair in her face he had no choice. Because he just couldn't put his story away and pretend nothing was wrong. For one, Izzy already knew there was something wrong, and for two, he had to be honest more than anything. Tell Izzy. Don't tell Izzy.

'I am a father.'

Her fingers tightened around her elbows as she turned to stare at him through wide-open eyes, but still she said nothing.

Am a father? Was a father? What was the protocol? Who cared? It was about his feelings. No one else's. 'Joshua. He died of SIDS at eight days old.'

Then she moved, came and sat beside him, reaching for his shaking hands. 'Oh, Rafe.' His name dragged across her shaky bottom lip. 'Raphael, I am so sorry.'

Don't show me pity. I'll fall apart.

And it would take for ever to get the pieces back together again. 'Cassie didn't tell me she was pregnant when she left me and returned to Los Angeles.'

'You didn't know?' Horror filled Izzy's face.

'No. All I knew was she went back for auditions in the movie industry. She was going to become the next big name in movies. Oh, and I was a stubborn bore who wouldn't move to Paris so she could have fun in the greatest city in the world.' Not that she'd ever shown any acting aptitude when he'd known her, except to pull off huge lies. And being pregnant hadn't helped her chances of getting her first break, something she'd told him was his fault.

'I didn't find out until two years later. We hadn't

communicated since she left France so I went over to see her, wanting to find closure. I couldn't wrap it up.'

'And you got the opposite,' Izzy whispered.

'I never met my son. Didn't know he existed until it was too late. Never held him, kissed him, hugged him. He didn't know I existed.' Raphael stared down at the floor. Hot tears slid down his face, dripped off his chin onto his chest. He did nothing about them. 'How could she do that to me?'

Warm arms wound around his back, tugged him close to Isabella's soft body. Her hands rubbed slow circles on his skin, her mouth brushed feather-light kisses on his neck.

'Did she hate me that much?'

'Cassie was always very selfish.'

'True. But she went beyond the realm of selfish into something so deep and hideous I can't believe it.'

Izzy tipped her head back to lock her troubled gaze with his. 'Have you talked to your family about it?'

'You're the only person I've told. I have been arguing with myself for days now over whether to say anything or to carry on as though it hadn't happened. But you deserve better than that.'

'Thank you.' With her thumb she wiped his damp cheeks. 'Is this why you've stayed away from your family?'

He nodded abruptly. 'They already disliked Cassie, they'd hate her if they knew this. And I'd always feel their wrath. It's not something they'd let go in a hurry, if at all. Also...' He breathed deep. 'I feel bad for the things she used to say about them to their faces. I made a monumental error when I fell in love with her, and I don't like seeing that in their faces every time I'm with them.'

'I think you're overreacting. Your family loves you, and that's what matters. I doubt they judge you for making a mistake. Who doesn't at some time of their life? More often than once.'

'Hell, Izzy, you're amazing. I've been dreading telling you and here you are being sensible about it all.' He really did love her, and now he'd cleared the way to follow through with that. But not now. She might think he was using her sympathy.

She leaned in to kiss him. 'Tell your parents. They'll understand.'

'It'd be cruel to tell them they were grandparents and didn't get the opportunity to be a part of Joshua's short life.' He couldn't do that to them. It was still so painful for him.

'They're tougher than you're giving them credit for, Rafe.' Izzy stood up. 'I'm going for a quick shower and then let's go see Grand'mère. You could practise on her, since she won't hear you.'

'Oh, right.' From somewhere deep inside, he found her a smile. 'Should've told you a long time ago.'

'Yes, Rafe, you should've.'

He reached for her hands, was shocked to feel them shaking too. Anger? Sadness? Knowing Izzy, it would be a combination of a lot of emotions—all for him. 'I was afraid that if I opened up and told you I'd never be able to get myself under control again.'

'And now?'

His heart slowed, but a weight had gone from it. 'I think I'm going to make it.'

Isabella wandered through the old city centre to the Halles d'Avignon again, Raphael beside her deep in thought. Not surprising after what he'd revealed earlier. She was still trying to get her head around it. They passed people eating on the sidewalk and today her mouth didn't water as the smell of a fresh croissant and piping hot coffee reached her nose from the endless cafés.

How could Cassie have done something so cruel? Unbelievable. She'd stolen his chance of knowing his child, of knowing he had been a father. He still was a father. Along with that she'd turned him away from the very people who could've supported him through the pain and grief. Including her. He'd said he was afraid to let the pain out, for fear it would grow and spread. She understood that.

They reached the market and she hesitated. Not even the spices of every variety at the market could distract her. Glancing at Rafe she saw him smile ever so slightly, despite the heaviness on his heart. This was something he missed in London. But then he was French. And this was France. Home. He could live here all too easily. If he told his parents about Joshua. He had to. She knew that, probably better than he did, because until he did it would still be hanging over him, affecting everything he decided to do.

'Come on. I promised you breakfast and you can't back out on me now.' He leaned in to kiss her cheek.

She nodded, afraid to speak in case she told him that she understood him better than he realised, probably better than he did at the moment. He would front up to his family with the truth, and then… Yeah, and then… She couldn't put it into words. It hurt too much.

The pastry was dry on her tongue and the coffee ordinary. Finally she pushed her plate aside and watched

Raphael. She loved him so much, and still couldn't find the courage to tell him.

'Come on, I'll buy you some Camembert and bleu d'Auvergne to take when you go home.'

'My favourite cheeses,' she agreed. Hopefully her appetite returned to enjoy them. 'Let's go.' Suddenly impatient to be moving she leapt up. 'I'd like to visit Grand'mère once more today.' Rafe's grandmother was still in a coma, though when they called in before coming here the doctor said she was responding a little to touch sometimes.

'I hope she has heard you talking to her. You hold a special place in her heart, as her lost Kiwi.'

Isabella felt her eyes tearing up. 'She's always been welcoming and kind to me. Even when I was a bumptious teen.'

'I think that's why she likes you. You don't take any nonsense from anyone.' Raphael's arm wrapped around her shoulders and he drew her against his side as they ducked around people to reach the cheese stall. 'Let loose, pick whatever you want.' He didn't let go of her as she chattered away to the woman behind the counter, nor when he handed over money to pay for her choices, nor as they walked back to the hospital.

She was glad, needing him, wanting him to want her.

'No change,' a nurse told them as they walked past the desk in Grand'mère's ward.

'To be expected,' Rafe said, though she could hear his despair.

'Gives you the opportunity to tell her what you don't want her to hear.'

Raphael stopped still, right in the middle of the corridor, and turned to face her. His gaze was serious and her heart lurched. She knew what was coming.

'You were right. I do need to tell the family about Joshua. I'll do it this afternoon.'

Reaching up on her toes, she brushed a kiss across his mouth. 'I'm proud of you.'

And I love you, but that's for another day.

The next morning Raphael bounced out of bed and into the shower at seven o'clock.

'Look at you, bouncing around like a kangaroo.' Izzy groaned. 'Some of us still need our sleep.'

'I had the best night in ages,' he told her. 'Slept right through. You were right. Telling Maman and Papa about Joshua was the right thing to do. I feel like a huge weight has been lifted from my heart.'

'Good. Sometimes I'm not so silly after all.'

'I'm going in to see Grand'mère and tell her, even if she is still unconscious. She'll probably wake up telling the world my story.'

'Then I'll stay here and have a lie-in.'

'See you later, then. I'll take you to the airport about two. How does that sound?'

'Awful. I don't want to go home yet.' What she really didn't want was to leave Raphael. It had been good spending time here with him, and joining his family.

'Sound like you mean it, will you?' Didn't he want her to go either?

She laughed. 'Say hello to Grand'mère for me.'

An hour later she rolled out of bed and into the shower before going to make a coffee and sit on the terrace overlooking the edge of the city and the Rhône beyond. It was beautiful with all the stonework and the wall that surrounded the city. But it wasn't home. That was London. She had to keep believing that or she'd be back at the beginning, not knowing where she was headed.

'Morning, Isabella.' Raphael's mother stepped onto the deck, a cup of coffee in hand. 'Beautiful morning, *oui*?'

'Stunning.'

'Where's Raphael?'

'He's gone into the hospital to see Grand'mère.'

'I can't believe what that woman did to him.' Celeste sat down beside her. 'It is cruel. He'll always wonder what his boy looked like.'

'Yes, he will.' It was the most hideous thing someone could do, and Cassie had once loved Raphael. Had that not counted for anything?

'It's good that he told us. We can understand why he's stayed away now. Not that he should've. We'd always support him.'

'I think he knows that.'

Celeste sipped her coffee and stared out over the balustrade. 'And what about you, Isabella? You're settling into London?'

'Yes, I am. I can't wait to move into my flat and start putting my own mark on it.'

'How long do you think you'll be there?'

Hello? What was this about? 'Long term.'

'I see.'

Isabella's stomach cramped. What did she see? 'Do you? It's been a long time since I've stopped in one place, and never for ever. I need to do this.'

'What about Raphael?'

'What about him?' The cramps turned to hard squeezing. Her heart began racing.

'He belongs here, Isabella. With his family. He misses Avignon and all of us, especially Grand'mère.'

She couldn't argue with that. 'He does.'

Now Celeste turned to face her. 'Thank you for understanding.' Then she got up and headed inside.

Leaving Isabella stunned. Of course his family would want him to return home. Face it, so did Raphael. It was her who had to either change her mind about where she'd live or give up on any thoughts of getting together with Rafe. Not that he was actively encouraging them. She was hanging her hope on the fact he hadn't stopped having sex with her. It had to mean something, didn't it? Or was she being naïve?

Damn it. She couldn't sit around here waiting for him to return from the hospital. She'd go for a walk.

But not even the stunning views of the river and city from the old fort could distract her. She felt as though she was walking in quicksand, getting deeper and deeper without any sign of a way out. She'd fallen for Raphael so hard she literally didn't know what to do with herself. To give up her own goals to follow him wherever he chose to live would be easier than fighting for what she wanted. But giving up her own dreams after finally starting to realise them was not being true to herself. But hey, she was getting way ahead of herself. He wasn't exactly reciprocating her love.

When Raphael stepped through the front door he heard voices coming from the lounge and headed towards them.

'Raphael, you remember Louis Fournier? From the hospital,' Papa said as he entered the room.

He put his hand out to shake the older man's. *'Bon-*

jour, Docteur.' From the smug look on his face, Papa was up to something. 'It's been a while since I talked to you.'

'It has. I've been keeping up with your career through your father though. You've done well.'

'Thank you. I've worked hard to get where I am, for sure. So what brings you out here?'

'Louis has some news for you.'

'I see,' said Rafe. But he didn't. Though he was beginning to suspect where this might be heading. 'Let's sit out in the conservatory.' There he'd be able to look out over the houses and the fort as he listened to what this man was about to say. He'd be able to see his hometown and think about a future here, compare it to what he had in London.

'I'll come straight to the point,' Louis said. 'There's a position for a gynaecologist coming up at the general hospital. I wondered if you might be interested.'

'Yes, definitely.' His heart rate sped up. Of course he was. His lifelong dream to practise medicine here was falling into place.

Izzy.

He couldn't walk away from her now. It was the only thing he was certain about. She'd been the one to convince him to talk about Joshua to his family. She'd come here with him when he was so worried about Grand'mère. She wasn't Cassie. He'd have to convince her she could start over—again—when he'd spent the last few weeks helping her realise she was where she really wanted to be. No, he couldn't do that to her.

Raphael closed his eyes, breathed deep, searching for answers. Found none. Or far too many. Look out for Izzy, the love of his heart? Or follow his own dreams and hope she'd tag along? No. He'd never ask that of her.

Nor did he want to give up this opportunity in Avignon where his family was. For the first time in years he was ready to live where he belonged. If he could figure out a way to keep everyone happy.

'So? What do you think?' Papa was back. 'Couldn't be better timing, eh?'

Oh, yes, it could. Damn it. He wanted to take it up. Desperately. *So do it.* Inside, his heart was cracking. Half for Izzy, half for Avignon. This couldn't be happening. But it was. Yet he'd never felt quite so strongly about returning here until now. Grand'mère's accident had brought home to him that if he was to spend time with his family, now was it. 'How soon do you need a decision?'

'Why don't we go in now and I can show you around, introduce you to our team, give you a general idea of how we run things here?' Obviously Louis had no intention of letting him make up his mind slowly. At least, not without all barrels being fired first.

What did he have to lose? Though he already thought he knew his answer. He wasn't destined to fly solo when his heart belonged to Isabella. 'Sure. As long as I'm back in time to take Isabella to the airport.'

Isabella watched Raphael change into a suit and comb his hair. 'Something you want to tell me?'

'I'm popping out but I should be back in time to take you to the airport. If not, Maman will give you a lift.'

'You're going to the hospital to look at an opportunity of a position there.'

He stared at her as though she'd done something wrong.

'If you didn't want me to hear your conversation with

Monsieur Fournier, then you should've stayed away from our bedroom window.'

He winced.

Her hands gripped her hips. 'So, Raphael, are you planning to move back here? Taking this job?'

'No… Yes… I don't know.'

'I see.' She didn't really. But she was angry. 'Thanks for not telling me about any of this. Was I supposed to wait and accept whatever you chose to do without hesitation? I know we've agreed to take our time working out where our relationship might lead, but not being open with me isn't going to help.'

'Izzy, we'll talk on the way to the airport.'

'No, thanks. I'll find my own way there. You go and see what's on offer at the hospital.' She turned her back on him and waited for him to leave the room.

'Isabella, I am sorry. I do need to make some decisions. I just don't know what they'll be.'

Less than an hour later Isabella paid off the taxi, slung her bag over her shoulder and went to check in. Her heart was numb.

Raphael had been offered a position at the hospital in Avignon. She should've expected it. He'd take it up. When asked by Monsieur Fournier if he might be interested he'd said, 'Yes, definitely.'

She boarded her flight and sank into her seat, closed her eyes and pretended to be asleep.

For the first time since meeting Raphael she wanted to hate him. He'd lied by omission. They were better than that. He should have told her the truth. But instead of hating him, she loved him.

Which hurt like hell.

CHAPTER TEN

THE EXPECTANT MOTHER who'd been admitted an hour ago with early contractions was reading a book and quite comfortable with her lot—for now. Isabella's heart hadn't been in her work all day so when sign-off time came around she was out of the ward like a rabbit being chased by a hound.

Once she finally staggered into Raphael's house, exhausted from lack of sleep, she headed for the fridge and the wine, rubbing the small of her back where a persistent ache had started up hours ago. 'What a day. It couldn't have got any slower if it tried.'

Taking her glass with her, she wandered outside to the deck and slumped into the first chair. Chienne was quick to jump and spread herself across Izzy's thighs. 'Hey, you. Lonely too?'

Purr, purr.

'Okay, so you'll settle for anyone as long as you have food and cuddles.' Next week she'd be moving into the apartment she'd rented and beginning to unpack the mountain of kitchenware and other things she'd bought. It would be the start of everything she'd hoped for. Except a life with Raphael. He wouldn't leave his house to move into a tiny one-bed apartment. But he might—

make that probably would—leave this place for Avignon and the family he'd started getting back with.

A sharp breeze skipped across the yard, lifting leaves and chilling her skin. 'Guess we're going inside, Chienne. Wasn't enjoying it that much out here anyway.'

After making sure she was locked in, Isabella headed upstairs, not to Raphael's bedroom but to the third floor where she crawled under the covers on the bed, still in her clothes. Who cared? The cat followed, and quickly made herself comfortable curled up against Isabella's leg. Looking around, she sighed. The room she'd used for the first weeks was cold and uninviting, the bed not welcoming. No hints of Rafe. There again, not even his bedroom had been warm and inviting when she'd popped her head in earlier.

'At the end of the day, without Raphael this place is only a house, not a home.' She blinked hard. 'I love him.' So much it was unbearable. Did she really want to give him up to live in a one-bed downstairs apartment? After seeing Raphael's enjoyment as he wandered around Avignon the idea of living in London so she could have her own home was turning cold. What was the point if she wasn't with the love of her life? An old saying slipped into her head. 'Home is where the heart is.'

It was like someone had turned the lights on. Blink, blink. She couldn't leave Raphael. She'd go to the end of the earth if it meant being with him. And yes, she'd travel to different countries, other cities, if she had to. Though that was unlikely. If they settled in Avignon, it would be for a long time, probably for ever. She could do this. And be happy about it. She was in love. Nothing could be better than that. Could it? No, it couldn't.

* * *

From the hospital Raphael went into the city centre for a look around. He rolled his shoulders as he walked, trying to ease the tightness brought on by the dismay in Isabella's eyes as she told him he hadn't been honest with her. He breathed in the scent of the place, recalling other times he'd been here, with Grand'mère, his parents, his cousins. He knew most corners and streets, not much had changed. It was familiar in a comfortable way. Old yet pulsing with new energy. Tourists and locals alike sitting outside cafés enjoying the sun and coffee.

As he passed a bar the sounds of a rugby game on the television reached him and he paused to look in. The French were playing the Italians. If it had been the All Blacks playing Izzy might've been watching.

His heart lurched. She'd gone. In anger. And pain. He'd let her down. Badly. It was time to tell her how he felt.

Which was why he was walking around his beloved city, taking in everything, storing up new memories.

He tugged his phone out of his back pocket and pressed her number.

'Raphael.' Her voice was flat.

'Izzy, I'm sorry.'

'Sure.'

Right. 'Can you pick me up from Heathrow tonight?'

'You're returning home?'

What she was really asking was, *Are you coming home for good?* 'Of course I am.' Except there was no of course about it. In reply to her question about if he was moving home he'd answered no and yes. Home was a new word for him. It wasn't just a house with a bed in it any more. It was where his heart lay. Except his heart had been torn. London and Avignon. Izzy and his family. Would it have been greedy to want it all?

'Okay.'

He tried another tack. 'Grand'mère opened her eyes for a few minutes this afternoon.' It should've been the first thing he told Izzy, but he'd been overwhelmed with his love of his city and had to say something about it before it consumed him. Telling Izzy his dilemma should be a priority, but he was afraid to put it out there until he knew for sure what he would do. 'I was doing my talking thing, chatting about anything and everything, and looked over and there she was staring at me.' His heart had gone into overdrive as he'd reached for her wrist to check her pulse.

'Hey, that's great news.' Finally some enthusiasm. 'Give her another hug from me.'

'Already did.'

'What time do you get in?' Flat again.

He told her the fight number and arrival time. 'I'll see you later.'

'Okay.'

Who knew if she'd turn up to collect him, but he had to believe she would. Tossing the phone on the bed, he quickly shoved his clothes into the bag, for once not folding anything. He had a flight to catch and missing it was not an option.

His phone pinged as he paced the terminal, waiting to board his flight.

Get it right, my boy.

Grand'mère. Nothing wrong with her brain after the coma.

His gut churned. What if Isabella turned her back

on him? What if she'd decided he wasn't worth the effort? Only one way to find out, and he had to endure two flights first.

Both flights were slower than a winter's day. At Heathrow Customs it took for ever just to reach the grumpy-looking woman behind the desk.

His phone pinged as he handed over his passport. Izzy.

I'm here.

'Excuse me, sir. I'm asking you to turn that off while you're here.' The grumpy official dragged out the questions like he was an illegal alien trying to get across the border. Finally his passport was approved and he was free to go.

Striding out into the arrivals hall he scanned the crowd, missed Izzy the first time. Then on a second sweep he saw her standing to one side, tired and sad. No human tornado tonight. His heart squeezed. 'Izzy,' he called as he crossed to stand in front of her. When he reached to hug her she stepped back.

'Did you take the job?'

'No. I didn't.'

'Why didn't you tell me that's what you were going into town for?'

Dropping his bag to the floor, he laid both hands on her shoulders. 'Because I didn't want to upset you when I had no idea if I'd take it or not. I wanted to be certain one way or the other before saying anything.'

She stared at him, her eyes wide and filled with a pain he'd never seen there before. 'Really?'

'Really. Really didn't know. And really turned it down. I live in London, Izzy.'

She blinked, bit her lip.

'I've come home to tell you I'm not moving away, that Avignon's a part of me but not all of me. I've finally come to my senses and see that returning there was a dream, and now that the opportunity has arisen to live and work there, it all feels wrong. I won't deny a part of my heart will always be there with my family, but...' He drew a breath. This was the moment he had to put himself out there. 'But really, my heart belongs with you. In London, in our house. I love you, Izzy.'

'Rafe? You do?' A tear snuck from the corner of her eye.

'Yes. I love you, Isabella Nicholson, with everything I have.'

'I love you, too,' she whispered. Then louder, 'I love you, Rafe, and it's been so hard thinking you wouldn't love me back.'

'Oh, Izzy.' He wrapped his arms around her familiar body and held on tight.

'I can't believe us.'

'Right pair, aren't we? Great friends, awesome lovers, and now for the future.' He pulled back enough to gaze down into her eyes, and he knew he couldn't wait until they got home. He dug into his pocket for the small box he'd put there hours ago, and dropped to one knee. 'Isabella Nicholson, will you do the honour of marrying me?'

She gasped. 'Raphael? Did I hear what I think I did?'

'Please marry me, Izzy? I love you so much I can't bear the thought of not being with you.'

She went quiet on him again, but he wasn't worried.

She wouldn't have lied about loving him. Just being typical Izzy, making him wait. 'Answer the question, will you, Izzy?' he pleaded.

Then her sweet, fierce voice whispered, 'I love you, Rafe, more than anything, but I am not asking you to give up your dreams for me.'

'I'm not. Yes, I adore my family and being back in Avignon has been wonderful, but I mean it. My heart is with you in London.'

'I can live anywhere if we're together,' she said. 'Yes, Rafe, I will marry you. Till death do us part in about sixty years' time.'

Phew. She was smiling right at him. Hadn't realised he was holding his breath.

'Are we seriously engaged?'

He slid Grand'mère's engagement ring onto her finger. 'As of now, yes.'

'Mummy, what's that man doing?'

'Asking the pretty lady to marry him.'

'Why?'

Raphael looked across to the little boy staring at him. 'Because I love this lady and want to be with her for the rest of my life.'

Loud cheers and lots of clapping drowned out anything else the child might have said. Raphael swung Izzy up in his arms and kissed her before he turned for the exit.

'Hey, mister, you've forgotten your bag.' A man ran after them, a silly grin on his face.

'Thanks.' He grinned back, happy as a man could get.

But at the car, his Isabella stood swinging the keys in her hand and looking slightly bemused. 'I can't promise you I'll settle easily, though I know it's you I want in my life more than a home in one place. If we move house every year I will be happy. And I certainly won't object to moving across to Avignon to be a part of your family.'

'*You* are my family, Izzy. I've got a home that as of now is ours. We both have jobs we love, though I'm going to look for something less time-consuming so I can have more time with you. There are our friends nearby we like to spend time with. We have everything that matters.'

A sob came across the rooftop of the car. 'You say the nicest things when you're not trying to annoy me.'

'Love you, sweetheart.'

EPILOGUE

Months later

HARRY TAPPED HIS glass with a knife from the dining table. 'Okay, everyone, please raise your glasses for a toast to the disgustingly happy couple.'

Isabella reached for Rafe's hand, and entwined her fingers between his. 'We did it.' It had taken time to organise a dinner in their London home with their friends. Everyone was so busy and a baby had been born, but eventually they'd managed it. If only they could get married now, but divorces took time, and she had to be patient.

'If you're half as happy as Esther and I, then well done.' Harry held his glass before him.

Raphael grinned. 'I reckon.'

'Cheers,' everyone shouted, before drinking to them.

Isabella felt the tears burning lines down her face, and grinned. They were happy tears. 'Thanks, everyone. I'm just glad we've joined you all in wedded bliss, or in our case, on the way to marriage.' This was the bliss, the wedded component to follow when she was single again. 'Less than nine months to go before the big day.'

At that, Raphael glanced at her, a question in his eye.

She nodded. They'd agreed about this before everyone got here.

His hand squeezed hers before he announced, 'We're going to join some of you in the parenting stakes too.'

The room erupted and Isabella found herself wrapped in Carly's arms. 'Go, girlfriend. That's awesome news.'

'Who'd have thought?'

'Everyone but you.' Carly smiled, and turned to Adem to scoop her daughter out of his arms and against her swollen breasts.

'She's gorgeous.' Izzy smiled.

'Here, have a hold. Derya Ann, this is your godmother.'

Izzy's heart swelled further as she took the warm bundle. 'She's so beautiful.' She sniffed. 'I'm so happy it's scary.'

'Not scary. Wonderful.' Carly grinned. 'Now, can I have my daughter back?'

Harry did his spoon-tapping-glass thing again. His smile was wider and softer as he focused on Esther, nothing but love in his eyes. 'We, too, are pregnant.' Once again the room exploded with joy and laughter and shouts.

Then Esther and Chloe were nudging Carly aside to give Isabella a hug. 'Go, you. A baby. No wonder you're looking so peachy.'

Peachy? Yuck. Isabella grinned and flapped her hand. 'I'm so glad Rafe suggested I come back to London.'

'The man had an ulterior motive,' Xander said.

'It worked, didn't it?' Rafe said.

Yes, it had. And she couldn't be happier. She had found her match, the man to go through life with, raise children with, laugh and love and do all the things she'd been hoping for. It didn't matter where, only that she was with Rafe. She took one more sip of her champagne and put the glass down. From now on water would suffice until their wedding day by which time junior would've put in an appearance.

Life couldn't be better.

* * * * *

BILLIONAIRE, BOSS...
BRIDEGROOM?

KATE HARDY

For Charlotte Mursell and Sheila Hodgson – with love and thanks for letting me have so much fun with this story. x

CHAPTER ONE

I'm coming to get you, Bella texted swiftly. Hold on.

For once, it looked as if she was going to be the rescuer instead of the rescuee. With her new job to boost her confidence, she thought she might just be able to handle it. For once she would be the sister who was calm, collected and totally together instead of the flaky, ditzy one who always made a mess of things and needed to be bailed out of a sticky situation.

She glanced around and saw a black cab waiting at the kerbside. Relieved, she rushed up to it and jumped in.

'Can you take me to the Bramerton Hotel in Kensington, please?' she asked the cabbie.

There was a dry cough from beside her, and she whipped her head round to discover that there was already a passenger sitting in the back seat.

She'd been so focused on getting to Grace that she hadn't even noticed the other passenger when she'd climbed into the taxi.

'I'm so sorry,' she said. 'I didn't mean to be rude. Look, I realise that you were here first, and technically I ought to leave right now and let you get on with your journey, but I really do need to get to the Bramerton as quickly as possible. Would you mind finding another taxi and...and...?' She waved a desperate hand at him. 'Look, I'll pay for your cab.' It'd mean extending her overdraft yet again, but what were a few more pounds if it meant that she could return the favour for once and help Grace? Besides, she was about to start a new job. Next month, her cash-flow situation would be a bit better.

'Actually, I'm heading towards Kensington myself,' he said. 'I'll drop you off at the Bramerton.'

Relief flooded through Bella. She'd found the modern equivalent of a knight on a white charger: a man in a black cab. She wouldn't have to let her sister down. 'Thank you. Thank you so much.' She gave in to the impulse, leaned forward and kissed him soundly on the cheek. 'You have no idea how much I appreciate this.'

'What's so urgent?' he asked as the taxi drove off.

'It's a family thing,' she said. It wasn't her place to tell anyone about her sister's situation, let alone tell a complete stranger.

'Uh-huh.' He paused. 'Did I see you just come out of Insurgo Records?'

She looked at him, surprised. The man looked like a businessman on his way home from a late meeting, and he was hardly the target market for an independent record label—even though Insurgo's artists were a real mixture, from folk singer-songwriters to punk and indie bands, with a few oddities thrown in. 'Yes,' she said.

'Are you one of their acts?'

In her black jeans and matching plain T-shirt, teamed with a shiny platinum-blonde bob, Bella knew that she probably looked as much like an indie musician as she did a graphic designer. 'No,' she said.

But the man had been kind enough to let her share his taxi, so she didn't want to be rude to him. Besides, making small talk might distract her enough to stop her worrying about whatever had sent her normally cool and capable big sister into meltdown. She smiled at him. 'Actually, I'm a graphic designer, and I'm starting work at Insurgo next week.'

'Are you, now?'

Something about the way he drawled the words made alarm bells ring in the back of her head. But he was a total stranger. She was making something out of nothing. 'Yes, and I'm really looking forward to it,' she said with a bright smile. 'I'll be designing website graphics, album covers and band merch. Actually, I'm still trying to get my head round the fact that I've just been offered my dream job.' In an ideal world she would've preferred to have Insurgo as a client rather than as her employer, but working for someone full-time again meant that she'd have a regular income for a while—and right now she needed a regular income rather more than she needed her freedom.

'You don't know who I am, do you?' he asked.

'Other than a stranger who's been kind enough to let me share his taxi? No,' she admitted.

'Allow me to introduce myself,' he said, leaning forward out of the shadows and holding out his hand.

Bella caught her breath. He was gorgeous. Dark hair that was brushed back from his face, cornflower-blue eyes, and the kind of jawline that would've made him a hit in any perfume ad. She really had to resist the urge to reach out and trail her fingertips down his clean-shaven cheek. And that mouth. Almost pouting, the sexiest mouth she'd seen in a while.

Almost in a daze, she shook his hand, noting how firm his handshake was. And she studiously ignored the fact that her palm was tingling; after the way Kirk had let her down, she was officially off men. Even if this one was very easy on the eye and was wearing a beautifully cut designer suit, what looked like a handmade white shirt, a silk tie and highly polished Italian shoes.

No involvement.

Full stop.

Because she was never going to let anyone make her feel as foolish and useless as Kirk had made her feel, ever again.

'Hugh Moncrieff,' he said, and he waited for the penny to drop.

It took five seconds.

'Hugh Moncrieff—as in *Insurgo's* Hugh Moncrieff?' Bella asked in horror.

'That would be me,' he said. And he looked as if he was enjoying her reaction.

He was her new boss? 'But—you can't be.' Even though it would explain why he'd asked her if she was one of the artists; he must've thought that his second-in-command had signed her up in his absence.

'Why not?'

'Because you—you—' She gestured to his suit. 'You don't look like an indie record label owner. You look like a stockbroker.'

'The bank always likes the company's MD to wear a suit,' he said mildly. 'If I'd turned up to the meeting in ripped jeans and an avant-garde T-shirt, with funky hair, they'd have seen me as less of a professional and more of a risk.'

The bank? That nasty feeling got a lot worse. If he'd been to the bank for a meeting, all dressed up, at this time on a Friday evening, did that mean the company was in trouble and her job would be over before it had even started?

Her fears must've shown on her face, because he said, 'It's our annual review, and I went for a drink with a business contact afterwards. Don't look so worried. So you're my new graphic designer?'

'Bella Faraday,' she said. 'And I'm very good at what I do.'

'I expect you are, or Tarquin wouldn't have hired you,' he said dryly.

'So what are you doing in a taxi, when you own a record label? Why don't you have your own car, or a limo or something to drive you around?' The question was out before she could stop herself and she groaned inwardly. Way to go, Bella, she thought. Just grill your new boss, two minutes after you insulted him by saying he didn't look like the owner of an indie record label. Carry on like this and you'll be picking up your cards on Monday morning instead of starting your job.

So much for never letting herself feel foolish again. Right now she felt like a prize idiot.

'That's an easy one.' He smiled. 'My car happens to be in the local garage, having something fixed. I'd rather put my money into the business than waste it by hiring a flashy limo to do little more than wait around for me all day. Hence the taxi.'

Bella could feel the colour swishing through her cheeks. 'I'm sorry. It's not my place to question you. Look, um, please ask the cabbie to pull over and drop me off, and I'll get out of your way and find myself another taxi.'

'You said it was urgent—a family thing.'

'It is.'

'Then let me get you to the hotel. Tarquin obviously

overran with the interviews and made you late in the first
place, so it's Insurgo's fault.'

'No, it's not,' she said. It wasn't anyone's fault. But
right at that moment she was more worried about Grace
than about making a good impression on her new boss,
so she'd accept the offer. 'But thank you for the lift. I really appreciate this.'

'No problem.'

She texted Grace swiftly.

In taxi now. Wait for me in Reception.

Finally the taxi driver pulled up outside the Bramerton Hotel.

'Thank you again, Mr Moncrieff,' she said politely.
'How much do I owe you for the cab fare?'

'Nothing. You're practically on my way,' he said.

'Thank you. Really. And I'll work late every night
next week to make up for it,' she said, and left the taxi
before she could say anything else stupid.

When she walked into the reception area, Grace was
waiting there, white-faced and silent. And there was no
sign of Howard. Why wasn't Grace's fiancé waiting with
her? Had something happened to Howard? No, of course
not, or Grace would've said something in her texts. Not
just that single word: Help, followed by rejecting Bella's
call and sending a second text: Can't talk now. And now
Bella was seriously worried. What on earth had happened?

But Grace had been right about one thing. They
couldn't talk about it here. Not with Howard's parents'
golden wedding anniversary going on in one of the func-

tion rooms. Whatever it was, Bella had her sister's back. And they were leaving. Now.

'Come on. Let's get out of here,' Bella said softly, put her arm round Grace and led her out of the hotel.

Back in the street, she looked around for a taxi.

Then she realised that the taxi that had dropped her off was still waiting at the kerb, exactly where she'd left it. And Hugh Moncrieff was still there too, though he'd moved seats so that his back was to the cabbie. He wound the window down and beckoned them over. 'Can I give you a lift somewhere?'

'But—' she began.

'Everything's clearly not OK,' he said softly, looking at Grace, 'so I'll drop you and…your sister, I presume?' At her nod, he continued, 'I'll drop you where you need to go. What's the address?'

Bella definitely didn't want to leave Grace alone tonight, and her own flat wasn't big enough for two. Biting her lip, she gave him Grace's address. 'Thank you so much,' she said. 'We both really appreciate this. Especially as you didn't have to wait.'

'No problem.'

She helped Grace into the car. Grace still hadn't said a word. Worried, Bella took her hand and squeezed it; but Grace didn't return the pressure. And this time nobody seemed disposed to make any small talk. With every second, Bella felt more and more awkward.

Then, just as the taxi turned into Grace's road, Grace threw up. All over Hugh's posh Italian shoes and suit trousers.

'I'm so sorry,' she mumbled.

She looked almost as mortified as Bella felt—and Bella had no idea what to say. What could you say when your sister threw up over your new boss? Apart from an equally apologetic, 'I'm so sorry.'

Hugh brushed it aside. 'These things happen. Do you need help getting her indoors?'

'Thank you, but no—I think you've done more than enough to help us, this evening.' Bella took a deep breath. 'Look, I'll pay for valeting the taxi and I'll pick up the bill for dry-cleaning your suit and replacing your shoes.'

'We'll sort it out later,' he said. 'Are you sure you can manage?'

'I'm sure,' Bella fibbed. At least she had Grace's spare door key, so actually getting into the flat wouldn't be a problem. 'And thank you. And sorry. And—'

'Just get your sister safely inside,' Hugh cut in. 'We'll sort out everything later.'

'Thank you. And I'm sorry,' Bella whispered again, and helped Grace out of the taxi.

This really wasn't how Hugh had expected to spend a Friday evening. Or how he'd expected to meet the newest member of his team.

The poor woman had looked horrified when her sister threw up everywhere.

Did Bella often rescue her sister like that? he wondered. Funny, the other woman had been dressed so soberly, in a navy linen dress and sensible shoes. Looking at them together, most people would've guessed that the younger woman was the one who partied too hard and would be most likely to throw up in the back of a taxi and need looking after.

Or maybe Bella's sister hadn't been drunk. Maybe

she'd been ill. But then surely Bella would've said that her sister was ill, or even called an ambulance?

But it was none of his business. He should just take a step back and ignore it.

'I'm sorry about all that,' he said to the driver. 'If you can drop me home, I'll pay for the cost of valeting the taxi and lost fares.' He gave the driver the address.

Though he still couldn't get Bella Faraday out of his head. Especially the moment when she'd kissed his cheek; it had felt as if he'd been galvanised. And then, when she'd shaken his hand, every nerve-end had been aware of the feel of her skin against his.

Hugh was definitely attracted to her. More attracted than he'd been towards anyone in a very long time.

But.

After the whole fiasco with Jessie, he'd learned his lesson well. Hugh would never, ever mix work and pleasure again. As Tarquin had just hired Bella as their new graphic artist, it meant that she came firmly under the category of work. So he'd have to just ignore the pull of attraction in future and treat her just the same as he did every single one of his colleagues—by keeping her at a professional distance.

Even if she did have the sexiest mouth and sparkliest eyes he'd ever seen.

No involvement.

No risks.

This time, he'd stick to the rules.

'I'm so sorry I was sick everywhere,' Grace said once they were sitting down inside her flat.

Bella frowned. 'Didn't you eat anything to line your

stomach before you started knocking back whatever it was that made you throw up?'

'Champagne. No,' Grace said miserably. 'My stomach was tied in too many knots to eat.'

And Grace hardly ever drank. It wasn't a good combination. Not to mention really worrying—what had been so bad that Grace had had to get drunk? She took a deep breath. First things first. She needed to get Grace sober. 'Right. First of all you're having water—lots and lots of water,' Bella said. Then she looked through Grace's cupboards. Please let there be something that she could actually cook. Or, failing that, cereal to soak up all that champagne.

Then she spied the box of porridge oats. Perfect. Even she could follow the instructions on the box and make porridge in the microwave.

While the porridge was cooking, she took a banana from Grace's fruit bowl and chopped it up. She added it to the finished cereal and put the bowl in front of Grace, who immediately pushed it away.

'I can't.'

'Eat it,' Bella said firmly. 'Your electrolytes are all over the place and bananas are great for sorting that out, and oats will help because they're bland carbs which will raise your blood sugar without upsetting your stomach.'

'How do you know all this stuff?' Grace asked, looking bemused.

Bella smiled. 'Remember I dated a doctor a couple of years back? He gave me the lowdown on the best food to eat for a hangover.'

'I'm sorry,' Grace said again. 'Was the taxi driver very angry?'

'Don't worry,' Bella said airily. 'My boss is sorting it.'

Grace did a double-take. 'Your *boss*?'

'Uh-huh.' Bella flashed her sister a grin. 'Guess what? I got the job.'

'I—oh, my God. Are you telling me that I just threw up over your boss before you even started the job?' Grace asked, looking horrified as Bella's words sank in. 'Oh, no. I'll talk to him and explain, so he doesn't sack you or—'

'Gracie, it's fine,' Bella cut in.

'It's not fine at all! I've messed things up for you. Look. I'll pay for the dry-cleaning.'

Bella smiled. 'I already told him I'd do that, and I said I'd pay for valeting the taxi as well.'

'My mess, my bill,' Grace said. 'I'll pay.'

'Gracie, just shut up and eat your porridge. I don't want to hear another word from you, young lady, until that bowl is empty.'

'You sound like Mum,' Grace muttered.

'Good,' Bella retorted. Usually Grace was the one who sounded like their mother and Bella was the one hanging her head in shame.

She made Grace eat every scrap and drink two more glasses of water before she resumed her interrogation. 'Right. Now tell me—what happened?'

'I can't marry Howard.'

It was the last thing Bella had been expecting. Her older sister had been engaged for the last four years. OK, so Howard was a bit on the boring side, and his parents were nightmares—Bella had dubbed them Mr Toad and Mrs Concrete Hair with good reason—but if Grace loved him then Bella was prepared to be as sweet as she could to them. 'What? Why not? Don't you love him any more?' And then a nasty thought struck her. 'Is there someone else?'

'Of course there isn't anyone else.' Grace shook her head. 'I wouldn't do that to him.'

'Not deliberately, no, but you can't help who you fall in love with,' Bella said. She'd fallen for Mr Wrong enough times, and Kirk had shattered her trust for good. She'd never trust another man with her heart again, no matter how attractive he was. It had taken her six months to re-build her life—and she was still angry with herself for being so naïve and trusting. Why hadn't she been able to see that he was stringing her along?

'I love Howard, but I'm not in love with him,' Grace said. 'There's a difference.'

'I know.' Bella squeezed her hand. 'And it's a big dif-ference. A deal-breaking difference.'

'He's never made me feel breathless and dizzy, as if he'd swept me off my feet.'

Not surprising: Howard was cautious and sensible. Which wasn't a bad thing, Bella thought, but the oc-casional bit of spontaneity wouldn't have hurt. And it might have made her sister's world complete—which clearly hadn't happened. On paper, Grace and Howard were the perfect match—both sensible and cautious—but there was a little thing called chemistry. Without that, life would be miserable. 'You can't spend the rest of your life with someone who doesn't make your world light up.'

Grace bit her lip. 'I think you're about the only per-son who'd understand that. Mum's going to be so disap-pointed in me.'

'No, she's not, and neither is Dad—they both want you to be happy, and if marrying Howard wouldn't make you happy then you definitely shouldn't marry him,' Bella said firmly.

'I'm not sure if he was in love with me, either,' Grace said.

'Of course he was—you're gorgeous and you're clever and you're nice. What's not to love?' Bella demanded, cross on her sister's behalf.

'I think we both loved each other,' Grace said softly, 'but not *enough*. I mean, we've been engaged for ever—who stays engaged for four years in this day and age?'

'A couple who's saving up the deposit for a house?' Bella suggested.

'Apart from the fact that we already have enough money for that between us, you know what I mean—if we'd really wanted to be together, we'd have got married years ago rather than waiting. We don't even live together,' Grace pointed out.

'Mainly because Cynthia of the Eagle Eyes and Concrete Hair wouldn't let her little boy shack up with someone,' Bella said. 'Is that why you got drunk tonight?'

'No. That was the cartoon you drew for me,' Grace said. 'Fifty Shades of Beige.'

Bella winced. 'Sorry. I meant it as a joke, to make you laugh and relax a bit. I knew you weren't looking forward to the golden wedding party.'

'But it was so accurate, Bel,' Grace said. 'I was the only woman there not dressed in beige.'

Bella couldn't help laughing. 'Ouch. I didn't think it'd be quite that bad.'

'Oh, it was,' Grace said feelingly. 'I really didn't belong there. I drank three glasses of champagne straight down to give me courage and I didn't even feel them, Bel.'

Which was really un-Grace-like. She always stopped

after one glass. Sensible, reliable Grace who looked after everyone else and was usually the one mopping up, not the one throwing up.

'I was just numb. And that's when I realised,' Grace said, 'that I was walking into a life I didn't actually want. In fifty years' time, I don't want to be sensible Grace Sutton, whose heart has never once skipped a beat, and whose mother-in-law directed the whole of her marriage.'

'If anyone could live until well past the age of a hundred, marbles intact and with an iron fist, it'd be Mrs Concrete Hair,' Bella said feelingly. 'You've done the right thing, Gracie. It's much better to call a halt now than to wait until after you married Howard and then have all the mess of a divorce to go through.'

'Really?' Grace didn't look convinced. She looked guilty and miserable and worried.

'Really,' Bella said firmly, 'and Mum and Dad will back you, too.'

'I just feel that I've let everyone down—all the work that's gone into arranging the wedding.' Grace swallowed. 'Not to mention the money.'

'But you haven't let anyone down,' Bella said. 'Well, except you should have told me all this a *lot* sooner, because I'm your sister and of course I'm going to support you. I hate to think that you've been miserable all these months when I could've listened to you and made you feel better. You're doing the right thing, Gracie. And cancelling the wedding won't be that hard.' This was slightly surreal; it felt almost as if she and Grace had swapped places and it was her turn to be the sensible, super-organised one instead of the one who needed rescuing. 'Just give me a list of the names and contact details of the people you've invited and your suppliers, and I'll ring them all and explain the wedding's off.'

'I can't make you do that!' Grace protested.

'You're not making me do it. I'm offering. That's what sisters are for.' She took a deep breath. 'Have you told Howard?' Was that why her no-longer-future brother-in-law had been so conspicuously absent?

'No. I'm going to do that tomorrow.'

A nasty thought struck Bella. 'Does he actually know you've left the party?'

Grace nodded and winced. 'I told him I had a migraine and was going home.'

'And he didn't even offer to take you home? That's atrocious!'

'How could he leave? It's his parents' golden wedding anniversary party.'

'OK, so he probably had to stay there with the Gruesome Twosome,' Bella allowed, 'but he still should've made sure you were all right first and at least arranged a taxi to take you home.'

'I'm sure he would've done, but I told him you were coming to collect me,' Grace explained.

'Hmm,' Bella said, though she wasn't mollified. What on earth was wrong with the man? Howard had been Grace's fiancé for four years and he hadn't even made sure that she got home safely when she'd told him she felt ill—whereas Hugh Moncrieff, a man Bella had met only a few minutes ago, had not only come to the rescue, he'd offered to help them indoors. So her new boss had a good heart as well as a gorgeous face.

Not that she should be thinking about that right now. Or ever, for that matter. Even if she wasn't officially off men, her boss was completely off limits. She needed this job, to get her finances back on an even keel. 'So what are you going to tell Howard tomorrow?' she asked.

'The truth—that I can't marry him.' Grace closed her eyes for a moment. 'And that means I'll lose my job and my home, too, Bel. No way can I go back to work at Sutton's, not when I've just split up with the boss's son—and in the circumstances I can hardly ask them to give me a reference to work anywhere else. Plus I've already given my landlord notice on my flat. I know he's already found my replacement and signed a contract, so I can't ask him just to ignore my notice and renew my lease.' She blew out a breath. 'I've really burned my bridges, Bel—and who knows how long it'll take me to find another flat?'

'You don't have to. Come and stay with me,' Bella said immediately.

Grace hugged her. 'I love you, sweetheart, and thank you for the offer, but your flat's barely big enough for one person. You don't have room for me to stay. I'll ask round my friends—one of them will put me up until I can find somewhere—and I'll sign on with a temp agency. If I explain the situation, I'm sure they'll understand about the problem with references and help me to find a way round it.'

This sounded more like her level-headed older sister, Bella thought. Planning. Being sensible. The oats were clearly soaking up what remained of the champagne. 'It'll all work out, Gracie. You know what Mum always says: when one door closes, another opens.'

'I know,' Grace said.

'I was going to take you out for sushi and champagne tomorrow, to celebrate my job—because I wouldn't have got it without you—but we can take a rain check on that, because I'm guessing you won't want to see champagne again for months.'

'Definitely not.' Grace winced. 'And you might've lost the job, because of me.'

'Of course I haven't. I'll talk my boss round,' Bella said, sounding slightly more confident than she actually felt. 'Go and have a shower, clean your teeth, get in your PJs, and then we're going to snuggle under a throw on your sofa and watch a re-run of *Friends*.'

'I love you, Bel,' Grace said. 'You're the best sister I could ever ask for.'

Even though they were total opposites, Bella thought. And, weirdly, tonight, it felt more as if she was Grace and Grace was her.

'You came straight to rescue me without asking any questions,' Grace said.

'Of course I did! You've done it often enough for me,' Bella said. 'And you're the best sister I could ever ask for, too, and I love you to bits—even when I don't understand you. Now go and get yourself sorted out. I'm going to raid your fridge because I'm starving, and I'm sleeping on your sofa tonight. Tomorrow, you can talk to Howard and we'll make that list and work through it together. And then things will start to look better. You'll see.' She hugged her sister. 'Nothing fazes a Faraday girl, right?'

'Right,' Grace said. 'Nothing fazes a Faraday girl.'

CHAPTER TWO

ON MONDAY MORNING, Bella left her flat at what felt like the crack of dawn. For the last couple of years, she'd been able to set her own working hours—meaning that she could sleep in until ten a.m. and work until late, which suited her body clock better—but she knew that she needed to make a good impression on her first day at Insurgo. Particularly given what had happened at her first meeting with the boss. She couldn't afford to put a single foot wrong from now on, not if she wanted to keep her job and get her finances back on track.

And getting up early would take her mind off what had been a truly lousy weekend. Seeing Grace—the person she'd always looked up to as a tower of strength, someone who knew exactly what to do to sort out any given situation—fall apart had shocked Bella deeply. Right now Grace was in the almost same position that Bella had been in six months ago: recovering from a wrecked relationship, worrying about her job and her home and her finances, and feeling as if the sun would never rise again.

OK, so Grace had been the dumper rather than the dumpee, in this case, and she hadn't lost her best friend and the contents of her bank account as well as her partner; but it was still going to be a huge change in Grace's life. Even though it had definitely been the right decision.

Privately, Bella thought her sister had had a lucky escape. Howard was a nice enough guy, but he was completely under his mother's thumb. Marrying him would've basically meant having the rest of her life run by Cynthia of the Eagle Eyes and Concrete Hair, the most cold and judgemental woman that Bella had ever met. And finding another job might just mean that Grace's new employer would appreciate her and give her the promotion she deserved. At Sutton's, Grace had been totally taken for granted. They'd expected her to work way more than her fair share of hours, under the guise of being 'almost family', but they hadn't actually given her any of the privileges of being 'almost family'.

Howard had barely raised a single argument when Grace had gone to see him on the Saturday morning and called off the wedding. So he clearly hadn't loved Grace enough to fight for her. And Bella thought her sister deserved a lot better than a man who was nice enough but didn't have a backbone and would never stand up for her.

Today was a new chapter in both their lives. And hopefully this one would be better for both of them.

Bella paused outside the Insurgo Records building. The basement was a recording studio and practice rooms that local bands could book as well as being used by the Insurgo artists; the ground floor and mezzanine comprised a seriously upmarket café—the sort that offered coffee made in a way that looked more as if it was some kind of laboratory experiment than a hot drink, but apparently brought out the floral notes in the coffee; and the top two floors were the record label's actual offices.

'All righty. Welcome to your new life,' she told herself, and went inside.

She was the first member of staff to arrive in the office after Tarquin, Hugh's second-in-command—to her relief, Hugh didn't seem to be there yet—and Tarquin handed her a design brief, a portable CD player and a pair of headphones. 'Welcome to Insurgo, Bella,' he said with a smile. 'We're doing a limited edition of coloured vinyl for Lacey's third single. She's one of our singer-songwriters. I've given you a rundown here of our target market; her career history, and the PR schedule. What I need you to do is have a listen to the album—the song we're releasing is the fourth track on the CD—and come up with some ideas for the vinyl cover and a promo T-shirt, based on what you hear. Or if you have ideas for other promo items, bring them along. If you'd like to have a second listen in one of the studios rather than working on headphones, just yell and I'll sort it out. And then maybe we can talk about it, later this afternoon?'

'That sounds fine,' Bella said, smiling back. She was being thrown in at the deep end, but she'd always thrived on that. And this was her chance to shine and prove they'd made the right decision in hiring her.

'This is your desk, over here,' he said, and ushered her over to a desk by the window with a drawing board and a computer. 'As soon as Shelley—our admin guru—comes in, we'll get you set up with a password and username. The meeting room's on the floor above, along with Hugh's office, the staff kitchen and the toilets. I'm over there in the corner, and I'll get everyone else to come over and introduce themselves as they come in.'

'That's great,' Bella said, trying to damp down the sudden flood of nervousness. She was good with people.

She knew she'd find her place in the pack and quickly work out how to get the best from the people she worked with. She always did. But these first few hours in a new role were always crucial.

'Is there anything else you need before you start?' he asked.

Yes, but she couldn't exactly explain why she needed to see the boss without making things awkward. But she'd just thought of the perfect excuse to go up to the next floor. Hopefully Hugh wasn't in yet, so she could leave the neatly wrapped parcel in her bag on his desk. Or, if he was at his desk, hopefully he'd be alone and she could snatch two minutes to apologise to him in person while the kettle boiled. She smiled. 'How about I make us both a coffee?'

'Excellent idea. Thank you.' Tarquin smiled back. 'Mine's black, no sugar. I'm afraid it's pretty basic stuff in the staff kitchen—tea, instant coffee and hot chocolate—but help yourself to whatever you want. If you'd rather have something fancier, you do get a staff discount downstairs at the café.'

'That's good to know. And instant does me just fine. At this time of the morning, any coffee works,' Bella said with a smile.

To her relief, she discovered that Hugh's office was empty. So she wouldn't have to confront him quite yet, then. There was a pile of post set neatly in the middle of his immaculate desk; she left the package and accompanying card on top of it. Then she boiled the kettle and made herself and Tarquin a mug of coffee before heading downstairs to her desk and making a start on the design briefs. And please, please, let Hugh Moncrieff accept her apology.

* * *

Hugh wasn't in the best of moods when he drove his car into the tiny car park behind the record label offices. His shoes had just about recovered from their ordeal on Friday night, and his dry cleaner had said that there would be no problem with his suit. But he hadn't been able to get Bella Faraday out of his head.

Worse still had been the slew of texts and emails and answering machine messages over the weekend from his mother, his brothers and their partners, all reminding him that his brother Nigel's engagement party was coming up and they couldn't wait to see him. Which meant that Hugh was in for another bout of familial nagging. Why was he still messing about with his record label? When was he going to treat it as the hobby it ought to be and get himself a proper job?

He knew what the subtext meant: he was the baby of the family, so they'd let him have his dream and do his degree in music instead of economics. Now he was thirty, they all thought it was about time he gave up his financially risky business and joined the long-established family stockbroking firm instead. Which was why Bella's comment about him looking like a stockbroker had really touched a raw nerve on Friday night.

He happened to like his life in London, thank you very much. He loved what he did at Insurgo—finding promising new talent and polishing their rough material just enough to make them commercially viable without taking away the creative spark that had caught his ear in the first place. Insurgo had made a name for itself as an independent label producing quality sound, from rock through to singer-songwriters, with a sprinkling of oddities who wouldn't fit anywhere else. Hugh was proud of what he did. He didn't want to give it up and be a stock-broker like his older brothers Julian, Nigel and Alistair.

But the question that drove him really crazy was when his family asked when he intended to find a nice girl and settle down. That wasn't going to happen any time soon. Jessie had cured him of that particular pipe dream. He knew his family meant well, but couldn't they see that they were still prodding a bruise?

His business, his heart and his music had all taken a battering. And finding a new, suitable girlfriend wasn't going to repair any of the damage. Sheer hard work and some quiet support from his best friends had rescued his business, but nowadays his heart was permanently off limits. And the music that had once flowed from his fingers and filled his head had gone for good. He didn't write songs any more. He just produced them—and he kept a professional distance from his artists.

He ran through a few excuses in his head. None of them worked. Even being in a full body cast wouldn't get him a free pass. He was just going to have to turn up, smile sweetly at everyone, and metaphorically stick his fingers in his ears and say 'la-la-la' every time his career or his love life was mentioned. Which he knew from ex-perience would be about every seven minutes, on average.

He collected a double espresso from the café on the ground floor—on a morning like this one, a mug of the instant stuff in the staff kitchen just wasn't going to cut it—and stomped up to his office, completely bypass-ing the team. What he needed right now was music. Loud enough to drown out the world and drown out his thoughts. A few minutes with headphones on, and he might be human enough again to face his team without biting their heads off even more than he normally would on a Monday morning.

And then he stopped dead.

On top of the post he'd been expecting to see, there was a neatly wrapped parcel and a thick cream envelope. It wasn't his birthday, and the parcel didn't look like a promo item. It was the wrong shape for a CD or vinyl, and in any case most unsigned artists pitching to him tended to email him with a link to a digital file on the internet.

Intrigued, he untied the ribbon and unwrapped the shiny paper from the parcel to discover a box of seriously good chocolates.

Whoever had sent them had excellent taste. But who were they from and why?

He opened the envelope. Inside was a hand-drawn card: a line-drawing of a mournful-looking rabbit with a speech bubble saying 'Sorry'. Despite his bad mood, he felt the corner of his mouth twitch. Whoever had sent this was saying they knew he wasn't a happy bunny—and Hugh had a very soft spot for terrible puns.

He opened the card to find out who'd sent it, and a wad of banknotes fell out.

What?

Why on earth would someone be giving him cash?

He scanned the inside swiftly. The writing was beautifully neat and regular, slightly angular and spiky—the sort you'd see on hand-drawn labels in an art gallery or upmarket bookshop.

Dear Mr Moncrieff
Thank you for rescuing us on Friday night and I'm
very sorry for the inconvenience we caused you.

*I hope the enclosed will cover the cost of valeting
the taxi, dry-cleaning your suit and replacing your
shoes. Please let me know if there's still a shortfall
and I will make it up.*
Yours sincerely
Bella Faraday

He blinked. She'd said something on Friday evening
about reimbursing him, but he really hadn't been expecting this. Since the parcel and the card had been hand-
delivered, that meant that their new graphic designer must
already be at her desk. Most of his team didn't show their
faces in the office until nearly ten, so she was super-early
on her first day.

And, although he appreciated the gesture, it really
wasn't necessary. His shoes had survived and the rest
of it hadn't cost that much. He really ought to return the
money.

He picked up his phone and dialled his second-in-
command's extension. 'Can you send Ms Faraday up?'

'Good morning to you, Tarquin, my friend,' Tarquin
said dryly. 'How are you? Did you have a nice weekend?
What's new with you?'

Hugh sighed. 'Don't give me a hard time, Tarq.'

'Get out of the wrong side of bed, did we? Tsk. Must
be Monday morning.'

Hugh knew he shouldn't take out his mood on his best
friend and business partner. Particularly as Tarquin dealt
with all the stuff Hugh didn't enjoy, and with extremely
good grace, so Hugh could concentrate on the overall
strategy of the label and actually producing the music.
'I'm sorry. All right. Good morning, Tarquin. How are
you? Did you have a nice weekend?'

'That's better. Good, and yes, thank you. I'll send her up. And be nice, sweet-cheeks—apart from the fact that it's her first day, not everyone's as vile as you are on Monday mornings.'

'Yeah, yeah,' Hugh said, but he was smiling as he put the phone down again.

Bella was leaning back in her chair, eyes closed, listening to the music. Lacey, the singer, had a really haunting voice, and the song was underpinned by an acoustic guitar and a cello. The whole thing was gorgeous, and it made Bella think of mountains, deep Scottish lochs, forests and fairies. Maybe she could design something with mist, and perhaps a pine forest, and...

She yelped as she felt the tap on her shoulder; reacting swiftly, she sat bolt upright, opened her eyes and pulled off the headphones.

Tarquin was standing next to her, his face full of remorse. 'Sorry, Bella. I didn't mean to give you a heart attack.'

Bella's heart was galloping away. 'You did give me a bit of a fright,' she said. 'I was listening to the CD—it's really good.'

'Yeah, we think so, too.' He smiled. 'Lacey's a bit of a character. She always performs barefoot.'

'Like a fairy.' The words were out before Bella could stop them. 'Sorry. Ignore me. Did you want something?'

'Yes. Hugh just called down. Can you go up to his office?'

Uh-oh. This must mean that Hugh had seen her parcel and her card. And she had absolutely no idea what his reaction was going to be. 'Um, sure,' she said.

'Don't look so worried. The boss knows it's your first

day, so he probably just wants to say hello and welcome you to Insurgo,' Tarquin said kindly.

Bella wasn't so sure. If that was the case, why hadn't Hugh come down to the open-plan office? She had a nasty feeling that she wasn't going to be hearing a welcome speech but a 'goodbye and never darken our doorstep again' speech. Clearly the parcel she'd left on her new boss's desk hadn't been anywhere near enough of an apology.

Her fears must have shown on her face because Tarquin said, 'His bark's worse than his bite. He just isn't a Monday morning person, that's all. Whatever he says, don't take it to heart, OK? Everyone else in the office will tell you the same—and if he does say something horrible to you, he'll come and apologise to you in the afternoon when he's human again. It's just how he is.'

'Right,' Bella said, forcing a smile she didn't feel. 'I'll, um, be back in a minute, then?' She switched off the music, scribbled the word 'mist' on a pad to remind herself what she'd been thinking about, and then headed for Hugh's office, her stomach churning. Hesitantly, she rapped on the closed door.

'Come in,' he said, sounding brusque.

Tarquin obviously hadn't been joking when he'd said that the boss wasn't a Monday morning person.

And then her jaw almost dropped when she walked in. The last time she'd seen Hugh Moncrieff, he'd been clean-shaven and wearing a formal suit. Today, he was wearing black jeans and a black T-shirt with the Insurgo Records logo on it, and his dark hair looked as if he'd dragged his fingers through it instead of combing it. Teamed with the shadow of stubble on his face, it made him look as if he'd just got out of bed. He should've looked scruffy and faintly disgusting. But the whole package made him seem younger and much more approachable—not to mention sexy as hell—and her mouth went dry. Oh, help. She really had to remember that he was the boss, not just another one of the team. That made him totally off limits. And, besides, she didn't want to risk her heart again. Which gave her a double reason not to act on the desire flickering through her—even if he was the most gorgeous man she'd ever met.

He indicated the box of chocolates sitting on his desk. 'Why?'

Hugh was clearly a man of few words when it came to work. Or maybe it was his Monday morning-itis. 'Why the gift? Or why chocolates?' she asked.

'Both.'

'The gift is to say thank you, because you went way beyond the call of duty on Friday night. They're chocolates, because I can hardly buy a man flowers,' she said. 'Did I give you enough money to cover everything, or do I still owe you?'

He handed her the envelope, which felt thick enough to contain most—if not all—of the money she'd enclosed with the card. 'My shoes survived, and the taxi and dry-cleaning bill weren't much,' he said.

She knew that wasn't true. The taxi firm would've charged him for valeting the cab and for lost earnings while the cab was out of action, being cleaned. 'I'd rather you kept it,' she said, putting the envelope back on his desk. 'To cover the inconvenience.'

'No need,' he said firmly. 'Is your sister OK? She looked terrible.'

Bella was grateful he hadn't mentioned the 'incident'. 'Grace barely even drinks, normally,' she said, not wanting him to think badly of her sister. 'Friday was totally out of character for her. She's the sensible and together one who sorts everything out; I'm the flaky and unreli—' She stopped mid-word, realising what she was about to blurt out. 'Not when it comes to my job, obviously. I'm very together where my work is concerned,' she added swiftly.

'But in your personal life you're flaky and unreliable?' he asked.

'Not unreliable, even—just the one who opens her mouth without thinking things through,' she said ruefully. 'As you've just heard.'

'But you rescued your sister when she needed your help,' he said softly. 'That definitely counts in your favour. Is she OK?'

'She will be,' Bella said. 'I've never known her to drink three glasses of champagne in a row, let alone on an empty stomach. I think that's why... Well. What happened, happened,' she finished, squirming slightly.

'Thank you for the chocolates. They're appreciated,' he said. 'And you have good taste.'

'I have good taste in a lot of things.' And then, when she saw the momentary flicker in those amazing blue eyes, she wished the words unsaid. 'I wasn't flirting with you,' she added quickly.

His expression said, *much*. 'Take the money,' he said. 'I don't need it. Use it to take your sister out to dinner or something.'

'Just no champagne, right?'

This time, he smiled. 'Right. Welcome to Insurgo, Ms Faraday.'

'Thank you, Mr Moncrieff.' Formality was good. It put distance between them. And it would stop her getting crazy ideas about a man with a mouth that promised sin and eyes that promised pleasure. Ideas she most definitely couldn't let herself act upon.

'Are you settling in all right?' he asked.

'Yes. Tarquin's given me my first brief and I'm working on it now. The limited edition single.' She paused. 'He said it was coloured vinyl. I have to admit, I don't know that much about how records are physically made. Can the vinyl be any colour you like?'

'Yes.'

'So you could do clear vinyl with little wisps of mist running through it?'

He looked surprised. 'Yes. Would that tie in with your design?'

'It's what the music makes me think of. Obviously it's just an idea at this stage,' she said swiftly, not wanting to put him off. 'I'll do some rough mock-ups of three or four ideas, and then I'm discussing them with Tarquin this afternoon.'

'Good. I look forward to seeing what you come up with.'

She blinked, surprised. 'You're going to be in the meeting as well?'

'Not that one,' he said. 'But when you and Tarquin have agreed which one to work on, then you come and convince me.'

'Challenge accepted.' The words were out before she could stop them. Oh, for pity's sake. This wasn't about a challenge. This was about…about…

Why had her brain suddenly turned to soup?

He smiled, then, and it felt as if the room had lit up. Which was even more worrying. She didn't want to start feeling like this about anyone, especially not her new boss.

'I think I'm going to enjoy working with you, Bella Faraday.'

There was a faint trace of huskiness in his voice that sent a thrill right through her. This was bad. She could actually imagine him saying other things to her in that gorgeous voice. Things that would turn her into a complete puddle of hormones.

No.

This was *work*. She was really going to have to keep reminding herself that her relationship with Hugh Moncrieff was strictly business. Maybe she'd ask her friend Nalini to put a temporary henna tattoo on her hand saying 'work'—written in Hindi script, so Bella would know exactly what it meant but anyone else would think it was just a pretty design. The last thing she needed was for anyone to guess how attracted she was to her new boss.

'Good,' she said. 'I'll get back to it, then.' She gave him what she hoped was a cool, capable smile, and forced herself to walk coolly and calmly out of his office. One foot in front of the other. One step at a time. She could run once that door was closed behind her.

She'd just reached the doorway when he said softly, 'Bella. I think you've forgotten something.'

Oh, help. She had to suppress the surge of lust. 'What's that?' Oh, great. And her voice *would* have to be squeaky. She took a deep breath and turned to face him.

He waved the envelope at her.

'Keep it.'

He coughed. 'As your boss, I'm pulling rank.'

If she was stubborn over this, she could lose her job.

If she took the money back, she'd be in his debt.

Caught between a rock and a hard place. Or maybe

there was a way out. 'Then I'll donate it to charity,' she said. 'I'm sure you can suggest a suitable one.'

'Bella, this isn't a war,' he said softly, and she felt horrible.

'Sorry. It's just... I don't want to be in your debt. And I don't mean just you—I mean in *anyone's* debt,' she clarified.

'The dry-cleaning bill wasn't much, and the taxi firm is one I use a lot so they were pretty accommodating. And,' he added, 'I'm not exactly a church mouse.'

'Church mouse?' she asked, not following. Then she remembered the proverbial phrase. 'Oh. Of course.'

'Take the money,' he said softly, 'and it's all forgotten. As far as I'm concerned—and everyone else at Insurgo, for that matter—today's the first day we've met. And I'm notorious in the office for not being a Monday morning person. Nobody usually talks to me until lunchtime on Mondays because I'm so horrible.'

That made her feel better. 'Thank you,' she said, and took the envelope.

'Have a nice day,' he said, and that smile made her feel warm all over.

'You, too,' she said. But this time she lost her cool and fled before she could drop herself in it any more.

CHAPTER THREE

EVEN THE IDEA was crazy.

Asking Bella was completely out of the question. She was practically a stranger; and she worked for him. Two huge reasons why Hugh knew that he should put this whole thing out of his mind.

Hugh paced up and down his living room. The problem was, now the idea was in his head, it had taken root. And he knew why. He could tell himself that asking Bella to play the role of his unsuitable new girlfriend was simply because she was vivacious enough to make it convincing. It was true enough. But he knew that the real reason was a little more complicated than that. Spending the weekend together in Oxford would give them a chance to get to know each other better. See where things took them.

Crazy. Stupid. Insane.

He knew better than to mix work and pleasure. Last time he'd done it, the whole thing had gone so badly wrong that he'd nearly lost Insurgo—letting down his business partner and the people who depended on them for their jobs. Only the fact that Roland, his other best friend, had bought into the business as a sleeping partner had saved him from having to shut the business down.

He'd worked stupid hours and he'd managed to stabilise everything, but he would never take that kind of risk again.

Strictly speaking, he knew this wasn't quite that kind of risk. Bella wasn't Jessie. She was part of the team, not one of his artists. She'd signed a contract with him rather than making a verbal agreement she could back out of because it would be her word against his. Getting to know Bella wasn't going to put Insurgo at risk.

But it still made him antsy. Since Jessie, he'd promised himself he wouldn't trust anyone with the battered remains of his heart. He'd keep an emotional distance. So why couldn't he get Bella Faraday out of his head? Why did he keep remembering that frisson of awareness when she'd kissed his cheek in the taxi? Why did her smile make him feel as if the room lit up?

And, more importantly, what was he going to do about it?

By Thursday morning, Bella felt as if she'd been working at Insurgo for ever. The rest of the team turned out to be total sweethearts, and they all shared a love of music, cinema and art. Everyone pitched in with ideas and suggestions, and nobody minded if theirs was passed over for a better one. And she absolutely loved working there.

The previous afternoon, they'd had a discussion in the office about which song fitted them, so that evening she'd made little name-cards for everyone's desk with a quick caricature of them and the title of 'their' song in place of their name.

It seemed mean to leave Hugh out just because he was upstairs rather than in the open-plan office with everyone else, so she made a card for him as well. 'I Don't Like Mondays' fitted him to a T, she thought.

That morning, as the rest of the team filtered in to the office and saw the name-cards on their desks, there was much hilarity.

Then Hugh walked into the office—clearly not in a good mood, again—and Bella rather wished she hadn't done a name-card for him after all.

'Ms Faraday—a word?' It was more of a command than a question, and his expression was completely impassive.

'Yes, Mr Moncrieff,' she said, and followed him meekly up to his office.

Even though he didn't say a word to her on the way up, she had a pretty good idea what this was about. He hadn't been amused at all by his name-card.

'I'm sorry,' she said as soon as he closed the door. 'We were messing about yesterday—' Then she stopped as she realised how incriminating her words were. 'Over lunch, that is,' she said swiftly, hoping that she'd saved the situation. She didn't want to get her new colleagues into trouble. 'We were talking about the song title that could be used instead of your name to describe you, and I drew the cards last night at home. It was just a bit of fun and I didn't mean anything by it.'

'You picked an appropriate one for me,' he said.

Though every single day seemed to be Monday, where his mood was concerned. He really wasn't a morning person. She winced. 'Sorry. Are you very cross with me?'

'No—and, just for the record, I don't mind a bit of messing about in the office. It helps creativity, and I know everyone on the team puts the hours in. As long as the job gets done on time and within budget, I don't actually care *how* it's done.'

'Then why did you want to see me?' Bella asked, now completely mystified. If he wasn't about to haul her over the coals for unprofessional behaviour, then what?

'Your hair.'

She frowned. 'What's wrong with it?'

'You were blonde, yesterday. Platinum blonde.'

'Ye-es.' She still didn't follow.

'And today your hair's red.'

A tiny bit brighter red than she'd intended, because she'd been so busy making the name-cards the previous evening that she'd left the dye in for a few minutes longer than she should've done, but she liked it. 'Yes.' Where was he going with this? 'Is there a problem with my hair colour?' she asked carefully.

'No, not at all.'

She really didn't understand. 'Then why did you call me into your office?'

'Do you have a boyfriend?'

Apart from the fact that you weren't supposed to answer a question with a question, what did that have to do with anything? She frowned. 'You're not supposed to ask me things like that. My relationship status has nothing to do with my job.'

'I know. I'm not asking you as your employer.'

She caught her breath. Did that mean he was asking her out?

No, of course not. That was totally ridiculous. Just because she had a secret crush on him, it didn't mean that her feelings were in any way returned. And in any case her boss was the last man she'd ever date. It would cause way too many problems, and she really couldn't afford to give up her new job. There was no guarantee that the receivers dealing with her former client would give her any of the money owing to her, because she'd be way down the pecking order in the list of creditors. And, with Kirk having cleaned out their joint bank account so she no longer had any savings to her name, she was stuck. 'Why do you want to know?' she asked, trying hard to sound polite rather than aggressive.

'Because I need you to do something for me, and I need to know whether I'm going to have to have a conversation with an overprotective boyfriend first.'

She was still none the wiser. 'Now you've really got me worried.'

He raked a hand through his hair. 'Bella, don't be difficult.'

That was rich, coming from him, she thought. Hugh Moncrieff was the walking definition of difficult. He was also the walking definition of sexy, but she had to keep a lid on that thought.

'Can you just answer the question?' he asked. 'Are you single or not?'

'I'm absolutely single,' she said crisply, 'and I intend to stay that way.' Just so it'd be totally clear that she wasn't trying to flirt with him—or anything else.

'Good.' He gave her a sweet, sweet smile. One that made a lot of warning bells ring in her head. 'Bella, remember when I helped you out last Friday night?'

The warning bells got louder. 'Ye-es.'

'Good.' He paused. 'I need a favour.'

So much for him saying that they'd forget what had happened. Clearly were strings attached, after all. How *disappointing*. 'What sort of favour?' she asked carefully.

'I need you to be my date for a family event.'

That was the last thing she'd expected. Had she misheard? 'To be what?' she asked.

'My date for a family event,' he repeated.

That was what she thought he'd said. The words 'date' and 'Hugh Moncrieff' were a dangerous combination. 'Why?'

'A more pertinent question, in the circumstances, is "when?",' he said dryly.

OK. She'd play it his way. 'When?' she asked sweetly.

'Next weekend.'

What? 'As in tomorrow or as in next Friday?'

'As in a week on Saturday,' he clarified.

Talk about lack of notice. Did he think that she didn't have a social life? 'Where?'

'Oxfordshire.'

'Right.' She stared at him. 'So let me get this straight. You want me to go to a family do with you in Oxfordshire and pretend to be your girlfriend.'

'Yes.'

She folded her arms. 'Now I think "why" might be pertinent. And I think I deserve a proper answer.'

'If you want to know the truth, it's because you,' he said, 'will annoy my family.'

She looked at him through narrowed eyes. 'That's not very nice—to me or to them.' And it made her feel as if he was using her. Just like Kirk had. Even though Hugh was being upfront about it rather than pretending he loved her, the way Kirk had, it still stung.

'Given that you told me you were flaky and unreliable in your personal life, I think that's a fair assessment.'

He had a point. Just. 'It's still not very nice,' she said.

'I didn't expect you to go all Mary Poppins on me,' he drawled.

She resisted the urge to slap him or to say something rude. Just. 'That's because you don't know me very well. What do you want to achieve?'

He frowned. 'I don't know what you mean.'

'You said you want to annoy your family. What do you really want to happen?'

When he still looked blank, she sighed. 'Look, you're at point A and you clearly want to be at point B. What do you need to do to get from A to B, and is having a fake girlfriend really the most effective way to do it?'

He raised his eyebrows. 'That's a bit sensible.'

'Coming from me, you mean?' She rolled her eyes. 'It doesn't come from me, actually. It's the way my sister looks at things.'

'Your sister Grace? As in the woman who downed three glasses of champagne on an empty stomach…?' he said, with mischievous emphasis.

She put her hands on her hips and glared at him. 'Don't you dare be rude about my sister,' she warned. 'I already told you: that was really unlike her. It was due to special circumstances—and don't bother asking what they were, because I'm not going to tell you. It's none of your business.'

'Absolutely,' he said, disarming her. 'Actually, I like the way you stand up for your sister. And you have a point.'

'So why you do want to annoy your family?' she asked.

'This,' he said, 'is even more confidential than anything commercial I talk to you about.'

'That's *obvious*,' she said, rolling her eyes at him.

'You're my boss, so anything you say to me in this room stays in this room unless you say otherwise.'

'Thank you,' he said. 'Since you ask, the reason is because I'm sick and tired of them nagging me to settle down. So if I turn up to my brother's engagement party with someone who looks completely unsuitable, maybe they'll shut up and get off my case.'

She digested this slowly. He was saying she was unsuitable because of her hair? 'So basically you're asking me to play the kooky wild child. You want me to turn up with a mad hair colour, wearing ridiculous shoes and a skirt that's more like a belt?'

'What you wear is entirely up to you,' he said. Then he looked thoughtful. 'But, as you mentioned it first, yes, I think you probably have the chutzpah to carry off that kind of outfit.'

She still couldn't quite work out if he was insulting her or praising her. Instead, she asked the other thing that was puzzling her. Well, apart from the fact that he was single. Even though he tended to be grumpy in the mornings in the office, she knew he had a good heart. He'd rescued her and Grace when they'd needed help, even though at the time they'd been complete strangers— and at the time it hadn't felt as if there were any strings. Plus he had beautiful eyes and an even more beautiful mouth. The kind that made you want to find out what it felt like to be kissed by it.

She shook herself. That was something she shouldn't be thinking about. 'So why does your family want you to settle down?'

When he didn't answer, she pointed out, 'If you ask me to design something for you, then I need a brief to know what your target market is and what you want the design to achieve. I need to understand *why* before I can design something to suit. This is the same sort of thing. If I don't understand why you want me to play someone unsuitable, I'm not going to be able to deliver the goods, am I?'

'So you'll do it?'

'I didn't say that. I still reserve the right to say no.' If saying no was actually an option. Would her job depend on this? 'But if you tell me why and I agree with your reasoning, then I might consider it.' She spread her hands. 'Anything you tell me is confidential. But I would also like to point out that I do have a social life, actually, and I did have plans for the weekend.'

'I'm sorry.' He raked a hand through his hair, suddenly looking vulnerable. Which was almost enough to make her agree to help him, regardless of his motives.

Weird.

Hugh Moncrieff was old enough and tough enough to look after himself. You didn't get to be the successful owner of an independent record label if you were a pushover. He didn't need looking after by anyone. But that expression in his eyes had touched a chord with her. It reminded her of the look in Grace's eyes when she'd confessed that she didn't fit in with Howard's family and didn't think she ever could. That she'd felt trapped and miserable.

Was that how Hugh felt about his own family?

And why did she suddenly want to rescue him, when she was usually the one who had to be rescued?

'Of course you have a social life,' he said. 'And I don't expect you to say "how high" every time I ask you to jump.'

'Good,' she said. 'I'm glad that's clear.'

He gave her a wry smile. 'And I know I'm out of order, asking you to play a part.'

'It does make me feel a bit used,' she admitted.

'I don't mean it quite like that. I need help to deal with a tricky situation.'

'Just like I did—and you helped me, so it makes sense that I should return the favour.' Put like that, she thought, his request was much more reasonable.

'If it's possible for you to change your plans for the weekend and you do agree to help me by being my date, just be yourself. That'll do nicely.'

'Because I'm unsuitable?' she asked. Just when she'd started to feel OK about it, he'd made her feel bad again. Stupid. 'That's a bit insulting.'

'That isn't actually what I meant. You're confident,' he said. 'You're direct. You don't play games.'

'But you're asking me to play a game. Well, play a part,' she corrected herself. 'Which is pretty much the same thing.'

'I guess. I don't mean to insult you, Bella. I apologise.'

'Apology accepted.' She paused. 'So why do you need a date?'

He sighed. 'I'm the youngest of four boys. The other three are all stockbrokers in the firm started by my great-grandfather. My family would very much like me to toe the line and follow suit.'

She winced. 'Ouch. That's what I called you on Friday. I said you looked like a stockbroker.'

'I'm not one, and I never want to be one,' he said softly. 'Don't get me wrong. I'm not saying that it's a bad career—just that it's not right for me. My brothers love what they do, and that's fine. I'd support them to the hilt, but

I don't want to join them.' He gave her another of those wry smiles. 'That's why the label has its name.'

'Got you. Insurgo's Latin for "to rebel".' She wrinkled her nose. 'And, no, I didn't go to the sort of school that taught Latin. I looked it up on the internet. The only Latin I know is "*lorem ipsum*"—the stuff used as filler text in a design rough, and that's not really proper Latin.'

He smiled back. 'Actually, "*lorem ipsum*" is a mash-up of Cicero's *De finibus bonorum et malorum*.'

'Trust *you* to know that.' The words came out before she could stop them.

He laughed. 'I'm afraid I did go to the kind of school that taught Latin.' He dragged his hand through his hair. 'I love what I do, Bella. I like hearing artists play me raw songs—and then a different arrangement flowers in my head, and I can see exactly what they need to do to make it a hit without losing their original voice. I've never wanted to do anything else but produce music that I love—music that makes the world a better place. But my family worries about me, because the music business isn't exactly stable. Insurgo's doing well—well enough for some much bigger labels to have offered to buy me out, though I've always refused because I'm not going to sell out my artists like that—but I'm still at the mercy of the markets. We've managed to weather a few storms, but all it takes is one wrong decision that loses the business a lot of money, or for a couple of my biggest customers to go bankrupt and not pay me, and we could go under.'

'Tell me about it,' she said feelingly.

'I knew you'd get that bit. You've been there,' he said.

So either Tarquin had told him that she'd once had her own business, or he'd read her résumé. Or maybe both.

'Small businesses fail all the time,' she said, 'and I kept mine going for two years. If my best client hadn't gone bankrupt, owing me the equivalent of three months' salary, I'd still be a freelance designer now. But when one door closes another opens—and now I have a job I like here.'

'I take it back about being Mary Poppins,' he said. 'You're Pollyanna.'

'I'm just me,' she told him firmly, 'not a stereotype. But, yes, I believe in looking for the good in life.' She whistled the chorus from 'Always Look on the Bright Side of Life' and smiled.

'It's a good philosophy,' he said.

'You're right—you're perfectly capable of being a stockbroker, but it'd make you miserable. You're doing what you love,' she said. 'And there's nothing wrong with that. Why doesn't your family see that?'

He sighed. 'They have this little box ready for me. I'm supposed to fit in with a sensible job, a sensible wife, and two point four children or whatever it's meant to be nowadays. A *pied-à-terre* in London for me during the week, and an ancient pile in the countryside for the family, where the kids can grow up until we send them to boarding school.'

Was he describing what his own childhood had been like? 'I guess I'm lucky,' she said. 'All my parents and my sister want is for me to be happy and fulfilled.'

'Are you?' he asked.

She nodded. 'Are *you*?'

'Yes.' But she noticed that he didn't meet her eye. So did that mean he wasn't? And what, she wondered, was missing from his life?

Not that there was any point in asking. She was pretty

sure he'd stonewall her. Getting the information so far had been like pulling teeth.

'OK. So you want me to pretend to be your girlfriend, to show your family that you have no intention of meeting any of the criteria to fit that little box they've made for you. You already have a job they don't approve of, so what you need is an outrageous girlfriend to horrify them even more. That will be the icing on the cake, if you'll excuse me mixing my metaphors,' she said, hoping that she'd summed up the situation without missing anything.

'That's pretty much it.' He paused. 'So will you do it?'

'It's one way to get from A to B,' she said. 'But I think a much better one would be to sit down with your family and talk to them. Make them see how much you love Insurgo. Show them your passion for it. Play them the raw stuff, and then the final version with all the changes you suggested, so they can hear exactly what you do. Then they'll understand and be happy just to let you do it.'

'Maybe,' he said. 'But, even if they listened to me about my job, that's only half the problem dealt with. There's still the sensible wife they want me to have.'

She shrugged. 'You could always tell them you'd like a sensible husband.'

He grinned. 'You mean, ask Tarquin to pretend that he's my life partner as well as my business partner? I think Rupert—his other half—might have something to say about that.' Then his smile faded. 'I don't want a sensible wife. Or husband, for that matter.'

'What do you want?' she asked.

What did he want?

Never to have his heart broken again.

Which meant no more serious relationships. And it

had suited him just fine over the few months, dating casually and making sure that all his girlfriends knew that a diamond ring and a change of name were never going to be on offer. That he was looking for fun, not for for ever. And most of the time he didn't even bother with that. He concentrated on work. Though it wasn't quite the work of his heart any more. Not since he'd stopped writing music.

'What I want right now,' he said, 'is to get through Nigel's engagement party without being nagged about my choice of career or lifestyle.'

'You know that's not going to happen,' she said. 'That's the thing about families. They're interested in what you do, so of course they're going to ask questions and give their opinions, whether you ask for them or not. It's part and parcel of family life.'

Clearly she didn't mind about that as much as he did. Then again, she'd said that her family just wanted her to be happy. And she'd gone straight to her sister's rescue last week; he had a feeling that Grace would've come straight to Bella's rescue, too, if the positions had been reversed. His brothers certainly weren't batting his corner. They thought he ought to give in and join them in the family business.

She shrugged. 'So. Realistically, what's the best you can hope for?'

'That an outrageous girlfriend will distract them enough to stop them nagging me about when I'm going to settle down. Just for the weekend,' he added, wanting to make it clear that this wasn't a long-term thing.

'Weekend? I thought you said it was a party?'

'It's a weekend thing,' he explained.

She looked shocked. 'You're telling me that this engagement party is going to last for a whole *weekend*? Wow. I thought that my friends and I could party pretty hard, but we're all amateurs compared to that!'

'It's not that big a deal,' he said. 'We turn up for afternoon tea and cake on Saturday with the older relatives, and then we have a cocktail party in the evening. It's black tie, by the way.'

She looked thoughtful. 'So you want me to wear an unsuitable dress to the tea party bit, and something even more outrageous for the evening do rather than a proper little black dress.'

Oh, good. She understood and she wasn't going to give him a hard time about it. 'That would do very nicely.'

'And then what?'

'Um, we stay overnight—but you'll have your own room, don't worry. I'm not expecting you to share with me or anything,' he added swiftly. 'We'll have breakfast in the morning, go for a walk, stay for Sunday lunch because Ma will insist—except that'll be just my brothers and their partners and us, plus maybe an aunt and uncle or two—and *then* we can go home.'

'A whole weekend,' she repeated.

'The food will be excellent,' he said. 'And there will be pink champagne.' And then a nasty thought hit him. 'Unless last weekend put you off champagne?'

She rolled her eyes at him. 'That's mean. I already told you, my sister doesn't normally drink more than one glass. Last weekend was exceptional circumstances.'

'I apologise. Again.'

'Apology accepted, but I have a three strikes and you're out rule,' she warned. 'Do it again and I'll stand on your foot. In spike heels. I might be only five feet four, but I'm heavier than I look.'

'Got it.' The more time Hugh spent with Bella, the more he liked her. She made him feel different—she brought back the crazy, spontaneous part of him that he'd kept locked away since Jessie. Which was dangerous. Maybe he should call this whole thing off. For safety's sake.

'So what colour do you want my hair to be?' she said, cutting into his thoughts.

'Any colour you like. It's your hair.'

She smiled. 'Good answer. You're learning.'

'I'll pay for your frocks,' he said, 'and your shoes, and whatever else you want. Just tell me how much you need.'

'It's very tempting to say yes and drag you off to the fashion department in Selfridges with your credit card,' she said, 'but I guess it'd be more believable if I wore a charity shop find.' She paused. 'Or am I playing a gold-digger who expects you to bankroll her fashion habit?'

'I don't think you'd be a believable gold digger, because you're too independent,' he said. Again, so unlike Jessie, who'd always had an eye on the main chance. Except he'd been so in love with her that he hadn't seen it at the time. With Bella, what you saw was what you got—and that was refreshing. It tempted him to relax the rules where she was concerned. Part of him thought this was a bad idea; but part of him was intrigued enough to want to know where this could take them. 'A charity shop find would be good, but I meant it about paying for your clothes and what have you. Just get anything you need and I'll pick up the bill. You shouldn't be out of pocket when you're doing me a favour.'

'OK. I'll make sure I get receipts for everything. So I need outfits for a tea party, a cocktail party, breakfast, a walk and lunch.' She raised an eyebrow. 'I hope your car has room for a lot of luggage.'

'The brasher the better—and add that to your shopping list,' he said with a grin. 'And thank you. I think I'm actually going to enjoy this now.'

'Is it really going to be so bad, spending time with your family?' she asked.

And now she'd wrong-footed him again. He wrinkled his nose. 'I love them, but they don't see me for who I am. They don't listen to me. They want me to fit in their nice little box. That's the thing I find hardest to deal with.'

'So my job is to be their wake-up call. To make them see that by pushing you so hard, they're actually making you run just as hard in the other direction. Whereas, if they leave you be, you might just come up with a compromise that will keep you all happy.'

'I'm beginning to think that you should swap places with me and be head of strategy at Insurgo,' he said.

'Hardly.' She scoffed. 'I was working on design principles.'

'They work for strategy, too.' He paused. 'Thank you. I think I'm in your debt.'

'Strictly speaking,' she said, 'and, as you pointed out, I was in yours—you rescued Grace and me when we needed help. This is my chance to return the favour. And then we're quits—right?'

'Quits,' he agreed. 'That sounds good to me.' He reached over to shake her hand, then rather wished he hadn't when his palm started tingling. He really shouldn't start thinking about Bella in that way. He'd learned from Jessie that business and love didn't mix, and he didn't want to repeat his mistake. He was attracted to Bella— she was gorgeous and vibrant and she would make any man look more than twice—but he really shouldn't take this any further. They were going to keep this strictly professional. 'I'll let you get back to whatever you were working on,' he said. 'And thank you.'

'Last thing,' she said. 'What about an engagement present?'

'It's all taken care of. And the card.'

'How much do I owe—?' she began.

'It's all taken care of,' he repeated, cutting in. 'Really. I don't expect you to pay a penny towards this.'

'Can I at least take your mother some flowers, as we're staying at your parents' place?'

He frowned. 'That's very *suitable* behaviour, Bella.'

'Actually, it's common courtesy to take a present for your hostess,' she corrected. 'I don't mind people thinking I'm an airhead and unsuitable, but I *do* mind them thinking I'm rude and selfish. So. Flowers or chocolates?'

'She's a chocolate fiend. Dark. But you don't have to—'

'Yes, I do,' she cut in. 'Or the deal's off.'

And hadn't he asked her to help him partly because she was so outspoken and independent? 'OK,' he said.

'Good. And now I'm going back to what you pay me to do,' she said, and sashayed out of the room. As much as you could sashay in jeans and flat canvas shoes.

But the images in his head wouldn't shift all day. The curve of her backside. The confident, brisk way she moved. That spark of merriment in her blue, blue eyes. The curve of her mouth.

How would her mouth feel against his? Would she make his lips tingle as much as his skin? And how would it feel to lose himself inside her?

There suddenly wasn't enough air in the room. He

walked over to the window, opened it and shoved his head out. Maybe the noise from the traffic would clear his head.

It didn't.

'Get a grip, Moncrieff,' he warned himself.

This was strictly business. Letting his imagination loose was a seriously bad idea. He wasn't going to let himself think about what it would be like to touch Bella. To kiss her. To hold her close. This pretend girlfriend business was just to get him off the hook with his family. And, the more he kept telling himself that, the quicker he'd start to believe it.

CHAPTER FOUR

'ARE YOU SURE this is a good idea, Bel?' Grace asked.

'Going to Oxfordshire and pretending to be Hugh's unsuitable girlfriend? Possibly not,' Bella admitted. 'I did tell him I thought it'd be a better idea to be straight with his family and get them to see his passion for his work. But he's adamant that this is the best way to get them off his back—and I guess they're his family, so he should know the best way to handle them.'

'I don't mean just that,' Grace said gently. 'I mean getting involved in your boss's personal life.'

'I'm not getting involved in his personal life,' Bella insisted. 'Apart from the fact that I'm officially off men for good, I'm just doing this as a favour.'

Grace winced. 'To make up for me throwing up over him in the taxi?'

'No,' said Bella firmly. 'No.' Though he had hinted at it. Which had made it easier for Bella to say yes. Not that she wanted Grace to worry about it, so she kept that information to herself. 'He just needs someone to help him make his family back off. And I kind of fit the bill.'

'So you're going to a posh afternoon tea party wearing a skin-tight leopard-print dress,' Grace said.

'Yup. And I've got tiny, tiny shorts and high-heeled

mules for the country walk the next day. And, best of all, for the cocktail party… Meet my alternative to the little black dress.' Bella produced the curtains she'd found in one of the charity shops, flapped one with a flourish and draped it over one shoulder. 'Ta-da!'

Grace blinked. 'You're wearing a *curtain* to a cocktail party?'

'Not quite—it's going to be a proper dress. Only I'm making it from a curtain instead of from normal dress fabric. Em said she'd come round tomorrow, measure me, and we'll cut it out and run it up together.' Bella grinned. 'This is where going to art school comes into its own. I know loads of people who can help. I just thought, what could be gaudier and more unsuitable for a black tie cocktail party than a mini-dress made out of a curtain?'

Grace eyed the orange flowers. 'Um. Very nineteen-sixties.'

Bella's grin broadened. 'And it's so *The Sound of Music*, don't you think?' She draped the curtain over the back of her sofa, pulled Grace to her feet, and danced her sister around the tiny living room, all the while singing, 'How Do You Solve a Problem Like Maria?' but substituting her own name in the song.

'You're impossible,' Grace said, but she was laughing.

'I'm a genius. And I've just had another great idea. We can have takeaway pizza tonight and watch *The Sound of Music* together. I love that film so much. And we can sing "Do Re Mi" in harmony—I'll even let you pick your part.'

Grace hugged her. 'I know what you're doing, Bel. You're trying to distract me. But I'm OK. Really. The hard bit was last weekend and breaking up with Howard. The temp agency's found me some work, I've got a couple of weeks to find a new flat before I have to move out of mine, and you've been the best sister and most brilliant support anyone could ask for. My new life starts now, and it's going to be just fine.'

'I still worry about you,' Bella said. She didn't quite dare ask if this was how Grace felt about her, most of the time. Grace had had to rescue her often enough from some scrape or other.

'I'm fine,' Grace reassured her again. 'But, yes, we can order a pizza and watch a film tonight. That sounds good.' She took a deep breath. 'And if this engagement party goes horribly wrong next weekend, just ring me and I'll drive straight down to get you, OK? It's only an hour and a bit from London to Oxford.'

'It won't go wrong,' Bella said. 'I'm just playing a part. Even if I wasn't officially off men, Hugh Moncrieff is the most unsuitable man in the world for me. He's my boss, and dating him would make everything way too complicated.'

'So why,' Grace asked, 'are my big sister antennae suddenly twitching like mad?'

'Force of habit,' Bella said with a smile. 'But nothing's going to go wrong.'

The following weekend, Bella's confidence in that statement had evaporated.

Had she gone too far with her outfit?

What if Hugh's family had a blazing row with him over her unsuitability and it ruined the engagement party? That really wouldn't be fair on Hugh's brother and his fiancée.

Maybe she ought to pack some suitable clothes as well, in case she needed to change at the last minute. Or borrow Grace's car so she could make a quick getaway if she needed to, rather than letting Hugh drive her down to Oxfordshire. Or maybe she should just make sure her mobile phone was fully charged and she'd got the number of a reliable local taxi firm.

Plus she and Hugh hadn't set any real ground rules. What did playing his unsuitable girlfriend actually mean? Holding hands, draping herself over him—or even kissing him?

The idea of kissing Hugh sent her into a flat spin.

He was her boss. She shouldn't even flirt with him, let alone entertain ideas about kissing him. Even if he was the most attractive man she'd met in years. Kissing was totally off the agenda.

So why, why, why couldn't she get the idea out of her head?

Her stomach was in knots by the time her doorbell rang, just after lunch.

When she answered the door, Hugh was standing there, wearing one of his business suits. He looked utterly gorgeous—and Bella felt completely out of place in her outrageous get-up. Particularly when his eyes widened in apparent shock as he took in what she was wearing: a tight leopard-skin mini-dress with a wide shiny belt cinched round her waist and spindly high heels, a chunky bead necklace, and she'd styled her hair so her normally sleek bob was in wild curls.

'This is a bit too much, isn't it?' she asked, indicating her outfit.

'It's, um, *interesting*,' he said. 'Very eighties. Especially the hair.'

In other words, he hated it. She'd gone way over the top. There was cutesy retro, and there was a total mess.

She'd clearly crossed the admittedly narrow line between the two. She took a deep breath. 'Sorry. Give me ten minutes and I'll change.'

He caught her hand. 'No, Bella, you're perfect as you are.'

A shiver ran through her at the feel of his skin against hers. She had to remind herself sharply that she was doing this as a favour to him—acting the part of his unsuitable girlfriend—and that was all. Any attraction she felt towards him was totally inappropriate and needed to be squashed. Like yesterday.

'Are you sure this isn't too much?' she asked, doubt still crawling through her. 'Are you quite, *quite* sure it wouldn't be better to switch to Plan B?'

'Which is?'

'Go to the party on your own and tell your family how much you love Insurgo, that you're perfectly happy being single and that you don't need a romantic partner to feel that your life's complete.'

'I could, but they wouldn't listen, so it has to be Plan A,' he said softly. 'And I want you to know how much I appreciate this, Bella. I don't know anyone else who could've carried this off.'

'Really?'

'Really. I'm not flannelling you.'

She could hear the sincerity in his voice. He really thought that she could do this. And to have someone believing her on a personal level, someone other than her family... That made her feel better about herself than she had in a long time.

'I'm truly grateful,' he said. 'Now, where's your luggage?'

She picked up her large, bright pink suitcase and

faked a confidence she didn't quite feel. 'OK. I'm ready. Let's go.'

His car was gorgeous—sleek and low-slung, with leather seats that were amazingly comfortable—and she wasn't surprised to discover that he had a really good sound system, too. She was happy enough to listen to music until they were out of London and on the motorway, and then she turned to him.

'Can I ask you some questions?'

'Sure you can ask,' he said, sounding as if he reserved the right not to answer.

'We'll start with your family,' she said. 'Even an unsuitable airhead girlfriend would know who she was going to visit. I know you're the youngest of four boys, and we're going to your brother Nigel's engagement party somewhere in Oxfordshire. Everyone else in your family is a stockbroker. And that's *all* I know. Do you not think that I might need to know everyone's names, at the very least?'

'I guess,' he said. His voice was totally expressionless, so she had no idea what was going through his head. 'OK. My parents are Oliver and Elizabeth. Pa's recently retired and spends half of his day on the golf course. Ma's in the WI and does charity work. My brothers—Julian's the oldest, married to Poppy, and they have a baby girl, Sophia. Alistair's the next and he's married to Harriet. Nigel's about to get engaged to Victoria, and they're getting married at Christmas. I'm the youngest, and I'm taking my new girlfriend Bella Faraday to meet the folks. Anything else?'

'Yes. Ground rules. What does playing your girlfriend actually mean?' she asked. 'Holding your hand? Draping myself artfully over you?'

He blew out a breath. 'I hadn't thought that far ahead, to be honest. I suppose they'd expect us to hold hands. And for me to dance with you at the cocktail party. Which is a point. Can you dance?'

She couldn't help smiling because he'd set up her answer so beautifully. And, with any luck, it would make him laugh and relax a bit, too. 'Would that be with or without a pole, Mr Moncrieff?'

As she'd hoped, he laughed. 'Without.'

'I don't really tend to go clubbing,' she said. 'But I go to a dance aerobics class, so I can move in time to music.'

'That's good enough for me.'

But he hadn't answered her question fully. 'Anything else?' she asked.

He frowned. 'Such as?'

'Normally, people who are dating tend to, um, kiss each other,' she said. 'Especially when dancing and parties are involved.'

'Ah. Yes. Kissing.'

The car suddenly felt way too small. And was it her imagination, or had the temperature just shot up by ten degrees?

'Chaste kissing would be acceptable,' he said.

Right at that moment, she didn't feel very chaste. And she wished she hadn't brought up the subject, because she could just imagine what it would be like to kiss Hugh Moncrieff. To cup his face in her hands and brush her lips against his, teasing at first, and then letting him deepen the kiss. Matching him touch for touch, bite for bite, until they were both dizzy with desire and he carried her off to his bed...

'Bella?'

'What?' She'd been so lost in her fantasy that she

hadn't heard him say anything to her. She felt colour flood into her cheeks.

'I said, are you OK with that?'

No. It was way too risky.

But she'd agreed to play his unsuitable girlfriend. And she was the one who'd brought up the question of kissing in the first place.

'I guess,' she said, trying to sound cool and calm and completely unbothered. 'Next question.'

'Hit me with it,' he said dryly.

'Why are you single?'

He blew out a breath. 'You're very direct. Why are *you* single?'

Because she'd put her trust in the wrong people. 'I asked you first.'

He shrugged. 'I was seeing someone and it didn't work out.'

That was obviously the need-to-know version of the story, she thought. She didn't think Hugh was the type to be a selfish love rat—someone like that wouldn't have come to her and Grace's rescue when they'd needed help, the other week—so she assumed that he hadn't been the one to end the relationship. Had his ex broken his heart? But there was no point in asking him. She knew he'd stonewall her.

'You?' he asked.

'You summed it up for me, too. I was seeing someone and it didn't work out,' she said. She didn't want to tell him the whole messy story. More precisely, she didn't want him knowing that she was so naïve and had such poor judgement in relationships. Her best friend and her live-in boyfriend. Just how had she managed to keep her eyes so firmly closed to what was really going on between them?

'Was it recent?' he asked.

'Six months ago,' she said. 'And you?'

'A year.'

'And you haven't met anyone else since?' That surprised her. When he wasn't being grumpy in the office, Hugh was good company. And he was very easy on the eye. Surely he had women lining up for him in droves?

'I've been too busy concentrating on my business.' He paused. 'You?'

'The same.' Except it hadn't just been her romantic relationship that had crashed. Kirk had dumped her for the woman Bella had believed was her best friend since sixth form, taking that support away from her, too. And Kirk had quietly cleaned out their joint bank account, the morning he dumped her—which was why Bella hadn't had her normal safety cushion of the equivalent of three months' salary when her best client went bust, and why her finances were in such a mess now.

And there had been next to nothing she could do about it, because the money had been in their joint names. She'd talked to the bank, but they'd said that any signatory to a joint account had the right to withdraw however much money they liked, no matter how much they'd actually put in.

Bella would never make that mistake again. And she was really glad that she'd listened to Grace's advice and put her tax money to one side in a different account rather than keeping it with her 'salary', or she'd be in debt to the Inland Revenue as well.

'Let's just say I'm tired of always dating Mr Wrong and I'm happier being single,' she said.

'Works for me. Any more questions?'

He was definitely in his Monday morning office mode now. Grumpy and difficult. She decided that any other questions could wait. 'I guess we've covered the basics.'

'Good. If you don't mind, I'd better concentrate on my driving.'

Given that they were going to his family home, he probably knew the route blindfold, so Bella was pretty sure that this was just his way of avoiding any more questions. And she supposed he had a point. She knew enough to play her role. Asking him anything else would be intrusive, wouldn't it? She let him concentrate on his driving and fiddled quietly with her phone, until he turned off the main road and drove them through narrower country roads to the outskirts of a village.

'Here we are, then,' he said as he turned into a driveway. The fences on either side were in perfect repair, and huge lime trees lined the fences and cast dappled shade on the driveway.

Bella had known that Hugh was from a posh background, but she hadn't realised just how posh. At the end of the half-a-mile-long driveway was the most beautiful house she'd ever seen: an Elizabethan manor house built from mellow Cotswold stone, with floor-to-ceiling sash windows on the ground floor, mullioned windows on the top floor, wisteria climbing the walls which wasn't in bloom yet but would look stunning in a couple of weeks, and a wide front door with a spider-web fanlight above it.

'That's gorgeous,' she said. 'And I've got this weird sense of déjà vu—I know I've never been here before, but somehow I feel as if I have.'

'You've probably seen the house on TV,' he said. 'It's been used as a location for a few period dramas.'

Before she had the chance to ask which ones, he parked on the gravelled area outside the house.

'I see my brothers are already here,' he said.

There were two sports cars similar to Hugh's parked outside the house, along with a Range Rover, a Daimler and a Bentley. It felt almost as if she was walking into one of the period dramas he'd mentioned. And it was a million miles away from her own background. Was she really going to be able to pull this off?

'The grandparents and the aunts are here, too, by the looks of it,' he said. 'We might as well go in and say hello. There probably isn't enough time to give you a proper guided tour of the house before tea's served, but I promise I'll do it tomorrow. Ma's probably in the kitchen fussing about. She said afternoon tea would be in the dining room and the cocktail party tonight's in the ballroom.'

'Your parents have a ballroom?' She smiled to hide the panic that trickled through her. 'That's very Jane Austen.'

'It's probably been in one of the Austen adaptations. I can't really remember,' he said with a shrug. 'Which sounds terribly snooty, but it isn't meant to be.'

'Of course not.' Bella had the feeling that he was much more nervous about this than he looked, and somehow that made her feel a little less nervous. A little less alone.

'Imagine the kind of house parties they had back in Austen's time,' he said. 'I'd be off fishing or hunting with my brothers, or playing cards and drinking. But the women in the house party wouldn't be allowed to do much more than read or play the piano. They'd be under constant scrutiny, and there were all the intricate manners...' He shuddered. 'I hate that kind of stuff. I'm glad it's not like that now.'

'Isn't it?' she asked softly—because that bit about constant scrutiny and manners sounded personal.

'No.'

'It was for my sister.' The words were out before she could stop them.

He looked at her. 'How?'

'I...' She sighed. 'OK. You're unlikely to meet her again, but if you do and you tell her you know why she drank all that champagne that night I might have to kill you.'

'Noted. What happened?' he asked, sounding curious.

'She was at the golden wedding anniversary party for her fiancé's parents. Let's just say that Cynthia of the Concrete Hair—'

He blinked. 'Who?'

'Howard's mother. You know the sort of woman I mean. Everything's all about appearances and she's so polished that her hair is set like concrete.' Bella waved a dismissive hand. 'And she watches you like a hawk and judges you—usually unfairly.'

'Yes, I've come across people like that,' he said.

'So I think Gracie finally realised that if she went ahead and married Howard, her life was going to be seriously miserable.' She grimaced. 'She tried to blot it out by drinking champagne. It didn't work. So, for the first time ever, I was the sister who did the rescuing—with a lot of help from you.' She bit her lip. 'The wedding was meant to be next weekend.'

'So Grace was a runaway bride?' He looked surprised.

'No. She didn't jilt Howard at the altar—she'd never do anything that mean. But they'd been engaged for four years and he never swept her off her feet, not *once*.'

'Being swept off your feet is overrated,' Hugh said. 'You're more likely to fall into a puddle of slurry.'

'Slurry?' she asked, not understanding.

He grinned. 'You're definitely a townie, then. Slurry is liquid manure. Used as fertiliser on fields.'

She pulled a face. 'That's vile.'

'Exactly how it smells. You always know when it's muck-spreading season.'

'It's not muck-spreading season now, is it?'

He laughed. 'No.'

'Good.' She took a deep breath. 'Righty. Time to play my part, I guess. Ditzy and unsuitable girlfriend with a terrible taste in clothes—that's me, right?'

'Right. And thank you for saving my bacon. I appreciate this. Even if it might not seem that way.'

He took their bags from the car and they went into the house. Bella noticed the sweeping staircase coming into the hallway and the Regency striped paper on the walls; the house really was gorgeous, and she itched to explore, though she knew it would be rude to ask.

Three dogs came rushing down the hallway to meet them, their tails a wagging blur.

'I forgot to warn you about the mutts,' he said. 'Sorry. Are you OK with dogs?'

'Very OK. I grew up with a dog,' she said, and bent down to make a fuss of the chocolate Labrador, Westie and Cocker Spaniel.

'This lot are Lennie the lab, Wilf the Westie and Sukie the spaniel,' he introduced them.

The dogs wriggled and shoved each other and tried to get closer to Bella. 'They're lovely,' she said, laughing. 'Hello, you ravening beasties. I'm sorry, I don't have any treats for you because I wasn't expecting to meet you, but

I can rub your ears and scratch your backs for you, and I'll play ball with you for a bit if you want.'

'Do that and they'll pester you for the whole weekend,' Hugh warned.

She smiled up at him. 'And that's a problem, how?'

A woman who looked so much like Hugh that she had to be his mother came into the hallway and hugged him. 'Darling, I'm so glad you could make it.'

OK, so now she had to be Miss Ditzy. Breathe, Bella reminded herself, and stay in character. She stood up and gave her best attempt at a goofy smile.

'Bella, this is my mother, Elizabeth Moncrieff,' Hugh said.

'Libby will do nicely,' Hugh's mother said. 'We don't stand on ceremony in this house.'

'Ma, this is my friend Bella Faraday,' Hugh continued.

'Like the scientist?'

Libby had perfect manners, Bella thought, and didn't even look the remotest bit fazed by Bella's outlandish dress. 'Yes, like the scientist,' she agreed, before remembering that she was supposed to be playing the part of someone who would probably never have heard of Michael Faraday, let alone known who he was.

'I'll just show Bella up to her room,' Hugh said hastily.

'She's in the Blue Room, next to yours. I hope that's all right?'

'Thank you, Mrs Mon—' Bella began.

'Libby,' Hugh's mother reminded her.

'Libby.' Bella opened her bag and took out the beautifully wrapped package of dark chocolates she'd bought earlier. 'And these are for you, to say thank you for having me.'

'How lovely.' Libby went pink. 'And I recognise that

packaging. These are my absolute favourites. That's very kind of you.'

'My pleasure. I'm glad you like them,' Bella said. 'Don't let Hugh anywhere near them. He's a chocolate fiend. But I guess, as his mum, you already know that.'

'Oh, I do,' Libby said feelingly.

'Let's go and put our things upstairs,' Hugh said.

'Come down when you're ready. Everyone will be in the dining room,' Libby said. 'And it's a pleasure to meet you, Bella.'

Bella followed Hugh up the sweeping staircase and all the way to the end of a corridor.

The Blue Room was enormous. It was very plain, with cream walls and a polished wooden floor with a navy rug in the centre, but what really caught Bella's attention was the ancient wooden four-poster bed. She'd always wanted to sleep in a bed like that. 'This is amazing,' she said.

'I'll put my things next door. I'll call for you in a few minutes,' he said.

Was Hugh's bedroom anything like this? she wondered. Were there things from his childhood that would give her a clue about what made him tick?

Not that she should be thinking about any of that. She was simply doing him a favour and playing a part. None of this was *real*, she reminded herself.

To distract herself, she went and looked out of the window. The room overlooked the garden at the back of the house: a perfectly striped lawn, with borders all full of tulips, and a stone wall at the end of the lawn with what looked like espaliered trees full of blossom. It was a million miles away from her own suburban upbringing. How wonderful it must have been to have a garden like that to run around in and explore as a child.

Then there was a knock at the door. 'Bella?'

'Come in.'

Hugh remained in the doorway. 'Ready?'

She nodded. 'I was just looking at the view. It's gorgeous.'

'Yes, it's pretty good. I guess I didn't really appreciate it when I was younger.' He took a deep breath. 'Let's go and face the hordes.'

She walked over to join him. 'Though you might have to roll your eyes at me to remind me to be Miss Ditzy. I already made a couple of mistakes with your mum.'

'It'll be fine,' he said. 'I know you're going to do a great job. That's why I asked you.'

'So you didn't ask me just because you were desperate?'

His eyes crinkled at the corners. 'That, too. But mainly because I think you'll do this brilliantly.'

Funny how the compliment warmed her all the way through. Maybe that was because he was being sincere.

Then again, she hadn't spotted Kirk's lies, had she? For all she knew, Hugh could be lying, too.

She took a deep breath. '"Once more unto the breach, dear friends."'

He laughed. 'It won't be that bad.'

Once they got downstairs, Bella wasn't so sure. The dining room held the biggest table she'd ever seen in her life. And every place was already filled, except two.

Hugh introduced her swiftly to everyone before they sat down. She'd already met his mother, but now there was his father, his brothers and their partners and baby Sophia, various aunts and uncles, and his grandparents. And it was all just a little bit overwhelming—especially as Bella could see the shock on all their faces, even though it was quickly masked and everyone was very polite to her.

She knew that she was playing a part and Hugh's intention had been to bring someone home who was so out of place that his family would stop pressuring him to settle down, but even so she didn't enjoy their scrupulous politeness. It looked as if this was going to be a very long weekend.

A maid came in carrying a tray with silver teapots and what Bella guessed were silver jugs of hot water to refresh the tea. Porcelain jugs of milk and dishes with slices of lemon were already on the table, along with a selection of finger sandwiches, tiny pastries, slices of cake and what looked like still-warm scones. A butler followed the maid, carrying a magnum of champagne; once everyone's glass was filled, Hugh's father made a brief speech and proposed a toast to Nigel and his new fiancée, Victoria.

The food was amazing, and in other circumstances Bella knew she would've really enjoyed it. It was a shame that she had to play a part. Until she'd had a chance to work out who was who and the best way to play it, she decided to keep quiet.

But then the old lady sitting next to her—Hugh's great-aunt Lavinia—went very pale and looked as if she was about to faint.

'Are you all right?' Bella asked her, worried.

'I do feel a bit odd,' Lavinia admitted.

'Can I get you a glass of water?'

Lavinia looked grateful. 'Yes, please.'

Miss Ditzy might not know what to do, but Bella couldn't possibly keep playing that part when the old lady clearly wasn't very well and needed help. Hugh wouldn't mind her breaking out of role for this, would he? So she had a quiet word with the maid to get some water, persuaded Lavinia to eat a sandwich, and sat quietly with the old lady until the colour had come back into her face.

'I think I might go and have a little lie-down,' Lavinia said.

'I'll see you up to your room,' Bella said. 'As long as you can direct me, that is. I'm afraid I don't know my way round the house.'

Lavinia patted her hand. 'Thank you, dear. That's very good of you.'

'My pleasure.' Bella helped the old lady back to her room, and stayed with her for a little while to make sure she was quite all right.

'You're a lovely girl, very kind,' Lavinia said. 'I can see what Hugh sees in you.'

Which was totally the opposite of what Bella was supposed to be doing. And she knew that Hugh didn't see anything in her anyway, apart from her being his graphic designer who was probably too outspoken and had been crazy enough to agree to help him in his even crazier scheme. She'd have to hope that her outrageous clothes would distract everyone else from seeing who she really was.

But going back to face everyone in the dining room felt really daunting. She didn't have a clue what to say. To her relief, Hugh met her in the hallway. 'Thanks for looking after my great-aunt. Is Lavinia OK?'

'She's fine—just having a little rest,' Bella said, and gave the same reassurances to Hugh's mother when Libby asked her the same question.

Libby gave her a searching look, then a nod of what looked very much like approval.

Oh, help. She'd really have to work at being unsuitable now. Hugh's mother wasn't supposed to approve of her. She was meant to stick out like a sore thumb.

After the tea party, everyone disappeared to get changed for the cocktail party.

'Come and knock on my door when you're ready,' Hugh said when they reached her bedroom door.

'OK.' Bella wished again that she'd brought a normal black dress with her, rather than going along with Hugh's plans, but it was too late now.

When she'd changed, she knocked on Hugh's door.

'Come in,' he called.

When she pushed the door open, she could see that he was sitting on the end of the bed, checking something on his phone. He looked up and burst out laughing. 'Well. I really didn't expect that. You actually found that in a charity shop?'

'The material, yes—it was originally a pair of curtains. One of my friends from art school specialised in textiles, so she ran this up for me.' She narrowed her eyes at him. 'Why didn't you expect it?'

'I guess I really ought to give you advance warning,' he said. 'The curtains in the ballroom are, um, exactly the same material as your dress.'

'The same material?' She stared at him in shock. 'No way. You're *kidding*.'

He coughed. 'Afraid not.'

She covered her face with her hands. 'Oh, no. I thought I was being so clever, having a Maria moment. It never occurred to me your parents might have curtains like this. I should've run this past you before we came. And I haven't got a spare dress with me.' She blew out a breath. 'Oh, well. I'll just have to change into the leopard-skin thing again.'

He came over to her and rested his hand on her shoulder. Again, her skin tingled where he touched her. 'Relax. Stay as you are. It'll be fine,' he soothed.

She rolled her eyes at him. 'I can hardly go to a party wearing a dress made out of the same curtains that are in the room, can I?'

'Actually, you can,' he said. 'You're the one person I know who can pull this off.'

She really wasn't convinced. And it didn't help that Hugh was wearing a dinner jacket with grosgrain silk lapels that matched the fabric on the buttons, a white pleated-front shirt, and a properly tied black grosgrain silk bow tie. He looked sleek, elegant and perfect.

She blew out a breath. 'You look very nice. Very James Bond, though I think you might actually have the edge on Daniel Craig.'

'Thank you.' He inclined his head in acknowledgement of the compliment. 'You look very nice, too.'

'In a dress that matches your parents' curtains and clashes with my hair?' she asked, raising her eyebrows. 'Hardly.'

'Remember, you have chutzpah,' he said.

'Maybe I should stay here. You could say I drank too much champagne earlier and have a headache.'

He shook his head. 'Have the courage of your convictions, Bella.'

She scoffed. '*Your* convictions, you mean. If we'd done it my way, I wouldn't be here and you would've shown your family how great you are at your job.'

'Let's agree to disagree on that one, because I know you can do this,' he said. 'Ready?'

No. But she had no other choice. 'Sure,' she said. 'Let's go.'

CHAPTER FIVE

BELLA'S FACE WAS pale beneath her make-up, but she lifted her chin high and pulled her shoulders back.

For a moment, Hugh thought about calling this whole thing off—someone in the house was bound to have a spare dress that she could borrow for the evening—but they'd agreed that the idea was to present Bella as Miss Totally Unsuitable. To the point where his family would all breathe a collective sigh of relief when he announced next week that the relationship was over, and they'd stop nagging him about settling down.

Bella was the only woman he knew who could pull off an outfit like this one. And he knew he was asking a huge amount from her. When they were back in London, he'd do something nice for her to make up for what he was putting her through right now. Maybe he could send her on a spa weekend with her sister or something.

He suppressed the thought that he'd like to take her away and make a fuss of her himself. She'd made it clear that she was single and wanted to stay that way. The same was true for him. Bella Faraday might make his pulse beat that little bit faster: but she was his employee, and that made her completely off limits.

They went downstairs and he ushered her into the ballroom. As they walked through the doorway, he felt her hand tighten on his arm just a fraction. And the gasps of surprise as people saw her and took in what she was wearing were actually audible.

The ground obviously wasn't going to open up and swallow her, and turning back time wasn't physically possible either. Bella glanced at Hugh for a cue about how to react and what to do—after all, this was his family and he knew them way better than she did—but he seemed to have frozen.

Nothing fazes a Faraday girl. The mantra she shared with Grace echoed through her head. Wrong. This had definitely fazed her.

Then again, Hugh had asked her to play the part of his unsuitable girlfriend. Which was exactly how she felt right now—awkward and out of place, absolutely not fitting in. What would an unsuitable girl do when she was the centre of attention? The only thing Bella could think of was to draw even more attention to her gaffe and ham it up a little.

She walked over to the curtains and did a little curtsey. 'I promise I didn't make my dress from these,' she said, gesturing to the curtains. 'Because my name isn't Maria and I'm fairly sure you're the Moncrieffs and not the von Trapp family—right?'

There was still an uneasy silence.

Had she gone too far? Or did she need to go further still? 'Well, then,' Bella said, and began to sing 'Do Re Mi' very softly.

Hugh looked at Bella, totally stunned. He'd had no idea that she could sing—especially this beautifully. It made him think of Jessie, and how his ex had bewitched him with her voice.

But Jessie wasn't half the woman that Bella Faraday was. Jessie was an ambitious, lying cheat, whereas he knew that Bella was completely open and honest. Even though at the moment she was playing a part: that was solely because he'd asked her to do it.

And right now all the heat was on her—Hugh's unsuitable new girlfriend in her even more unsuitable dress. He could hear Bella's voice faltering and he knew he ought to rescue her. Especially because this whole fiasco was his fault. He needed to step in and take the heat off her. Now.

She'd even given him the perfect cue.

Yet that would mean performing in public. Something he hadn't done since Jessie had walked out on him. And singing a duet... The whole idea of it made him feel sick to his stomach, bringing back the misery and disappointment he'd felt when he'd learned the truth about how much of a fool he'd been, and the dismay when he'd realised the ramifications for Insurgo. He really didn't want to do this.

Yet how could he be a snake and leave Bella to face everyone's disapproval alone? This whole thing had been his idea, and she was doing him a favour. It wasn't fair that she should bear the brunt of it.

It left him no real choice.

Taking a deep breath, he walked over to Bella and took her hand. 'Von Trapp, you said? I believe that's my cue.' And then he began to sing 'Edelweiss'.

Bella smiled, and to his surprise she joined him in the song.

It had been a long, long time since Hugh had sung a duet with someone. Jessie. Who'd sung like an angel, promised him paradise, and left him in hell. This should've made him want to run for the hills as fast as possible. Instead, it felt as if something in the region of his heart had just cracked a tiny bit, enough to let in some unexpected warmth. His hand tightened just that tiny bit more round hers; and when she squeezed his fingers back the crack around his heart grew just that little bit wider.

When the song finished, everyone clapped and the tension in the ballroom had dissolved.

Then Nigel came over to him. 'Hugh, I need a favour.'

Considering that he'd just almost wrecked his brother's engagement party, Hugh felt guilty enough to agree to whatever it was. 'Sure. What do you need?'

'Excuse us, Bella,' Nigel said, and led Hugh off to a quiet corner. 'The band I hired for tonight just called to say that their van's broken down and they're running an hour late. Would you play for us until they get here?' He inclined his head towards the baby grand piano in the corner of the ballroom.

'You could've had the pick of my artists. And they would've been here on time,' Hugh said mildly.

'I know, but the singer of the band happens to be Vicky's friend. Vicky asked her to do it before I had a chance to suggest asking you to recommend someone.'

Hugh laughed. 'Nice save.'

'I know I'm asking a lot of you,' Nigel said softly. 'I know why you don't play in public any more.'

Because of Jessie's betrayal. It had sucked all the joy out of music for him. He didn't write songs any more. Today was the first time he'd sung in public since she'd left. Right now though, he was punch-drunk, not quite sure how he felt—happy and sad were all mixed up together, with him smack in the centre of the whirlpool.

'Yeah.' Hugh took a deep breath. This was a big ask. But, in the circumstances, there wasn't a nice way to say no. And Hugh did love his brother. This was his chance to help, to do something nice for his family. How could he turn that down? 'All right. I'll play until the band gets here. But I'm not singing any more, and neither is Bella, OK?'

'OK.' Nigel patted his shoulder. 'Thanks. I appreciate it.'

Hugh walked back over to Bella. 'Will you be OK if I play the piano for Nigel and Victoria until the band turns up?' he asked.

'Sure,' she said, giving him what looked like a brave smile. Clearly she didn't think she'd be OK at all.

'Of course she will. I'll look after her,' his mother said, coming over and catching the end of the conversation.

That was almost what Hugh was most afraid of.

But before he could say anything his mother had swept Bella away and Nigel was looking anxiously towards the piano. What could he do but give in and sit down at the baby grand? 'Let's get your party started, O brother mine,' he said and began to play.

'I think you need some champagne after that, Bella,' Libby said, and snaffled a glass from the nearest waiter.

'I'm so sorry, Mrs Moncrieff,' Bella said, accepting the glass. 'About the dress. And… And…' She shook her head, not knowing where to start. Just that she needed to apologise. She'd thought she was being so clever, making a dress out of a curtain. And she'd ended up being horrifically rude. This wasn't who she was. At all. And it made her squirm inside. She'd come here under false pretences and she'd behaved appallingly.

'It's Libby,' Hugh's mother reminded her gently. 'My dear, I can see exactly why Hugh fell for you.' Libby patted her arm. 'What you did just now—that was very brave.'

'Or very foolish in the first place,' Bella said softly. There was a huge lump in her throat. She really hadn't expected Hugh to come to her rescue like that. The last time a man had left her in a sticky situation, he'd left her to deal with it alone. Yet Hugh had been right there by her side, supporting her and sorting it out with her. 'I didn't know Hugh could sing like that—or that he could play the piano.' Considering that Hugh owned a record label and he'd told her how much he loved producing the songs and turning them from raw material to the finished product, she should've guessed that music was more than just a money-making venture to him. But Hugh wasn't listed on Insurgo's website as one of the label's artists, and nobody in the office had even hinted that he'd ever been any kind of performer. He hadn't even sung along with the music in the car on the way to Oxfordshire.

But she'd overheard Nigel saying something about knowing why Hugh didn't play in public any more. Something really awful must've happened. And there was no way she could possibly ask Hugh about it, not without opening up what might be some very painful scars. She'd have to tread very carefully.

'Hugh was very cagey when I asked him about how you'd met,' Libby said. 'Are you one of his artists?'

Bella winced. 'Not *quite* in the way you think. I'm not a singer and I don't play an instrument.'

Was it her imagination, or did Libby Moncrieff suddenly look relieved? And why? Did that have something to do with the reason why Hugh didn't play in public?

'So how did you meet?' Libby asked.

Bella could hardly be completely honest about that, either. Not unless she wanted to tell a story that made her sister look bad, and that wasn't fair. The best she could do was give the bare bones of the truth. Which would probably be the safest thing in any case, because then she wouldn't have to remember which fibs she'd told and end up in a muddle. 'I'm an artist—and by that I mean a graphic designer, not a recording artist—and Tarquin interviewed me for the job at Insurgo.'

'Ah.'

That earlier look of relief hadn't been her imagination, then, because Libby suddenly looked wary again.

Was Insurgo the problem? Hugh had said that his family worried about him because the music business was so risky. Maybe this was her chance to bat his corner for him and get his mother to see just how good he was at his job and how much the recording label meant to him.

'As I said, I'm not a singer,' Bella said, 'but I do like music, and Insurgo produces some of the very best music around. I used to be a freelance designer, but my best client went bust a few months ago, owing me rather a lot of money. My parents would've bailed me out if I'd told them, but I wanted to stand on my own two feet rather than rely on them—so that's why I applied to Insurgo when I saw the job advertised. Hugh had nothing to do with me getting the job. Tarquin interviewed me.' She spread her hands. 'I didn't even meet Hugh until after I'd accepted the job.'

To her relief, Libby looked a bit less wary again.

She took a sip of champagne. 'It's a good place to work. I've never been anywhere with a sense of team spirit like there is at Insurgo. Everyone looks out for each other. And the musicians all love coming in to the office because they feel we listen to them. Hugh doesn't treat them just as cash cows or as if they're stupid. He listens to what they want, and he gives them advice—and they listen to him because they know he wants to help them be the best they can be. They know he'll take their raw material and polish it—but he'll still keep their vision.'

Libby nodded, but said nothing.

'Insurgo wouldn't be the success it is without Hugh. He's its heart,' Bella said. 'And he really loves what he does. There aren't many people who can say that nowadays.'

'But the music business is so precarious,' Libby said.

'It is,' Bella agreed. 'But Hugh doesn't take stupid risks. He's really sharp and he makes exactly the right business decisions—though nobody in the office will ever ask him anything on a Monday morning.'

'Why not?'

'He's, um, not really a Monday morning person. Though I guess, as his mum, you already know that.' She smiled, and told Libby about the name-cards she'd made for everyone in the office.

Libby laughed. 'You didn't do that on a Monday morning, I hope.'

Bella laughed back, feeling properly at ease for the first time since she'd arrived. 'I wouldn't have dared. No, it was a Thursday. And he was still pretty grumpy.'

'So you can sketch people really quickly?'

'Not just people.' Bella fished in her bag and took out a pen and a small spiral-bound notebook. 'Give me a few seconds,' she said with a smile. She sketched swiftly. Then she handed the notebook with the line drawing to Libby. Sitting patiently next to a cake and wearing hopeful expressions as they stared at it were Lennie, Wilf and Sukie.

'Oh, that's wonderful,' Libby said. 'May I keep it?'

'Of course.' Bella detached the page and handed it to her.

'Thank you. So what exactly did you draw on Hugh's name-card?' Libby asked, sounding intrigued.

'You're his mother. I can hardly show you.'

Libby laughed. 'I used to have to get him out of bed on Monday mornings when he was a teen. I think I've seen him at his very grumpiest.'

'Well, if you put it that way,' Bella said, 'how can I resist?' She drew another sketch. And, before she realised it, she had a circle of people around her, all wanting to see her drawings and all asking for a sketch.

Oh, help. She was supposed to be playing Miss Ditzy and Unsuitable, not making friends with everyone the way she always did. Hugh was going to be furious. She'd just have to work out how to extract herself from this before the band turned up and he could leave the piano.

Hugh finally managed to get away from the piano when the band turned up, all flustered and apologetic. He went to rescue Bella from his mother, only to find her right in the middle of a crowd. Everyone around her was laughing and joking, and he noticed that she had a pen and paper in her hand.

She looked as if she belonged.

Oh, no. That wasn't supposed to happen. His bright idea was going completely pear-shaped. His family had obviously seen way beyond Bella's surface unsuitability. And Bella herself had clearly forgotten that she was playing the part of Miss Ditzy and Unsuitable.

Then again, hadn't he also told her just to be herself? Which was exactly what she was doing. Bella, the graphic artist, the woman who'd fitted in to their team at the office as if she'd been there since day one.

Right now, she lit up the room. Which scared him and drew him in equal measures. He wanted her—but he didn't want to risk his whole life imploding again, the way it had after Jessie. He needed to be sensible about this. And right now the sensible thing to do would be to get her out of there before she said anything that made his family guess at the truth.

And she was meant to be his girlfriend, so everyone would expect him to walk over and drape his arm round her shoulders. 'Sorry to desert you like that, darling.'

She looked up at him, her beautiful blue eyes wide. 'Hugh!'

'But I'm here now. Shall we dance?'

'I...' She looked flustered. Which was pretty much how he felt, too, so close to her that he could smell her perfume and feel the warmth of her body against his.

'May I finish my sketch first?' she asked.

'Sure.' He took a step back. Putting a bit of distance between them was probably a good idea, given that right now he wanted to pull her closer.

Hugh had seen what she could produce at the Insurgo office, but he'd never actually watched her working before. And he was amazed by how deft her hands were. He also noticed how she caught the tip of her tongue between her teeth when she was concentrating, and it made him want to kiss her.

Maybe dancing with her would be a bad idea after all. It would make her way, way too tempting.

But then she finished a sketch of Lennie with his father—lightning fast and seriously good—and handed it over to Oliver with a smile.

'Thank you, my dear. That's marvellous.' Oliver kissed her cheek. 'And maybe I could ask you to sketch Libby with Sukie for me, later?'

'Of course,' Bella said, smiling back. 'But I'll require payment in advance, you know. You'll have to dance with me first.'

He positively beamed at her. 'With absolute pleasure, my dear.'

Amazing. Even wearing a dress made out of a curtain which matched the ones in the ballroom and which clashed badly with her bright red hair—two things that Hugh was sure should've annoyed Oliver Moncrieff immensely—Bella had still managed to charm his father. Just, Hugh thought, by being herself. She couldn't help it. Bella was the kind of woman who brought out the best in people.

He led her off to the other side of the dance floor. 'I was going to apologise for throwing you to the wolves, but it looks to me as if you've managed to turn them all into little fluffy-wuffy lapdogs.'

She laughed. 'Hugh, don't be so mean. Your family's nice.'

He scowled. 'Maybe. When they're not nagging me.'

'Really, Hugh. They're *nice*.' She blew out a breath. 'And I should be apologising to you. I'm afraid I kind of forgot to be unsuitable. I was telling your mum about the name-cards I did in the office last week, and I ended up drawing the dogs for her, and...' She bit her lip, and Hugh had to suppress the urge to kiss the sting away. 'It snowballed a little bit. Sorry. I'll remember to be dim and scatty and unsuitable for the rest of the weekend, I promise.'

'Hmm,' Hugh said. He didn't think she'd be able to remember it for very long. Because he realised now that Bella wasn't a natural deceiver. What you saw was what you got. There were no hidden agendas. 'It's as much my fault as it is yours. I shouldn't have left you on your own.'

'But you couldn't have refused to help your brother.' She paused and gave him a curious look. 'I didn't know you could play the piano.'

'Lavinia taught me.'

'Lavinia, as in your great-aunt I sat next to this afternoon?'

He nodded. 'Before arthritis wrecked her hands, she was an amazing pianist.'

She frowned. 'So your family does understand about music, then.'

'Lavinia does,' he admitted. 'The rest don't. They still think I should give it up and join the family business.'

She looked thoughtful. 'So you play and you sing— I've heard that for myself. I'm guessing that you probably write your own stuff, too.'

He had. Once upon a time. Not any more.

She wasn't letting it go. She ignored his silence. 'And you own a record company. Do you ever record anything of your own?'

'No,' he said, knowing that he sounded abrupt and rude, but not being able to help himself.

But it didn't seem to put Bella off. 'Why not?' she asked. 'You're good. And I'm not just saying that because you're my boss. You, a piano and a love song— you'd have women swooning all round the globe. You'd make gazillions for the label.'

Hugh had written songs for Jessie, and he'd thought about recording them as duets with her. Then Jessie had dropped her bombshell that she was moving to another record label instead of signing the new contract with Insurgo, and by the way she'd met someone else...who just so happened to be the head of her new label.

And then Hugh had realised that maybe Jessie had never loved him at all. She'd just seen him as a stepping stone in her career, and it looked as if she was doing exactly the same with her new man. He'd been so shocked and hurt that he hadn't written anything since, and he couldn't remember the last time he'd touched the piano; the joy he'd once found in playing felt tainted with memories of her betrayal. Tonight was the first time he'd sung with anyone since he'd broken up with Jessie. The first time he'd played in public again.

And he didn't want to analyse that too closely. Or why it had felt so natural to sing with Bella, after the initial shock.

'I don't want to be a performer,' he said. 'I prefer being a producer. Seeing the rough diamond of the songs and how I can make them shine. You know, like Lacey's album—putting the cello in and a double bass made it just that bit more haunting and gave the sound some depth.'

'Fair enough.' She shrugged. 'I think I understand where you're coming from, because for me it's the other way round. I absolutely love designing, but I wouldn't want to own or run a gallery. The idea of having to organise a bunch of creative people...' She groaned. 'It'd be like herding cats. No, thanks.'

He smiled. 'It's very satisfying when it goes right.'

'Each to their own,' she said.

Hugh danced with her all evening, only stepping to

one side when his three brothers and his father all demanded a dance with Bella. And then he found himself dancing with his sisters-in-law and his mother, all of whom were singing Bella's praises loudly.

'She's perfect for you,' Victoria said. 'Even if her dress sense is a little, um, unusual.'

There was nothing he could say to that. If he protested, everyone would take it as a token protest; if he agreed, they'd have a date set for the wedding within the hour.

'I really should rescue her from Pa,' he said, and fled in Bella's direction.

'Is everything all right?' Bella asked when Hugh was dancing with her again.

'I think our plan might have crashed and burned a bit,' he said ruefully.

She winced. 'Sorry. That's my fault.'

'No. You were right. It was a daft idea in the first place.'

'I'm glad you can admit when you're wrong,' she said with a smile. 'That's a good thing.'

'Mmm.' He wasn't convinced.

She stroked his face. 'Hugh. Let's just forget it for now and enjoy the party.'

Her touch made every nerve-end sit up and pay attention. He had to stop himself from turning his head and pressing a kiss into her palm. Distance. He needed a tiny bit of distance between them, before he lost his head completely and gave in to his body's urging. He snagged a couple of glasses from one of the waiters and toasted her. 'I still can't believe you stood up there in front of those curtains, in that dress, and sang "Do Re Mi".'

'Says Captain von Trapp,' she retorted with a grin.

'Oh, please.' He rolled his eyes. 'Ma loves *The Sound of Music*.'

'So do I. It's one of the best films ever.' She hummed a snatch of 'My Favourite Things'.

'I hated that film,' Hugh said.

She blinked at him, clearly taken aback. 'Why?'

'The way the guy just ignored his kids made me so angry. And it wasn't so much a stick the guy had up his backside as a whole tree.'

'And you don't?' she teased.

What? Hugh stared at her in surprise. Was she saying that she thought he was stuffy? 'No, I don't,' he said, faintly put out.

'Prove it,' she challenged.

He narrowed his eyes at her. 'How?'

'Dance the samba with me.' She raised her eyebrows at him. 'After all, this is a party, and the samba is the best party dance I know.'

'Sorry.' He spread his hands. 'I would, but I'm afraid I don't know the steps.' It was a feeble excuse, but a valid one. If the samba meant dancing close to her and touching her... That would be way too risky. He needed to be sensible about this, not getting closer to her.

'It's easy. I'll teach you. Gracie and I go to a dance aerobics class where half the moves are based on samba.' She grinned. 'Just follow my lead.' Then she paused, batted her eyelashes at him, and drawled, 'Unless you can't take direction from a woman?'

He had the distinct impression that she was flirting with him. Even though he knew he ought to resist, he found himself flirting right back. 'I can take direction.' He stared at her mouth. 'When it's *appropriate*.'

Her skin heated, then, clashing spectacularly with her hair. 'Hugh!'

And her voice was all breathy. He was about to tease her when he realised that he couldn't speak, either, because right now his head was full of the idea of kissing her. And that breathiness in her voice was incredibly sexy. His mouth was actually tingling. All he had to do was lean forward and touch his lips to hers...

They ought to stop this.

Right now.

As if she was channelling his thoughts, she muttered, 'Back in a moment.'

But what she did next was to go and speak to the band. He recognised the song from the first couple of bars: 'Livin' la Vida Loca'.

So Bella wasn't going to let him off. To pay him back for making her blush, she taught him how to samba, making him repeat the basic steps and arm actions until his movements were fluid. He was surprised by how much he enjoyed the bouncy, shimmery nature of the steps.

Other people were watching them, but when Bella realised that she was having none of it. As the band continued to play songs with a similar beat, she went round and taught everyone else in the room how to do the basic steps. The women seemed to cotton on much quicker than the men—which didn't surprise him that much, because hadn't Bella said something about learning this kind of thing at an aerobics class?—but finally the whole room was dancing. Including relatives Hugh had never actually seen get up on the dance floor before.

How on earth had she managed that?

'You certainly know how to get a party going,' he said when she came back over to him.

She laughed and tossed her hair back. 'I *love* parties.'

He could tell. She was really lit up from the inside, and it was infectious. Being with her made him smile and forget just about everything else. How long had it been since he'd last felt this happy and carefree?

Then the band slowed it all down again. He held out one hand to her. 'May I have this dance, Ms Faraday?'

She gave him a shy smile and took his hand. 'Of course, Mr Moncrieff.'

He drew her into his arms and held her close, swaying with her. Weird how she fitted perfectly into his arms, all warm and soft and sweet. Maybe the romance of the engagement party had got to him, or maybe he'd drunk too much champagne, but he couldn't resist holding her just that little bit closer, dancing cheek to cheek with her. He could smell the soft floral scent she wore—gardenia, perhaps? It was enchanting: much like Bella herself.

And from dancing cheek to cheek it was the tiniest, tiniest move to kissing her. All he had to do was twist his head ever so slightly and brush the corner of her mouth with his lips.

Should he?

And what would she do if he did?

If she moved away, he'd stop, he promised himself.

Except she didn't move away. When he kissed the corner of her mouth, she twisted her head ever so slightly towards him, so her mouth brushed against his properly.

And Hugh was completely lost.

He tightened his arms round her and kissed her again, teasing her mouth with tiny, nibbling kisses until she let her lips part and he could deepen the kiss. It felt as if he were floating on air. Every sense was filled by her. And it had been a long, long time since he'd felt anything even approaching this.

He wasn't sure how long it was until he broke the kiss. But her mouth was reddened and her eyes were wide and bemused; he was pretty sure he looked in a similar state.

They needed to get out of here, before someone noticed or commented.

'Come with me?' he asked softly. 'Away from the crowd?'

She nodded, and he tangled his fingers with hers and led her quietly out of the ballroom and down the corridor to a room he knew would still be in darkness.

'Where are we?' Bella asked when Hugh led her into a darkened room.

'The orangery,' he said.

Once her eyes grew accustomed to the light, she realised that one whole wall was made of glass, and the moonlight shone through onto an ancient chequered red and cream flagstone floor. All along the walls were massive terracotta pots containing what she presumed were citrus trees; there were a couple of what looked like wrought-iron benches between the pots.

'Wait,' he said, and let go of her hand.

A few moments later, she heard a soft click, and then suddenly the room was glowing softly with dozens of tiny fairy lights twined round the stems of the trees.

'Hugh, this is amazing,' she said in delight. 'It's magical.'

'Isn't it just?' he said. 'We had a film crew here when I was in my teens, and the set designer said this was where people would sneak off for some privacy at a Regency house party, among the lemons and limes and oranges.

She reckoned they'd have had candles and it would've been beautiful.'

'Just like this.'

He nodded. 'Someone suggested fairy lights as a modern take on it without the fire risk. Since then, we've often sat out here after the sun sets, just watching the stars, with the fairy lights on. And a heater, in winter, because otherwise it's absolutely freezing.' He came back to hold her hand, and drew her over to one of the benches. 'This is probably my favourite place in the house. Even in the daytime, it's lovely.'

He'd promised her a guided tour of the house tomorrow, and she intended to hold him to that. But right now, when he sat down on one of the wrought iron benches and drew her onto his lap, she couldn't think straight. All she could do was to put her arms round his neck for balance. And from there it was one tiny step to kissing him again.

Time seemed to stop. It was just them, the moonlight and the fairy lights. Nobody came out to find them or ask Hugh to play the piano or Bella to sketch. They could've been light years away from anywhere.

But they could still hear the music.

'Dance with me?' he asked.

Even though part of her knew that this wasn't sensible—it was too intimate, just the two of them in the orangery among the fairy lights—how could she resist?

They swayed together in the room.

Any moment now, she thought, he'd say something to remind her that they were both playing a part.

And yet he didn't. He just danced with her. Held her close. Cherished her.

It was so long since she'd been held like that. It made her feel warm inside. Warm all over. And when Hugh rested his cheek against hers, even though she'd promised herself she'd be sensible, she found herself moving that little bit closer to him. Turning her head so her mouth made contact with the corner of his. His arms tightened round her and he moved his head too, so his lips brushed against hers. Once, twice: and then he was kissing her with abandon, and she was kissing him right back.

She was dizzy with desire when he broke the kiss.

'Hugh—I, we...' She couldn't think straight. There was something important she had to say, but for the life of her she couldn't remember what it was. She just wanted him to kiss her again.

She trailed her fingertips across his cheek, liking the very faint scratch of stubble. 'You're beautiful,' she said. 'Poster-boy beautiful.'

He turned his head and pressed a kiss into her palm. 'Less of the boy, thank you.'

Oh, yes. He was all man. 'I didn't mean it that way,' she said. 'Just that you're beautiful.'

'So are you.' He kissed her again. 'You make me ache.'

She dragged in a breath. 'Ditto.' An ache of wanting, of need. He was driving her crazy with his nearness.

'I know this isn't supposed to be happening, but right now,' he said softly, 'I don't want to go back and join the others. I want to carry you up the stairs to your bed.'

The big, wide four-poster.

'I want to make love with you, Bella.'

A shiver of pure desire ran down her spine.

She knew they shouldn't be doing this. It wasn't what they'd agreed. She was his pretend girlfriend, not his real one. He was her boss. It could have major repercussions and she could end up in another financial mess. They really ought to stop this right now and remember who and where they were. She opened her mouth, intending to say that they shouldn't.

Then again, this wasn't real. And she knew neither of them was looking for for ever. Kirk had wiped out her trust in relationships, and from the little Hugh had said about his ex she was pretty sure that he felt the same way. He wasn't looking for The One, any more than she was.

They were both adults.

There was no reason why they shouldn't act on the attraction between them, just for one night.

So instead, she said softly, 'Tonight's just tonight. A one-off.'

His eyes looked almost navy blue in the soft light. 'No strings.'

'No promises.' She didn't believe in promises any more. 'No for ever.'

'No promises and no for ever,' he echoed.

'Then do it,' she said softly.

He kissed her once. Hard. And then he scooped her up into his arms, pausing only to switch off the fairy lights, and carried her down the corridor and up a quiet flight of stairs to her bedroom.

CHAPTER SIX

THE NEXT MORNING, Bella woke to find a warm body curled round hers. For a moment, she couldn't place where she was and why on earth a naked male body would be in her bed at all, let alone wrapped round her.

Then she remembered.

Hugh.

She went hot as she thought about the previous night. The way he'd kissed her in the orangery among the fairy lights until she'd been dizzy. The way he'd actually carried her up to her bed. The way he'd undressed her, and then made love to her until she'd seen stars.

Right now, the way he was holding her made her feel special. Even though she wasn't really Hugh's girlfriend, and they weren't in any kind of relationship other than that of employee and boss—just for a moment, Bella could imagine what it would be like if this was the real deal instead of an elaborate fiction. She'd spent the last six months feeling stupid and useless and pathetic, after Kirk's betrayal. Last night, Hugh had made her feel good again. Not just the sex, either. He'd danced with her, laughed with her—*believed* in her.

Would last night have changed everything between them? They'd agreed that this was a one-off. No strings.

No promises. No for ever. But could they still work together after this? Or would she have to resign?

They'd have to talk—*really* talk—and maybe redraw
the ground rules.

Nothing fazes a Faraday girl, she reminded herself.

Except the mantra felt hollow.

Right now, she really didn't know what to do. Did
she stay where she was and wait for him to wake up? Or
did she creep out of bed and get dressed—or would that
make facing him even more awkward?

Hugh woke to find himself curled round a warm female
body.

Bella.

He remembered the previous night in full Technicolor,
and panic slid down his spine. Why had he been so stupid?

It was a physical thing, that was all, he told himself.
It was obvious why it had happened. He hadn't satisfied
any physical urges for a while. Maybe it'd been the same
for her. They'd both drunk too much champagne, they'd
danced together, they found each other attractive, and
they'd just given in to the temptation.

He sighed inwardly. Just who was he trying to kid?

If he was honest with himself, he'd been attracted to
Bella since the first moment he'd met her. Her bright
blue eyes, her bubbly personality, the way she opened
her mouth and just said what was in her head without
thinking it through. Not to mention the way she'd been
there for her sister; Bella Faraday had a good heart. He
really liked that about her.

But he still shouldn't have let things go this far between them. They were going to have to talk, *really* talk,

and redraw the ground rules. Because Bella was a great designer, perfect for Insurgo, and Tarquin would have his guts for garters if she left the company just because Hugh hadn't been able to keep his hands—or anything else, for that matter—to himself.

He lay there, trying to think what to say. Even though they'd both agreed that last night was a one-off, would she feel differently this morning? And, if she did, how was he going to handle it?

He knew that Bella wasn't like Jessie. But he just didn't trust his own judgement any more. He didn't want to take the risk of getting involved with anyone, so it was easier not to start something that was likely to end up in a mess.

Eventually he became aware that Bella's breathing was no longer deep and even, and her body was slightly tense. Clearly she was awake.

Was she, too, remembering what had happened?

Did she, too, think about turning round and kissing him hello, the way he wanted to kiss her right now?

Or was she full of regrets and awkwardness and embarrassment?

Right now, he didn't have a clue. But he knew he was going to have to do the right thing rather than ignoring the rest of the world and making love with her all over again. They had to talk.

'Bella?' he whispered.

'Uh-huh.' She sounded worried.

He resisted the urge to kiss her bare shoulder. No matter how much he wanted to touch her, taste her, he had to keep himself in check. Carefully, he withdrew his arms from round her. Odd how cold it made him feel. 'I think we need to talk.'

'Uh-huh,' she said again, and turned to face him. 'OK. I'll say it first. I know we agreed that last night was a one-off, but it really shouldn't have happened at all.'

Relief coursed through him. If she knew it, too, then it meant that things weren't going to be awkward between them. They could still work together. He wouldn't have to find another designer.

He tried to ignore the fact that another emotion under-pinned the relief. It was ridiculous to feel disappointed, especially as he didn't want to risk starting another re-lationship. He knew he was better off on his own, con-centrating on his business.

'Last night was last night,' he said.

'Exactly. You know the Vegas principle?'

'The Vegas principle?' he asked, not quite following her train of thought.

'You know—what happens in Vegas, stays in Vegas,' she explained.

'Ah. Yes.'

'I think we should apply that to last night,' she said carefully.

He agreed. Completely. 'So you're not going to resign because I couldn't keep my hands to myself?' he asked.

'And you're not going to sack me because I didn't stick to our plan?'

Clearly she didn't want to leave her job, either. Which was a very, very good thing. 'Apart from the fact that I don't have any grounds to sack you, you're good at your job. Tarquin would kill me if I made you leave.'

Was it his imagination, or was there a flash of disap-pointment in her eyes?

He wasn't going to analyse that too closely. Much bet-ter to let each other off the hook instead than to get tied up with all the complications. And he definitely shouldn't tell her that he didn't want her to leave because he liked having her around. That'd be way too much pressure on both of them.

'What happened last night—we don't talk about it ever again. And it's not going to be repeated,' she said.

'Agreed,' he said.

She took a deep breath. 'So we stick to the plan from here on, and I'm back to playing Miss Ditzy this morning.'

'Uh-huh.' Even though he knew she wasn't very good at it. Yesterday, although she'd tried, her true self had just shone through the play-acting. And his family had responded in kind: warmth generating warmth.

If only he'd met her years ago. When he was still able to trust. But there was no point in wishing for something he couldn't have.

'What's the agenda for today?' she asked. 'You promised me a guided tour of the house.'

And he'd make very sure that the orangery wasn't part of that. Because then he'd remember how it had been last night and he'd want to kiss her again. It would be very stupid to put himself back in the path of temptation. 'Of course,' he said, 'and everyone's going for a walk between breakfast and lunch.'

'I have a really unsuitable outfit for that,' she said. 'Totally impractical spike-heeled mules that I can totter about in.'

'They sound perfect.' He paused. 'I guess we ought to, um, get up and face everyone downstairs for breakfast. I'll, um, go next door and have a shower.' Even though part of him would much prefer staying here and having a shower with her.

'Uh-huh.'

Was she relieved or disappointed that he was going? He hadn't a clue. And he wasn't going to ask. 'I'll knock for you when I'm ready, shall I?'

This time she definitely looked relieved. He winced inwardly. Did she really think that he'd leave her to find her own way through the house, and then face his family on her own? Or maybe that was the way her ex had treated her. Again, he couldn't really ask. Not without maybe ripping open some scars, and he didn't want to hurt her.

'See you in a bit, then,' she said. And then she closed her eyes.

Was she feeling shy? Or was she trying to spare his blushes?

He climbed out of bed, pulled on his boxer shorts, grabbed the rest of his clothes—and then made the mistake of glancing back at the bed. She looked so cute, lying there. Warm and sweet. He almost dropped his clothes back on the floor and climbed back in beside her again. Especially as he remembered last night so clearly. Touching her. Tasting her. The look of sheer pleasure in her eyes just before she'd fallen apart. The soft little cry she'd made when she'd climaxed in his arms.

No, no and absolutely no.

Common sense won—just—and he managed to get back to his own room without bumping into anyone in the corridor.

Showering helped to restore a little more of his common sense, once he'd turned the temperature of the water right down. Once he'd dressed, he stripped the bed, threw everything into his case, and knocked on Bella's door.

'Come in,' she called.

She was just closing the lid of her suitcase, and she was wearing a strappy top and the shortest pair of denim cut-offs he'd ever seen. Her legs went on for ever. And his tongue felt as if it was glued to the roof of his mouth.

It grew even worse when she gave a little wiggle. Her bottom had the most perfect curve, and it made him want to touch her again.

'Is this ditzy enough?' she asked with a grin, seemingly oblivious to the desire coursing through him.

'Uh—yeah.' And now he sounded like a total troglodyte. He didn't want her to guess the effect she had on him, particularly as he knew she wasn't doing it deliberately. Bella wasn't a game-player. 'I need some coffee,' he gabbled wildly. 'You know I'm not a morning person.'

'Coffee sounds good. Would you mind, um, showing me where I can make some?'

'There's probably already a pot on the go downstairs.'

Though now they had to face his family at the breakfast table. Please don't let any of them start asking questions about where he and Bella had disappeared to last night, he begged silently.

When he ushered Bella into the kitchen, his brothers and their partners were all sitting there, along with Sophia in her high chair; his mother was bustling around and his father was deep in the Sunday newspapers. He narrowed his eyes at them all in warning that they were absolutely not to say a single word, and to his relief they actually went along with him, saying nothing more awkward to her than a cheerful, 'Good morning.'

Without another word, he pulled out a chair at the table for Bella, then sat down next to her.

'Would you like tea or coffee?' Libby asked, coming over to them.

'Coffee, please,' Bella said. 'Can I do anything to help?'

'No, sweetie, it's fine. Bacon sandwich? I'm just about to do another batch.'

'Yes, please.' Bella smiled. 'Bacon and sandwich have to be the two most perfect words for a Sunday morning.'

'And coffee,' Nigel added with a smile. 'Don't forget coffee. Especially where Hugh's concerned.'

'I reckon it'll be another twenty minutes before we get a civil word out of our Hugh,' Julian teased.

'And the rest! He only ever grunts before midday,' Alastair added. 'Even *with* coffee.'

'Now, now, children,' Libby said, mock-warning.

Bella was really enjoying the byplay between Hugh and his brothers. She missed chatting in the kitchen with her mum and her sister on Sunday morning, when her dad would be deep in the Sunday papers in the living room and they would talk about anything and everything—from films to books to seriously girly stuff that would make her dad squirm.

Then her smile faded. If any of her family knew what had happened last night… Well. Nobody would be surprised. If there was a way to mess things up, Bella would be the one to find it. But she and Hugh had agreed that they'd act as if last night hadn't happened.

She just hoped that he meant it.

The kitchen was amazing, a huge room with cream cupboards and tiled floors, with an Aga and an island workstation as well as the breakfast area with the massive table looking out onto the garden. There were comfortable-looking dog beds next to the Aga, but Bella had already worked out that the Labrador, the Westie and the spaniel were all sitting under the table, waiting patiently for treats to be sneaked down to them. 'Your kitchen's really lovely, Libby,' she said.

'Thank you,' Libby replied, putting a plate of bacon sandwiches onto the table. 'Has Hugh shown you the rest of the house yet?'

Only the orangery. And Bella had to fight to prevent the blush that threatened to betray her. 'Not yet,' she said.

'I promised I'd do that before we go out for our walk,' Hugh drawled.

'Make sure you do,' Libby said.

Bella noticed that little Sophia was fussing in her high chair; both Poppy and Julian looked exhausted, and she guessed that Sophia had slept badly during the night, meaning that so had her parents. 'Can I give her a cuddle?' Bella asked.

Poppy looked torn between wariness and gratitude.

'One of my friends does music classes for babies and toddlers,' Bella said. 'So I know a few things that might help distract her—then you might be able to have your breakfast in peace.'

'You haven't had your own breakfast yet,' Poppy said.

'I'll be fine.' Bella shrugged and smiled. 'So can I?'

Poppy smiled back at her. 'Thank you.'

Bella didn't quite dare look at Hugh as she scooped Sophia out of the high chair and then settled the baby on her lap. But Sophia clearly enjoyed being bounced to 'Humpty Dumpty' and 'Row, Row, Row Your Boat' and the other nursery songs Bella could remember, and she was gurgling with delight when Julian picked her up from Bella's lap again.

'Eat your bacon sandwich before it gets cold,' he said, patting her shoulder. 'And thank you for cheering up Miss Grumpy here.'

'Any time,' Bella said with a smile.

'Can I help with the washing up?' Bella asked when she'd finished her sandwich.

Libby shook her head. 'No, sweetie. Thank you for the offer, but it's fine.'

'The kitchen is Ma's domain,' Nigel explained.

'My mum's the same, except we all pitch in and help when we have family over for lunch, because it's really not fair to make someone peel all the veg on their own,' Bella said.

'Well, if you really want to, you can help me with the veg,' Libby conceded. 'But let Hugh show you round first.'

'Hint taken,' Hugh said and stood up. 'Come on, Bella.'

She took his hand and let him lead her out of the kitchen.

He dropped her hand again, the minute they were out of sight. 'Guided tour,' he said, and proceeded to whisk her through the house. The house was glorious, with mullioned windows upstairs and floor-to-ceiling windows downstairs.

'Hugh,' she said when he'd taken her swiftly through the library, not even letting her browse a single shelf in the acres of shelving.

'What?'

'What did I do wrong?' she asked.

'Nothing.' But his voice was clipped.

She sighed. 'Was it because I cuddled the baby? I *like* babies, Hugh. And I like your family.'

'You're meant to be unsuitable,' he reminded her.

'Even unsuitable girlfriends can like babies.'

'Hmm,' he said. 'Drawing room.' There were comfortable chairs and amazing artwork on the walls, and a den with a state of the art television and music system.

'Dining room.'

She'd already seen this the previous day, and the ballroom—though it was much less intimidating now it was empty. She was almost tempted to ask him to play something for her on the piano, something soft and gentle for a Sunday morning, but there was an odd expression on his face and she didn't quite dare.

So much for the Vegas principle. He was clearly finding it hard to ignore what had happened between them.

And that was probably why he didn't show her the orangery in daylight. It would've been too much of a reminder of how reckless they'd been.

'Do you want your family to think we've had a fight?' she asked when he'd finished the tour and was leading her back to the kitchen.

'Fight? Oh.' The penny clearly dropped, and he took her hand again.

Except it felt grudging.

Considering that *he'd* been the one to come up with the idea of the unsuitable girlfriend in the first place, Bella wanted to shake him by the scruff of his neck. 'You have to be the most difficult man in the universe,' she muttered.

He didn't disagree with her. And she had the nasty feeling that she was going to be looking for another job, pretty soon. She just hoped that Tarquin would give her a decent reference—she certainly wasn't going to ask Hugh. And she wasn't telling Grace about any of this. So much for standing on her own two feet and getting her life in shape. She'd just messed up again. Big time.

In the kitchen, everyone was still drinking coffee.

Libby looked at her shoes. 'You need to borrow some wellingtons, Bella, or you'll risk ruining those lovely shoes.'

'I guess they're probably not that suitable for a walk in the garden,' she said, playing Miss Ditzy—though her heart really wasn't in this any more.

'Hugh will find you something in the boot room,' Oliver said.

She blinked. 'You have a room just for *boots*?' Hugh hadn't shown her that.

'It's for boots, coats and muddy dogs to dry off in,' Hugh explained.

The boot room turned out to be just off the kitchen. The room had a stone chequered floor that reminded Bella a bit of the orangery, teamed with white tongue and groove panelling on the cabinets. There were shelves of wellington boots, pegs for coats, and a couple of wicker picnic baskets on shelves; there were also a washing machine and tumble dryer, and she guessed that there would be an iron and ironing board in one of the cupboards.

Hugh checked her shoe size and came up with a pair of green wellington boots and an ancient waxed jacket that was too big for her. 'You'll need socks,' he said, and rummaged in one of the wicker baskets for an old but clean pair of what looked like rugby socks.

And at least borrowing a jacket meant she had pockets to shove her hands into and she wouldn't have the temptation of being hand-in-hand with Hugh—or the awkwardness if she tried to hold his hand and he rejected her, which she thought would be the most likely outcome.

Hugh's brothers and their partners all joined them on the walk, along with Sophia in her pushchair, and the dogs romped along happily beside them.

'So we're going for a walk in the nearby woods or something?' she asked.

Hugh nodded. 'They're part of the estate.'

Well, of course a huge manor house like this would come with an estate rather than just a garden. How stupid of her not to think of that before.

But her awkwardness turned to delight when they walked through the narrow paths in the woods and she could see bluebells everywhere. 'That's gorgeous!'

'It's still a bit early for them yet,' Hugh said, 'but they're like a blue haze when they're fully out.'

'A real bluebell carpet—how lovely,' she said. It made her itch to sit out here with a pad of cartridge paper and a box of watercolours. 'I love the colour of new leaves, that really bright lime-green that means spring's really here.'

'Yeah.'

Somehow, Hugh was holding her hand again, and it sent a shiver of pure desire through her.

He met her gaze. 'I'm not coming on to you,' he said in a low voice. 'Everyone will expect me to hold my girlfriend's hand.'

'Of course,' she said, but she had to swallow her disappointment. Which was ridiculous in any case. She didn't want a relationship and she didn't want to mess up her job. Hugh was off limits and this was simply a bit of play-acting for his family's benefit. They'd agreed. And the fact that he was holding her hand simply meant that the bluebells had just got rid of his Monday morning-itis, which was actually more like *every* morning-itis.

Back at the house, the others all disappeared to sort out various things, and Hugh's father called him to come and help with something. Feeling a bit like a spare part,

Bella went in search of Libby in the kitchen. 'I promised to help you with the vegetables.'

'You really don't have to,' Libby said. 'You're a guest.'

'Even so,' Bella said. 'Is that beef I smell roasting?'

'Yes.'

'I could make the Yorkshire puddings, if you like.' She laughed. 'I admit I'm a terrible cook, but I'm actually quite good at cupcakes, pancakes and Yorkshire puddings. I guess it's because they're light and fluffy, like me.'

Libby gave her look as if to say that she knew there was much more to Bella than that, or Hugh wouldn't be dating her. 'You're playing a part, this weekend, aren't you?'

Uh-oh. She hadn't expected Libby to call her on it. 'A part?' Bella asked, trying not to panic. 'What makes you say that?'

'Because the real you keeps shining through. The way you brought me my favourite chocolates, the way you looked after Lavinia yesterday afternoon, the way you drew those pictures for everyone, the way you haven't minded a muddy dog draped all over you, the way you sat and cuddled Sophia this morning during breakfast and sang nursery songs to her.' Libby ticked them off on her fingers. 'If you were the dreadful airhead that you and Hugh clearly want us all to think you are, I'm not so sure you would've done any of that.'

There was no way she could keep up the pretence any more. 'Busted, I guess. But please don't tell Hugh you know.'

'I won't,' Libby said softly. 'But what I don't understand is why you both feel that you have to play a part.'

'I did tell him Plan B would be better,' Bella said with a rueful smile.

Libby's frown deepened. 'What's Plan B?'

Bella held up both hands in a surrender gesture. 'Just ignore me. I'm rambling.'

'No, I think this is something I need to know,' Libby said.

Bella bit her lip. 'Please, please don't shoot the messenger, because you've all been so kind and I don't want to be rude and ungrateful. Even though I've already been rude and obnoxious.'

'Now you're really worrying me,' Libby said. 'What's plan B?'

'To tell you the truth about his job and make you see how he feels. Hugh isn't a stockbroker at heart,' Bella said, 'he's a music producer. He loves his job and he's really, really good at it. I really don't mean to be rude or to offend you, but he seems to believe that you all want him to toe the line—to sell Insurgo Records to the highest bidder and join the family firm instead. If he does that, you're going to break his heart and his spirit. He'd hate it so much and he'd spend all his time wishing he was somewhere else. And then he might grow to resent you all instead of loving you like he does now.'

Libby was silent for so long that Bella thought she'd gone too far.

'Mrs Moncrieff? Libby?' she asked anxiously.

Libby's eyes were glistening with tears. 'Those were very wise words,' she said softly. 'And they came from the heart.'

Hugh was halfway down the corridor to the kitchen when he heard his mother ask, 'So are you his real girlfriend pretending to be his fake girlfriend?'

What?

Oh, no. He knew his mother was perceptive. He needed to go in and head her off. Or had Bella already caved in and told her the truth?

To his horror, he heard Bella say, 'That all sounds so complicated. But I was telling you the truth when I said I'm the designer at Insurgo.'

Oh, hell. She *had* caved in. She'd blown their cover completely. And he was shocked by how hurt and disappointed he was. He'd been telling himself that Bella wasn't like Jessie—and yet she'd let him down, too. She'd promised to play a part and she'd gone back on her word. Betrayed his trust. Ratted him out to his mother, so his subterfuge was well and truly uncovered. So much for thinking that she was different. Obviously his judgement was still way off.

'That,' Libby said, 'figures.'

'What does?' Bella asked.

Hugh went cold. Please don't let his mother start talking about Jessie. He only realised he was holding his breath when Libby said, 'If he hasn't told you, I won't break his confidence.'

'That's not very fair, given that I've just done that,' Bella said.

She'd even admitted what she'd done. And it made him feel sick. How far had she gone?

He strode into the kitchen. 'Breaking my confidence?' he asked.

Bella went white. 'Hugh. I didn't know you were there.'

'Obviously.' He shook his head in disgust. 'Well, thanks a bunch. I guess that'll teach me to trust you. So do you blab Insurgo's business all over social media, too, the same way you've just blabbed my personal business to my mother?'

'Hugh, that's not fair,' Libby said. 'She was trying to help.'

'She was gossiping about me.' And that hurt.

'I wasn't gossiping at all,' Bella said. 'Right now, I want to tip this Yorkshire pudding batter all over your stupid head. But I'm not going to waste food and put your mum in an awkward position. Instead I'm going to walk outside in the garden, in this stupid outfit I found to fit your even more stupid idea. And *you*,' she said, walking over to him and stabbing her finger into his chest, 'are going to sit down with your mum and talk. Really talk.'

He was too taken aback to say anything. Not that he could've got a word in edgeways, because Bella was on a roll.

'You're going to tell her how you feel about your business and how it's not just your job, it's your passion, and for you it's like breathing. And you're going to tell her that you're great at business and you don't take unnecessary risks—that you save being a total idiot for the other bits of your life. You three,' she added to the dogs, 'you're coming with me and we're going to find some tennis balls, and I'm going to pretend they're Hugh's head and kick them as hard as I can.'

'Bella—' he began, knowing that he needed to apologise.

'No. Talk to your mum,' she said. 'Right now, I don't want to talk to you. I'm going out with the dogs.'

'Take whatever you need from the boot room, love,' Libby said. 'And I'll shout at him for you.'

Bella shook her head. 'I'd much rather you listened to him,' she said softly. 'Even though right at this moment I don't like him very much, I respect him when it comes to business—and I think you both need to listen to each other.' And she walked quietly out of the kitchen, followed by the dogs.

Hugh found himself talking—*really* talking—to his mother about the most important thing in his life. And she listened. Understood. Just as he could now see that the worrying and fussing were driven by love rather than a need to make him toe a family line that didn't actually exist.

Without Bella's intervention, this would never have happened, and he knew it.

When he'd finished, Libby said, 'You owe that girl—'

'—a huge apology,' he cut in. 'I know.'

She hugged him. 'You're my youngest son, Hugh, and I love you, but I don't like you very much today.'

'I don't like myself very much, either,' he admitted.

'She isn't Jessie,' Libby said softly.

'I know.' Jessie would never have offered to help prepare the vegetables. Yes, musicians had to look after their hands, because an accidental cut or burn would affect their ability to play an instrument—but Jessie wouldn't have offered to do something that didn't risk her hands, either. She wouldn't have played with Sophia. He knew that his family hadn't taken to her—they'd been polite but reserved. But everyone had instantly warmed to Bella, from his great-aunt to his brothers and even his father. 'I need to go and talk to her.'

'Be nice,' Libby said softly. 'She's got a good heart. She didn't break your trust. She found a better way to deal with things than any of us did.'

Hugh hugged his mother back. 'I know.' And he'd messed this up. Big time.

He went outside to find Bella. She looked as if she'd

been crying, and he felt a total heel. How could he have been so unkind to her?

'Bella. I'm sorry,' he said.

'Hmm.' She didn't look in the slightest bit mollified by his apology.

'You were right and I was wrong.'

She folded her arms. 'That's rather stating the obvious.'

'And I'm sorry I was obnoxious to you. I shouldn't have said any of that.'

'Also stating the obvious,' she said.

'I can't even blame it on Monday morning-itis.' He sighed. 'How do I make it up to you?'

'You've made it clear that you don't trust me. So, actually, I don't think you can,' she said.

He blew out a breath. 'I don't have a clue what to say or what to do. Only that I'm sorry for hurting you. And, without you, I don't think my family would ever have understood what Insurgo means to me. And I wouldn't have understood how they really feel, either. I appreciate that.'

She shrugged. 'Even so, I'm not your personal punchbag. Hugh, I don't enjoy people lashing out at me. I was only playing Miss Ditzy because you asked me to. I'm not an actress. Your mum saw right through the whole thing. And I did tell you it was a stupid idea.'

'You were right,' he said again. 'I know you probably want to be a million miles away from here right now, so if you want me to drive you straight home, then I'll do it. But I think my family would like you to stay for lunch. They like you. And I mean they like the *real* Bella Faraday,' he clarified. 'The one who looks out for elderly aunts, cuddles babies, plays ball with the dogs, is an amazing artist and brings out the best in everyone. The woman who really is the life and soul of the party— because I've never seen my entire family get up on the dance floor before you came along.'

Her eyes sparkled with tears; he brushed away the single one that spilled over her lashes.

'They don't hate me for lying to them?' she whispered.

'No. They really, really like you.' And so did he. Though now wasn't the time to say so. After the way he'd hurt her, she wouldn't believe him—and he couldn't blame her.

'Come and have lunch,' he said.

'For your mum's sake. Not yours.'

'I know,' he said softly. 'And thank you.'

Although Bella didn't say much to him once they were back in the house, she sparkled all the way through Sunday lunch. She insisted on helping to clear things away and on cuddling Sophia again when his niece had another fit of the grumps. And when his family said goodbye to her, it was with a warm, heartfelt hug rather than the formal handshakes they'd always given Jessie.

'Come back soon,' Libby said. 'And I mean *really* soon. You have to see the bluebells when they're at their best.'

'I'd love to,' Bella said, hugging her back. 'Thank you so much for having me.'

His brothers and their partners all got hugs, too, along with the baby. And so did his father, who then shocked Hugh immensely by saying, 'Come and paint the bluebells for my study, and I'll cook you my famous chicken biryani.'

Since when had his father ever cooked? Let alone something as exotic as biryani?

Hugh was so stunned that he didn't say a word until they were halfway home. And then it was only because Bella was the one to start the conversation.

'I think we need to talk,' she said carefully.

'Talk?'

She took a deep breath. 'I'm sorry I messed up your plans. If you want me to resign and go quietly from Insurgo, I'll accept that and write you an official resignation letter as soon as we're back in London.'

'No, that's not fair.' And he didn't want her to leave.

'You asked me to play your unsuitable girlfriend, and I didn't do it right.'

'I also told you to be yourself,' he said. 'And you were. Though I don't get how you do it.'

'How I do what?' she asked, sounding confused.

'Fit in so effortlessly. When you joined Insurgo, within a couple of days it was as if you'd been one of the team right from the start. And my family. They took to you like they never did to—' He stopped abruptly.

'Never did to whom?' she asked softly.

'Never mind.'

'The girl who broke your heart? The one you worked with?'

He gave her a sidelong glance. 'Fishing, Bella?'

'No—but I can hardly ask you straight out about it, can I? You're not exactly approachable.'

'My past isn't any of your—' he began, then stopped, knowing that he was being completely unfair to her. 'Sorry. That was rude and unkind. Especially as you've just given up your whole weekend to do me a favour, and I've already treated you badly. I apologise unreservedly. And you have the right to stamp all over me in spike heels.'

'Spike heels?'

'Your "three strikes and you're out" rule. I've broken that several times.'

'That's bravado,' Bella said, sounding sad. 'I don't really stomp on people.' And he felt even guiltier when she added, 'Besides, you're right. Your past isn't any of my business.' She sighed. 'Did you hear everything I said to your mum?'

'Only from when she asked you if you were my real girlfriend pretending to be my pretend girlfriend.' He gave her another swift look. Guilt was written all over her face. 'Is there more I should know about?'

'I told her that you're Insurgo's heart—and joining the family firm would break your spirit and make you resent them instead of loving them and being exasperated by them as you do now.'

If Hugh hadn't been driving, he would've closed his eyes in horror. 'We never talk about that sort of stuff.'

'I think you might do, in future,' Bella said softly. 'But, as I said earlier, I understand if you want me to resign.'

'Right now,' Hugh said, 'I think the best thing would be if neither of us said another word until we get back to London.'

'OK,' Bella said, and lapsed into silence.

Which made Hugh feel even more mean and guilty. He knew she'd said everything with the best of intentions. But his head was in a whirl. Bella Faraday knocked him seriously off balance, and he didn't trust himself to say what he really meant. He wasn't even sure what he really felt, other than being completely mixed up, so it was better to say nothing.

It didn't help that he could still smell her perfume, and

that made him remember kissing her in the orangery last night. That kiss—and what had happened afterwards—was something he really couldn't dare to repeat. So it was better to put a little bit of metaphorical distance between them. Wasn't it?

Finally he pulled up in the road outside her flat. 'I'll see you to your door.'

'There's no need,' Bella said. 'Thank you for the lift. And I won't ask you in. Not because I'm being rude, but because I'm sure you're busy. And, tomorrow morning, when we're back in the office, this weekend never happened.'

'Agreed,' he said.

Even though he didn't see her to the door, Hugh waited until she'd closed her front door behind her before he drove away. That was the very least he could do. And as for the damage to their working relationship... He'd better hope that he could fix it. Because the only way he could keep Bella in his life was as a colleague—and he didn't want to lose her.

What a weekend, Bella thought as she closed the front door behind her.

She changed swiftly into a more comfortable—not to mention demure—pair of jeans and a normal T-shirt, and bustled about sorting out things in her flat. There was a message on her phone from Grace.

Give me a ring when you're back and let me know how it went xxx

Yeah, right. Bella rolled her eyes. She could hardly admit to her sister what she'd done: slept with her boss, gone completely off brief, interfered and told his mother the truth, and then had a huge row with Hugh. Even though he'd apologised, she still hated the fact that he thought he couldn't trust her. Maybe his ex had broken his ability to trust, the way Kirk had broken hers; but it still hurt that he could think of her in that way. Did he not know her at all?

So she left it until late in the evening to text a reply to Grace: Just got back. That was stretching a point, but it was only a tiny fib. Too late to call. That bit was true. All fine. That bit might not be true. But she hoped that Grace wouldn't push her for more details—and that things would be OK in the office tomorrow. That she and Hugh could pretend that nothing had ever happened. Because, otherwise, she'd be looking for another job.

And, if she left Insurgo, it wasn't just the job she'd miss.

CHAPTER SEVEN

ON MONDAY MORNING, Bella was slightly nervous as she walked in to the Insurgo offices. She bought a double-shot cappuccino from the café downstairs to give her courage. Would Hugh be the same with her as he usually was, or would he avoid her? Would he be more difficult than he usually was on Monday mornings?

But he wasn't in the office. He'd left Tarquin a message to say that he was in a meeting across town and probably wouldn't make it in to the office until very late that day, if at all. Bella wasn't sure if she was more relieved at not having to face him or disappointed at missing him; though she knew that she couldn't let anyone guess how she was feeling. Nobody knew she'd been in Oxfordshire with Hugh, and it had to stay that way. As far as everyone at the Insurgo offices was concerned, he was the boss and she was simply the graphic designer. Full stop.

By Wednesday, Hugh knew that he had to show his face in the office or Tarquin would start working things out for himself. But he wasn't sure if he could do what Bella had suggested and work on the Vegas principle.

On paper, it was easy. What had happened in Oxfordshire should stay in Oxfordshire.

The problem was, he could still remember what it felt like to wake up wrapped round her. And, worse still, he wanted to do it again.

But he couldn't see a way of making this work. He already knew that from his experience with Jessie. Even though Bella wasn't anything like Jessie, the equation was the same: business plus relationship equals disaster.

So either he dated her and she left the company—which wouldn't be good for Insurgo, because she was a great designer—or she stayed in her job and he'd have to keep a lid on his feelings. It made business sense for it to be the latter. Plus he was used to keeping a lid on his feelings.

But that had been before Bella Faraday exploded into his life. Before he'd taken her home as his 'unsuitable' girlfriend. Before she'd turned his world upside down.

Bella was aware of every time Hugh walked into the room, even when her back was to the door.

She looked up several times from her work when he was in the main office, talking to Tarquin, and caught his eye. He looked away again almost immediately. And, because Hugh was so good at being impassive, she didn't have a clue what he was thinking.

Was he thinking about what had happened between them? Did he feel the same pull, the same awareness, as she did? Or was he regretting every single moment?

She was half tempted to text him and suggest that they talked. But that would be needy and pathetic, and that wasn't who she was. She'd got through Kirk's betrayal, and this situation with Hugh wasn't anywhere near that on the scale of awfulness.

Things would all settle down, soon enough. She

would get to the stage where she could look at Hugh without remembering how it had felt when he'd touched her and kissed her. Where she could look at him without wanting him to kiss her again. It would just take a bit of time, that was all. Until then, she'd just have to keep a lid on her feelings. This wasn't appropriate, and she wasn't in a position where she dared do anything to jeopardise her job.

Hugh sat in front of his computer with his elbows resting on the desk and his chin propped in his hands. This was ridiculous. He never, ever let anything distract his focus from his work.

But he couldn't stop thinking about Bella.

Maybe he should call her. Text her. Tell her he'd like to change his mind about the Vegas principle and see her now they were back in London. Ask her out to dinner or to a show.

But then things would start to get complicated in the office, and he didn't want that. He knew that keeping his distance from her was the sensible thing to do.

All the same, he was antsy. He couldn't settle to anything. And he knew it was making him snappy with everyone.

On the Thursday, he was glad that one of his artists was in the studio in the basement, recording an album. It gave him an excuse to stay out of the office and focus on producing the music—the part of his job he loved most. That would keep his head too busy to let him think about Bella Faraday.

And he actually managed it…until lunchtime, when Tarquin brought Bella down to meet the band and talk about the cover art concept.

She'd changed her hair colour again, Hugh noticed. Today she was brunette. It was a huge change from the almost fire-engine-red she'd sported in Oxfordshire, but it suited her and it brought out the depths of her eyes. It made her look seriously pretty.

How he wanted to twirl the ends of her hair round his fingers. Feel how soft and silky it was. And then touch his mouth to hers...

What made it worse was that she was dressed in faded jeans which hugged her curves, and spike-heeled ankle boots. She'd teamed it with a black T-shirt with the In-surgo logo on the front, clearly going for the rock chick look. And she carried it off beautifully.

He wasn't surprised that she charmed the band as quickly as she'd charmed his family. Just by being her-self: bright, vivacious Bella with her ready laugh, and the way she touched people's hands or arms or shoulders when she spoke. She was very tactile; and yet she didn't make you feel as if she'd invaded your personal space. It felt natural. Easy.

Hugh caught her eye. Was it his imagination, or was there the faintest blush in her cheeks as she looked at him? Probably his imagination, he decided, because she was totally professional and almost cool with him. Clearly she didn't have a problem with the Vegas prin-ciple.

They discussed the album concept and cover with the band, and Bella made a few sketches and notes. Hugh could barely take his eyes off her hands. He remembered how they'd felt against his skin, and it made him ache.

When would he stop wanting her?

Tarquin had also organised a buffet lunch for all of them, sent down by the café on the ground floor. Being together in a more social setting would be awkward, Hugh thought, but no way could he or Bella get out of this. He hadn't said a word to Tarquin about the situation and he was pretty sure that she hadn't said anything, either, or his business partner would've had quite a lot to say about it.

Well, they'd just have to roll with it and pretend that everything was normal. Even though it wasn't.

He noticed that Jet, the band's lead singer, was flirting with Bella during lunch. She wasn't encouraging him at all; she was professional and polite and made sure that she included the rest of the band in the conversation. Hugh couldn't fault her behaviour. But he really wanted to snarl at Jet and tell him to back off, because Bella wasn't available. Which would put her in an impossible situation, so he kept his tongue firmly under control.

But then he reached for the plate of sandwiches at the same time as Bella did. As his fingers brushed against hers, he felt the heat zing through him. And when his gaze caught hers, her pupils went just that little bit darker and wider. So was it the same for her, too? This crazy, raging need that sent him into a flat spin?

And just what were they going to do about this?

The more time Hugh spent with her, the more he wanted her—and this wasn't fair to either of them. But right at that moment he couldn't see a way of making things better. Not without complicating things or risking things getting a whole lot worse.

To his relief, after lunch Bella made an excuse to go back up to the office with Tarquin, which left him to concentrate on the music and the band and working on the arrangements.

Jet turned to him at the end of the next song. 'I was going to ask you—could you give me Bella's number?'

'To discuss the album cover?' Hugh asked, deliberately misunderstanding the other man. 'Just call the usual office number and someone will put you through to her.'

'No, I meant…'

'What?' Uh-oh. He really hoped that Jet hadn't picked up how short his tone was.

But the singer didn't seem fussed in the slightest. 'Dating her, man,' he said with a grin. 'I know you're dedicated to your work, Hugh, but surely even *you* have noticed how hot she is?'

Of course he'd noticed. More than noticed. 'She's my colleague,' he said crisply. 'I never mix business and relationships.'

Jet gave him a look as if to say, *more fool you.* 'So can you give me her number?'

'She might already be involved with someone.'

Jet held his gaze. 'And she might not.'

'I'll let her know you asked, and leave it up to her if she wants to call you,' Hugh said. And he seriously hoped she didn't. Even though he knew he was being a complete dog in the manger, given that he wasn't actually in a relationship with Bella. For all he knew, she might actually want to date Jet. But he'd be much happier if she didn't. 'Now, let's get back to work and go through the next song, shall we?'

Later that afternoon, when the band had left, Hugh walked back into the office. Bella was working at her desk, but he knew by the sudden tension in her shoulders that she knew he was there.

'Jet asked for your number,' he said abruptly.

Her head snapped up and she stared at him. 'Jet?'

'The lead singer of the band. You were talking to him at lunch.' And Jet had most definitely been flirting with her. Surely she'd been aware of that?

'Oh.'

'I told him to ring the office and someone would put him through, if he wants to discuss the album cover.'

'Uh-huh.'

He couldn't tell anything from her expression. Which left him with no choice; he'd have to raise the issue. 'Jet didn't want to discuss business.'

'Then what did he want?'

He gave her a speaking look. Wasn't it obvious? 'I told him that relationships and business don't mix.'

And now there was the tiniest, tiniest glint in her eyes. Amusement? Anger? Pity? He wasn't sure. There was no way he could ask without betraying himself, and until he knew what was going on in her head he didn't want her to know what he was feeling.

'Did you, now?' she drawled.

'I said I'd tell you he'd asked.'

'I might,' Bella said, 'already be committed to someone.'

'So you might,' he said. And he had to suppress the wish that it was him.

'I'll make sure he knows that,' she said.

So she wasn't going to date the guy? He was shocked by the way it made him feel as if a massive weight had been lifted from his shoulders. 'Thank you.' But he didn't want her to realise he was glad for selfish reasons. 'I like the office to run smoothly,' he added coolly.

'Noted, Mr Moncrieff.'

And then she did something that nearly finished

him off. She moistened her lower lip with the tip of her tongue, so her lips looked as shiny as if she'd just been kissed. *Just as she'd looked when he'd kissed her.*

'Right,' he said, and left for his own office. While he still could.

Back at his desk, he rested his elbows on the table and propped his face in his hands. When was he going to stop wanting this woman? When was his common sense going to come back? He knew it wouldn't work between them. It couldn't.

Yet he still wanted her.

By the end of the next week, Hugh was near to going insane. Throwing himself into work wasn't making any difference at all. And when he was at home he actually found himself sitting down with a guitar in his hand or at the piano, something he hadn't done in a long time. There were little snatches of songs buzzing round in his head—nothing he recognised, so he knew they were his own compositions. There were bits of melodies, bits of introductions, and bits of a middle eight. None of them fitted together and none of the melodies had proper words to go with them, but Hugh knew that he was starting to write songs again.

And that worried him even more.

It had taken him a year to get over the mess that Jessie's betrayal had caused. He didn't want to leave himself open to the risk of feeling that low ever, ever again—even though part of him was glad that the music he loved so much was bubbling up inside him again, and he knew it was all due to Bella.

But this was all too complicated.

He was just going to have to get over these growing

feelings for Bella and ignore them. And ignore the hints from his parents that the bluebells were starting to look really pretty and the dogs would love to go for a run with him. They might just as well have texted him in capitals to say WE WANT TO SEE BELLA.

Well, it wasn't happening.

What happened in Oxfordshire, stayed in Oxfordshire. They'd agreed it. Their relationship had been strictly business from that Sunday afternoon onwards.

So why couldn't Bella get Hugh out of her head? Why could she still feel the warmth of his body wrapped round her? Why, every time she closed her eyes, did she remember him kissing her among the fairy lights until they were both dizzy?

'Are you OK, Bella?' Tarquin asked.

'Fine.' She smiled at him. 'Just a bit of a headache.' A headache called Hugh Moncrieff. Not that she would ever admit that to anyone at Insurgo. Since they'd been back, Hugh's cool and professional behaviour towards her had made it clear that their relationship was strictly business. And she didn't want to cause tension in the office. Even so, she couldn't help asking, 'Tarq, have you known Hugh for very long?'

'We were at school together, so yes. Why?'

'I just wondered,' she said, 'why he has this thing about not mixing business and relationships.'

'Ah. That's not my story to tell, sweet-cheeks,' Tarquin said softly. 'Why? Are you…?'

Oh, no. He hadn't guessed how she felt about Hugh, had he? 'No, no, not at all,' she fibbed hastily. 'It's just something he said when Jet from the band asked for my number.'

'OK.'

But Tarquin looked curious, and Bella wished she hadn't said anything. 'Just being nosey,' she said sweetly. 'Obviously something's happened in the past that made things difficult for everyone in the office, so he doesn't want people to get involved with people they have to work with. I get it.'

'Something like that,' Tarquin said.

But he still looked oddly at her, and she knew she had to do something to distract him. 'I'm going to do a tea and coffee run. What do you want?' Even if that did mean going upstairs to the staff kitchen and being even closer to Hugh's office, it would hopefully distract Tarquin and he wouldn't start working things out or leaping to conclusions.

'I'd love a coffee, thank you, sweetie,' Tarquin said, and to her relief the sticky moment was over.

On Friday evening, Tarquin walked into Hugh's office and tapped the face of his watch with an exaggerated motion. 'Right, you. Time to turn the computer off.'

Hugh frowned. 'Not now, Tarq. I've got a couple of things to do.'

'They can wait. We're meeting Ro, or had you forgotten?'

Roland was their other best friend from school. And both Hugh and Tarquin had been worried about him for months; their regular fortnightly meeting was their way of keeping an eye on him, under the guise of rescuing Hugh from being a total workaholic. 'I'd forgotten what today was,' Hugh admitted. He glanced at the screen. 'OK. Let me save the file and shut the computer down, and we'll go.'

* * *

Roland walked into the bar at roughly the same time they did, and raised his hand to show he'd seen them.

But although Hugh had thought this was all about keeping an eye on Roland, he was in for a surprise when Tarquin turned to him after ordering two beers and a mineral water for Roland.

'All righty. You're being more of a nightmare than usual in the office, Hugh. I'm pretty sure it's got something to do with your brother's engagement party—and, as I haven't been able to get it out of you, Ro's going to do the thumbscrews.'

Roland spread his hands. 'That pretty much sums it up. So you can tell us now, or we can nag you until you tell us. Your choice, but I'd advise saving all the drag of us droning on at you and just telling us.'

Hugh raked a hand through his hair. 'Nothing's wrong.'

'Or,' Roland suggested, 'I could call your mother and tell her that Tarq and I are worried about you. She'll tell us what you're not saying.'

Which was what Hugh and Tarquin had done to Roland, the previous year, out of sheer desperation. It had worked, but they'd had an unspoken pact since then that calling any of their mothers was off limits.

'No. *Don't* call Ma. Please.' Hugh had been avoiding his mother's calls, too, returning her answering machine messages with a brief text to say he was up to his eyes at work and would call her soon. If his two best friends tag-teamed her and she told them the information he'd been keeping back, he wouldn't stand a chance. He put his hands up in a gesture of surrender. 'OK. I'll talk.' At least then maybe he could do some damage limitation.

Tarquin handed him a beer and gestured to one of the quieter tables in the corner.

They really weren't going to let him off this, were they? He suppressed a sigh and went to sit down.

'Tell us, sweet-cheeks,' Tarquin said. 'What happened at Nigel's party?'

Hugh blew out a breath. 'I thought I was being so clever. I took someone with me. A pretend girlfriend. Someone unsuitable. The idea was that they'd all be so horrified by her that they'd be glad when I told them it was all over—and then they'd back off.'

Tarquin and Roland exchanged a glance. 'But?' Tarquin asked.

Hugh grimaced. 'They saw through it. And they liked her. A lot.'

'Hmm. If you liked her enough to ask for her help, and she liked you enough to go along with it, and your family all liked her, then it sounds to me as if you're looking at this from completely the wrong direction,' Roland said. 'Why don't you just date the girl properly?'

'You know why,' Hugh said. 'After Jessie, there's no way I'm getting involved with anyone again. Nothing serious. I'm concentrating on the business. That's how I like my life.'

'Not all women are like Jessie,' Tarquin said. 'There's no reason why you can't try again with someone else.'

Hugh folded his arms. 'I *know* not all women are like Jessie. But I don't trust my own judgement any more. I was stupid enough to let her fool me, so what's to say I won't make the same mistake again?'

'Because you're too bright to do that,' Tarquin said. 'Think about it. You earned a first class degree.'

'Plus you own the hottest indie record label in the

country and the business is going from strength to strength,' Roland said.

It was now. Thanks to a lot of hard work—and Roland's investment. But Hugh knew just how much damage had been done to his business by letting his heart rule his head over Jessie.

'Tarq has a point,' Roland continued. 'It's been a while. Surely you're lonely?'

Yes. He was. And he wanted Bella. Hugh's temper flared. 'That's rich, coming from you.'

'That's a different kettle of fish altogether,' Roland said, his voice very quiet.

Hugh saw the emptiness in his best friend's eyes and flinched. 'Ro, I'm sorry—that was way, way below the belt. I apologise unreservedly. I shouldn't have said that.' Roland was single, but not from choice; his wife had died in a car crash eighteen months ago, and he was still mourning her. Some well-meaning friends had tried matchmaking over the last few months, but every attempt had failed spectacularly.

'Apology accepted.' But Roland's voice was completely neutral, and Hugh knew he'd overstepped the mark. Big time. Exactly the way he'd lashed out at Bella—and for exactly the same reason.

The only way he could think of to make amends was to tell the truth. Well, some of it. 'I *am* sorry, Ro. This whole thing makes me antsy, and I shouldn't have taken it out on you. I'm just as horrible at work, and...' He shrugged. 'I hate being like it. Everyone else hates it just as much. But I don't seem to be able to stop myself.'

Tarquin patted his arm. 'You're in Monday morning mode. We get it. Now spill.'

'I like her. A lot. And it scares me stupid,' he admitted. 'The way I feel about her is like nothing else I've ever known. Not even Jessie. I just can't get her out of my head.'

'Are you going to tell us anything about her?' Roland asked.

Hugh squirmed. How could he do this without giving away too much? 'She's bright, she's funny, and she makes me feel as if the world's full of sunshine.'

'Which sounds perfect. So why aren't you dating her officially?' Tarquin asked.

'It's complicated,' Hugh hedged.

'Complicated how?' Roland asked.

Hugh put his face in his hands. There was no way out of this, any more. He was going to have to bite the bullet. 'Because she works for Insurgo,' he muttered. '*Now* do you get why it's a problem?'

Tarquin groaned. 'No. Please. Not Bella. Tell me you didn't take Bella with you to Oxfordshire.'

'Who's Bella?' Roland asked, looking mystified. 'And why would it be so bad if Hugh was with her?'

'Bella's our new designer,' Tarquin explained. 'She's really good at her job, and she makes everyone in the office laugh for all the right reasons. She fitted in from the moment she walked in to Insurgo. She's adorable. If I was straight, I'd be tempted to ask her to marry me. Which gives you an idea of just how great she is.' He looked at Hugh, unsmiling. 'All righty. Bottom line. How does she feel about you?'

'I don't know.' Hugh looked away.

Tarquin groaned. 'I've got a bad feeling about this. I thought she'd been a bit wary of you in the office, this last week or so. And you've been grumpier than usual. I assumed it was because of your family—but it's not, is it?'

'Bella Faraday and I are not an item,' Hugh said calmly. 'Don't worry, Tarq. It'll be absolutely fine. Things will settle down. We talked about it.'

'Did you tell her about Jessie?' Roland asked.

'No. The subject didn't come up.' Which was a big fat lie. The subject *had* come up, but his family hadn't told her quite enough for her to work it out for herself, and Hugh had refused flatly to discuss it. He'd even been rude to Bella when she'd asked. Unkind. Unfair.

Tarquin rolled his eyes. 'Great. So now I'm going to have to scour London for a new designer—one as good as she is and who'll fit in as quickly as she has. Which is practically impossible. You *idiot*. I could shake you until your teeth rattle.'

'It's fine,' Hugh repeated. 'She's staying. We understand each other.'

'You mean you've both said all the right words,' Roland said. 'And neither of you have said what you're really thinking.'

'Neither of us wants any complications,' Hugh insisted.

'But you complicated it anyway?' Tarquin asked dryly.

'Yes,' Hugh admitted. He told them about her dress and the curtains in the ballroom, making them both laugh. 'And I sang with her.'

His best friends both went still. 'She sings?' Roland asked, his voice very soft.

'Not professionally,' Hugh said. 'Tarq already told you that she's a graphic artist. She really loves what she does. She doesn't want to be a pop star.'

'Ro, this isn't a re-run of the Jessie situation,' Tarquin said. 'Bella's nothing like Jessie at all. If someone came and offered her ten times her salary to work for them instead of for Hugh, she'd tell them to get lost. She's loyal, she's sweet and she's utterly lovely.' He looked at Hugh. 'And you know it, too. Actually, now I think about it, she's absolutely perfect for you and she might even make you into a nicer man. Except you're such an idiot that you won't give her a chance.'

Hugh folded his arms. 'You know how I feel about the situation, and you know I'm right. Mixing business and your love life is a recipe for disaster.'

'No. Getting mixed up with Jessie was a recipe for disaster,' Roland corrected. 'How many people meet their partners at work and there's a happy ending?' He paused. 'I met Lynette at work. And, if it hadn't been for the car accident, we'd still be together now.'

Hugh patted his shoulder awkwardly. 'What happened to her was beyond awful, Ro.'

'Yeah. But,' he said, surprising Hugh, 'I've decided it's time to make the effort. Lyn wouldn't have wanted me to spend the rest of my life on my own, missing her and being lonely. She would've wanted me to live life to the full.'

'So you're going to date again? Have you actually met someone?' Tarquin asked.

'No. But I'm going to try,' Roland said. 'Jessie, on the other hand, would want you to be on your own and miserable, Hugh. Which is because she's totally self-absorbed and wants the universe to revolve round her. Are you really going to let her make the rest of your life as lonely and empty as it's been for the past year, when you've met someone you actually like and you have a chance of grabbing happiness with both hands?'

'You,' Hugh said, 'are trying to pull a guilt trip on me.'

'No,' Tarquin said. 'He's telling you that it's OK to feel let down by Jessie, but it's not OK to wallow in it. Talk to Bella. Find out how she feels about you. Then, if she feels the same way you do, just sweep her off her feet.'

Could he?

Should he?

Would it all go wrong anyway?

'Maybe,' Hugh said. 'Now, can we please change the conversation and lighten this evening up a bit?'

'Flowers for the best sister in the world,' Bella said, dumping a large bunch of flowers into Grace's arms. 'And pudding.' She swung the carrier bag from one finger, and added with a grin, 'I bought it rather than made it, so it'll be edible.'

Grace simply laughed. 'Oh, Bel. You're going to have to learn to cook, one day, you know.'

'No, I won't. I have an excellent plan. I'm going to win a million on the lottery and have a housekeeper,' Bella retorted.

'In your dreams,' Grace teased back. 'Come and sit down. The kettle's on.'

'Just what I wanted to hear. So how's the flat-hunting going?' Bella asked.

Grace wrinkled her nose. 'I'm still looking. But when I have to leave here at the end of the week, Charlene's letting me use her spare room because her flatmate's spending a month in Australia. And that'll hopefully give me enough breathing space to find somewhere.'

'You can stay at mine, any time,' Bella said. 'I know it'll be a squeeze, but I'll never see you out on the streets, Gracie.'

Grace hugged her. 'I know. And the same goes for you.'

Bella enjoyed dinner—until Grace made them both a cappuccino and said, 'So when are you going to tell me?'

'Tell you what?' Bella asked, feigning innocence and trying frantically to work out how she could distract her sister.

'About what really happened in Oxfordshire? You've been way too quiet about it.'

Bella laced her fingers together. 'There's nothing to tell.'

Grace coughed. 'Try the truth.'

'I messed it up,' Bella confessed.

'So does that mean you're looking for another job?'

'Yes and no,' Bella hedged.

'You're not making a lot of sense.'

'I know.' Bella sighed. 'I don't know where to start.'

'Try the beginning?' Grace suggested gently.

'OK. I managed the afternoon tea bit OK, and I looked after his great-aunt when she wasn't feeling well.'

Grace frowned. 'That doesn't sound like messing up, to me.'

'It's not what an unsuitable girlfriend would do,' Bella pointed out.

'I guess—but it's what a decent person would do, and I know you, Bel. You couldn't have just left her to be unwell. So then what?'

'My dress for the cocktail party.' Bella blew out a breath. 'It turned out that the curtains in the ballroom were the same material as my dress.'

Grace put her hands up in a 'stop' gesture. 'Wait. Let me get my head round this. They have a *ballroom* in their house?'

Bella nodded. 'They live in an Elizabethan manor house—it's been used as a location for a few period dramas, Hugh said. Oh, Gracie, the house is utterly gorgeous, and his family's so lovely. Libby—his mum—

she's so like our mum. And his oldest brother and sister-in-law have the cutest baby, and they have three dogs.'

'I think I'm beginning to see what you meant about messing up,' Grace said. 'They didn't think you were unsuitable at all, did they?'

'Um—no.' Bella squirmed. 'I guess they kind of liked me.'

'Of course they liked you. Everyone who meets you likes you,' Grace said.

'Except Mrs Concrete Hair,' Bella said, referring to Grace's almost mother-in-law.

Grace laughed. 'I don't think she likes anyone. So his family are nice and you get on. Was that a problem for Hugh?'

'Possibly,' Bella said. 'We haven't exactly spoken much since we've been back.'

'It's difficult between you at work?'

'We pretty much ignore each other—unless we're in a meeting together, which isn't that often,' Bella said. 'And I'm just hoping that nobody in the office has noticed that it's a bit strained between us.'

'Maybe they haven't,' Grace said. 'So—back to your dress. What happened?'

'I brazened it out,' Bella said. 'I said I hadn't cut it from their curtains because they weren't the von Trapps—and then I sang "Do Re Mi".'

Grace laughed. 'That's *so* you, and I bet everyone joined in.'

'No. It was a bit awkward. And then Hugh sang "Edelweiss".' She bit her lip. 'That's something else odd, Gracie. The band his brother booked for the party was late, so Hugh played the piano until they turned up. He's really talented. And he has a gorgeous voice. I can't understand why he doesn't release records as well as produce them—and his brother said something about knowing why Hugh doesn't sing or play in public. His mother kind of let something slip, too. And Tarquin in the office, this week… I was subtle when I asked.'

Grace laughed. 'Bel, you don't do subtle.'

'Subtle for *me*, then.' She frowned. 'I might be putting two and two together and making ten, but I think Hugh fell for someone he worked with and it went pear-shaped.'

'Have you asked him about it?'

'Sort of—and he said it was none of my business. Which is quite right,' Bella added hastily, seeing Grace's eyes narrow in annoyance. 'It was rude of me to ask. And I wasn't subtle when I asked him. Anyway, we danced together. And he sneaked me off to the orangery—Gracie, it was the most romantic place ever, just the two of us and the darkness outside and fairy lights wrapped round the base of the orange trees, and he k—' She stopped, realising that maybe she shouldn't have admitted that much.

But Grace had clearly realised anyway. 'He kissed you?' she asked softly.

There was no point in trying to deny it. Especially as Grace was sensible enough to help her work out how to deal with it, and her sister could only do that if Bella told her the truth. She nodded. 'And it was like seeing stars—it's never been like that for me before.'

'Me, neither,' Grace said, sounding wistful. Then she frowned. '*Just* kissing?'

Bella winced. 'No. But we took precautions. And the next morning we agreed it'd be like the Vegas principle—what happened there, stayed there.'

'Uh-huh,' Grace said. 'So what's the situation now?'

'I don't really know,' Bella admitted. 'I like him, Gracie. I mean *really* like him. Which is crazy. We've only known each other for a few weeks. And yet in some ways I feel I've known him for ever. He's a good man. Look at the way he rescued us. And I know from talking to some of the artists that he's gone way beyond the call of duty for them. He's one of the good guys. He'd never do anything like what Kirk did.'

'Not if he wanted to keep all his bits intact, he wouldn't,' Grace said crisply.

Bella gave her sister a wan smile. 'I don't know what to do, Gracie. After Kirk, I don't really believe in love any more. And I don't want to mess up my job by falling for my boss, knowing that he doesn't believe in mixing work and relationships. One of the bands came in to record an album and the lead singer wanted to ask me out, and Hugh told him straight out that work and relationships don't mix.'

'Because he wants you for himself?'

That was the big question. Bella dragged in a breath. 'I don't actually know,' she said miserably. 'I don't know what to do, Gracie. I mean, I know I'm scatty and disorganised outside work and it's usually fine, but right now I feel as if I'm in the middle of a whirlwind, and it's really not very comfortable. I don't like feeling this way.'

'I think, love, you're going to have to take a risk and talk to him,' Grace said. 'If he likes you and you like him, then it's simple.'

'But what if he doesn't like me?'

'Bel, you're sweet and you're warm and you're funny and you're beautiful. What's not to like?'

'You're my sister. You're supposed to think that.' Bella folded her arms. 'And I don't know what he thinks of me.'

'For what it's worth,' Grace said, 'you've already said he's not like Kirk. And from what you said he's not like Howard, either—he was right there by your side when you sang "Do Re Mi". So it sounds to me as if he likes you.'

'And his family's definitely not like Mrs Concrete Hair and Mr Toad,' Bella added, referring to Howard's parents.

'Well, then. Talk to him. What's the worst that could happen?'

'That he turns me down and then it's too awkward to work with him,' Bella said.

'But isn't it already awkward working with him?' Grace asked.

'A bit,' Bella admitted. 'So I've been half thinking that I might need to find another job anyway.'

'And if you don't say anything, what's the worst that could happen?' Grace asked.

Bella knew that her sister wouldn't let her get away with being feeble. 'I'll always regret not talking to him and seeing if we could make a go of it. And maybe he'll meet someone else, and he'll never know how I felt about him because I was too much of a coward to try.'

'And you're not a coward, Bel. You're brave and you're honest and you're lovely,' Grace said. 'Talk to him.'

'I'll try,' Bella promised.

But would Hugh talk to her? Or would he keep himself shut off?

CHAPTER EIGHT

'ARE YOU SURE you don't want to leave this until the morning, sweet-cheeks?' Tarquin asked, the following Tuesday evening. 'It's late and you've already put in a lot of hours.'

'I'm sure,' Bella said firmly. 'It won't take me very long to get this finished and I really hate leaving things.'

'OK. Just let Hugh know when you leave, so he can lock up,' Tarquin said. 'I'll let him know you're working late so he doesn't accidentally lock you in or anything.'

A frisson went through her. So she and Hugh would be alone in the building?

Well, not completely alone—she knew that there would be people downstairs in the café—but there would be just the two of them in the office.

Maybe she could be brave and talk to him tonight…

'See you tomorrow, Tarq,' she said brightly. 'Have a nice evening.'

'You, too—and don't work too late, do you hear?'

She smiled and blew him a kiss; smiling back, Tarquin left her to it. Bella managed to concentrate on what she was doing and finished the piece of art she'd been working on all day. Once she'd turned off her computer and checked all the other switches in the main office, she paused by the staircase. Time to face Hugh.

Would she have the nerve to talk to him about the unfinished business between them?

She took a deep breath, headed upstairs and rapped on Hugh's closed door.

'Yes?' he called.

She opened the door and leaned against the door jamb. 'Tarquin said to tell you when I was leaving so you could lock up.'

'OK. Thanks.' He barely glanced at her, concentrating on a file on his desk.

He looked tired, she thought, as if a gazillion things were on his mind and stopping him sleeping. She knew the feeling. He clearly wasn't going to bring up the subject, because he was too stubborn. Which meant that she'd have to be the one who initiated the conversation. She walked over and sat on the edge of his desk. Hugh looked up at her again and glowered. 'What?'

She wasn't fooled by the brusqueness. 'You were in earlier than everyone else, and you're here later than everyone else. It's been like that ever since we got back from Oxfordshire. Carry on like this and you're going to risk burn-out.'

'Thank you for your concern, but my mother doesn't need anyone to help her nag me.'

His tone was snippy enough to make her back off. Except she'd seen that tiny glint of vulnerability in his eyes before he'd looked away. So maybe Grace was right and he was feeling as antsy as she was, and for the same reasons. She knew she was taking a huge risk here and it could all go horribly wrong, but on the other hand if she didn't try then she knew she'd always regret it. She leaned over and stroked the hair back from his forehead. 'Hey,' she said softly.

He looked at her again, and his pupils were huge. So he *did* react to her then.

'You've done enough for today,' she said. 'Come and have dinner with me.'

He was silent for so long that she thought he was going to refuse. She was about to back away and tell him to ignore anything she said because she was sleep-deprived and that meant her mouth wasn't in sync with her brain, when he asked softly, 'Are you asking me out on a date, Bella Faraday?'

His voice was deep. Slightly raspy. Just as he'd sounded when he'd made love with her and whispered her name. And it sent a thrill right the way through her.

'I'm asking you back to my place,' she said. 'There's not going to be anything super-fantastic on the menu, just a stir-fry, because I'm really *not* a very good cook. But it does mean that you won't have to make anything for yourself when you finally leave here and go home.'

He looked at her, wide-eyed with surprise. 'You're mothering me?'

She gave him a rueful smile. 'As you said, your mother doesn't need any help.'

He grimaced. 'Sorry. That was rude and unfair of me.'

'And a defence mechanism. You're snippy when you want people to back off.'

He raised an eyebrow. 'So you're a psychologist as well as an artist, now?'

'Nope. Just someone who also uses a defence mechanism. Except mine's sunshine rather than grumpiness.'

He smiled, then, and rested his hand against her cheek. 'Bella. Go home.'

His touch made heat zing throughout her body. And

maybe short-circuited her brain, because she said, 'Not without you.'

'Bella—I've already told you, I don't do relationships.'

'Neither do I.' She dragged in a breath. 'But you and I, we've been circling each other in the office ever since we went to Oxfordshire. And I think we need to…'

He was staring at her mouth. 'Need to what?'

She twisted her head to one side and pressed a kiss into his palm. 'Talk.'

His pupils dilated even more, making his eyes seem completely black. 'Uh-huh.'

'Maybe among other things,' she admitted. Because talking wasn't all she had in mind. Particularly when he was this close to her.

He moistened his lower lip with the tip of his tongue. 'Do you really think it's a good idea for you and me to be alone in a room that might have a bed nearby?'

She smiled. 'Who needs a bed?'

He groaned. 'Bella, you're killing me.'

'Maybe,' she said, 'we need to get this out of our systems. Unfinished business and all that.'

'I don't do for ever,' he warned.

'Neither do I.' And this time she leaned forward and touched her mouth to his. Really, really lightly. Every nerve-end in her lips tingled.

Was he going to kiss her back? Pull her into his arms and really kiss her? Anticipation danced through her. Any second now. Any second…

Hugh dragged in a breath. 'Bella. Right now, my self-control is hanging by the thinnest thread. We can't do this. Go home.'

It was enough of a confession to give her the courage to ignore his protests. She curled her thumb and fingers into her palm and widened the gap between her first and middle finger, as if her hand were a pair of scissors, then smiled at him and 'snipped'. 'Come home with me,' she said softly.

She could see the struggle in his face. Hugh the honourable man, who wanted to do the right thing and keep his employee at a respectable distance, versus Hugh the lover, who remembered how in tune their bodies had been and wanted to do it all over again.

Then he pulled her into his arms and she knew that the lover had won.

When she surfaced from the kiss, she whispered, 'Ready?'

'Not in a million years.' He kissed her again. 'We need to lock up.'

His head and heart were still warring, she guessed.

She waited for him to lock up, then took his hand.

'My car's outside,' he said.

She nodded, and followed him out to the tiny car park behind the offices. He actually opened the passenger door for her; she loved his old-fashioned good manners.

Then he drove her home and parked outside the road by her flat.

'Do I need a parking permit or anything?' he asked.

Yes, but she didn't want him to have time to think about this and change his mind. 'There won't be any traffic wardens around at this time of night,' she said.

He kissed her. 'I wouldn't bet on that, but OK. You're worth a parking ticket.'

She grimaced. 'Now you've made me feel guilty.'

'Good.' He gave her a slow, sensual smile. 'You can make it up to me.'

He held her hand all the way between the car and her

front door. Once they were inside, he slid his hands into her hair and kissed her until she was dizzy. 'I can't get you out of my head,' he said, holding her close.

'Me, too,' she admitted. She slid her hand under the hem of his T-shirt and splayed her hands against his abdomen. 'Every time I close my eyes, I see you. And I want you, Hugh. It's driving me crazy.'

'Me, too,' he admitted. 'Let's do something about it.'

She took his hand and led him to her room. Slowly, she took off his T-shirt; then she took a step backwards, looked at him and sucked in a breath. 'I want to paint you.'

'Oh, yes?'

'Like Michelangelo's David.'

He grinned. 'I'm hardly a fourteen-foot-tall statue.'

'Scaled down,' she said, grinning back. 'But you're still wearing too much.'

'So are you,' he pointed out.

She spread her hands. 'Do something about it, then.'

He kissed her, then stripped off her T-shirt; and then it was her turn to get rid of his jeans. He followed suit, stroking every inch of skin he uncovered as he removed the soft denim, then making her whimper when he kissed the soft undersides of her breasts and drew a path downwards.

Bella wasn't sure who finished stripping whom, but finally they were naked and in her bed and he was inside her. And the world felt very right indeed.

As they lay curled up together afterwards, her stomach rumbled. 'Sorry,' she said, feeling the heat flare into her cheeks.

He laughed and kissed her. 'It's not just you. Sorry. I was hungrier for you than I was for food.'

'Me, too,' she admitted. 'It's been driving me crazy this last couple of weeks, seeing you in the office and knowing I was supposed to keep my hands off you.'

'That's why I've been skulking in my office instead of coming downstairs with the rest of the team,' he said, and kissed her again. 'Bella, we need to talk. We need to work out how we're going to deal with this.'

'The Vegas principle again?' she asked.

'Maybe,' he said.

'Let's eat, first,' she suggested. 'It might get some brain cells working properly.'

'Good idea.' He climbed out of bed and started to get dressed.

Bella was tempted to tell him not to bother putting his T-shirt back on, but a wave of shyness stopped her; she, too, scrambled out of bed and pulled on her clothes.

'Take a seat,' she said in the main room of her flat, gesturing to the little bistro table in her kitchen area.

'Now I think I know why your desk is so untidy,' he teased.

'Because there's more room on it than there is in my flat?' she asked wryly.

'It's, um, bijou,' he said.

'I like it.'

He stroked her face. 'It's a nice flat.'

'But the whole thing's hardly bigger than the boot room in the house where you grew up.'

'Isn't there a saying that lovely things come in small packages?' he asked. He kissed her lightly. 'Starting with you.'

'Hmm. Sit down and I'll feed you,' she said.

Except when she was making the stir fry, she managed to burn the chicken slightly, and then the noodles caught on the bottom of the wok as well, and the vegetables had somehow gone watery. The whole thing looked disgusting and smelled disgusting—and she dreaded to think what it would taste like. Even a sachet of sweet chilli sauce wouldn't be able to disguise the burned or watery bits.

No way could she serve him this.

'I'm so sorry,' she said, and bit her lip. 'This has all gone a bit wrong. I wish I was more like Gracie—she's a great cook and I've never got the hang of anything more than cupcakes, pancakes and Yorkshire puddings,' she finished miserably.

Hugh came over to her, gave her a hug and kissed her frown away. 'It's no big deal. Actually, I'm an OK cook. Ma taught us all before we left for uni. Do you mind me taking over your kitchen?'

'But I was supposed to cook for you, because you're tired. I can't make you cook for me.'

He kissed the tip of her nose. 'The thought was there, and it's appreciated. But right now you're stressed, and cooking relaxes me anyway. Let me do this for you.'

'OK. And thank you. But I need to get rid of this mess first.' She gestured to the wok.

'Sure.'

She scraped the ruined stir fry into the bin and put the burned pan to soak in the sink. 'Would you like a glass of wine?' she asked.

He shook his head. 'Thanks for the offer, but I'm driving.'

Obviously he wasn't planning to stay the night, then. Well, she shouldn't have expected it. He'd made it very clear that he didn't do relationships. Neither did she, really; so this was just unfinished business to get it out of their systems. 'You'd still be under the limit with one glass,' she pointed out.

'My best friend's wife was killed by a drunk driver, eighteen months ago,' he said softly. 'Since then, none of our group of friends touches a drop of alcohol if we're driving.'

Her eyes widened. 'Oh, poor Tarquin! But I thought he was…' Her voice faded. 'Um. Well.'

'Not Tarquin,' he said. 'His partner—who is indeed male—is just fine. I was talking about Roland. He went to school with Tarq and me. He's a silent partner in Insurgo.' He gave her a sidelong look. 'Though I guess it's a bit greedy, having two best friends.'

Just lucky, Bella thought. She'd been perfectly happy with one—until it had all gone wrong. 'There's nothing wrong with having two best friends,' she said. 'So can I get you a coffee instead?'

'Thanks. That'd be good.'

'I'm afraid it's instant,' she warned. Because Kirk had taken their posh coffee machine as well, and replacing it had been a wee bit out of her budget.

'Instant's fine,' he reassured her.

She made coffee for them both while he rummaged in her cupboards and her fridge. Within ten minutes he'd made the best pasta carbonara she'd ever eaten in her life.

'Is there anything you're not good at?' she asked.

He laughed. 'My ego says thank you.'

'Seriously. You're good at business, you're good at music, you can dance, you're good in b—' She stopped, feeling her face heat. 'Well.'

'Have you gone shy on me, Bella?' His eyes glittered with amusement, but she knew he was laughing with her rather than at her.

'I'm going to shut up and eat my dinner. Which really I should've made for you, except there's no way I could produce anything as excellent as this.'

They ate in silence that wasn't quite companionable but wasn't quite awkward either, then shared a tub of posh ice cream from her freezer.

'I guess,' he said when they'd sorted out the washing up, 'we need to deal with the elephant in the room.'

'You and me.'

'Yeah.' He blew out a breath. 'Bella, I don't do relationships—nothing more than casual, anyway. And I never, ever mix work and relationships.'

'Something obviously happened to make you feel that way,' she said. She'd picked up that much from his family and Tarquin. But would he trust her enough to tell her?

There was a long, long pause. Then he nodded. 'It was a couple of years ago. Insurgo had just hit the big time, and this woman came to the offices to ask if I'd sign her. I said no, because right at that moment my list was full, and she asked me for two minutes to change my mind. And then she sang for me.' He looked away. 'She sang "The First Time Ever I Saw Your Face". She was good. Seriously good. I fell in love with her voice.'

'I love that song,' Bella said. 'There was a version a while back that I really liked—who sang it?' She thought about it. 'Oh, I remember now. Jessie Harrison.'

'That would be her,' Hugh said softly.

'Jessie Harrison? Seriously?' She stared at him. 'But she isn't one of your artists.' Jessie wasn't on the list that Tarquin had given her. Bella would've recognised her name.

'Not any more, she isn't.'

Bella had a nasty feeling where this was going. 'You were dating her?'

'Yes. It happened one night when we were in the studio. She'd been working on a song and couldn't get it right, and she wanted my help.' He paused. 'I played piano for her and did the harmonies, and suggested a few changes to the music—and then somehow I ended up taking her home. A couple of months later, she moved in with me.'

Now Bella was beginning to understand what his brother had been getting at. Obviously the reason why Hugh didn't play the piano or sing in public was because it reminded him of being with Jessie. Working with her, loving her, having his heart broken by her.

Yet he'd sung 'Edelweiss' with Bella, to take the heat off her when their plan to make her his unsuitable girlfriend had gone wrong. And she realised now that it must have brought back memories and hurt him.

'I'm sorry,' she said softly.

'I loved her, and I thought she loved me,' Hugh said, 'but it turned out I was her stepping stone to a bigger label and a bigger career. Six months after she moved in with me, I did something very stupid. Because I was in love with her, I assumed she was just being scatty and hadn't got round to signing her new contract. I'd already put a lot of work into her new album, and I'd put a lot of money into promotional stuff.'

'And it didn't happen?' Bella asked softly.

'It didn't happen,' he confirmed. 'She told me she was leaving Insurgo for another label.'

'What about all the work you'd done—all the things you'd paid out for?'

'It was her word against mine. She hadn't signed any-thing and I'd gone ahead on an assumption I should never have made. There was nothing I could do except absorb the losses.' He dragged in a breath. 'But it was a really bad business decision that put the label at risk for a while, until Ro decided to invest. I hate that I let everyone down because I let my heart rule my head.'

'I know that feeling,' Bella said. 'It's not much fun.'

'Jessie didn't just leave Insurgo. She left me, too.' He shrugged. 'I found out she'd been having an affair with the head of her new label. That's how, she, um, got him to sign her.'

'That's a really vile way to treat someone.' Bella could understand now why Hugh didn't want to mix work and relationships. He'd been badly burned. But she wasn't Jessie and she would never behave like Jessie had. Surely Hugh could see that?

'I've kind of lost my faith in relationships since then,' he said.

She could appreciate that, too. 'Yeah. It's hard to get your trust back when someone lets you down.'

'That sounds personal.'

She nodded. 'You told me the truth about your past, so I guess I should tell you about mine. Even though it makes me feel so stupid.' She sighed. 'I'd been living with Kirk for six months, though we'd been dating for a year before that. He'd gone all secretive on me for a few weeks. I thought he was going to ask me to marry him, and he was planning this amazing proposal—which was why he was acting oddly, because he wanted it to be a surprise—and I was so happy. I was going to say yes.'

She blew out a breath. 'Except it turned out he'd been seeing my best friend. Instead of proposing to me, he went off with her.'

Hugh winced. 'Your boyfriend and your best friend? That's a double betrayal. Nasty.'

She might as well tell him the worst. Just so he knew how naïve and stupid she'd been. 'He cleared out our bank account as well. Which is why it hit me so badly when my client went bust a couple of months back.' She grimaced. 'Thankfully Grace is an accountant. When I went freelance, she told me that I should always put my tax money to one side in an account I never touched as soon as a client's payment cleared, and to keep a cushion of three months' salary in my bank account. So, although Kirk wiped out my cushion, at least I can still pay my tax bill without worrying where to find the money.'

'But how did he manage to take all the money out of your account?' he asked.

'Online banking—he just transferred all the money to a different account. When you have a joint current account, it seems it doesn't matter how much you each put in to the account; you can both take out however much you like because the bank treats it as jointly owned money,' she explained. 'The bank said if it'd been a savings account, that would've been different and I could've taken him to court for theft. But it was a current account, so I couldn't because he had as much right to the money as I did.' She sighed. 'And how stupid does that make me?'

'Not stupid. Naïve, perhaps,' Hugh said. 'But you loved him and you had no reason not to trust him. Were there any signs that he was going to take all your money?'

'No. He'd been seeing a lot of my best friend, but I thought it was all to do with the secret proposal and that she was helping him plan it. It was the same as you and Jessie, really. You loved her and you had no reason not to trust her, either.' She looked levelly at him. 'You and I—we both made the same kind of mistake, and we both paid for it.'

'Very true.'

'So where does that leave us now?' she asked.

He blew out a breath. 'I'm attracted to you, Bella. Seriously attracted.'

And it was mutual, she thought.

'You're the first person I've really wanted to date since Jessie.'

'And you're the first person I've wanted to date since Kirk.' The first person she'd slept with since Kirk. 'But?' she asked. Because it echoed as loudly in her head as if he'd actually said the word.

'But,' he said softly, 'I learned from my mistakes. I'm never going to mix business and relationships again.'

She narrowed her eyes at him. 'Are you saying, if we start dating then I have to find another job?'

He paused for a long, long time. And then he said, 'Yes.'

She frowned. 'That's totally unreasonable, Hugh. I'm not Jessie, just as you're not Kirk.'

'I know.'

'We can keep it strictly business in the office and see each other outside. There's no reason why we can't separate our relationship from work. We're both grown-ups.'

'You came up to my office tonight and kissed me,' he pointed out.

She blinked. 'So you're saying that this is all my fault?'

He raked a hand through his hair. 'No. Just that it's not negotiable. If we see each other, we can't work together.'

'So I have to choose between seeing you and keeping my job.' She frowned. 'Can you not see how unreasonable that is?'

'Yes,' he said. 'But it doesn't stop me feeling it. I can't keep working with you and seeing you.'

'I admire the fact you have strong principles,' Bella said, 'but actually, right now I think you're being really stubborn and inflexible. You're not taking into account that life doesn't stay the same all the time. Things *change*, Hugh.'

'Not this.'

She stared at him. 'Think about this, then: whatever I decide to do, I lose something. According to your rules, I have to give something up—either you or my job.'

'We can't work together,' he said again.

And he didn't have to give anything up. Admittedly, Insurgo was his company and his last relationship had put it all at risk, so she could understand why he was so antsy about getting involved with someone he worked with. But she was going to be the one making all the sacrifices—which wasn't fair. 'I need time to think about this,' Bella said. 'And I think you, do, too.'

'Yes.' He looked at her, unsmiling. 'So I guess I'll see you tomorrow. Or not.'

Depending on whether she chose him or his job. Or neither, though he hadn't seemed to consider that as an option. Which made her even antsier.

'I guess,' she said.

Unless she could find an argument to convince him

that there was another way. One that didn't involve either of them making a sacrifice. But would he be able to compromise? Or had he been hurt too badly to let himself try again?

CHAPTER NINE

BELLA SAT MISERABLY on the sofa with her knees drawn up and her arms wrapped around her legs for half an hour after Hugh left. Then she pulled herself together and went to splash her face with water.

She needed to think about this—and, better still, to think aloud and work out what to do. Right now there was only one person she knew who'd let her talk and help her see her way through this. She picked up the phone and called her sister. 'Gracie? It's Bella.'

'Are you OK, sweetie?' Grace asked.

'Sure,' Bella fibbed.

'You don't sound it. What's happened?'

Bella sighed. 'I talked to Hugh.'

'I'm coming straight over,' Grace said. 'Hold on. I'll be with you in twenty minutes.'

'You don't have to—' Bella began, but the phone line was already dead.

Twenty minutes later, Grace used her spare key to Bella's flat, walked in and gave her a hug.

'You didn't have to come over,' Bella said.

'I most certainly did,' Grace corrected her. 'You're my little sister, and there's no way I'm letting you cry yourself to sleep.' She hugged Bella. 'Right. Cake and hot chocolate.'

'I don't have any cake,' Bella said miserably.

'I do,' Grace said, and took a wrapped cake from her bag. 'Emergency ginger cake.' While the milk for the hot chocolate was heating in the microwave, Grace cut them both a slice of cake, then finished making the hot drinks and sat down with Bella on the sofa. 'Right. Tell me everything.'

Bella did so, ending with, 'So it seems I have a choice. Either I lose him or I lose my job.'

'Maybe,' Grace said carefully, 'you might be better off without both of them.'

'How do you mean?'

'If you choose the job, it's going to be hard to work with him.'

Bella sighed. 'He's being totally unreasonable about this.'

'Which is why I'm worried,' Grace said. 'Supposing you choose him and you find another job—and then he lets you down?'

'I'm not exactly planning to live with him and open a joint bank account with him,' Bella said dryly.

'OK. You've already told me he's not like Kirk. And, although I wasn't in a fit state to remember much when I met him, you've said he has a good heart and I trust your judgement. So I guess, when it comes down to it, the real question is what do *you* want?' Grace asked.

'I want Hugh,' Bella said. 'But, because he's being stubborn about it, that means losing my job—which I can't afford to do.'

'I've got savings,' Grace said immediately. 'I can cover

your bills. So you don't have to worry about money. Not now and not ever.'

'That's so lovely of you, and I appreciate it,' Bella said, 'but I'm going to say no. Not because I'm an ungrateful, spoiled brat, but because I want to stand on my own two feet. I want to be able to hold my head high, instead of having to rely on you or Mum and Dad to bail me out all the time.' She sighed. 'I want Hugh, but I can't be with someone who's not prepared to even consider meeting me halfway. Having principles is a good thing—something that Kirk didn't have—but Hugh's at the opposite extreme of the spectrum. And if he can't learn to compromise, then we don't stand a chance.' She looked plaintively at her sister. 'Why can't life be simple?'

Grace squeezed her hands. 'I wish I could wave a magic wand for you, Bel.'

'You already have. You came straight over when I called, you brought me cake and you listened.' Bella swallowed hard. 'The only person who can sort this out is me.'

'Together with Hugh.' Grace bit her lip. 'I feel guilty, because I'm the one who told you to talk to him in the first place.'

'No. You were right. We needed to talk.' Bella lifted her chin. 'And now I have to think about it. Long and hard. And then…' She sighed. 'Then I need to make a decision.'

'Sleep on it,' Grace advised. 'And if you want to talk to me about it, even if it's stupid o'clock in the morning and you've just woken up, then just pick up the ph—. No, actually, scratch that,' she corrected. 'You don't need to call me, because I'll be right here. I'll stay with you tonight.'

Bella hugged her. 'I love you. But you really don't

have to stay.' Her bed was only big enough for one and her sofa wasn't big enough to sleep on, which meant that one of them would have an uncomfortable night on the floor. And she knew that Grace would be the one to insist on taking the floor.

'I can sleep on the fl—' Grace began, unconsciously echoing her younger sister's thoughts.

'No, you can't. And, although I can lend you pyjamas and toiletries, my clothes would be totally unsuitable for a day at your office. Not to mention the fact that you're four inches taller than I am, so nothing I own would fit you properly anyway,' Bella pointed out.

'True,' Grace said. 'In that case, go and have a shower and get into your pyjamas. We're going to snuggle up on your sofa under a throw and watch a rerun of *Friends* for a bit.'

Exactly what Bella had done with Grace on the very first day she'd met Hugh—the day when Hugh had rescued them from the Fifty Shades of Beige party. And she was pretty sure her sister remembered that, too. Tears pricked her eyelids. 'Oh, Gracie.'

'It'll work out,' Grace said gently. 'You're strong and you're brave, and you'll make the right decision when you've slept on it.'

Snuggling up with her sister on the sofa—with the help of their favourite comedy, more cake and more hot chocolate—made Bella feel marginally less miserable. But she knew that Grace needed to be up early tomorrow for work and it wasn't fair to keep her up late. Especially as she could see her sister's eyelids drooping.

'Go home, sweetie,' she said. 'You've got work tomorrow.'

Grace shook her head. 'I don't want to leave you.'

'I'll be fine,' Bella reassured her. 'Really. I'm already a lot better than I was.'

'I'll go,' Grace said, 'but only on condition you promise to ring me if you need me. Any time. And I mean *any* time.'

Bella knew she meant it. 'I will, and thanks.'

'And I meant it about covering your bills. Even if you insist on it being a temporary loan,' Grace said. 'If you decide to leave Insurgo, I can help you out until you find another job. It doesn't mean you're stupid or pathetic or needy—it's what sisters do. You had my back when I called off my wedding to Howard. And I've got yours now.'

Bella had to blink back the tears. 'I love you,' she said.

'I love you, too.'

'Text me when you get home.'

Grace laughed. 'You sound as if you're turning into me.'

Good, Bella thought. Maybe Grace's capable, calm togetherness would rub off on her and help her make the right decision.

She didn't sleep much that night. Every time she looked at the clock, the minute hand barely seemed to have moved. The next morning, she felt groggy and her head ached. She washed her hair, drank two big glasses of water and took some paracetamol.

Time to make her decision. Hugh or her job? Whatever she did, she'd lose.

She thought about it for a long time, and eventually came to the conclusion that this was the only way forward. She typed a text to Hugh on her phone, but didn't send it; she needed to bite the bullet, first.

She rang the Insurgo office, hoping that Hugh wouldn't

be the one to answer. She actually crossed her fingers as the call connected and she heard the ringing tone, and then to her relief Tarquin answered.

'Hi, Tarq, it's Bella.'

'You sound terrible,' he said immediately. 'Are you calling in sick?'

'I, um—no, actually.' She sighed. 'I'm, um, afraid I'm resigning. For personal reasons. With immediate effect. Anything of mine in the office, just give to the local charity shop if nobody else wants it.'

'What?' He sounded utterly shocked. 'Bella, sweetie, are you all right? What's happened? Is there anything I can do, anyone I can ring for you?'

His concern and kindness nearly undid her. But she lifted her chin. She needed to do the right thing and stand on her own two feet. 'No, I'm fine.' As fine as you could be with a broken heart. 'I'm sorry to let you down. To let everyone down.'

'Sweetie—I don't know what to say, but I'm worried about you.'

'I'll be fine. Really. And I've loved working at Insurgo. I'm sorry to let you all down.' She'd call the café later, wield her credit card and get them to deliver cake to the team on her behalf to say goodbye. 'I need to go now, Tarq.' Before she let herself down by bursting into tears. 'All the best.'

Once she'd hung up, she pressed the button on her phone to send the text to Hugh.

And then she switched off her phone.

Hugh's phone buzzed as he was walking up the stairs to his office. He checked the screen.

Bella.

His heart skipped a beat. So she'd made her decision? He flicked into the message.

Am leaving Insurgo

She'd chosen him. Thank God. He closed his eyes with relief, realising just how much he'd wanted her to make that choice.

His phone beeped again, and he looked at the screen. Another message from Bella.

Am leaving Insurgo but I can't be with someone who gives me impossible ultimatums. I wish it could've been different. Sorry.

What the hell? But she'd just said...

He looked at the previous message. At the bottom, in a different script, it said: This message has only been partially downloaded.

Yeah. And how.

He really hadn't expected this. He'd given her the choice of a working relationship or a proper relationship. He'd never dreamed that she'd pick a different option: neither.

He was still trying to get his head round it when his best friend stormed in to his office and slammed the door behind him.

'What the hell did you do?' Tarquin asked. 'Bella's resigned and, after the conversation we had with Ro, I know it's your fault. What did you do?'

'Something very stupid. Don't worry. I'll find you another designer,' Hugh said wearily.

'Not like Bella, you won't. And nobody can believe

she's just left like that. Just what did you do?' Tarquin asked again.

Hugh shook his head. 'You know how I feel about things. I can't mix work and relationships.'

'So you're seeing her?'

That had been the plan. But he'd got that wrong. 'No.'

'Then what the…?' Tarquin shook his head. 'I don't understand what's going on.'

Hugh handed over his phone. 'Here. Read it for yourself.'

Tarquin read the text, then stared at Hugh with narrowed eyes. 'What was the ultimatum?'

'Work and relationships don't mix,' Hugh said.

'You mean you actually asked her to choose between you and Insurgo?'

Hugh winced. 'Put like that, it sounds bad.'

'Sounds bad? It *is* bad, Hugh. Really bad,' Tarquin said. 'I can't believe you did that.'

Hugh was rather beginning to wish that he hadn't, either.

'You,' Tarquin said, 'are my best friend as well as my business partner. Which is why I can tell you that you're also the most stupid, stubborn, *unreasonable* man I've ever met, and right now I don't want to work with you. I don't want to see your face in the office this week. I don't want to speak to you—and, quite frankly, you're lucky the rest of us aren't all walking out on you as well. As of now, you're taking a week's leave.'

Hugh coughed. 'I'm the senior partner.'

'True. But I'm in charge of personnel,' Tarquin reminded him, 'which means that in this case *you* do what *I* say.'

Hugh had never seen his best friend so angry. And he

knew he only had himself to blame. 'I can't take a week off. We've got people in the studio.'

'Most of them are outside bookings. There's only one Insurgo artist due in, and I'll rearrange that for at least a week's time—when your head might be in a fit state to deal with it. I'm not letting you do any more damage this week,' Tarquin said firmly.

'Ouch,' Hugh said, but he knew that he deserved it— and that Tarquin was telling the truth. 'OK. Call me if you need anything.'

'From you? I'll tell you what I need,' Tarquin said. 'I need you to go and have a long, hard think. Look at yourself, look at your life, and think about what you really want. And when you come to your senses and realise that Bella Faraday is the best thing to happen to you—as in the best thing *ever*—you'd better find a fantastic way to apologise to her. And you'd better hope that she's a better person than you are and will actually forgive you. In her shoes, I'm not so sure I would.'

'Noted,' Hugh said dryly.

'Don't you try your Mr Grumpy-in-the-mornings act on me,' Tarquin said, scowling at him. 'Now go home and sort your life out.'

Sorting his life out was easier said than done.

By the time he got back to his house, Hugh was half surprised not to have had a barrage of calls from his family to ask him what he thought he was doing. He was grateful that Tarquin clearly hadn't told his mother or his brothers; though he knew Tarquin had told Roland because his other best friend simply sent him a text saying, You are *such* a moron.

Nothing felt right. Everything felt two-dimensional.

And he knew exactly why: it was because Bella had walked out of his life.

He picked up the phone and called her. A recorded message informed him that her mobile phone was switched off, so please try later or send a text. He tried her landline next, but it went through to voicemail. Which didn't exactly leave him much of an option. Awkwardly, he said, 'Bella, it's Hugh. I'm sorry. I've been a complete idiot. Can we talk? Please call me.'

But she didn't return his call.

He tried both lines again later, several times, with the same result: her mobile was switched off and her landline was switched through to voicemail. Was she avoiding him? Or was she just busy?

Going to her flat in person didn't help, either. Although he rang the bell, there was no answer. He knew Bella wouldn't refuse to answer the door, so clearly she was out. He had no idea where she was and no idea how else to contact her; she was close to her sister, but an internet search to find a phone number for Grace Faraday in London when he couldn't narrow it down to any particular part of the city left him frustrated and grumpy.

It looked as if he'd just have to wait for Bella to contact him. Even though waiting wasn't something that sat well with him.

He paced round the house for a bit, flicked through various television channels without finding anything remotely interesting, and couldn't even lose himself in music. Though he found himself wide awake at three a.m. with music filling his head. He lay there for a bit, trying to ignore it, but the urge was too strong.

In the end, he pulled on a pair of jeans and padded downstairs to his piano. Luckily the houses in his road

were well insulated, and he'd installed soundproofing
in his music room when he moved in, or the neighbours
wouldn't be too happy with him playing the piano at stupid o'clock. He grabbed a manuscript book and a pencil,
scribbled down the words in his head, and then started
to work out the tune to go with them. By the time it was
light again, he'd finished the song.

And he knew exactly what he was going to do.

He showered and changed, though he didn't bother
shaving; he just wanted the rest of his life to hurry up
and start now. He drove to Bella's and rang the doorbell.
There was no answer, but the curtains were still closed—
so surely she was there? He rang again and waited, but
there was still no answer. Panicking slightly, he leaned
on the doorbell.

She opened the door abruptly, rubbing her eyes. 'All
right, all right, give a girl time to wake up... Oh,' she
said, taking in who was standing on her doorstep.

'I'm sorry. I'm an idiot, please forgive me and—' He
broke off, not quite ready to say the three little words yet.
'Come for breakfast.'

'Breakfast?' She blinked, looking confused.

'Breakfast,' he confirmed. 'At my place, and I'm cooking.'

'Hugh, it's the crack of dawn,' she protested.

'It's half past seven,' he pointed out.

'Same thing.'

'No, it isn't. I saw the sun rise this morning, and I'm
pretty sure it was about five o'clock.'

She frowned. 'But you're not a morning person. What
on earth were you doing up at five o'clock?'

'Finishing.'

'Finishing what?'

'Come for breakfast and I'll show you.'

'Hugh…'

'You don't have to dress up,' he said. 'Just grab some clothes. Please.'

She paused for so long that he thought she was going to say no. But then she gave a weary nod. 'Come in and make yourself a coffee while I have a shower.'

'Thank you.' Though he didn't bother with coffee. He simply paced around her tiny flat, music running through his head. He felt more alive than he'd been in months. Than he'd ever been, if he was honest with himself. And once he'd opened his heart to Bella, told her how he really felt about her, he just hoped she'd give him a second chance.

At last, Bella emerged from the bathroom wearing jeans and a T-shirt. Clearly she'd taken the time to shower, as her hair was damp and not styled, but she hadn't bothered with make-up—and she'd never looked more beautiful to him.

'Ready for this?' he asked softly.

She nodded, and he drove her back to his house. Once he'd made coffee and they'd gone through a stack of pancakes with maple syrup, he said, 'We need to talk.'

'I thought we did all our talking the other night, back at my flat,' she said.

'No, we didn't, because I wasn't thinking straight,' he said. 'I was wrapped in panic because I was so scared of repeating my past mistakes—even though I know you're not Jessie and you'd never behave like her in a million years.' He dragged in a breath. 'I wrote a song for you.'

She looked surprised. 'You wrote a song for me?'

'That's why I was up in the middle of the night. I had music in my head—music you inspired—and…oh, look, why am I blathering on about it? I need you to hear something. That's why I brought you here.'

He led her into his music room and she curled up on his easy chair. Then he sat down on the piano stool and played the song to her.

It was the most beautiful song Bella had ever heard and she knew it came straight from the heart. Hugh's voice kept catching with emotion as he sang, 'You're the missing piece of my heart.'

When the last chord had died away, he turned round to face her. 'I love you, Bella. Yes, I have issues, and I'm probably not going to be the easiest person to share your life with, but I love you and that's not ever going to change. I think I fell in love with you when I saw you bouncing out of Insurgo and into my taxi, that Friday night. I love everything about you—your warmth and your vitality and your brightness. You make my world feel a better place. And I meant everything I sang to you, because you really are the missing piece of my heart,' he said simply.

She simply stared at him. 'I can't believe you wrote this song for me.'

'You took down all the barriers I'd put round myself and set the music free again.' He smiled at her. 'I'm a nicer person when I'm writing music. And you make me a better man.' To Bella's shock, he moved off the piano stool and dropped to one knee in front of her. 'I was totally wrong about not being able to mix business and a relationship. With you by my side, I can do anything; and without you everything just feels wrong. Will you marry me, Bella Faraday?'

She stared at him, not quite sure she was really hearing this. 'But the other night you wanted me to choose between you and my job.'

'Because I was scared. Because I was stupid. But a few hours on my own to think about it and what I could be losing means I've worked through that,' he said. 'I admit, you might still need to tell me I'm stubborn and unreasonable at various points in the future, but I promise I'll listen to you and I'll take it on board—and, more importantly, I'll talk things over with you instead of brooding. So will you give me a second chance? Will you come back to Insurgo?'

'You really think you can work with me?'

'I work a lot better with you than without you. And you're a great designer. Everyone misses you. And they're all pretty mad at me for being an idiot and driving you away,' he admitted.

'So do I still have to choose between you and my job?' she checked.

He shook his head. 'And you took the option I never even considered—not because I'm arrogant but because being without you in any way is so unthinkable. I was wrong, and I'm sorry. Please come back to Insurgo. And—even more importantly—please will you marry me?'

Words she'd expected to hear six months ago from someone else—from a man she'd thought she'd known but she'd been so wrong. So foolish.

And now Hugh—a man she'd known for only a few weeks—was saying those words to her. Offering her for ever. Sweeping her off her feet.

She knew he'd still be grumpy in the mornings. And obstinate. There would be days when he'd drive her crazy.

But, the very first time she'd met him, he'd been there

for her. He'd given her help when she'd needed it, without any strings. And he'd believed in her, been there right by her side when the pretend girlfriend plan had gone wrong.

With Kirk, she'd had dreams. Castles built on sand.

With Hugh, she had reality. Something solid.

'We haven't known each other very long,' he said, as if picking up on her worries, 'but I think you know when you've met the right one. It feels different with you. Like nothing else I've ever known.'

'Me, too,' she whispered.

'And I think that's why I asked you to come home to Oxfordshire with me,' he said. 'Because, even then, I knew you were the right one. The woman who'd just be herself and my family would love her as much as I did— even though I was in major denial at the time.'

'And you let me wear a dress made out of the same curtains your parents had.'

'That's when I knew.' He coughed. 'May I point out that I'm still on one knee, waiting for an answer?'

She leaned over and stroked his face. 'You're not Kirk. You're not going to run off with my best friend and the contents of my bank account. Though you did run off with my heart. Which I guess is why I agreed to go to Oxfordshire with you instead of sending you off with a flea in your ear.' She smiled. 'The answer's yes.'

'To coming back to Insurgo? Or to marrying me?'

'Both,' she said, 'because I love the job—and I love you.'

'I love you, too. So much.' Hugh kissed her, then stood up, scooped her out of the chair, sat down in her place and settled her on his lap. 'One thing. You might have noticed that I'm not very good at waiting.'

'Meaning?' she asked.

'Meaning that I don't want this to be a long engagement.'

'Gracie was engaged to Howard for four years,' she said.

'Way, way, way too long,' he said. 'This is going to be a very short engagement. As short as we can possibly make it.'

'So you're telling me I don't get an engagement party like Nigel and Victoria's—a tea party with your older relatives, a dress made out of curtains and a sneaky dance in the orangery?' she asked.

'How about a wedding in a tiny parish church in Oxfordshire, a party afterwards in my parents' ballroom, and as many sneaky dances as you like in the orangery and a walk in the bluebell woods with the full carpet out?' he countered.

She blinked. 'But the bluebells are out now.'

'And they'll still be out for the next three weeks,' he said softly. 'I reckon we can organise a wedding in three weeks—don't you?'

She grinned. 'I see what you mean about not being good at waiting. Yes, we probably can organise a wedding in three weeks, but we're going to need help.'

'I have a feeling that the Moncrieffs and the Faradays are all going to be very happy if we ask them to help us sort things out,' he said. 'Plus Tarquin and Roland.'

'Hmm. It sounds to me as if we're going to have two best men,' she said.

'Is that OK?' He looked worried.

She kissed him. 'It's very OK. I haven't met Roland yet, but if he's anything like Tarq we'll get on famously. Though, Hugh, if we're working to a deadline of three weeks, we're going to have to start asking people now.'

He grabbed his phone. 'OK. We'll start with a synchronised text to our parents, siblings and best fr—' He stopped. 'Um. Sorry.'

'Don't apologise. You haven't brought back any bad stuff. I do still have a best friend,' Bella said softly, 'but she's usually known to the world as my sister.'

'And I hope also as our chief bridesmaid.' He paused. 'How many bridesmaids can we have? Can we ask my sisters-in-law? Because, um, they all told me you were perfect for me at Nigel and Victoria's engagement.'

'Oh, bless.' Bella smiled. 'Of course. And we need Sophia—she'll be perfect as the flower girl.'

'You are utterly wonderful. And I intend to tell you that every single day. As well as telling you how much I love you.' He typed in a message on his phone.

Bringing Bella to see the bluebells this weekend. Need everyone there for family meeting to plan our wedding.

'How about this?' he asked, and handed the phone to her.

She read it swiftly. 'Perfect. OK.' She handed his phone back and grabbed hers from her pocket. '"Going to see the bluebells at Hugh's parents' in Oxfordshire at weekend. Need you to come with us as is also family meeting to plan our wedding,"' she said as she typed.

'Perfect,' he said.

They both put all the phone numbers in to the right place and smiled at each other. 'Ready?' he asked.

She nodded. 'Go.'

Simultaneously, they pressed Send.

'What do you think—maybe ten seconds before we get a response?' Hugh asked.

'About that,' Bella agreed.

They counted.

On cue, both their phones started ringing and beeping with texts from the people who were obviously trying to call and discovering that the line was engaged.

'And let the wedding planning craziness begin,' Bella said with a grin.

EPILOGUE

Three weeks later

WHEN THEIR PARENTS had gone down to the hotel reception to wait for the other bridesmaids to arrive, Grace turned to Bella. 'Are you absolutely sure about this? Because if you've got even the *slightest* doubt, you walk away now and we'll all support you.'

'I'm absolutely sure,' Bella confirmed. 'Hugh's everything I want.'

'Then I wish you both a lifetime of happiness together,' Grace said softly. 'And you look amazing.'

'So do you. And I can't believe we've organised everything in less than three weeks.'

Grace laughed. 'With Team Faraday and Team Moncrieff joining together—of course we've managed to organise everything in the shortest space of time possible between us!'

'You're all pretty awesome,' Bella agreed.

'And your new in-laws are fantastic,' Grace said. Neither of them said it but both were thinking, the Moncrieffs were so unlike the Suttons, and how nearly Grace had been trapped in a lifetime of misery.

'Thankfully you're not a Bridezilla, so it was relatively easy to sort everything out,' Grace said.

'It's not the dress or the food or even the venue that's the most important bit of a wedding,' Bella said. 'It's the vows and the people there.'

'Totally,' Grace agreed. 'Though I have to admit I'm glad it's the perfect day for an early summer wedding—much better to have bright sunshine than trying to dodge the showers.'

Bella hugged her. 'Sorry. I'm being selfish. This must be so hard for you, considering that right now you should've been just back from your honeymoon.'

'Actually, no,' Grace corrected. 'You're not selfish at all, and today's confirmed for me that I did the right thing. When you and Hugh are together, you both glow—and that's not how it was for Howard and me. I think we both owed it to each other to let ourselves find the person who'd make us light up and who we could light up in return.'

'But you just blinked away tears,' Bella pointed out.

'Those are tears of happiness,' Grace said softly, 'because I'm so glad for you. You've got the kind of love you deserve.'

There was a knock on the hotel room door and their parents came in, followed by Hugh's sisters-in-law and little Sophia, all dressed up in their wedding finery.

'Look at you all—you're gorgeous,' Bella said in delight.

'Bel-Bel,' Sophia cooed, and Bella scooped her up for a kiss.

'My little Sophia.' She grinned. 'We're so going to do "Row, Row, Row Your Boat" later.'

'Bo!' Sophia said happily.

'Careful,' Poppy said, 'or she'll have us all singing that down the aisle.'

'What an excellent idea.' Bella laughed. 'So are we all ready to get this show on the road?'

'We certainly are,' Harriet said. 'Even though we still can't quite believe how fast this is all happening.'

'Sorry. I did kind of steal your and Nigel's thunder, Victoria,' Bella said.

'No, you didn't. It's good to see Hugh happy,' Victoria said. 'And it could be worse. You could've made us all wear bridesmaid dresses made out of curtains.'

In response, Poppy started singing 'Do Re Mi', and everyone joined in, ending in gales of laughter.

Finally it was time to go downstairs, where the bridal cars were waiting to take everyone to the tiny country church where Hugh and Bella were getting married—the church where Hugh's parents had been married and Hugh himself had been christened.

'I'm not even going to ask you if you're sure about this,' Bella's father said when they were in the car. 'Apart from the fact that I know Gracie's already asked you, I can see it in your eyes. Hugh's the right one for you.'

'Absolutely yes,' Bella said.

'Will you please stop checking your watch, sweet-cheeks?' Tarquin asked in exasperation. 'She'll be here. She might be a couple of minutes late, because it's traditional, but she'll be here.'

'She loves you to bits,' Roland added.

'I know. I'm just antsy.' Hugh dragged in a breath. Standing here by the altar, waiting, was much more nerve-racking than he'd anticipated. He'd been there before as Roland's best man, but being the groom gave you a totally different perspective. The ancient Cotswold stone church was full to bursting, there were flowers everywhere he looked, and the sun was shining through the stained glass in the windows, spilling pools of colour over the congregation. Everything was perfect.

Or it would be, when Bella was here.

And then a memory surfaced that made him even more antsy. 'Did I ever tell you, her sister cancelled her wedding three weeks before the big day?'

'And you've had three weeks to organise yours,' Tarquin said. 'But, from what Bella told me, Grace would've been donning a ball and chain instead of a wedding ring, and she did absolutely the right thing in calling it off.'

'Even so, cancelling it just three weeks before the actual day—surely she must've known earlier that she didn't want to get married?' Roland said with a frown. 'She sounds a bit princessy to me. Obviously she's nothing like her sister.'

'Grace is all right, actually—but she is pretty much the opposite of Bella,' Tarquin agreed.

'You would've met her and found out for yourself if you hadn't been off on a conference when the rest of us were doing wedding organising stuff,' Hugh pointed out mildly.

Roland rolled his eyes. 'If you will insist on getting married with practically no notice, Moncrieff…'

'We wanted the rest of our lives to start as soon as possible,' Hugh said softly. 'There was no reason to wait.'

'Hang on. You're not…?' Tarquin asked.

'Expecting a baby?' Hugh finished. 'No. We just didn't want to wait. Because we're sure this is the right thing for us.'

'I remember that feeling,' Roland said softly.

Hugh patted his shoulder. 'I know. And I'm sorry.'

'Don't be sorry. It was the best day of my life. Just as this will be yours,' Roland said.

Suddenly, the organ music changed from Bach to the processional music from *The Sound of Music*.

'So very Bella to choose this one to walk down the aisle to,' Tarquin said with a grin. Then he looked over his shoulder. 'Oh, my. Ro. Look.'

Roland looked. 'Hugh, you definitely need two best men, one either side—because otherwise your knees are going to go weak and you'll fall flat on your face when you turn round and see her. She looks incredible.'

Fortified by their warnings, Hugh looked round to see Bella walking down the aisle towards him on her father's arm. She looked absolutely amazing. Being Bella, she'd made a few alterations to the traditional wedding gown. Her dress was in cream silk and chiffon, with a strapless sweetheart neckline and a ballerina-type skirt which came to just above her ankles and showcased her strappy high heels—which were exactly the same dark red as the bouquet of sunflowers she was holding, the bridesmaids' dresses and the waistcoats and cravats of the men in the wedding party. He knew that Grace had talked her out of dyeing her hair the same colour as the sunflowers, but today she'd gone back to being platinum blonde. Just like the first day he'd seen her.

And she looked like an angel.

'I love you,' Hugh mouthed at her as she joined him at the altar, and was rewarded with a smile that felt as if it lit up the whole church.

They both pledged to love, honour and cherish each other, in front of a whole church full of family and friends. And then came the bit he'd been waiting for. The moment when he could kiss his beautiful bride.

Signing the register and walking back down the aisle as man and wife passed in a blur, and then they were walking on the path outside the church with dried white delphinium petals raining down on them. Hugh's face was aching, but he didn't care because he couldn't stop smiling. Even posing for endless photographs, both at the church and back at his parents' home under the wisteria, didn't try his patience: Roland had been absolutely right, he thought, because this was really the happiest day of his life.

'Libby, Oliver, this is so perfect—thank you so much,' Bella said, hugging them both inside the marquee on the lawn in the back garden.

'It was a team effort between the Moncrieffs and the Faradays,' Oliver said. 'The men put up the marquee and the women did the flowers and the table arrangements.'

'And what gorgeous flowers,' Bella said happily. There were alternating arrangements of red and yellow sunflowers in the centre of the table.

'Come and see the cake,' Hugh said. 'Victoria says the top tier is red velvet, the middle one's vanilla and the bottom one's chocolate.'

In keeping with the rest of the theme, red sunflowers made from fondant icing spilled down the side of the cake in a cascade. 'Just brilliant,' Bella said. 'We're so lucky, Hugh. We have the best joint family in the entire world.'

'We do indeed,' Hugh said.

The meal was perfect, too, and Roland and Tarquin did the perfect double act for the best man's speech, teasing Bella about her ever-changing hair colour and Hugh about having to learn to be less grumpy in the morning now he was married. Oliver welcomed Bella to the Moncrieff family. 'Though I still have to stop myself calling her Maria,' he teased at the end, 'and I'm going to have to check the curtains for cut-outs before she and Hugh leave tonight.'

Bella laughed and raised a glass to him. 'I promise—no scissors, so your curtains are safe. For today, at least!'

Ed welcomed Hugh to the Faraday family. And Hugh's own speech was simple but heartfelt. 'I do enough talking in my day job, so I just want to say that Bella's made me the happiest man alive and I intend to make her the happiest woman alive, I'm glad you're all here to celebrate with us, and I hope everyone else has as happy a day as we're having.'

After the speeches were over and the cake had been cut, the party moved to the ballroom for the dancing. Oliver and Libby had decorated the room with fairy lights, so it looked completely romantic and utterly gorgeous.

Hugh took Bella's hand. 'You know we don't always do things the traditional way,' he said, 'and the first dance is no exception—because we're not actually going to dance to the first song. We also know most of you are pretty sure we're going to use "Edelweiss" or something else from *The Sound of Music* as "our song", because of the first time a lot of you met Bella in this very room. But instead,' he said, 'it's this.' He sat down at the baby grand piano, pulling Bella onto his lap, and began to play the song he'd written for her—'The Missing Piece of My Heart'.

She joined him when he sang the chorus.

And there wasn't a dry eye in the house when they'd finished.

'That's our song,' Hugh said softly. 'The one Bella

inspired. Because she really is the missing piece of my heart. Now, please, I want you all to dance and drink champagne and enjoy yourselves—because today's all about celebrating.'

'Today and the rest of our lives,' Bella said softly.

'The rest of our lives,' Hugh echoed.

* * * * *

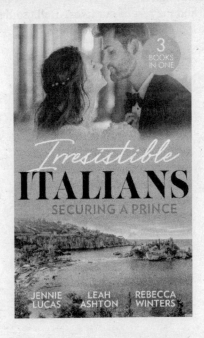

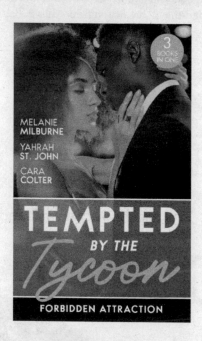

JOIN US ON SOCIAL MEDIA!

Stay up to date with our latest releases, author news and gossip, special offers and discounts, and all the behind-the-scenes action from Mills & Boon...

 @millsandboon

 @millsandboonuk

 facebook.com/millsandboon

 @millsandboonuk

It might just be true love...